Defying Destiny

By Andrew Rowe

This is a work of fiction. All characters, organizations, and events portrayed in this book are fictional.
Copyright © 2019 Andrew Rowe
All rights reserved.
ISBN: 9781692331269
Version: 1.09102019

DEDICATION

For every player, game master, artist, writer, editor, and creator that helped contribute to this world. Thank you.

TABLE OF CONTENTS

Table of Contents iv
Style Notes vi
Introduction vii
Recap – Dominion Sorcery viii
Recap – Species x
Recap – Major Characters and Events xii
Prologue I – Edon – Senses of Irony 18
Prologue II – Jonan I – Partners 31
Chapter I – Velas I – Old Friends 38
Chapter II – Lydia I – Sorcery Burns 50
Chapter III – Taelien I – Forest of Blades 59
Chapter IV – Jonan II – A Nested Series of Traps 76
Chapter V – Lydia II – Crowns 95
Chapter VI – Taelien II – Relics of the Past 123
Chapter VII – Velas II – False Families 137
Chapter VIII – Taelien III – Prime Nobility 153
Chapter IX – Jonan III – Hints of Things to Come 183
Chapter X – Lydia III – Eyes Everywhere 196
Interlude I — Venora — Rendalir Remembered 200
Chapter XI – Lydia IV – The Scholar 207
Chapter XII – Velas III – Dual Identities 220
Chapter XIII – Taelien IV – Soul Survivor 226
Chapter XIV – Lydia V – Immortal Sorcerer 237
Chapter XV – Jonan IV – Branches 249
Chapter XVI – Velas IV – A Variety of Silks 264
Chapter XVII – Taelien V – Blighted Woods 280
Chapter XVIII – Lydia VI – Winter 300

Interlude II — Venlyra — Seasons 306

Chapter XIX – Jonan V – Wounded by a Thorn 319

Chapter XX – Taelien VI – Lord of Stone 331

Chapter XXI – Velas V – The Second Silk 345

Chapter XXII – Lydia VII – A Path to Victory 361

Chapter XXIII – Taelien VI – Clean Up 381

Epilogue – Velas – Legacy 385

Epilogue – Jonan – Travel Plans 391

Epilogue – Lydia – Home 398

Epilogue – Taelien – Endings and Beginnings 402

Appendix I – Magical Items 413

Appendix II – Notable Personages 415

A Note From the Author 422

Preview Chapter – Six Sacred Swords 423

Acknowledgements 442

About the Author 444

Other Books by Andrew Rowe 445

STYLE NOTES

Some characters within the story communicate telepathically. To indicate this, rather than using quotes, I use different forms of punctuation based on the character initiating the telepathic communication.

I use square brackets to indicate telepathy for most characters, such as Vendria, the crystal that Lydia obtained in the first War of Broken Mirrors book (see the recap if you don't remember Vendria). For example, [This would be her form of telepathic communication.]

I use angle brackets for the telepathy for a new character. For example, <This is what that would look like.>

Finally, I use inverted angle brackets for one other new character. For example, >That looks like this.<

This formatting difference is to make it immediately obvious which character is sending the telepathic message without repeatedly using dialogue tags or other indicators. The specific characters in question should be clear once the story actually reaches them.

I use the singular "they/them" for agender and non-binary characters, as well as characters that have not had their gender determined by the narrator yet. For example, "I didn't know who wrote the note, but they had a peculiar style of writing".

For this book, I've chosen to use lower case for species names (e.g. rethri, delaren, esharen). This is a deliberate change from early versions of some of the previous books in the series. Names that refer to national origins (e.g. Xixian, Selyrian) still are capitalized.

Finally, I use spaces before and after em dashes (AP style). This is purely because I find this style easier to read.

INTRODUCTION

The first few sections of this book are a recap for readers who have not read the previous two *War of Broken Mirrors* books recently.

Any of these sections can be skipped if you've read one or both of the other books recently, or feel like you have a good memory of what happened.

There will be some minor reminders within the story itself as well.

RECAP – DOMINION SORCERY

Dominion sorcery involves drawing on the power of other planes of existence (dominions) to influence the world. Practitioners of dominion sorcery are called sorcerers, and each sorcerer tends to have a few different dominions they can draw from.

Prime dominions are considered the easiest to access, and the most commonly practiced. They include things like flame, water, knowledge, and life.

Deep dominions are more complex, and generally require proficiency at one or more connected prime dominions to learn. For example, metal is a deep dominion connected with flame and stone. Lightning is a deep dominion connected with flame and air. It is possible to learn to use a deep dominion without the connected prime dominions, but somewhat uncommon.

Each type of sorcery has a different cost related to the dominion the sorcerer is drawing from. For example, flame sorcerers expend their body heat, and knowledge sorcerers lose memories. The more powerful the spell, the greater the cost.

The amount of energy used by the sorcerer does not directly match the output; most of the power is coming from an external source (the dominion), not the sorcerer. This means that a sorcerer conjuring a ball of fire doesn't actually need to use the same amount of body heat that would equate to a fireball — they're just providing a small portion of it, like lighting a match to ignite a bonfire.

As sorcerers use their dominions, their bodies acclimate, allowing them to cast more and stronger spells over time. Overuse of sorcery can cause permanent damage, however, rather than growth. This is very much like physical exercise; you grow stronger if you train in moderation, but if you overdo it, you could tear a muscle. For example, overusing sight sorcery can cause permanent vision loss.

Dominion sorcery is broken into two main categories.

Dominion calling involves directly conjuring matter or energy from a dominion. Materializing a metal sword would be metal calling, for example.

Dominion shaping is the process of modifying material that is already present. For example, changing the shape of a metal sword into a spear would be metal shaping.

Many practitioners of sorcery tend to have a little bit of both calling and shaping ability for each of the dominions that they practice, but some exclusively practice one or another.

Essence is the term used for the sorcerous power that people contain in their bodies. As people practice sorcery, their bodies develop more essence of that particular type over time. This essence not only allows them to cast more and stronger spells, it also improves their physical capabilities.

For example, practicing stone sorcery and generating more stone essence in the body can permanently increase the body's resilience to physical harm. Notably, this also works in reverse; physical exercise, for example, can help develop stone and motion essence in the body.

This is generally a slow process. It often takes years to develop a meaningful amount of essence for a new type of sorcery, or to significantly increase your essence capacity for a type that you already practice. More extreme forms of training can accelerate this growth, and new spells, potions, and other techniques for enhancing training speed are being developed and tested all the time. Some species develop essence more quickly than others, and there is also variation on a person-by-person basis.

DEFYING DESTINY
RECAP – SPECIES

Humans are a diverse, short-lived species with a notable potential for being able to learn a broad variety of types of sorcery, sometimes even including opposing types, which is rarely possible for other species.

Rethri are virtually identical to humans in appearance, save for their eyes, which are full pools of color without any sclera. The color of their eyes is determined by a dominion that they were born with a strong connection to. This connection is reinforced through a coming of age ceremony when they reach maturity. When this occurs, the rethri ceases to physically age, although they can still accumulate permanent injuries and may suffer effects similar to aging from overuse of dominions.

Uvar are rethri children who are born without a connection to a dominion. They suffer severe physical disabilities and rarely survive more than a few years without the aid of powerful sorcery. As such, they are often "returned to Vaelien" — meaning killed — by their parents as babies. A number of uvar were being studied in secret in the city of Orlyn during the events of *Forging Divinity*. It is unclear how much research was being done to look for a "cure" for their malady, and how much they were being used as tools for other magical research.

Esharen are a physically powerful species with the ability to rapidly adapt to both environmental conditions and offensive magic. Their Xixian Empire ruled the continent for millennia, but a combined human/rethri/delaren uprising gradually sapped away their strength over time. The battle that finally crushed their capitol city was only decades ago. In the region around Selyr, children are taught that the esharen are essentially extinct, but other nations believe there to be survivors — especially off the coast of the continent on small outlying islands.

Delaren are shapeshifting humanoids with strands of crystals rather than hair. The crystals are sources of tremendous magical power, but when used up, they permanently drain away a portion of the delaren's life force. During the days of the Xixian Empire, delaren were often enslaved to be used as batteries for powerful spells.

Elementals are beings that originate from one of the many dominions. "Elemental" is not a specific species; rather, it is an umbrella term that encompasses several different species. These range from creatures that are barely sentient to species with intelligence comparable to humans. **Harvesters**, for example, are humanoid entities that are focused on spreading the power of their dominion throughout the material world, then later collecting that power after it spreads. They are generally tremendously powerful, comparable to some of the strongest human and rethri sorcerers.

Vae'kes are the immensely powerful "children" of Vaelien, the King of Thorns, the primary deity worshipped in the region near Selyr. It is unclear if they are literally Vaelien's children, some sort of new species made with sorcery, or something else entirely. They are nearly invulnerable to conventional weapons and spells, and capable of permanently stealing sorcery from both objects and people. They are believed to be immortal.

DEFYING DESTINY
RECAP – MAJOR CHARACTERS AND EVENTS

Lydia Hastings, also known as **Lydia Scryer**, is an officer in the Paladins of Tae'os, the military branch of an organization that worships seven deities (the Tae'os Pantheon). While the paladins worship all seven deities, members are assigned to a branch indicating their focus. Lydia serves Sytira, the goddess of knowledge. She is a practitioner of knowledge, protection, and dream sorcery. She specializes in calling, rather than shaping, in all three disciplines. She's also demonstrated very basic use of sight sorcery.

During *Forging Divinity*, Lydia was working as a spy in the city of Orlyn, investigating the local government's claims that they had the ability to raise ordinary humans into gods. After learning that this "godhood" was actually the product of a rare form of enchanting that involved bonding people to enchanted objects, Lydia was instrumental in overthrowing the leader of the local "gods", **Edon**.

At the end of *Forging Divinity*, Lydia obtained a green gemstone that appeared to be intelligent. It refers to itself as "Vendria". Lydia has been studying the object while keeping it safe in the main base of operations for her paladin organization, the Citadel of Blades.

During the events of *Stealing Sorcery*, Lydia was severely injured in battle with **Jonathan Sterling** (see below), who crippled one of her legs and stole some of her sorcerous abilities. At the end of the book, Lydia went to train with **Blake Hartigan**, one of the three "immortal sorcerers", in order to regain her abilities and potentially learn new sorcery to help battle Sterling in their next encounter.

Lydia has two younger brothers, one of whom (**Dyson Hastings**) is a fellow paladin.

Taelien Salaris is a swordsman from near the city of Selyr. He was raised by rethri and underwent mandatory military training due to his sorcerous talents, but never joined the local military (the Thornguard). His "first" name is actually a title, rather than a name.

When he was left with his adoptive parents, a legendary sword — the **Sae'kes Taelien** — was left along with him. As the wielder of this weapon, he has taken on the "Taelien" title. This has religious significance to the Tae'os Pantheon, where the sword is the symbol of their organization. As a result, his use of this title is considered sacrilegious by some, and many believe that his weapon is a replica or fake.

Taelien is an extremely talented swordsman, in part due to his natural proficiency at metal shaping, which he uses to modify his weapons in combat. While he has a great deal of raw power with metal shaping, he requires physical contact with metal to reshape it, either directly or by touching it with another metal object. This means he can reshape an opponent's sword during a moment of contact, for example, but not from a distance.

In addition to metal shaping, Taelien has demonstrated a limited degree of proficiency at flame calling and flame shaping. He also has some degree of stone sorcery ability.

Jonan Kestrian is an agent of **Aayara**, the Lady of Thieves, one of the deities (or demigods, depending on who you ask) worshipped in the Forest of Blades. Since Aayara is supposedly a child of Vaelien, Jonan also frequently works with Vaelien's agents, such as the Thornguard.

While working with Aayara's other agents, Jonan uses the alias "Scribe". This is an "ess" name, meaning it starts with the letter "S" — the naming convention that all of Aayara's personal servants use for their pseudonyms.

Jonan is immensely proficient at sight sorcery and capable of using it to create convincing illusions in wide areas. He can also make multiple people invisible, blind himself or others, and modify his eyesight in other ways. As a consequence of repeated overuse, however, his eyesight has gradually been deteriorating. He carries several different pairs of glasses and wears the type he currently needs for any given situation.

During *Forging Divinity*, Jonan obtained the research notes of Donovan Tailor, a man who had set himself (and three others) up as the new "gods" of Orlyn. He has been studying this information, which contains notes on a rare form of enchanting called dominion marking, as well as a means for permanently tying humans to magical items to remotely draw from the powers of the object.

Velas Jaldin is Aayara's apprentice, primarily serving as an infiltrator into major organizations. She utilizes the alias "Silk".

During *Forging Divinity*, she was one of two people who played the role of "Myros", the local "god of war". She was the warrior who fought in physical demonstrations of Myros' abilities, while someone else played Myros' public persona. As Myros, she wielded the Heartlance, the sacred weapon of the city of Orlyn. She regained this weapon at the beginning of *Stealing Sorcery*, but kept it concealed until the end of the book.

During *Stealing Sorcery*, Velas participates in a series of tests to join the Paladins of Tae'os. Her prior identity as Myros is revealed, but the paladins do not learn about her loyalties to Aayara. She is sworn into the organization at the end of the book.

Velas is a tremendously powerful physical fighter, unmatched until her battle against Taelien in *Forging Divinity*. Encouraged by finally having a rival, she trained obsessively during *Stealing Sorcery*, finally defeating and seriously injuring Taelien in their final match during the paladin exams.

Velas is a practitioner of motion calling, allowing her to manipulate kinetic energy into bursts of force to quickly move herself or others around the battlefield. She also demonstrates some ability with sound sorcery.

Donovan Tailor is a former Priest of Sytira, the same deity that Lydia worships. He was cast out of the priesthood for preaching that humans should aspire to become gods themselves. Shortly thereafter, something stripped away his sorcerous abilities. One of his personal spells was active at the time that this occurred, however, and allowed him to comprehend the nature of the effect that took away his sorcery. He believed that his power had been stolen by Sytira herself, and that the strange power he had sensed was the magic of the gods themselves.

In the following years, Tailor researched the mysterious magic that had taken his sorcery away, and eventually used that knowledge to develop a new form of spell casting. This new magic required drawing power from magical items and artifacts. He developed a connection with the rulers of the city of Orlyn, and eventually took on the identity of "**Edon**", a new god, and promised "divine" power to those who served him. The queen of Orlyn, Tylan, was the first person gifted this new "divine" power.

Edon continued his research for many years, sending expeditions into the "Paths of Ascension" — a dangerous vault filled with traps and monsters left behind by the Xixian Empire — in order to find more magical items to use for his research. He also performed experiments on uvar, rethri children who were generally considered to be terminally ill. It is possible he was searching for an actual cure for their condition, but he also appears to have been using them as research subjects for determining how to safely give magical powers to others.

At the end of *Forging Divinity*, he was defeated by Lydia and arrested. Tylan and her son, Byron, took control of the kingdom of Orlyn in the aftermath.

Rialla Dianis is a rethri sorceress and the older sister of one of the uvar that Donovan Tailor was experimenting on. She managed to keep her brother alive for many years on her own after fleeing home as a teenager with her infant brother. Initially, she was convinced that Tailor could find a cure for her brother's illness, and willingly gave her service to Tailor in exchange.

When she discovered that Donovan seemed to be using her brother and other children for testing other types of magic, she was convinced to help overthrow him and take her brother to Aayara for help.

Rialla is now in Aayara's employ, serving with the name "Shiver".

She has demonstrated a broad variety of magic, including deception, travel, and ice. Some characters have noted that her eye color has changed over the years, which indicates that Edon may have performed experiments on her as well.

Jonathan Sterling is the assumed name of a vae'kes who infiltrated the Trials of Unyielding Steel, the series of tests taken to join the Paladins of Tae'os. His goal was apparently to assassinate Landen of the Twin Edges, one of the candidates in the exam. While he was stopped from killing Landen, he killed multiple others, including paladin Lieutenant Garrick Torrent.

During the battle, he also severely injured Lydia, and stole some of her sorcerous abilities. He escaped unharmed, with none of the weapons or spells used against him proving effective.

Cassius Morn is a former member of the Thornguard's Bladebreaker division, the group dedicated to countering sorcerers. Cassius participated in the Trials of Unyielding Steel as Susan Crimson, and also trained with the legendary warrior **Herod** under the identity of Morgan Stern at some point in the past. It is unclear which of those three identities, if any, is the original. Cassius was working with Sterling during the exams and escaped along with him after the assassination attempt.

Landen of the Twin Edges is a skilled swordsman, as well as a close friend of Taelien and Velas. He once had the name Larkin Theas, of the legendary house Theas, but changed his name and identity at some point after leaving his home city. Unlike most members of House Theas, Landen has never demonstrated any sorcerous talents.

Nakane Theas is the surviving child of Edrick Theas and a talented young sorceress. She is one of the few survivors of an attempt to wipe out her family by assassins, along with her cousin, Landen, and her absentee father, Edrick Theas.

Edrick Theas is one of the three legendary "immortal sorcerers", human sorcerers who have found a means of extending their life far past the normal capability of human survival. He specializes in defensive magic and is responsible for the powerful wards on the walls and gates of the city of Velthryn.

Blake Hartigan is one of the other three "immortal sorcerers", and specializes in offensive magic and alchemy. At the end of Stealing Sorcery, he agrees to take Lydia as a student.

Erik Tarren is the last of the three "immortal sorcerers", and a famous scholar and world traveler. His books on history and magic theory are used throughout the continent. He specializes in teleportation magic.

Asphodel is a delaren "oracle" who took the Trials of Unyielding Steel along with Taelien and Velas. She sees a few seconds into the future simultaneously with the present, allowing her to easily avoid most attacks. With concentration, she can divine further into the future, but looking at Taelien shows her someone else entirely, and looking at Velas shows her nothing at all.

Aladir Ta'thyriel is Lydia's partner in the Paladins of Tae'os. He is one of the most skilled healers in the organization, blessed with the Gifts of Lyssari, the Goddess of Life. He is capable of casting the "Spark of Life" spell, which can bring someone back from the brink of death. It is not guaranteed to succeed, however, and failed when he attempted to save Kalsiris Theas' life.

The Shrouded One is the leader of a dangerous cult (The Disciples of the First) that was responsible for ordering the assassination of the Theas family. While the attempts on Nakane and Landen were unsuccessful, their organization successfully killed Nadelya and Kalsiris Theas, Nakane's mother and brother. Members of the organization believe The Shrouded One can see the future, and that certain people must be eliminated to save the world. While the future-sight is suspiciously similar to Asphodel's, currently no connection between the two has been found.

PROLOGUE I – EDON – SENSES OF IRONY

Donovan Tailor's jail cell was surprisingly well-furnished.

There was a wooden table toward the center, piled high with books and scrolls he dearly wished that he could read. An unused chair sat beside it, looking temptingly comfortable.

The bed looked like an excellent place to rest, in spite of the dust. No one had changed the blankets or pillows in some time, it seemed. This was unsurprising, since it was little more than a prop to illuminate the potential for comfort just beyond his reach.

None of those things drew his attention like the mirror, however. It was a tall standing mirror with a golden frame, the surface clean and bright. That, at least, was being properly maintained.

He stared at it with the full knowledge that someone somewhere might be staring right back at him.

How had he failed to see it sooner?

It was a shame that he had no way of taking action. He couldn't approach the mirror to write a message or smash it apart.

He was, of course, chained to the wall on the furthest side of the room.

All it took was one mistake. One minor miscalculation.

How many decisions will it take to fix things?

Before he could answer himself, the room's solitary door began to open.

"No knock?" Donovan inquired. "How rude."

A familiar woman stepped inside, her flame-red hair pulled back into a neat bun. She was not wearing the robe of a court sorcerer, however, as she had when she'd worked in his service.

No, she wore the colors of a Paladin of Tae'os now. Her true affiliation from the beginning, if his suspicion was not mistaken.

"Lydia Scryer." A thin smile played across his lips. "I'm a tad surprised. I'd expected you to flee the country after deposing me."

The woman stepped fully inside, waited a moment with a glance toward the doorway, then shut the door. She turned her gaze toward him. "Deposed implies rulership. You were never the true ruler of this kingdom, Edon."

He shrugged a shoulder as best he could with the restraints. "Ruler? Not in the sense of being a king, certainly. But a king is a thing of birthrights and bloodlines. I was something greater, something purer. I was a god to the people of this city, and that godhood was *earned*."

"You were a charlatan who took advantage of the population's ignorance to spread your false doctrine. Then, when there was a threat — the prince coming of age — you never intended to allow him to earn his rightful throne."

Donovan's lips twisted into a frown. "Is that what you believe? I had no intention of denying Byron the throne. I delayed the coronation because of the assassination attempt. I was working to discover who was responsible."

Lydia leaned back against the wall opposite from him, her expression neutral. She glanced away for just a moment and then turned back to him. "Regardless of what your intentions were with Byron, you were misleading the people of this city. Why? You believed in sharing knowledge once, didn't you?"

Donovan nodded, feeling exhaustion seeping in, deeper than the cold of the chains. "Of course...but they cast me aside. Everyone did. Even the gods themselves. *Especially* the gods." He shook his head. "The people of this city needed someone...something to believe in. A god who actually cared for them. Someone who would be present in the world, willing to tend to their needs. I intended, at first, to tell everyone how my new form of magic worked, but as I learned more, I began to see the limitations...and those same limits are why I could not take the risk."

"You were hoarding magical items." Lydia folded her arms. "Because you needed them to fuel your sorcery. If you spread the word that anyone could gain access to magic by linking themselves to enchanted objects, it would have created fierce competition. Moreover, if the queen regent could reproduce what you'd learned, it would have rendered you expendable."

"Ah." Donovan's eyes gleamed as he gave Lydia a closer look. "You do understand. You read my notes, then."

Lydia waved a hand. "Some of them. The queen regent denied me access to your library after we'd apprehended you. But I understood the basics." She shook her head. "I understand a degree of what you were doing and why. I might have even been convinced to agree with parts of it. But you crossed a couple lines."

"Oh? Tell me, Miss Scryer, what invisible lines were so important to you?"

Lydia pointed to the sigil of Sytira pinned to her tunic. "One. You outlawed other religions in your city and persecuted anyone who wouldn't follow you."

He leaned against the chains, tightening his jaw. "People spend their entire lives with knees bent in hope of being the one in ten thousand that will be blessed by divine gifts. But there is no amount of prayer that will bring the gods to your rescue. Eratar will not visit you and bring you knowledge from his travels. Lissari will not heal your ill. And Lysandri will not cry over your grave when you die." He turned his head aside. "She won't even notice. Because she abandoned you, and everyone else, long ago."

"You may believe that, but it doesn't give you the right to deny others the ability to worship as they choose."

"Pah. I never sought to punish those who were foolish enough to continue worshipping the absent. Who someone wants to whisper to in the dark of night is their own business, even if I don't approve."

Lydia raised an eyebrow, waving at the chains. "Then why put Taelien in here when he arrived?"

Donovan laughed. "Is that what this is about? A bit of ironic revenge for how I treated your champion? Please. I didn't even know your swordsman was in the city until after he'd escaped. If I had, I'd have invited him for dinner, not thrown him into a cell."

"I have no reason to believe that." Her expression showed hesitation in spite of her words. Doubt.

That was good.

She never should have let him talk.

"Believe what you will, but from the moment I heard the Sae'kes was available in the city, I knew it was a potential asset. You understand my style of sorcery, at least to some limited degree. Can you imagine what would be possible with a link to a weapon of that kind?"

"Unfortunately, I can. That's part of why I assume you wanted to steal it."

"Steal? Quite the opposite. I doubt my body could have handled the strain of connecting with an object like that. I would have made a god of that man, someone malleable. A sign of the old giving way to the new." He sighed. "It's a shame that things ended the way they did. I'm still not certain you understand how completely you were manipulated. Tell me, who controls this city now?"

"King Byron," she answered automatically.

Donovan smiled. "It's cute that you think that."

"You refer to his Thornguard contacts?"

Ah, excellent. That confirms one thing. Let's see how much deeper I can go.

"You say 'Thornguard', but do you believe a mere Thornguard was the mastermind?"

She shrugged. "It doesn't matter. Byron is king, and he's reopened the option to worship anyone the citizens please. Even you, amusingly enough."

"Ah, yes. They dress me up every once in a while, keeping void-imbued shackles within my robes, and parade me about the kingdom to assure everyone I'm still watching over them." He let out a bitter chuckle. "I'm sure they'll find a good enough actor to replace me eventually."

"I don't think acting is the issue." Lydia glanced to her side again, then shook her head. "I think they're still hoping to pry how your magic works out of you to make a real replacement."

"Oh, they've tried, I assure you. But interrogating me has proven less than useful."

Lydia frowned. "Why?"

"I've forgotten some pertinent details." His smile turned victorious.

"Forgotten..." She frowned. "Knowledge sorcery. Or memory, perhaps? You either overused them...or, lost those memories deliberately?"

"A bit of both, truly. The intent was to make certain that the full depths of my secrets could only be discovered through a combination of my own knowledge and Morella's, as well as access to our notes. We did not wish to take the risk that others could steal our work simply by capturing one of us. We were, it would appear, at least somewhat successful."

"Such a waste..." Lydia sighed.

"I agree, dear. I agree. And you can take a bit of responsibility for that loss."

Her hands tightened. "I did what I needed to do. You were experimenting on *children*."

Donovan felt an old anger building inside him. "To cure them of a fatal illness. If I'd had enough time—"

"I read enough of your notes to know that's not the full story. You weren't *just* looking for a cure. You were testing the limits of applying dominion marks on living creatures. The *uvar* children were a unique opportunity for you, since they had practically no dominion essence to start with. They were even easier to work with than human children would have been...and you always had the pretense of saying you were trying to fix their condition. Moreover, that was only the first step of your plan."

"I—"

"I'm not done. You learned early on that linking them to a single dominion wouldn't fix their problem — the child's body would simply be flooded with essence of a single type, which would be fatal. Linking them to items with multiple dominions was the next step, and you made progress by using items linked to protection and stability. That was real progress. Perhaps if you'd continued down that line, you would have found a cure. Maybe linking them to several different items, each containing a fraction of what they needed to live." Lydia shook her head. "But you abandoned that line of research in favor of another. You were working on linking the children to each other — and to humans."

"I didn't have the kind of resources necessary to find or construct dozens of dominion marked items for every child. But if I could pair a human with a rethri child, sharing their essence..."

"You might be able to stabilize the child that way, at some cost to the human essence donor." Lydia nodded. "A reasonable enough plan. Perhaps it could have worked. But that's not what you were doing, was it?"

She reached into a pouch at her side, removing a piece of paper.

On that paper was a six-by-ten grid, with a single rune representing a dominion in each section.

In the center was a single circle, with lines stretching outward to every single grid space.

There were scribbled notes on the side and the bottom of the page, illegible to Donovan without his glasses.

But he knew what they said.

"A reproduction of one of the pages in your notebook. At first, I thought it was a simple cosmological map. One of many attempts to organize the dominions into a coherent format." Lydia shook her head. "But upon examining the notations," she waved a hand at the text on the bottom, "I realized it was nothing of the kind."

"Is this what you're here for?" Donovan deflated. "To chastise me for ideas that never came to be? It was a concept, a hypothetical. Nothing more."

"You were planning to use children as *batteries*, Edon. You'd mark them with a dominion, keep them in some form of stasis, and link them to yourself. And rather than giving them a fraction of your strength to make them stable, you'd draw on their power whenever you needed it."

Donovan set his jaw. "Only the ones I couldn't save." He shook his head. "There were those among them that would not have survived even with the best care I could have provided. This would have given them meaning. Purpose."

"Right. The purpose of making you more powerful." Lydia wrinkled her nose in disgust.

"I never sought power purely for its own sake." Donovan paused, his breath stolen by the now-familiar pangs of regret. "With one child serving as a self-replenishing source for each dominion, I would have had the means to enchant items of any type that I needed. Eventually, I would have found the necessary combination of items to treat the other children, and I would have had the means to produce them in high quantities."

Sadly, Lydia showed no sign of acknowledging how eminently reasonable his plan had been. Her eyes simply narrowed, focused with an intensity he could not understand. "Rialla's brother. Was he one of the ones you 'couldn't save'? Were all those years she spent in your service going to be rewarded by turning her brother into another item to power your sorcery?"

She sounded...oddly invested in that line of questioning.

How does she know Vorain's real name? Or how long she worked for me?

Was it in the notebook...? No, I didn't keep personal details of that nature in the same book as my sorcery notes. Another book, perhaps, but...

It had been over a year since he'd been deposed. Lydia could have learned much in that time.

But there was a better explanation.

Subtle things began to click together in his mind. He tried not to allow his calculations to play across his expression.

Should I change my approach? I need to test a bit.

"Of course not. She'd managed to sustain him quite effectively by herself for years. He was in better condition than most. He would have been healed as soon as possible, securing Rialla's loyalty and silence. It's a shame you stopped me when you did. I *would* have cured those children. But that's not the answer you wanted, is it? You wouldn't have come all the way back here just for my sake. Perhaps you're looking to clear your conscience? Has Byron done something so awful that you're wishing that you'd kept me in charge?"

Lydia narrowed her eyes. "No." She balled up the paper, stuffing it back in her bag. "I don't need validation. I need answers."

"Ah. Trying to finish my research, then?" He smiled. "Perhaps you think you'd make a better god than I did." He looked her up and down, scanning for more details. Just the slightest things: the way she leaned against the wall with a single foot pressed against it, the way she leaned downward like she was taller than she appeared to be... "Or perhaps you think you already did?"

Lydia smirked. "What gave me away?"

"Balling the paper was the confirmation I needed. Lydia never would have wasted paper in such a fashion. There were other small things as well. Mannerisms, ways of speaking...but you generally mimicked her well enough that I couldn't say for certain. The greatest hint was talking about Rialla. That was out-of-character for Lydia Scryer. They were never close. But you...you were willing to switch sides at her behest, Velas."

Velas Jaldin clapped her hands softly. She retained Lydia's appearance, but when she spoke next, it was with her own voice. "I'm going to be honest, I was hoping you'd catch it. Maybe not this soon, though. Makes the talk a bit more awkward."

"Does it? I can understand why you wanted some answers. You didn't need a disguise."

Velas made a dismissive gesture. "Wasn't really about you. The old queenie thinks it's Scryer in here. If she knew it was me, well, another former god showing up in town might be a bit difficult for her. And I wouldn't want to end up as your cellmate." She paused, scanning the room. "They can't have had you in here long. Just moved?"

Donovan nodded. "This morning. I suspect Tylan was looking for some sort of symmetry with Taelien's imprisonment. I spoke truthfully when I said I had nothing to do with that, however."

"Oh, sure. I don't really care about that, anyway. We both know he could have snapped those chains anytime he wanted." She glanced up at the exposed runes on his skin. "Imagine that'd be a bit harder for you without any of your toys, though."

"Indeed. I'll admit I'm entirely at your mercy." He straightened up as best he could. "But you're not here for simple revenge. What are you scheming, Velas?"

"Might be that I wanted a few answers, like I said." She bit her lip. "Might be that I'd actually trusted you at some point, and that it hurt when I found out what you'd been up to."

"Don't play me for a fool, Jaldin. You're no innocent yourself."

"No." She shook her head. "You're right. I have another reason I'm here."

"Well, then I'd be pleased to negotiate with you."

Velas rolled her eyes. "You don't exactly have a lot of bargaining room at this point, old man."

"I do have the knowledge that you're impersonating Lydia Scryer, at least. I imagine you wouldn't want the queen regent to know about that."

Velas shrugged. "I'll be long gone before you have a chance to chat with queenie. And I'm pretty sure I'm off her Dawnsday card list, so I'm not exactly afraid of hurting her feelings."

"I'd imagine that your reputation with Lydia might be more of a concern. If you're leaving the city, and you're wearing a paladin insignia..."

Velas chuckled. "You're reaching now. I could have gotten this old thing anywhere."

"Perhaps. But I also have nothing to lose by making an effort to find leverage. You present the best opportunity I've had in some time to facilitate change."

"We can talk about it. What is it that you want?"

Donovan laughed. "Isn't it obvious? I'd like you to break me out of here. And if you felt like looking like Lydia at the time, I would be *deeply* amused by the symmetry in that."

"As much as I might enjoy making Red deal with the aftermath of that, I don't think so. But we'll see how useful you are, and I'll consider it."

There's no chance she'll actually break me out of here, but it means something that she's trying to give me the impression that there is one. She's always been the calculating type. It's part of why we got along so very well.

"Tell me what you need, Velas, and I'll see what I can supply."

Velas pushed herself off the wall, walking closer to him.

He tensed. If she chose to attack him in this position, he truly had no defense against her.

Velas made no such move. She just walked close, turned, and then walked to the mirror. "Seems a bit gaudy, don't you think? Ruins the décor." She moved to the bed next, yanking the top blanket off of it, then draping it over the mirror. "Much better."

Donovan's eyes narrowed. He had no doubt she was aware of the mirror's function, but he felt the need to address it regardless. "You may have just limited the time we have available."

"I have a feeling that was already running short, and I'd prefer to have a degree of privacy for this portion of the chat." She stretched. "Never know who can read lips."

Edon wrinkled his nose. "Shall we address why you're here, then? I've already made it clear that I can't provide you with how to reproduce my dominion marking process."

"No, you mentioned losing your memories, but that doesn't mean you couldn't offer *some* more information than I have available. But I'm not here about that. Tell me, what do you know about the Disciples of the First?"

Donovan blinked, sincerely surprised for the first time in the conversation. "You could be asking me about immortality, about divine sorcery...and you're here about a cult?"

"Never really cared much for your brand of life extension. Wouldn't do much for me. If I die, it's going to be in a pile of my enemies, not ancient and decrepit." Velas smirked. "I'm sure the real Lydia would love a sorcerous theory lecture, but my tastes tend to run a little simpler. In this case, my flavor of the day is revenge."

"What makes you think I know anything about a cult?"

"You've already shown you recognize the name, at least. Besides, you *ran* a cult. I figured you'd want to be familiar with the competition."

"My religion was far from a cult. We had—"

Velas waved a hand. "I remember. I was a part of it, remember? Let's skip the semantics and get to the point. Do you know anything about them?"

Donovan nodded slowly. "Yes...but I'm afraid my information is significantly out of date. They followed someone called the Shrouded One with apparent prophetic abilities. This 'Shrouded One' claimed that the world would end if specific conditions were not met, often at precise places or times. Typical cult tactics — a bit of cold reading mixed with fearmongering and prestidigitation. I didn't consider them a significant threat."

Velas nodded slowly. "I have reason to believe they may be our mutual enemy."

"Mutual enemy? Well, I suppose I should pack my bags and gird myself for battle, then." He glanced left and right toward his chains. "Ah, there seems to be a small problem with that, however."

"I'm not convinced freeing you would be worth the headache. But I do think you could get a degree of closure if you help me with this."

He raised an eyebrow. "Closure?"

"Your notes said that Sytira removed your sorcerous abilities as a result of your teachings."

Donovan grunted. "It was her betrayal that led me down this path. The hypocrisy of a goddess who sought to keep the secrets of true power to herself."

"I'm not going to point out how ironic that statement is...oh, wait. Just did." Velas shook her head. "But that's not my point. You were wrong from the beginning. Sytira had nothing to do with it."

"What, you think some charlatan with a name like the 'Shrouded One' did? Their title sounds like something a twelve-year-old would come up with."

Velas snorted. "No, I don't think the Shrouded One did anything to you personally. But they did, at one point, have a vae'kes in their employ."

"No." Donovan shook his head. "I was a priest of Sytira. A vae'kes wouldn't have dared to provoke—"

"A vae'kes calling himself Jonathan Sterling was involved in a series of assassinations in Velthryn a few months back. He escaped, but not until after stealing some of Lydia's sorcery."

Velas paused for dramatic effect. "When he did, she was under the effects of a Comprehensive Barrier spell. A variation of your own Intuitive Comprehension, with the same spell identification effect. It took some time for her to process what had happened, especially since she was being choked near to death at the same time. Later, she used memory sorcery to enhance her recollection of those moments, and what the spell had told her. She didn't give me the whole phrase, but it contained something like '*Eru ravel lares taris*'. Sound familiar?"

"No..." He felt his hands tightening. "It's...that isn't..."

His mind raced. Was that phrase in his books? Could she have identified that it was the foundation of his studies?

...It wasn't impossible. But the story she was telling mirrored his own so closely, it had such close proximity to something he knew to be true...he couldn't dismiss it outright.

"Now, I'm sure you're dealing with a bit of surprise—"

"...Surprise?" Donovan's tone turned sharp, his body trembling. "No, child. Not surprise. You've cracked a foundation I did not realize existed." He turned his head toward her, meeting her eyes. "If you constructed this story, I've underestimated your talents."

"We all have our flaws." Velas smiled. "And you did underestimate me, but not in this regard. The story is true. It may not have been Sterling in specific that stole your sorcery, but it was probably a vae'kes, not Sytira. Your anger has been misdirected. Would you like to correct that?"

He continued to meet her gaze. "Of course. But what's in this for you?"

"Sterling made the mistake of hurting someone I care a great deal about."

"Oh? Scryer?"

Velas smirked. "No, silly. Me." She cracked her knuckles. "And I'm going to pay him back for that tenfold. Maybe a hundred. Does a hundred seem excessive to you?"

"No." He shook his head. "Not in the slightest." Donovan took a breath. "Free me, and I will help you with the full extent of my abilities."

Velas glanced to her side, looking tentative, then back to him. "Sorry. Doesn't seem like that's in the stars. Not for now, at least. I'll keep the idea in mind. For the moment, if you'd like a bit of revenge by proxy, fill me in on everything you know about the Shrouded One. If I can find them, I can use them to get to Sterling. And maybe Sterling will know who did this to you."

"That leaves several potential points of failure between me and any sort of justice. I dislike dealing in such uncertainties."

"Sometimes a bad deal is better than no deal at all." Velas glanced toward the mirror, then back to him. "I can give you my word that I'll make an effort to find out who took your sorcery and why. That's the best I can do right now. And I think we're running out of time."

So soon?

But there's so much more I need to know now...so many more details that are missing.

Donovan sighed and straightened himself.

He glanced at Velas, a goddess he'd forged himself, and for a moment, he felt a remnant of pride.

You've beaten me, he realized. *I have no good options left.*

"Very well." He lowered his head in a gesture acknowledging his opponent's victory. "I'll tell you what I know about the Disciples of the First. And about the Shrouded One. But under one condition."

Velas tilted her head to the side. "Oh? What'd that be?"

"You have the Heartlance, I presume?"

"Been a bit of a mess, but yes, it's currently accessible to me."

Edon examined his former disciple, feeling the hint of a smile that mirrored her own. "Good. When you find the one who took my power, I want you teach them how the Heartlance earned its name."

Velas' grin widened. "With pleasure."

PROLOGUE II – JONAN I – PARTNERS

Jonan slipped out of the jail cell right after Velas, allowing her to close the door behind them.

Well, this is nostalgic.

He nodded to her, making a gesture to indicate his use of sight sorcery.

She made a hand-sign for 'understood' in return, then spoke aloud. "You got us both hidden?"

"Of course. What sort of amateur do you take me for?" He glanced back at the door. "I assume you cut off the sound around us?"

Velas scoffed. "Please. I did it the moment the door was closed."

"Good." Jonan reached out an open palm.

Velas rolled her eyes. "Ugh, fine. You win. I don't think he noticed you at all. But for what it's worth, I should get credit for being extremely distracting." She reached into a pouch at her side, fishing out a silver coin and pressing it into his palm.

"I never doubted your performance abilities. That was a part of why I made the bet in the first place." He tucked the coin away. "Are we going to help him?"

Velas shook her head. "Not directly. Too much risk, too little potential for reward. And given what I just told him, he might even cause some trouble for us."

"That's a pragmatic response, but I know you were close to him at one point. You don't feel bad about his situation?"

"He's a good talker, but he knew the risks with what he was getting into. And they'll let him out of this particularly gilded cage soon enough and throw him somewhere he'll be more useful. I think Tylan just moved him in here to give Lydia the impression she was in complete control. Edon would be dead if she didn't have further uses for him."

"Very well, then. Shall we continue this chat somewhere more comfortable?" Jonan gestured to the hallway that led back toward the keep's entrance.

"Sure, but you should make me visible again. I think that went smoothly enough that people should see Lydia leaving. We don't need an emergency exit."

Jonan made another unnecessary gesture. "It's done." He considered telling her to make sure she adjusted the sounds around them again, but he stopped himself. She knew what she was doing.

They made their way to the exit without any difficulty. Jonan smirked as Velas checked in with Captain Shaw to let him know she had finished her visit. Shaw had been one of his first contacts in the city, and the one who had helped him arrange for Taelien to be put in that particular cell along with the mirror.

He'd felt pretty good about how things in Orlyn had turned out, at least initially. He'd accomplished his goal of overthrowing Edon with minimal difficulty. Rialla had been his biggest threat, and he'd ended up recruiting her to his cause. He'd maneuvered Taelien and Lydia into doing the heavy lifting, and thus the Thornguard hadn't been implicated in the slightest in the regime change. He'd even managed to secure the Heartlance, a valuable artifact.

But every victory was earned on behalf of someone else. Every resource he'd obtained had lined Aayara's coffers further, just as they always did.

And given Velas' presence in the city, and the fact that Edon's sorcery had likely been taken from him by a vae'kes many years before, it was abundantly clear that he was just one of many pieces Aayara had in play.

How many more opponents would Aayara have to take off the board before the game was over?

And, perhaps more importantly, what was her true goal?

Even as one of her personal servants, he had little idea of her true motivations. There were too many masks. Was she Vaelien's loyal daughter, securing entire kingdoms on his behalf? Was she the Lady of

Thieves, delighting in organizing heists of impossible scale? Was it her rivalry with the Blackstone Assassin that motivated her?

Without knowing that, he couldn't determine what her next moves would be. And, on a more personal note, he could never be certain how expendable he was.

Velas finished talking to the guard captain without incident. Jonan followed her out of the keep, down a familiar path toward the city proper. After that, they made their way to a small house. Not the same one Jonan had used during his last time in Orlyn, fortunately. That would have been far too reckless.

Jonan unlocked the door and they stepped inside. After closing the door, Jonan dropped his invisibility and the illusion over Velas. His eyes itched, but that was nothing new. He'd have to change his glasses if he wanted to read anything, but that wasn't an immediate concern.

Velas stretched and laid down on the nearby couch. "Not a bad use of a day. You get what you needed?"

Jonan pulled up a chair next to her, retrieving a notepad from his pouch. "Copies of all the runes on his skin. We can compare them with his notebook later to figure out his exact capabilities, as well as whether or not there are any on his body that weren't listed elsewhere. Both will be useful for determining what sorts of other items he had access to."

"Nice. I still think it's hilarious you made a spell to look through his clothes. And I'm glad you had to be the one to do it. Don't think I could have kept from laughing. Barely managed it just knowing you were there. I kept wondering if you'd make his clothes totally invisible by accident."

"Right. Now, let us never speak of that again." Jonan tucked his notebook back away. "Do you still happen to have access to any of Edon's other enchanted items?"

Velas winced. "I have the dominion marked armor he gave me, but I have no desire to put that back on."

"Memories you'd rather let go of?"

Velas snorted. "Nothing so sentimental. That armor was a trap. One of the functions was teleportation, and he used it to drop me miles outside of the city when I tried to team up with Taelien to fight him. Now that I know it was sabotaged, I'm not wearing it. Kept it because it was too valuable not to, of course."

"It may not have been a trap. He could have just added that function in case he needed to teleport you to safety or something."

"Doesn't matter. I don't like the idea of wearing something that can be remotely activated by someone else. Not worth the risks, even if it had some other nice enchantments."

"Such as?"

"Sound modification on the helmet. I can use sound shaping on my own, of course, but it saved me some effort and boosted my effective range. It also had some high-end durability enchantments. Held up against virtually anything that hit me. Not against Taelien, but well, that's Taelien for you." She sighed.

"That sword of his is a problem." Jonan shook his head. "We'll worry about that another time, however. For the moment, the armor. What if you didn't have to wear it?"

Velas frowned. "You want to rune me up?"

Jonan grinned. It was refreshing to have someone who could follow his line of logic for a change. "Both of us, in fact."

"You sure you can manage that? I know you've read some of his notes, but dominion marking on humans is..."

Jonan rolled up his sleeve.

Velas blinked. "How long have you had that?"

"Better part of a year. It works. No noticeable side effects."

Velas gave an appreciative whistle. "Gotta say, that's unexpected. It took Morella and Edon years to crack making those."

"The notes contained almost everything I needed, at least for artifacts that they'd already tested. Making a mark for any other item would be exponentially more difficult...but I suspect the armor will be in the notes. And now that we know which marks were on Edon's body, we can narrow things down significantly. He clearly had a mark for the armor's teleportation rune, at least, since he used it on you."

"Wait, hold on. What's that rune connected to?"

Jonan winced. "Um..."

"That's from the Heartlance, isn't it? Have you been robbing my *baby*, Jonan?"

He raised his hands in a defensive gesture. "In fairness, I haven't really used the mark much. But yes, it's from the Heartlance. The motion function."

Velas frowned. "Hm."

"Hm?"

"Well, if you've been stealing essence from the Heartlance, has that helped you figure out what else it can do?"

Jonan gave a wave of his hand indicating 'sort of'. "That process didn't, but I found some notes. It really does interfere with healing, for example, it just doesn't prevent it entirely. It's a blood sorcery effect."

"Boring. What else?"

Jonan shrugged his shoulder. "There's a big one, but I haven't tested it. I'd have to physically hold the lance, and, uh, it's kind of creepy."

"Creepy how?"

Jonan dug into the bag at his side. "The activation phrase. Don't read it out loud, obviously."

Velas read the note.

Blood of the fallen, ignite my spirit.

"A little theatrical, isn't it?" Velas snorted, tucking the note away. "Less creepy, more, uh, like something a child would come up with. Or Sal, maybe."

"Maybe, but I'm still a little concerned about anything that might set our spirits on fire. Sounds uncomfortable."

Velas rolled her eyes. "Think you're being a little too literal there."

"Obviously. But I don't like the idea of messing with spirit sorcery in general, and mixing it with blood sorcery sounds even worse. Keep in mind the Heartlance was probably built for esharen — and they're a different species. Something that was beneficial to them, like say pulling spirit and blood essence from inside the Heartlance, could, you know, kill us. Like a lot."

"Worth considering. I can handle a lot of things that kill ordinary folks."

Then it was Jonan's turn to roll his eyes. "I'd still advise against it. Maybe get a spirit sorcerer to look at it, at least?"

"Eh, maybe. I'll think about it." Velas shrugged, indicating she would not, in fact, think about it. "In the meantime, yeah, let's rune me up. Wouldn't mind one for the Heartlance, even if that phrase is ludicrous.

We can tinker with the armor stuff, too. Could have started this earlier if you'd told me about it sooner."

"Perhaps, but looking at Edon will reduce the number of attempts we need to make. I prefer to minimize trial and error when it comes to potentially fatal sorcerous experiments."

"And you didn't trust me."

Jonan shrugged. "Well, yes."

"Does that imply you trust me now?"

"Don't be absurd, of course I don't trust you. But I do *like* you a good bit more now." He gave her an exaggerated wink.

Velas laughed. "Fair enough, Kestrian. Fair enough." She took a breath. "One problem. I do have the armor, but it might be, uh, somewhat damaged."

"Damaged?"

"I was...unhappy about being teleported."

I guess Taelien wasn't the only one capable of breaking the armor after all.

Jonan sighed. "We'll take a look at it later. Hopefully some of the runes are salvageable, at least."

Velas gave him a nod. "Right. For now, maybe we should discuss the main thing we were here for?"

"Not much to talk about, I'm afraid. He knew very little about the Shrouded One."

"Eh, pretty much what I expected. We knew any connection with Edon was tenuous at best. At least we've planted an idea in Edon's head that we can grow later if we need to. I don't think freeing him later would be difficult."

Jonan rubbed his temples. "Sure, if we think we can point his ire in the right direction."

"Seems like you did a pretty good job of getting *all* of us pointed the way you wanted last time around." Velas gave him an accusatory look.

Jonan simply shrugged. "I had a good amount of prep time for that. And for what it's worth, you weren't one of my targets. Your involvement was incidental."

"Should I be flattered that I didn't warrant your consideration?" Velas laughed, then seemed to notice Jonan's growing concern and waved a hand. "Relax. I don't hold it against you. I didn't know you were involved, either. It does say something that Auntie Ess deployed both of us into the same city at the same time, though. I wonder if she was expecting us to have to play against each other?"

"Guess we'll never know." Jonan leaned back in his chair. He was being dismissive, but he did have some ideas of his own on the subject. Not the types of ideas he wanted to share, of course. Velas seemed much more talkative about these sorts of matters than he was.

Maybe she could afford to be — he wasn't any sort of physical threat to her, and she clearly knew it. Conversely, if she decided that he was an obstacle, he was going to have more than headaches and eyestrain to worry about.

"Right. I suppose so." Velas whispered wistfully. She frowned, then blinked it away and returned to the conversation with renewed cheer. "Okay, where're we headed next?"

"*We* are not headed anywhere, I'm afraid." He reached into the bag at his left hip, retrieving a mirror. It was the wrong one, so he sighed and dug through the rest of the mirrors in the bag until he found the right one. "New orders." He offered the mirror to Velas and she accepted it.

Velas took a moment to scan over the text of the letter that was visible in the mirror's surface. "Bah. We had a good thing going, you know? It was nice to finally have a partner that could keep up with me."

Jonan blinked. He was not accustomed to dealing with any sort of flattery. "...Yes. It was, uh, pleasant."

Velas snorted. "You're a strange one, Kestrian. But I think I'll miss you." She handed the mirror back to him. "Especially because heading back south on my own is going to be *incredibly* boring."

"Well, at least that'll be a temporary problem. You're apparently getting a new partner for a while once you arrive."

"Oh?" Velas looked sincerely curious. "That wasn't in the letter."

Jonan smiled, tucking the mirror away. "No. I heard from your partner-to-be. I'd tell you who it is, but I'd hate to ruin the surprise."

CHAPTER I – VELAS I – OLD FRIENDS

Seven months later, Velas Jaldin cautiously stepped through the beginnings of a vegetable garden and arrived at the front door of a small home. It was too large to call a hut, too small to call a house, at least in her mind.

She knocked on the door politely, waiting with a hand by her side.

A timid looking young girl answered it a few moments later.

Velas gazed down at the girl, perplexed, and hesitated just a moment before regaining enough of her bearings to ask a question. "Is your mommy home?"

The little girl shook her head. "I don't have a mommy anymore. Daddy is here, though."

"Can you go get your daddy, then?"

The little girl nodded and gave her a bright smile. "One minute, please!"

Velas took a couple steps back from the door, her hand still hovering near her hip.

This complicates things.

But not much.

The figure that arrived at the door a few moments later was familiar in spite of some minor alterations.

Hair trimmed and dyed, loose fitting clothes, a simple peasant cap. Enough to pass a casual inspection, certainly.

Velas' hand rested on her hilt, but she didn't draw her weapon just yet. The little girl was still right behind her target.

Irritating.

Velas grinned brightly. "Cassius! It's so good to see you. It's been too long. Can we talk outside for a moment?"

The figure's eyes narrowed. "It's Morgan Stern right now, actually. But I applaud your effort. As for your request, I'll have to politely decline. Good day."

Cassius Morn — or Morgan Stern, or whoever his current identity was— moved to shut the door.

Rude.

Velas blurred forward, putting a hand on the door. "But I've come such a long way! Surely, you can spare a few moments for an old friend."

Cassius tightened his jaw, then tilted his head toward the little girl. "Head back inside, Elizabeth. Go play with your sister. I need to talk to my old friend for a few minutes."

"Kay!" The little girl headed deeper inside.

Cassius waved a hand for Velas to move, so she stepped back.

He stepped outside and closed the door.

Velas scratched her chin. "Okay, humor me. Cassius Morn? Morgan Stern? Susan Crimson? All basically anagrams, or close to them, but which is the original?"

Cassius shook his head, giving Velas a sad smile. "If I answer that, will you leave me in peace?"

Velas laughed. "Oh, gods, no. But I am curious. You're much better at the disguise bit than I've ever been. I don't know which—"

Velas saw the glint of metal in a sleeve as Cassius' hand moved upward. It wasn't a quick motion, no jerk of an abrupt shoulder rising.

With less experience, it would have been easy to miss.

Velas didn't bother parrying — she just stepped to the side and let the hurled needle miss her entirely. "That was a mistake."

Cassius raised both hands. "Had to try. You have me at a sincere disadvantage, and I have children to protect."

"Nope, not going to go easy on you because you've picked up some strays. I'm not Taelien, remember?"

Cassius tilted his head to the side. "No, but I did assume you'd still behave like a paladin."

"Oh, Sterling never told you?" Velas stepped back, out of reach, then bowed theatrically. "You can call me Silk."

Cassius' eyes narrowed. "You're an 'ess'? I suppose that explains how you found me, but not why you're here. I told Sterling I wanted out. He signed the papers. I'm clear."

Velas' tilted her head to the side. "Wait, did you actually think we could *retire*? After working for vae'kes? Serious question, I need to know if you're sincerely that naïve."

"I figured there might be an extra assignment here or there, true. I was hoping to at least have a few years, get these kids into a school."

"They yours? I'm guessing not, but…"

Cassius shook his head. "Strays, as you said."

"I can respect that. Wouldn't want to deal with them myself, mind you, but someone has to do it. You know, Luria sincerely believed you'd come back for him."

Cassius flinched, that statement seeming to affect him more than threat of violence. "I looked into it. Too secure. If I'd known we had someone else on the inside… Did you take care of it?"

Velas shook her head. "By myself? I'm not crazy. That's why I'm here. You're coming with me."

Cassius sighed. "I can't. Like I said, I'm done. If you'll check with the Thornguard office in Selyr—"

Velas tilted her head downward, then made a show of glancing side to side.

This home was located a good two hundred miles west of Velthryn — on the side of a mountain.

Selyr was hundreds of miles in the *other* direction. And also north.

Cassius pressed his hands together. "Look, I'd really like to help Luria out, but I've got responsibilities now."

"We can drop your kids off with Bertram. Don't worry, he's fine. He got out of town before the paladins could catch up to him."

"Shame, Mythralis would be a better place with that bastard in a cell." Cassius tightened his jaw. "Sorry you came all this way, but the answer remains the same. You could check in with the Thornguard office in Velthryn for some muscle?"

Velas waved a hand dismissively. "You know I can't get quality that way. I'm looking for subtlety, not a raid on the facility." She folded her arms. "Maybe I could get Sterling to help get Luria out of this mess? Do you know where he is?"

Cassius shook his head. "Not a word. Let me ask you something, though. What's a shadow mean to you?"

"Loyalty. And loyalty is like a crystal blade, yes, yes. I know the speech. Good of you to check, even if you're a bit late."

Cassius nodded slowly. "Luria *did* mention that he'd seen you use some of our hand signs, but he couldn't figure out who you were. I'm surprised they had more than one group of us in there."

Velas ran a hand through her hair. "You aren't the only one. Sterling is lucky *my* vae'kes didn't come calling after the resh job he pulled with that last assassination attempt."

Cassius frowned at that. "You think your vae'kes set us up to fight each other? Before I got out, I heard there was some kind of schism going on in Liadra."

"Doubt it was deliberate, unless you've heard something about 'esses' going up against each other specifically. We tussle with the jewelers every once in a while, but I've never seen any conflict between 'esses'."

"Ah, I see what you mean." Cassius nodded thoughtfully. "And I think I've about sorted this out."

"Oh?" Velas put a hand to her chin. "Thought of something helpful?"

"Maybe. The name Silk has something of a reputation." Cassius stretched his arms. "Is it true that you're one of Aayara's personal apprentices?"

Velas nodded, noting *something* still inside one of Cassius' sleeves as he moved. No, both sleeves. "Quite true. Where'd you hear that?"

"Heard all sorts of stories about Silk when I was growing up. Or several Silks, really. All sorts of daring escapes, training exercises...think I might have even read a book about one of them."

"Most people would be humble and say it's nothing like the stories. Truth is? It's just like the stories."

Cassius laughed. "That's wonderful. Thing is, though, there's no chance that Aayara's personal apprentice needs my help to break someone out of prison."

A knife slid from a sleeve into Cassius hand. "So, what are you actually here for?"

"Information, mostly." Velas waved at the knife. "No need to be rude."

"I prefer to be prepared, thank you. Especially since you've already been lying to me."

Velas shrugged, taking a step back. "It's the business."

The conversation wasn't going the way she'd wanted, but that was fine. She'd already picked up a few pieces of information.

And she never minded a good fight.

The knife isn't much of a threat, unless it's enchanted. He's a former Thornguard, so it might be, but I doubt it.

Her hand sat on the hilt of her sword, but she didn't draw just yet. "As I said, just here for information. Aayara wants to know where Sterling ran off to. He's supposed to be an 'ess', but he's misbehaving."

Mostly true, at least from what Aayara claimed.

"Sorry, not selling him out. Nothing personal, but Sterling is much more likely to come back here and chop me to bits than Aayara is. Your mentor is too busy to bother with someone like me."

Velas tapped the hilt at her side meaningfully. "That's what I'm for, silly."

"I'll take my chances—"

Velas didn't let him finish the sentence; she just blurred forward with a burst of motion sorcery and punched him in the gut. While Cassius was falling back, she grabbed the wrist of his knife hand.

He twisted even as he recoiled, trying to slip her grip. He was stronger than she'd expected, but she just hit him again with his free hand and the knife slipped free.

After that, she swept the knife out of the way with a foot and pressed him back against the door.

He smashed his forehead downward. She twisted, but not fast enough, and his head collided with her upper lip rather than her nose.

Velas stumbled back, tasting blood, and Cassius took that moment to turn and run.

So much for family.

A blur of motion and Velas was in front of him. She punched him in the face.

He staggered back a step, taking the punch surprisingly well, and then raised his fists into a high guard. A flick of the wrist and he had *another* knife in his hand.

Velas waved a hand downward. "Drop it or I drop you."

"Sorry, Jaldin. I'll take my chances with you over Sterling." He walked to the right. She mirrored him, not bothering to draw her sword.

Instead, she tried something new.

"Eru volar proter taris." She felt a momentary jolt as the rune concealed on the back of her shoulder flared, and Velas felt essence surge through her body. She'd activated the safer of her two new dominion marks.

Cassius lunged as soon as she started speaking, clearly understanding that a spell was being cast. Velas raised her arm, and the knife impacted against it just after she finished her phrase.

A shower of sparks flashed from the surface of her skin as the knife skidded across it harmlessly. The sound of impact was like the dagger was scratching against a metal plate rather than bare flesh.

Velas grinned.

Guess the armor is going to do me a bit of good after all.

Her opponent hopped back, wary. He was alert now, more aware of the threat that Velas presented. It hardly mattered.

Cassius was a good fighter, but he wasn't Velas.

She waited, let him circle a bit, enjoying the dance. She sidestepped a thrust toward her throat, then struck him again.

When he recoiled this time, his nose was bleeding freely. He spat blood.

Seems like this helps me hit just a smidge harder, too. Not a bad side effect.

Velas raised her arms, keeping them in the way of any future attacks while she talked. Drawing from the armor's power reinforced her entire body, but she wasn't going to risk seeing what would happen if he hit her in the eye or another vulnerable spot. "I can always go back and beat the answers out of Luria. Inconvenient, but the paladins still have him in a cell."

"Luria doesn't know where Sterling is." Cassius took a couple steps back, then wiped his nose with a sleeve. "In fact, he didn't know where I am, either. How *did* you find me?"

"Went back to where you fought Asphodel in the woods with her and a travel sorcerer. She pointed out the exact spot. We found some dried blood. Some was yours, from when she broke your ribs." Velas grinned. "How are those feeling, by the way?"

Velas stepped in and punched him in the ribs.

He'd had nearly a year to heal, but even so, he bent over double from the strike. Maybe it was lasting damage, or maybe she'd just hit him *that* hard.

He managed a quick counter-swipe with the knife, but Velas was ready, and she just stepped back out of reach.

Velas changed her mind. This wasn't enough of a challenge, even without the sword. The rune was stealing any fun she might have had from the challenge.

She briefly contemplated turning it off, just to make things more sporting, but she doubted even that would offer her enough of a challenge to bother.

Velas swept his right leg while he was still recovering from the hit to the ribs, then drew her sword and planted it atop his chest. "Now, we're going to have a conversation. If it's any comfort, by the time I'm done with Sterling, he's not going to be in any condition to come back for you."

Cassius was too busy coughing to reply, and for a moment, Velas wondered if she'd managed to punch a rib into something vital.

That would be awkward.

Gonna have to be a careful about where I hit people while this rune is on.

She took the moment to kick his hand, dislodging the hopefully final knife, and then moved back into position.

"I don't know where he is," Cassius managed after several moments of coughing.

"You've got an idea, otherwise you wouldn't have risked fighting me." Velas pushed downward on her sword, just a little. Not even enough to pierce through his shirt. Just enough to give him a little motivation.

"I haven't seen him in months. I can tell you where he *was*, but I don't—"

Velas shook her head and sighed. "This isn't getting anywhere. Do we have to do this the hard way?"

Cassius coughed, then looked Velas up and down. "Now you're just bluffing. You're not going to hurt the children, so there isn't much more you can do to threaten me. We both know torture isn't effective at getting true answers."

Velas nodded thoughtfully. "You're right. I'm done here."

She lifted the sword. For a moment, it looked like she might plunge it straight back down...

...but when she jammed it down, it was just into the weapon's scabbard.

Cassius lifted his head, coughed again, and then stared at Velas' retreating form. "What? You're just going to leave?"

Velas turned her head back. "Oh, no. You were right, I'm not going to get anything more out of you. I'm just backing off to give her a turn."

The shadows at Velas' side coalesced into the form of a thin rethri woman. The newcomer strode forward with clarity of purpose.

Velas smiled, retrieving the Heartlance from where it was leaning against a tree nearby. "All yours, Rialla."

***

Velas winced as she dipped two fingers into a container of foul-smelling paste, then wiped it against the thin cut on her neck.

She wasn't sure exactly *when* Cassius had managed to cut her. Probably right when the fight had first started?

Doubt he managed to cut me after I'd turned on the rune, but...ugh. I need to be more careful.

I hate poison.

Fortunately, she remembered Taelien's solution to their little assassin's test. And it was true; Thornguard always carried an antidote to their poisons somewhere on their person.

Unlike the prop used in the tests, though, this one was *awful*. If they hadn't interrogated Cassius thoroughly, she would have suspected it was just some kind of half-decomposed fruit or something.

"Could have saved us both some trouble if you'd let me talk to him from the start." Rialla was leaning up against a tree nearby, her arms folded. Her indigo eyes were narrowed in what Velas presumed to be a combination of worry and frustration.

Velas waved her other hand dismissively. "What fun would that have been? You have no idea how long I've been waiting to punch that guy in the face."

"Eradae 14th, last year."

"Hm?"

"That's the day that Sterling, Cassius, and Luria murdered those paladins."

Velas paused treating her wound to stare in Rialla's direction. "You actually remember that?"

"I remember that week for different reasons."

Oh. The whole killing her own father thing. Yeah, that'd stick with someone.

Velas shrugged, replaced the cap on the bottle of paste, and shoved it aside. She took out her waterskin from her pack and poured the entire contents on her fingers, trying to get rid of the foul smell. It mostly worked.

She tossed the waterskin to Rialla next. "Fill her up for me?"

Rialla sighed. "I'm not a sink."

Velas grinned. "But you could be!"

Rialla shook her head, putting a hand over the top of the bottle and concentrating. A steady flow of water trickled down from her palm into the bottle. When it was full, Rialla coughed, wiped her forehead, and walked the bottle back over to Velas. She could have tossed it back, but that wasn't her style.

Velas accepted the bottle and put it back in her pack. "Thanks, Ri. So, what do you think?"

"I think you should have killed him."

"Wasn't what I meant. But anyway, I've always had a soft spot for kids. Must have picked it up from Auntie Ess. And I wasn't going to take care of them myself, so…"

Rialla walked back over to her tree. "You gave him your 'ess' name."

"Hardly a problem at this point. Sterling already knows it, and Cassius really is trying to get out of the business. Wonder how long it'll be before the clean-up crew comes knocking. Maybe ending it now would have been a mercy." Velas lifted her pack, slipping it back on. "Okay, think I'm ready to go."

Rialla lifted her own backpack. "Good. I'm tired of being here, and we have a long way home."

"Home? Is that what we're calling Velthryn these days?"

"I grew up there."

With a father that wanted to kill your brother, yeah. Doesn't sound like home to me.

Velas put the thought aside. "Fair. I suppose it's a nice enough city, if you can deal with the arrogance of the nobility."

Rialla didn't take the bait. "As for what you were asking about earlier, I think it's pretty straightforward. Last Cassius heard, Sterling was in Selyr. That's one of the main Thornguard headquarters, and it's also where Aayara usually does business. I think she's been running us in circles on purpose."

Velas tightened her jaw. "Or he's found a way to slip around without her noticing. He's got void sorcery, after all."

"It's possible, but I think we need to consider the fact that your esteemed teacher might be wasting our time."

"That's not like her." Velas shook her head. "Even if she knows where Sterling is located, she's got an objective behind where she's been sending us. Maybe the real goal was just to get us to remind Cassius of his place. Or maybe she expected us to follow this lead toward something else."

"I think we might want to fill Scribe in about this. Isn't he up near the Selyr area?"

Yeah, and he's not the only one.

Velas felt the scar under her right arm itch. It was distracting.

"Fine. We'll contact Scribe. But if he's already in the area, he might already know."

It was Rialla's turn to frown. "You think he found Sterling and didn't tell us?"

Velas shrugged. "You never know with him."

If I had a good enough reason, I might keep that sort of thing to myself.

...But Jonan doesn't seem to have the motivation. He wasn't close with any of the targets. He'd probably be more professional.

"There's a good chance this is a trap. If Sterling knows we're following him, going to Selyr is a considerable risk. He'll be at the height of his power and resources in Thornguard territory."

"Agreed. It sounds lovely. Best news I've had in months." Velas cracked her fingers. "Let's hit Velthryn first. Our paladin friends are going to want to know that we've picked up the trail."

"When do you plan to tell Lydia about your *other* identity?"

"Ah, such a deliberate way of phrasing that question. You're learning, Ri. The answer is never."

Rialla paused in her tracks. "I don't think that's wise, Vel. If you keep referencing information coming in from outside sources, she's going to know something is amiss."

"Red knows I was Myros, but unless Jonan has been indiscreet, she still doesn't know about our ties to Symphony. I'd rather keep it that way. Wouldn't you?"

"I think we can trust her. I think she's a good person." Rialla sounded wistful, but resumed walking behind Velas.

Velas rolled her eyes. "Lydia *is* a good person. That's precisely why we can't tell her. You think she'd let me keep this shiny paladin badge if she knew I'd been working with a vae'kes from the start?"

"Maybe, if you volunteered the information..."

"Bah. I work better keeping this stuff separate. If you're worried about arousing suspicions, we can pass information to Jonan, and he can funnel it through to her."

Rialla frowned, but she nodded after a moment. "Very well. But there will come a time when you need to tell her the truth."

"That's a problem for the future. Today, I can just relax and enjoy the poison. Mmm, poison."

"If you actually start to feel anything get worse, let me look at that. Antivenoms aren't miracle cures."

"Aww, I'll be fine. 'Preciate that you're worrying about me, though. I would feel better if we had comfy beds to sleep in tonight..."

"No, Vel. I'm not going to try teleporting us that far. I've only tried line of sight, and even that makes me dizzy for hours. It takes years to get the proficiency to go any serious distance."

"We could go to the side of a cliff where you can see the bottom of the mountain. That's line of sight, yeah?"

"Sure, if you want to land at the velocity of falling off a cliff."

Velas tilted her head to the side. "Wait, really? Doesn't teleporting skip everything in between?"

"I don't know much of the theory behind how it works. Maybe veteran sorcerers can get it to work that way. But when I've tried going up or down a flight of stairs, it feels like I jumped and landed."

"Huh. What if you take us to about ten feet above the ground, then I use motion sorcery to cushion our fall?"

"No, Vel. We are *not* teleporting off a cliff."

Velas sighed and rolled her eyes. "Fine. But I'll have you know that you are no fun at all. In fact, I hereby dub you, 'Funslayer.'"

Rialla stopped to bow theatrically. "I'm honored by your beneficence, oh-great-taker-of-unnecessary-risks."

"Now that's more like it." Velas laughed, then slowed her walk to put an arm around Rialla's waist. "Now, what if you just took us down part way?"

"Not happening."

"Aww."

CHAPTER II – LYDIA I – SORCERY BURNS

Lydia stood on the circular roof of a tall stone tower, nearly fifty feet across. She was precariously close to the edge, with a hundred foot drop awaiting her if she took a step too far.

Careful...wait for it...

She watched as a serpentine coil of flame descended from the sky, hissing as if it was alive. It was moving too erratically for her to be certain that any evasive action would succeed, and the tower's edge limited her range of motion. Instead, she held her ground, raising her left hand, palm-outward.

"Flames, I command you to disperse."

The flames shivered even as she did, the spell extracting a toll on her body. It was not enough — the sirocco hovered above her, its downward movement arrested, but it shook as if struggling to break free from her command. Narrowing her eyes, she lifted her other hand and pressed her palms together, focusing on the fire. Her spell was still active, a connection still in place — she reached out for that connection with her mind, touching the original source of fire.

Vendria, buy me some time.

[Understood, Lydia.]

Lydia couldn't see the gemstone in her pack flash, but she sensed the power of the stone activate.

A many-faceted green barrier appeared around Lydia just in time to stop a handful of flaming arrows hurled by her opponent. The arrows vanished, leaving deep furrows in the barrier where they'd impacted, but the tornado of flame remained.

It shifted closer to her.

"**Disperse**," she commanded, pulling her hands apart. She tore the flames asunder with her word and gesture, separating the heat until it faded harmlessly.

That gave her only a moment of respite, however. Her opponent was a determined one.

The older man stood about fifteen feet away, closer to the center of the rooftop. His hands were pressed together, his half-dozen bright metal rings shining in the morning light. He closed his eyes for a moment in concentration, then pulled his hands apart and pointed skyward. "Lightning, descend and strike!"

Lydia hissed, drawing and throwing her sword in the instant before the spell took effect. A perfectly guided spell would have ignored the metal and stayed true to its course, but her opponent was not giving it that degree of focus — the lightning arced downward and struck the metal weapon, which clattered harmlessly to the ground. Layers of protection sorcery prevented the weapon from being damaged by the blast.

"Interesting, but not—"

She threw a rock at him.

The sorcerer had a momentary look of confusion as he stepped to the side, avoiding the projectile. "What do you—?"

Her hand was already in her pouch, then back in motion, hurling a handful of rocks — each glowing a soft purple.

"Wall."

The stone floor of the tower rumbled as a thin section of granite rocketed upward, blocking her hurled projectiles and her line of sight.

That was good. It blocked his vision of her, too.

She rushed closer, nearing the wall as a fiery snake — a literal snake, this time, not merely a spiraling flame — circled around the wall. The elemental hovered a few feet off the ground, hissing at her as it lunged.

Lydia grabbed it around the neck with her right hand, her ring flaring to life as it suppressed the creature's flames. "Go to sleep, Tythus. Sleep."

The snake stared at her for a moment, then fell limp. She set the familiar down gingerly, turning just in time to see her opponent leveling a ring-laden hand in her direction.

"Voidlance."

A trio of glowing black javelins appeared behind her opponent, hovering for a moment before shooting forward.

Her first instinct was to raise another barrier, but she brushed it aside. Void spells were designed to counter protection sorcery. For her, there was very little that could be worse.

She hurled herself forward, landing on the other side of the wall as the spears punctured the air behind her, the stone wall providing protection where sorcery could not. Her right leg screamed as she impacted against the ground, reminding her of the one type of sorcery she hated even more than void: the sorcery that had stolen much of her old power, leaving her vulnerable enough for Sterling to shatter her limb.

Even after Aladir's healing and months of rehabilitation, she still suffered with every step. It was unlikely she would ever walk properly again.

Vendria, ideas?

[I do not currently sense any protections against sorcery on your opponent.]

Lydia nodded once in gratitude. She could work with that.

Pushing herself from the floor with a groan, Lydia reached deeper into her pouch, retrieving a vial as her opponent circled the wall. She flicked off the cap and smiled at her opponent. "Air, push him back."

A jet of wind blasted the older man, pushing him back several steps. He lowered his stance, attempting to steady himself, but he frowned as the winds continued to buffet him and press him closer to the tower's edge.

"That's new. Stone, wall behind me, thank you."

The rooftop shook again as another section of stone rose from the floor, forming a barrier directly behind the sorcerer. Lydia's wind continued to blow, but the wall prevented him from slipping back any further.

Fortunately, it also prevented him from moving to avoid the vial that Lydia hurled through the air.

Purple sand spilled out of the vial, spreading in the air as the wind whipped it toward him. He waved a hand, blasting the vial itself to the side with a burst of kinetic energy, but that didn't deflect the grains of sand.

Lydia smirked as she saw a moment of confusion cross the man's face just before he slumped into a sitting position against the wall. He blinked rapidly, shaking his head. "What...why am I sitting?"

The paladin circled the wall, picking up her fallen sword and cautiously stepping closer.

"Ah, ah, I see. Sand... How very traditional for dreams." One of the rings on his right hand flared. He shook his head again, pushing his hands against the stone as Lydia took a cautious step backward.

"Quite a good trick there." He stood, still unsteady on his feet. "One of the best demonstrations you've made. But you're still taking too long with your incantations. Especially when you're wearing a vulnerability." He raised a hand and pointed at the ring on *her* hand. "Eru volar—"

Lydia covered the ring with her other hand instinctively, but she knew that blocking his sight wouldn't stop the effect. In a moment of panic, she spoke a word. "Shield!"

A spherical barrier flickered to life around her hand. It was a feeble thing, nothing compared to what she might have wrought before Sterling had stolen so much from her.

But when Hartigan spoke the final word of his incantation — "shen taris" — nothing happened.

Lydia shook her head. "That was a shaded trick, Master Hartigan. Virtually no one else has a bond to my ring, using it against me isn't exactly going to be a common tactic."

The older man folded his arms, which meant he planned to lecture her again. Lydia rolled her eyes as he began. "Oh? And exactly how short is that list? Edon, of course, the man you...acquired the ring from. Presumably also some of his former court sorcerers? You never found out what happened to Veruden or Morella, did you? And what about the former Queen Regent. Could she have ever used the ring, perhaps? Not unlikely, I would think. Edon only had a few trinkets to pass about for his 'gods' to make their miracles. Oh, and what about his other former gods? It's not like you see two of them on a regular basis..."

Lydia raised her own hand, felt the barrier expire, and waved her hand at him. "You've made your point. Fine, it's a relevant lesson. Fire storm."

A swarm of tiny spheres of blue-white flame manifested right above Hartigan, streaking downward. He waved his left hand upward and they vanished, nullified with only the slightest effort on his part.

Gods, he's still so far beyond me.

"Well, that was unexpected. I rarely see such initiative. That emergency shield was good work. Focus on using quick incantations like that regularly."

She stepped forward, smacking him in the arm with the flat of her blade. "Sleep." The weapon glowed purple as the spell took effect, surging into to him. "Short enough for you?"

"Rude. And I'm protected from that now." Hartigan raised his hand, showing her the still-glowing ring he'd activated after she hit him with the sand. "But, given that you've managed to get within reach of me...I'm prepared to call this one your victory."

Lydia's blinked. "...You are?"

The immortal sorcerer brushed her weapon aside, laughing in his characteristic way. "Don't let your head get too big for your neck. I'm sure I'm still a bit ahead of you."

Lydia sheathed her weapon. "Fifty-eight to one isn't an insurmountable advantage. I'll catch up."

Hartigan's eyes narrowed as he looked at her, his lips tightening into a more serious expression. "Yes. I do believe you will."

***

Eleven months had passed since Sterling had shattered Lydia's leg and stolen much of her sorcerous power.

She had spent much of that time training with Blake Hartigan, one of the three legendary immortal sorcerers. As his latest apprentice, Lydia had a rare opportunity for a glimpse at the secrets of one of the greatest minds of the civilized world.

She also assisted him with his own "research".

Hartigan stared at the bubbling cauldron on his work bench, heated by a tiny enchanted device that sat just below it. Without taking his eyes off the purplish fluid, he reached out a hand vaguely in Lydia's direction. "Lion's bane."

Lydia frowned. "When you mix that with the lifestrand, won't it explode?"

"Quite possibly."

Lydia sighed. It was going to be another one of *those* experiments. Dutifully, she walked to a nearby shelf, eyeing the dozens of containers that she had labeled and organized — Hartigan's own "organization" had been dubious at best — and found the vial he had asked for.

She placed it, still stoppered, in his hand.

Then she stepped back. Repeatedly. She'd learned to stand as far as possible when he was adding something to a volatile mixture.

Hartigan unstoppered the vial and poured the whole thing in.

"...Shield." Lydia whispered. A barrier flickered to life around her, forged from her own protection sorcery. She'd regained some of the power Sterling had stolen from her, but not nearly as much as she would have liked.

Vendria must have heard her, and a *second* barrier appeared beneath that one, formed of the same angled green plates as usual.

Thank you.

[It is my pleasure.]

If Hartigan ended up soaked again, that'd be his own problem.

The cauldron's contents churned and bubbled fiercely, and Hartigan let out an echoing laugh as something started to *crackle* inside.

But it didn't explode. The cauldron's contents churned for another few moments, then settled.

From Hartigan's frown, Lydia might have once thought this meant he was disappointed.

Now?

She knew that was his *considering* frown.

"This is...unexpected. But marvelous! Quite marvelous. Don't you agree?"

He turned his head toward her for the first time in hours.

"I do quite like the lack of explosions, but I'm not certain at the significance. I was under the impression you were attempting to make a powerful healing potion until you added the lion's bane."

"Oh, yes." He waved a hand. "I started out that way, but while you were studying last night, I added something extra. Two and a half units of goldroot and one unit of the protection essence you've been making."

Lydia frowned. "Wouldn't goldroot decrease the efficacy of a healing potion?"

"Yes, but did you see what just happened when I added the lion's bane?"

Lydia considered that. "Nothing. Well, a few moments of conflict, but no explosion." She found herself nodding as she tried to follow Hartigan's logic. "Goldroot is tied to the Dominion of Stability. You were testing if adding it would be sufficient to allow two antithetical dominions — life in the lifestrand and death in lion's bane — to be utilized in the same potion without causing a violent reaction. I'm not certain I understand the role of the protection essence."

He nodded fiercely. "Using stability dominion herbs to try to mix antithetical dominion compounds is hardly a unique concept. I've tried several similar compounds previously, but they are always inert. The opposing dominions were simply canceling each other out, rather than causing a violent reaction. I believe adding protection essence may have allowed the two components to mix without losing their effect."

Lydia took a step closer, tilting her head to the side to look inside the cauldron. "How do you know this compound *isn't* inert?"

"The smell. It's acrid, with a hint of the sweetness of the lifestrand. If the components had cancelled each other out it would smell...worse."

She sniffed at the air, taking in the sharp scent he was describing. "What do you think the potion's effect would be?"

He shrugged. "Not much, I suspect. A stomach ache? Would you like to try it?"

Her eyes widened in horror.

Hartigan laughed. "Just teasing. Even I wouldn't drink *that*. And believe me, I've tested a lot of potions I shouldn't have. This specific potion wasn't the goal, it was just a simple test of the concept." He waved a hand, disabling the enchanted burner beneath the cauldron. "I'd be more interested in seeing if we can mix two antithetical deep dominions safely to create a new category of beneficial elixirs."

Lydia raised a hand to her lips as she considered. "Sight and secrets, perhaps? The combination could result in a new form of sensory enhancement. Or, rather than something directly in opposition, perhaps only a single opposing prime dominion in the mix would be safer? We do have both dream and insight essence on-hand."

They worked late through the night on new combinations, too excited by the possibilities to go sleep. It was only when dawn's light crept through the window that an irate Sara Hartigan burst into the chamber and dragged her weary husband off to bed.

Lydia, finally feeling her own exhaustion, headed to the guest bedchamber for some sleep of her own.

She had one last bit of her routine before she slept, however. She reached into her pouch, finding a familiar mirror alongside a more recently procured one, and glanced at the reflective surface to see if Jonan had sent her a message.

A hint of alertness returned when she realized that he had. It had been three months since his last letter, in spite of her sending several to him. She had begun to worry.

Lydia,

Apologies for not writing sooner. I assure you that I am alive and intact, at least for the time being.

More of interest to you, however; I have a lead on Sterling's location.

His last whereabouts were in the vicinity of the city of Selyr. I am inquiring for further details, and I will plan to either meet you there personally or send a trusted ally to do so.

I would strongly advise you to bring Velas. Will provide more details if you agree.

-Jonan

Now she was *more* worried, but that was overshadowed by her excitement.

Finally, a lead on Sterling! As dangerous as this might be, it's excellent news.

Bringing Velas sounds even more dangerous, given that Sterling very nearly killed her in their last encounter. She is not the type to ignore a chance at revenge.

But Jonan knows that. That implies he's either anticipating a fight against Sterling, or deliberately pushing for one. That's unusual, given what I know about his employers.

But even if he has ulterior motives, he's right that I'm going to need muscle. Even after all this training, I'm not foolish enough to think I have good odds against Sterling on my own.

She wrote him a reply.

Jonan,

I'm glad to hear you are safe. What has been keeping you so busy?

Are you in danger? Do you need help?

I will, of course, be glad to meet with your contact. I will make the necessary arrangements with the Paladins of Tae'os... provided this is a matter I can discuss publicly?

I would be quite pleased to have Velas' company if you believe it would be wise. I will contact her upon my return to Velthryn.

I hope you are well,
-Lydia

Lydia waited a few minutes for a reply, but none came immediately. Finally, she succumbed to her exhaustion, a hint of a smile on her face.

She'd been training for nearly a year for this. Planning, researching, and developing new techniques.

Spirits of the lost, forgive me for taking so long.

It's finally time. We're going after Sterling — and we're going to make him pay for every life that he's stolen.

CHAPTER III – TAELIEN I – FOREST OF BLADES

Taelien closed his eyes and focused on the soothing sound of the rain. He'd spent countless nights falling asleep to that same sound, sometimes in even less hospitable environments than this one.

Taking in a deep breath, he slipped off his tunic and laid it down across the floor of the tent. His trousers came next. He shivered as he reached into his backpack to retrieve a new set of clothes, but they were very nearly as soaked as the clothes he had been wearing.

That was fine. He set them down alongside the ones he'd just taken off, then knelt down for some work.

Heat.

A warm glow enveloped his right hand, casting light across the interior of the tent. Taelien shivered as the spell extracted its cost. It wasn't much, but he was already taxed from long days of marching and soaked to the bone. Even a comparatively simple spell was enough to force his eyes shut for a few moments.

The warm glow around his hand persisted, beginning to heat the interior of the tent. Taelien had to be careful not to touch his hand to anything flammable. He could shape the heat he'd created to prevent it from burning him, but it would be much more difficult to manage if he started spreading flames around the tent.

First, he carefully waved the hand over his body, gradually evaporating some of the water that had soaked him.

Next, he began to run his hand over the soaking clothes. Properly judging the distance to evaporate the water without burning them was always tricky, but he'd done this several times before. After a few minutes, he'd finished drying the set of clothes that had been in his backpack.

Good enough for the night.

He pulled the dry clothes closer, nudging the wet ones into a corner of the tent to deal with in the morning. If he was lucky, the rain would be over by morning and he'd be able to dry them out in the sun without any further sorcery being necessary.

It would have been nice to dry his hair, too, but he didn't have the energy for it. The rain had plastered his black hair to his back. It had gotten even longer over the last several months, but still didn't quite reach his waist.

Still shivering, he slipped the dry clothes on, pulled his blanket out of the bottom of his backpack. Thankfully it was only damp, having been shielded by his clothes.

Better get some sleep. Tomorrow is going to be a long day. I—

He felt an itch at the back of his mind just before the blades pierced his tent.

His hand moved faster than conscious thought, ripping the Sae'kes free from its scabbard.

Three swift motions sundered swords, shattering them into harmless fragments.

He grimaced, immediately slicing through the heavily damaged remains of his tent to get a clearer view of his attacker.

Two more swords flashed toward him as he stepped outward; he deflected these with equal ease. In the moments before they shattered, Taelien saw that they were enshrouded in blue-green flame.

From that, he knew his attacker even before he saw the towering figure enshrouded in a heavy cloak.

"War." Taelien took a defensive stance, trying to keep his feet on top of the remains of his tent to prevent them from sticking into the muddy ground. "I'd invite you into my tent to get out of the rain, but, well, you sort of wrecked it. What are you doing out here?"

The Wandering War lowered his hood, revealing coppery skin. Raindrops sizzled and evaporated as they struck his face. "I go where I choose, cousin. Is that not the freedom you gave me?"

Taelien gave him an approving nod. "Of course. But we're a long way from Velthryn, and I have an assignment. I wasn't expecting to see you for a while."

War raised a single hand. A half-dozen more phantasmal blades appeared, floating in the air above him. "You kept me waiting too long. I require sustenance."

For an entity that fed on conflict, the meaning behind that was clear enough.

"Now War, you know I love fighting you. But it's the middle of the night, and I'm cold and wet. This isn't the best time."

War raised a hand and pointed. "You should use that anger to strike at me fiercely and prove your strength."

"I'm not really angry, War. Just mildly irritated."

"You should use that mild irritation to strike me fiercely and prove your strength."

Taelien sighed. "Can I at least get my boots on?"

Six swords flickered forward.

"Didn't think so."

Taelien moved.

His heart beat faster.

It's been a while since I've had a real fight.

The weapons were too close together for him to reliably dismantle them all at once, so he rushed left, toward a large tree.

War moved his hand, altering the trajectory of the swords, but they couldn't all approach Taelien from the same angle.

Taelien slashed the first two apart, while another brushed against the side of the tree and slowed. He grabbed that one by the hilt with his off-hand, twisted it to deflect another, and then smashed the remaining two apart with the Sae'kes.

The deflected sword rose again, but Taelien stepped forward and slashed it in half. It faded into nothing a moment later.

War lowered his hands, moving them together to form a triangle between his fingers.

Taelien hurled the sword he'd captured in War's direction.

War seemingly ignored it entirely; it shattered in mid-air about ten feet away from him.

Taelien felt a twinge of warmth in the air around him.

That was his only warning.

The heat that enveloped him a moment later wasn't precisely fire.

If it had been, he could have defended himself with comparative ease; flame sorcery was one of the two types he had the most practice with.

These seeming-flames burned black.

Disperse, he commanded as they rose to envelop them. He could sense them in the same way he could feel the swords that were not truly metal.

But, much like the false metal swords, the incendiary sorcery did not respond as easily to his command.

His entire body was surrounded by flame, and his will was the only force that prevented him from being consumed.

Disperse, he attempted again, but the heat only pressed closer. His skin and hair began to burn.

Agony, and with it, anger.

Through the anger, instinct.

End, he commanded.

The false flames ceased to be.

Taelien growled, his fist tightening around his weapon's hilt. His pain was distant in his mind. His focus was on his enemy now.

He stalked forward, raising the sword over his right shoulder. "You're going to have to try harder than that." A smile crossed his face in spite of the pain.

As The Wandering War began to draw his own weapon, Taelien charged.

Not this time.

Taelien raised his weapon in a high stance, preparing to swing.

War swept a hand through the air. A wave of invisible force blasted Taelien backward several feet, and he fell short of striking range.

It didn't matter. Taelien swung his blade downward in an arc, projecting a silvery wave of cutting force.

War frowned, side-stepping the attack.

Taelien twitched his off-hand.

The shockwave followed War's movement, slicing through a boulder to reach its target.

War reacted at the last instant, sending a burst of motion out of his hand to knock the wave off its trajectory. The shockwave passed behind him and dissipated harmlessly.

"Fascinating. It would appear you've learned to control your weapon's aura."

Taelien raised the Sae'kes and pointed the tip directly at his opponent. Only a single rune was glowing on the surface. For years, he had mistaken the number of runes for an indication of his degree of mastery over the weapon. In truth, their function was quite different.

The runes were not a display of his power over the weapon; they were designed to restrain the annihilating essence within it. They would glow only when the sword's destructive power was being properly contained.

Taelien smirked. "I've been training. Satisfied?"

The Wandering War laughed. "Oh, dear cousin, I'm only getting started." He stretched his hands out wide. "You're not the only one who has new tricks."

The ground below Taelien began to ripple. Taelien recognized the feeling of stone sorcery at work.

Taelien jumped forward just before the stone spikes burst from the ground.

I'll need to remember that trick.

He landed in a crouch ten feet away from War, swinging as he stood and projecting another shockwave from his blade.

War had drawn his own sword, a black-bladed weapon with ruby runes glowing on the surface. The harvester braced to deflect Taelien's attack.

Split, Taelien commanded the cutting wave.

The shockwave separated into three, spreading out and converging on War from different angles.

As Taelien expected, War spun and managed to disperse each of the three attacks with swings of his own weapon.

That, however, gave Taelien all the time he needed to close the distance.

He has the advantage at a distance, but not here.

Taelien swung downward. War stepped back, avoiding the swing entirely, and sent a burst of flame at Taelien with his free hand.

Taelien slashed through the fire, dispersing it, and parried War's follow-through thrust. The motion brought the two of them closer together: enough for Taelien to thrust his left hand forward.

An ordinary punch wouldn't have had any chance of damaging a Harvester of War, but Taelien wasn't using a fist. His left hand was enshrouded in the same type of aura that surrounded his weapon, forming a blade-like point a few inches in front of his fingers.

The aura cut.

War stumbled back in surprise, an open wound bleeding freely on his right arm. "Unexpected." A grin crossed his face. "Delightful."

His counterattack was, for the first time, too fast for Taelien to stop.

He blurred forward and slammed a fist into Taelien's chest, knocking the wind out of him. His next strike hit Taelien in the jaw with his pommel, snapping the swordsman's head back.

Taelien fell to the ground, his ears ringing and his vision swimming. He barely managed to roll to the side as War swung his sword downward, then failed to block the follow-up cut.

War left a gash on Taelien's right bicep, a near match to his own injury.

For Taelien, the cut was a painful one, making it difficult to continue to lift his sword. He pushed through the pain, but with the knowledge that every moment would continue to drain his strength.

War showed no sign of even slowing down.

I can't beat him in a battle of attrition, Taelien realized. *And he seems to have a counter for almost every skill I've developed.*

I'm going to have to improvise.

War took a step back, allowing Taelien to slowly rise to his feet and assume a defensive stance. For a moment, it looked as if he was granting the swordsman a reprieve.

Then War lunged.

Taelien stepped forward, gripping his hilt with both hands to withstand the force of the parry. The wound on his right arm screamed on the impact, and his left-hand's grip was already weak. He barely maintained his hold on the weapon.

Barely, fortunately, was enough.

Shatter, he commanded War's sword as the blades met.

He knew that breaking an enchanted weapon with metal sorcery was nearly impossible. He'd never succeeded at it before.

And so, when he issued that command, he drew from something else. Not his ability to manipulate metal.

He called on the power in his right hand, the same essence that matched the cutting aura of his blade. The power that he'd used to break War's false flames apart.

War's sword *shivered*.

The Harvester fell backward in shock, breaking the contact between the two blades. His weapon remained intact, but Taelien had felt *something* happening within it.

War was a blur as he flew backward, a dozen floating weapons appearing in his wake.

I scared him, Taelien realized.

Unfortunately, he considered as the whirling blades approached, *I don't think he's going to give me a chance to finish the job.*

The spectral weapons were easy enough for him to sense and counter now, but he was exhausted. He willed them to break, but nothing happened. His body no longer had the strength to pay the cost.

He had to settle for just trying to throw himself out of the way.

The swords twisted in the air and arced toward him.

Taelien's first parry was lethargic, but adequate. The wound in his arm deepened.

The second was barely deflected, loosening his grip. The third knocked the Sae'kes out of his hand.

Nine more swords descended, inches away.

His strength was gone.

He knew a way of reaching for more.

For nearly a year now, he'd known that the Sae'kes' aura was somehow leaking into his body. It seemed to be the source of the strange dominion in his right hand — or perhaps that dominion was the reason he was capable of wielding the sword at all, and it had grown stronger through decades of use.

It had only been in the last several months that he had been actively practicing the use of that dominion, learning to use it to control his sword's aura and to mimic it without using the sword at all.

His connection with the sword was stronger now than it had ever been.

He knew he could draw more of the weapon's power into himself intentionally.

He also knew that would have a terrible cost.

The aura he had developed was already disruptive to defensive sorcery, prematurely shattering spells that were designed to defend him. That had grown worse. His aura seemed to be gradually wearing away at anything he was in contact with, causing items to degrade more quickly than they normally would.

But that side effect was trivial in comparison to the true cost; as that dominion grew stronger, Taelien changed.

Even now, he could feel it — the urge to destroy his enemy utterly, leaving nothing behind that could threaten him in the future.

And he knew that in the destruction of a powerful entity, he would gain new strength.

The sword's desire. Annihilation.

I can't risk losing control.

Nine swords approached, and he refused the strength to stop them.

Instead, he turned to War and raised his hands. "I concede this round."

The swords didn't stop.

Body of Stone.

Stone essence flooded into his body, empowering his muscles and skin. It was one of his least favorite techniques to use in a fight, since the stone essence slowed his movement, but it was an effective last-minute defense.

The first three swords impacted against him, but left only shallow scratches against his reinforced body. After that, War waved a hand and the remaining swords dissipated.

Taelien took a step forward, his eyes narrowing. He couldn't fight effectively in this state, but showing weakness seemed unwise. "I'm done fighting for now. We can resume this another time."

War scowled. "You injured me." His voice was uncharacteristically introspective in tone.

Taelien pressed his left hand over the wound on his arm. He needed to word this carefully. "Yep. I think I'm catching up to you. I'll give you an even better match next time."

He had some ideas for how he might accomplish that. There was a technique he'd been practicing for gathering as much destructive essence as possible around the blade, compressing it, and then releasing it in a single powerful strike — but it was both time consuming and too inaccurate to use in a fight. He needed several seconds just to charge the essence to use it, and ordinarily, no opponent would give him that much time to simply concentrate his power.

Maybe with more practice, I can get that technique into a more usable state.

War tilted his head downward. "I will look forward to seeing what you are capable of next time, cousin."

Taelien gave a curt nod, trying not to make his relief evident.

Fighting dangerous opponents was among his favorite activities, but he was in a poor place to continue.

It was dark, but even in the minimal light from his fallen weapon, he could see that the gash on his arm was severe. Not deep enough to cut to the bone, fortunately — he never would have managed to continue holding the sword at all if that had been the case — but bad enough that it could be crippling if left untreated.

"I need to treat my wound now," he told War.

"I will assist you."

Taelien blinked. He thought he understood War relatively well, but occasionally, the entity managed to surprise him.

It made sense when Taelien considered it for another moment. War wanted him in fighting shape so they could battle again as quickly as possible.

The cloaked figure sheathed his sword and approached. Taelien lowered his guard just a bit; he found it unlikely that War would launch a surprise attack now that their fight was over. This wasn't because War was honorable — rather, War simply had a completely different idea of morality, and whatever led to the best combat would please him the most.

That didn't mean Taelien was going to let his guard down entirely, however. He knelt and retrieved the Sae'kes, sheathing the weapon and belting it back on.

His arm could barely handle even that bit of use.

"I am capable of searing the wound shut," War offered.

Taelien shook his head. He had made that mistake before. "I have a medical kit in my bag. Do you know how to sew a wound shut?"

"Yes. Treating battlefield injuries is an acceptable application of my dominion."

Interesting.

Taelien tore through the wreckage of his tent to find his backpack, then pulled out the medical kit.

"Sit," War instructed.

Taelien complied.

"Hold your arm still and use your other hand to press the wound together. I will clean it first, then sew the wound."

The Wandering War was nothing if not efficient.

He gave Taelien a series of curt instructions as he repositioned him, then used the medical kit to clean, stitch, and dress the wound.

Taelien shivered as the rain continued to pound on the pair throughout the process. The Wandering War appeared unbothered.

"You are suffering from both blood loss and hypothermia."

Taelien nodded weakly. His vision was swimming again.

"Drink your water and put this on."

The Wandering War shrugged off his massive cloak and offered it with a hand.

Taelien blinked. "You won't be cold without it?"

War's expression was neutral. "No."

Taelien accepted the cloak and slipped it on without any further hesitation.

The inside was warm. Not just the warmth of clothing that had been pressed against skin; it radiated heat, almost enough to cause discomfort.

He could sense a hint of *power* within the cloak, the same type of sorcery that War used to conjure his floating blades. The Dominion of War itself, Taelien suspected.

Does that imply the cloak is actually a part of him? Or is it something he enchanted, deliberately or simply through close contact?

At the moment, it didn't matter.

It was warm.

He took a drink of his water, as commanded. The water sent another chill through him, but the cloak helped to compensate.

"Now, we must go."

Taelien blinked. "...Go?"

War nodded. "The others are waiting."

Taelien pulled the cloak tighter around him. "I'm not sure I'm in much of a condition to move."

War gave him an appraising look. "That is regrettable, because you will have to. Your assignment cannot be delayed."

The swordsman quirked an eyebrow at that. He didn't bother pointing out the fact that War had caused that delay. "What do you mean?"

"The man of many mirrors will know. I am simply to bring you to him."

Jonan?

I shouldn't be surprised. Being ambushed at night in the middle of nowhere? I should have suspected his involvement from the beginning.

Taelien sighed, pushing himself to his feet. He salvaged his supplies from his ruined tent, changing his socks for the soaked-but-not-mud-encrusted pair he had worn earlier, and then slipped on his boots.

His right arm still throbbed, but the salve that War had applied diminished the pain somewhat.

"Very well. Take me to Jonan."

***

Miles passed.

Taelien's wound burned.

The rain continued to pour down on the pair. The Wandering War's cloak helped alleviate the chill, but it was insufficient to evaporate the water that already clung to Taelien's clothes.

The swordsman trudged on. If he was alone, he would have found shelter for the night, but the present situation did not permit rest. The Wandering War had no need for sleep, and Taelien suspected that displaying weakness would be a potentially fatal mistake.

It was in the deepest part of night, where the nightfrost was hidden by the trees and the dawnfire still slumbered, that they reached the building.

It was a three-story wooden structure, alone among the trees. There was no paved road to the door, only a dirt path barely distinct from those used by game animals.

Nevertheless, there was light visible within, and that might have meant they had a fire going.

Taelien approached with more haste than caution.

The sign over the door read, "The Perfect Stranger". Taelien's lips tightened, the name triggering a memory.

I've seen a tavern with that name before... in Orlyn, maybe?

He shook his head. It didn't matter right now.

Before his hand reached the door, it swung open.

Asphodel stood in the doorway, the purple crystals that served as her hair glimmering in the tavern's light. She looked much the same as when he'd last seen her, with a thin frame and moderate height hiding tremendous physical strength. The hints of grey in her hair reminded him of how much she had sacrificed in their last clash with Sterling and his followers.

Taelien blinked. "How...?"

She tapped a finger to her forehead. "Oracle." From her tone, it was clear she felt that was a sufficient answer.

Taelien was too tired to care.

A louder voice came from behind Asphodel. "Scrape your boots off before you come in! If you get mud on my floor you're going to clean it yourself. You can use the rag next to the door."

Asphodel gestured downward, then stepped out of the doorway.

Taelien found an already-muddy rag next to the door, sighed, and bent down to begin wiping off his boots.

Another figure brushed past Asphodel to lean over him while he worked.

Her black eyes immediately signaled her as rethri — and one of the rarer varieties. Black eyes usually signaled a bond to shadow, death, or one of the deep dominions connected to them.

More unusual were the tattoos that stretched across nearly all of her exposed skin. To Taelien, they looked like they might be runic, but he hadn't seen this particular style on anyone or anything else.

Some looked like letters in a foreign language glowing softly in varying colors, but the largest mark was a single tendril-like sigil of black that wrapped around her hands and slipped under her sleeves. She had similar black markings that spread up her neck, but he couldn't tell if that was an extension of the same mark or another tattoo in a similar style.

At this distance, it was a trivial thing for him to sense the metal hidden within her sleeves. And her bodice, both front and back. And her skirt. And her boots.

She was carrying enough weapons for a platoon of soldiers.

He recognized her immediately, but her presence here was even stranger than Asphodel's.

The heavily armed woman smiled as she met his gaze. "Wow, those are rough. Here, you might need a stick to get some of that off." She knelt down next to him and handed him a stick, then leaned closer and whispered in his ear. "You do *not* want to get mud on my floor."

Taelien let out a tired sigh. "Of course. I wouldn't dream of it, Wrynn."

"Good!" Wrynn beamed, putting her hands together in front of her. "Then welcome to my humble establishment. Can I take your cloak?"

"It's his, actually." He waved at The Wandering War, who was still standing in the rain nearby. "Not sure if he'd want me to hand it off to someone."

"If it's soaking wet—," Wrynn paused, frowned, and leaned closer to the cloak. "Huh. Enchanted cloak? Okay, if it's not dripping, you can hold onto it."

"You may hang it up." War folded his arms. "I have no need of it here, and he should recover by the flame."

Taelien slipped the cloak off and handed it Wrynn. "Thanks."

She grinned as she accepted it. "Ooh, this is warm. You'll have to tell me where you got it. Keep wiping those boots, I'll be right back."

When Wrynn returned a moment later, she knelt back down and spoke in a more serious tone. "You're injured."

"He'll survive," Asphodel added helpfully.

Taelien gave Asphodel an irritated look. From most of his friends, a line like that would have sounded conciliatory. From Asphodel, it was merely matter-of-fact.

"He's the one you've been waiting for?" Wrynn asked. "Never mind, rhetorical question. Okay, Sal. That's good enough. Go get warm."

Taelien nodded gratefully, setting the cloth down and turning to face the tavern's entrance. "Thank you...but why are you here? I just saw you at your shop in Selyr a few weeks ago."

"Girl's gotta keep busy somehow." Wrynn winked at him.

That answer told him nothing, but that wasn't a surprise. Wrynn never gave anything away for free, information least of all.

Taelien wiped his face, pushing away an errant lock of hair. "Since you're here, I may have some things to trade later. And a present for you, too."

Wrynn gave him a knowing smirk. "A present? I love presents! I'd say you shouldn't have, but I'd be lying. I'm curious what you have to trade, too." She moved back into the tavern. "I have other customers to serve, but I'll want to hear what you brought later." She pointed a finger at War. "And you. Clean your boots next."

War nodded in silent assent.

Taelien might have questioned War's willingness to follow the instruction without any hint of complaint, but he knew who he was dealing with.

Apparently, even War could sense how dangerous she was.

Taelien stumbled as he attempted to stand, but Asphodel caught him and helped him. Fortunately, she had the foresight to grab his good arm. "Sorry," he mumbled.

"Come on." She half-maneuvered, half-carried him to an empty chair next to a roaring fireplace.

They passed a number of other patrons on the way, most of whom seemed to be either eating or playing various table games. Taelien counted ten other people in total. A pair of hunters playing cards. A few ordinary looking civilians. One white-haired man, flirting with a barmaid that was *almost* as heavily armed as Wrynn herself.

A table of Thornguard near the corner, all in uniform. He'd have to keep an eye on them.

This place is almost certainly some kind of front, either for one of Wrynn's businesses or a Thornguard operation. Possibly both.

No sign of Jonan, but that could mean anything. Invisible or asleep are equally likely.

Exhausted, he sat in a chair by the flames.

The fire didn't seem warm enough.

Taelien shivered.

This time, it was the cold.

Asphodel sat down in a chair next to him, frowning. "Your injury makes this more difficult."

Taelien started to fold his arms in frustration, winced as the movement hurt too much, and then reverted to his previous posture. "I have no idea what you're talking about or why you're here, Asphodel. I'm supposed to be alone."

She shook her head. "I have your new orders."

He clenched and unclenched his hands. "And those involved sending War to drag me into this tavern?"

"No. That was his idea. He was impatient to see you."

"And you couldn't have come with him, or gotten me a warning message?"

Asphodel hesitated, her face showing lines of worry. "Perhaps. I still cannot see you properly. It is...uncomfortable at times."

"Fine." Taelien put his good hand over the bandage, trying to will the aching to stop, but the movement only made it worse. "What's this new assignment?"

"Ah, it would appear I have excellent timing."

Jonan's voice came from behind Taelien, unmistakable.

The swordsman sighed, turning around. "If this was your idea, you owe me a new arm."

Jonan was wearing a heavy robe and leaning on a walking stick. It was definitely *not* the Heartlance disguised as a walking stick this time, at least. Taelien couldn't sense any metal within. He looked haggard, his face showing several days of unshaved growth and an angry scab on his forehead. "You have my sympathies, but it is beyond my capabilities to stop our tall friend when he wants something."

Taelien gave a groan of acknowledgement. Jonan had a point.

"Now, then, if you're as excited as I am about our reunion, you'll want to get this over with as quickly as possible. To business, then?"

Taelien waved a hand. "Business."

Jonan smirked. "Excellent. No doubt you recall that while I am not a member of the Thornguard, I am employed by one of their... benefactors?"

Jonan gave a meaningful glance toward the Thornguard table, then back to Taelien.

Taelien quirked a brow. "I don't think you ever said explicitly who you work for, but I'm aware of your ties to the organization. Are you bringing me in for some sort of joint operation?"

Jonan twisted his lips until he ended on a thoughtful expression. "Not...exactly? More like a proposition from one of our higher-ups for a mutually beneficial arrangement."

Taelien narrowed his eyes. "Could you say that in a way that sounds any *more* suspicious?"

"Hey, don't eviscerate the messenger. Or mutilate him in any fashion, really. Leave the messenger intact." Jonan raised his hands in a defensive gesture. "I'm here as your escort. *Your* superiors have already accepted. Your friend," he pointed at Asphodel, "can confirm that."

"Yes." That was all Asphodel said.

Such a helpful contribution.

He turned his head toward Asphodel. "And what of my previous assignment, then?"

"Postponed. You may hold the items for now, or use them for this assignment as needed."

Taelien made an effort not to glance at his backpack. Knowing Jonan, he probably had some way of knowing about the dominion bonded objects that Taelien had spent the last several months collecting, but he didn't want to make it any more obvious that he was carrying something valuable.

He felt fortunate that War had given him the chance to retrieve everything he could from the tent before they'd left. Otherwise, some hunter would have probably eventually stumbled on a bag full of priceless relics.

That was an amusing image, but not exactly a good scenario as far as his career as a paladin was concerned.

"Very well. What's this hilariously suspicious arrangement we're being offered, Jonan?"

Taelien tossed a glance back toward Wrynn, but she was currently serving other customers. Still, he doubted the presence of an information broker at his meeting place with Jonan was any kind of coincidence.

The fact that she seemed to *own* this tavern was even stranger. He knew she owned a shop in Selyr, but that was a half-day's walk away.

That's not important right now. He looked back to Jonan.

Jonan took off his glasses, wiping them against his shirt to remove some of the moisture. "Well, I've been telling my superiors a great deal about you. And, as it happens, one of them has a job that you're uniquely suited for."

Taelien quirked his eyebrow again. He was trying to break the habit of doing that so often, but it was *hard*. "Oh? And who is this superior you're referring to?"

Jonan opened his hands and stretched out his arms in a magnanimous gesture. "Why, who else, but Aayara, the Lady of Thieves?"

CHAPTER IV – JONAN II – A NESTED SERIES OF TRAPS

Jonan Kestrian checked his mirrors in the relative discomfort of The Perfect Stranger tavern.

One message was of particular interest, mostly because it was the worst news out of the bunch.

Scribe,
En route to meet with Scryer. I'm bringing Shiver, because of course I am.
Please advise if you have further intelligence on the Selyr situation.
-Silk

There was something disturbing about one of Aayara's agents referring to Lydia by an "ess" name. Velas had probably just found it amusing — there was no chance Lydia was actually an agent of a vae'kes — but it felt like a continuation of a disturbing trend.

Aayara's agents were everywhere. He was no exception, but that didn't mean he was comfortable with seeing how far her influence was spreading.

And he knew enough to know that he only had seen a fraction of her true level of influence.

Sterling operating in Selyr was a serious problem if it was true. That was one of the centers of Aayara's power, and Sterling certainly knew that. He'd worked for Aayara at one point — that was clear enough just from the "ess" in his name.

Maybe he *still* worked for her. Aayara had insisted that Sterling was acting on his own when he'd assassinated Kalsiris Theas, but that didn't mean a thing. She fed him lies like mother's milk.

It was also possible that Sterling had found some sort of power or influence that was sufficient that he thought he could compete with Aayara directly. That was a somewhat terrifying prospect, since any war between Sterling and Aayara would put him on the front lines.

It also begged the question of what sort of resource or benefactor could give Sterling the confidence to operate in her territory. The Blackstone Assassin was the obvious choice — he'd been Aayara's rival for centuries — but individual vae'kes rarely picked one side and then switched. It wasn't strictly impossible, but the explanation didn't *feel* right to him.

Should I ask Aayara about this when I see her?

There were risks involved with that. If Sterling and Aayara were cooperating, asking Aayara would lead to tipping Sterling off to the fact that Velas knew where he was. That could put Velas, Lydia, and Rialla into more danger.

Should I warn Lydia that Sterling may have Aayara's support?

That was a better question.

No, he concluded. *There's no hard evidence of that yet. And if she starts trying to pry into Aayara's business for connections to Sterling, that could lead to undermining my other plans.*

Jonan rubbed his temples, then sat down to write a reply.

The problem was that he wasn't sure how much he wanted to say.

He hesitated, tensed his jaw, and then lifted the quill to write.

Silk,

My business near Selyr is unrelated to Sterling. No details on his present location or disposition. Would advise extreme caution, however, given the possibility that he may have family members in the area.

-Scribe

Jonan knew she'd catch the implications of "family members". He didn't know how likely it was that other vae'kes would be working with him, but they had to be prepared for that possibility.

He set the quill down, sending the message to Velas through the same mirror she had used to contact him.

Now, how much should I tell Lydia?

He glanced at the mirror that matched Lydia's, considering.

Not much. I can't jeopardize my position in Aayara's inner circle, and even if I did, I don't have much reliable information.

He picked up the mirror, wishing for a moment that he could just look at *her*, rather than the letter she'd written to confirm acceptance of his meeting.

Can't tell her much, he concluded.

But I can't leave her with nothing.

The note he sent her was brief. Just enough to make him feel like he'd said something, even if it wasn't much.

Lydia,

Recently met with Taelien and arranged for a meeting between him and Aayara. He will be in our general area, but working on a different assignment. Your paladin leadership should already be aware of this.

You should plan for him to be too busy for us to utilize as a resource in dealing with other matters.

-Jonan

She'd probably be getting that information from another source soon, maybe even from Taelien himself.

But if something happened, at least he could lie to himself and say he'd given Lydia some sort of useful information.

Lying to himself was just as easy as lying to others.

Maybe easier.

Will Lydia and Velas be enough handle a vae'kes?

That question weighed on Jonan's mind as he extinguished his candle and crept into his borrowed bed.

***

The sound of a knock on his door woke Jonan from his nightmare, but it didn't quite manage to send the last images out of his mind.

Lavender again.

Will she ever stop haunting me?

Probably not.

He wiped his eyes, then searched for a pair of his glasses. "Just a minute."

Is it morning already?

I suppose so.

Time to manipulate my friends, then.

After knocking the glasses case off the nearest table, he managed to find it on the floor and remove his standard pair. His vision was still blurry, even with them. His vision had been declining further from years of overusing his sight sorcery, but he compensated by getting stronger and stronger spectacles.

Blindness would come eventually if he kept abusing his sorcery, but that was a problem for the future.

He was still dressed from the night before, so he didn't bother with anything else before he opened the door.

It wasn't who he was expecting.

The delaren girl had a cheerful expression. "Good morning."

"Mmm." He managed. "Can I help you?"

He didn't know what to make of Asphodel. He'd met her briefly after the paladin exams had concluded, and he'd heard a considerable amount about her, but hadn't interacted with her on a personal level until recently.

When he'd delivered his message to the Paladins of Tae'os, they'd insisted that he take paladins as an escort when he went to relay the orders to Taelien. The lack of trust had been obvious. That was smart.

They seemed to expect the combination of Asphodel and The Wandering War to keep Taelien out of trouble somehow. That was a perplexing decision. Were Asphodel's oracular abilities that potent?

Potent enough to spot a trap? If so, how far in advance, and with what level of detail?

Jonan didn't know, and that bothered him.

She continued to smile, though. If she had any indication of Jonan's anxieties, she gave no hint. "The rain stopped. We should eat and leave before it starts again."

"Thank you."

Predicting the weather, or just acting based on a basic observation? Hm.

"I'll head downstairs after I pack my things."

"Good." She turned and started to walk away.

She seems nice. I hope she survives all this.

After a few more steps, she paused and turned back. "Jonan?"

He blinked. "Yes?"

"When the time comes, open the other door."

There was a brief pause. "Okay, you're going to have to translate that from vague oracle speak into Velthryn."

Asphodel smiled. "I can't."

"Why? Some of that infamous difficulty with interfering with fate?"

She shook her head. "No. I don't know. I only learned to call the dreams for myself recently. They're very vague." Asphodel shook her head. "But I'm sure you'll know what it means when the time comes." With that, she bowed, turned again, and walked away.

Jonan stared after her.

Let me revise my earlier statement. She seems nice, but also utterly infuriating.

For the moment, he decided he had bigger things to worry about than vague and useless prophecies.

Jonan was true to his word, packing his belongings while he considered his next moves. He didn't know what Aayara was planning to do with Taelien, but he needed to be ready for as many scenarios as possible.

After packing, he headed downstairs. The others seemed prepared to leave, so he ate a simple breakfast and said his goodbyes to Wrynn. She assured him that she'd see him again soon, which he wasn't sure about, but he agreed so that he sounded friendly.

He said goodbye to the Thornguard group staying at the inn, too. They had other business, so they were staying a bit longer.

Jonan's sole company for the next few days would be the strangest paladins he'd ever seen.

Asphodel's cheerful demeanor had subsided, and now she was back to wearing a more typical introspective look. He found her crystalline hair fascinating, but he suspected that asking to study it might be a social blunder.

The Wandering War looked even stranger now that he wasn't wearing his cloak. His height was conspicuous, but at least tall humans existed. No human's flesh had a metallic sheen like his.

Taelien looked miserable. His long hair was wildly askew, and from Taelien's sunken eyes, it looked like he'd slept even worse than Jonan had. He was the only one of the paladins that looked human.

If Jonan had to guess, Taelien was probably the least human of any of them. He hadn't confirmed his suspicions, but perhaps the meeting with Aayara would be illuminating, provided she even allowed him to stay and listen.

They left on foot, rather than by horseback. Their destination was only a day's walk away, still far from either of the main cities in the region.

They approached the village at nightfall, after a few stops due to Taelien's injuries. It was too small to even have a signpost indicating its name.

It reminded him of home.

He pictured it ending the same way as his home had, with broken bodies littering the dirt paths and buildings burning until they collapsed.

Nothing I can do if she wants that, he told himself. *But burning villages isn't in Aayara's character. Her horrors are of a completely different variety.*

It wasn't hard to find their destination. It was the largest building in the town, and the exterior was swarming with Thornguard in full uniform.

Jonan paused and turned to the others. "Wait here for a moment."

He approached one of the Thornguard members and waved. "Hey, Conrad. This is the group that Lady Aayara asked for. Is she in?"

Conrad nodded. "Yep, she's in there. Looked like she was in a pretty good mood, too. You can head on in if you're ready."

"Thanks, just give me a minute to, um, brief the others on proper decorum."

The Thornguard gave him a knowing look. "Of course."

Jonan wandered back to where the others were standing. "We're clear to head in."

Taelien folded his arms. "That's it? I expected a bit more security for someone as high profile as she is."

Jonan laughed. "What would the point be? Even the guards there aren't for her protection. They're mostly to keep her from being annoyed."

Asphodel nudged Taelien in the arm. "Do not be rash."

Taelien raised his hands in a defensive gesture. "I'll be on my best behavior. Aren't you more worried about what War will do?"

The Wandering War tilted his head down toward Taelien. "You are...concerned about my behavior?"

Jonan turned toward the towering giant. As much as he hated to admit it, Taelien actually had a point. The Wandering War was a potentially dangerous factor to introduce into a meeting with Aayara. "Please do not take any violent actions in Aayara's presence. She would react poorly, and not in a way you would enjoy."

War stood up straight, speaking toward nothing. "I would not dare to insult one such as she. She is the architect of great things both past and present, and I would not survive antagonizing her."

That...was not the response he had expected.

He'd have accepted that answer from almost anyone without a thought. Aayara was, in his opinion, probably the most dangerous entity on the planet. He included gods in that evaluation — because gods were predictable.

Aayara was just as physically dangerous, but every time he thought he understood her, she'd find a way to defy his expectations.

The idea that The Wandering War — an entity from another plane with a completely different way of evaluating the world — was intimidated by her?

That was a little terrifying.

"Right. Good. Let's not make her mad. Let me introduce you, then she'll guide the conversation. I'll try to smooth over anything that gets awkward. Any questions?"

Taelien glanced at the Thornguard, then back to Jonan. "Can we trust her?"

"Of course not. She'll honor an agreement if she makes one, but she won't make a deal unless it's advantageous to her. That may mean that you're offering her more than you realize, or it may mean that what she's giving you is worth less than you wanted."

"Sounds like a typical merchant. I can handle that."

Jonan rolled his eyes. *You go ahead and think that.*

"All right. Any other questions?"

There weren't, so Jonan waved a hand and led them to the building. They weren't escorted inside. One of the guards simply opened the door and gave them a look of sympathy.

Jonan led them to the door at the end of the hall where Aayara would be located. He'd only been in this particular location once, but he remembered it.

He knocked once for propriety's sake. Aayara probably knew they'd arrived the moment they stepped foot in town. Possibly sooner. "It's Jonan. I've brought Taelien, as you requested, and he is accompanied by two companions."

"Come in, the door is open."

Jonan opened the door.

Aayara was sitting behind a desk, running a cloth along an unsheathed rapier. It wasn't necessary; the blade was already pristine. *Luck's Touch in one of its guises*, he realized. *Oh, this is not going to end well.*

He suppressed the urge to flee, pausing in his tracks instead of stumbling back like he might have when he was younger.

She was dressed in an unremarkable gray tunic and pants, with her hair pulled back in a neat bun. With the bandolier of tools stretched across her chest, she fit the image of a young thief ready to break into some wealthy noble's mansion.

This was ridiculous, of course, because Aayara owned virtually every mansion in the region — and most of the land in general.

The image was pure theatrics. She was presenting the image that most people imagined when they thought about the *legends* of the Lady of Thieves. If he didn't know any better, he might have thought she was trying to recapture some of the fun of her youth.

But he did know her better. She was the closest thing he had to family.

Fortunately, that meant he knew how to play her games, even if he knew she'd always be a few steps ahead. "Symphony."

He greeted her by her old guild "ess" name to acknowledge her current guise, and bowed at the waist. "Allow me to present Taelien Salaris, the current bearer of the Sae'kes, as you requested. He is accompanied by Asphodel, a Paladin of Tae'os, and The Wandering War, a Harvester of War."

Aayara stood up, set down her polishing cloth, and sheathed the rapier at her hip. "Thank you, Scribe. And thank you all for coming at such short notice. Please, have a seat."

There were three seats across from her. Not enough for all of them, if Jonan included himself. But he understood the intent, and instead drifted to Aayara's side of the table to stand next to her.

The others took seats. Taelien, to his credit, managed to keep his hand off the hilt of his own weapon — a rarity.

Aayara drifted around to the opposite side of the table, extending a hand to The Wandering War first. "A Harvester of War. It's been some time since I've seen one of you. I thank you for the visit."

The Harvester hesitated.

He's afraid. A moment later, he realized why. *She's a vae'kes — she can absorb dominion essence. He's primarily, if not entirely, composed of that essence.*

Could she kill him outright, just by touching him?

He's probably wondering that same thing right now.

Moments passed. The Wandering War accepted her hand. "It is an honor to meet one such as you."

Aayara smiled. "Likewise." She moved to Asphodel next, extending her hand. "And a delaren! How delightful."

"You're wrong." Asphodel's expression sank into a frown.

"Pardon?" Aayara tilted her head to the side.

"Everything about you...it's wrong. Your destiny is...I don't understand."

"Oh, you refer to your oracular insights! How fascinating. May I see what you see?"

Asphodel visibly recoiled. "I..."

Taelien shifted to the side, offering a hand toward Aayara. "Lady Aayara, I've been hearing about you since I was a child. It's such a pleasure to finally meet you."

Aayara turned her head just slightly toward Taelien. "I'll get to you." She turned back toward Asphodel, grinning broadly enough to show teeth. "About those visions."

"You would not like them." Asphodel shook her head, then reached out and took Aayara's hand. "But in any case, they are mine."

"A pity. Perhaps later." Aayara accepted the handshake, patting Asphodel's hand softly with her other hand.

Jonan stepped back into the corner of the room, trying to get as much distance as possible, just in case something happened in the next exchange. Sadly, the plain room didn't offer any protective cover.

"Taelien Salaris. An unusual name, don't you think?" She accepted his offered hand by clasping it at the wrist. "Full of so many layers of meaning."

Taelien nodded. "Unlike Aayara, which is largely a meaningless combination of syllables in any modern language."

Aayara laughed. "Quite so! I do get tired of the excessive vowels at times, but it suits me."

"More than your original name?"

Aayara released his wrist and waved her hand. "Oh, you're a bit devious, aren't you? I hadn't expected that. But you won't win that little tidbit out of me, I'm afraid. Certainly not today."

"A shame, I was hoping to get to know you a little bit better." Taelien gave a sharp grin of his own.

Taelien was *not* devious.

Not normally, anyway.

But Aayara loved it when people tried to tease things out of her.

Has he been coached for this more than I'd expected?

It wasn't impossible. *He'd been close with Velas for a time...but that was before their fight. And before that, she hadn't told him who she was, had she?*

Jonan put his pondering on hold to continue watching the exchange. The others seemed content to listen to Taelien and Aayara, too.

"Oh, I'm sure you will." Aayara sat atop the table. "A little bit, at least. But forgive me, I'm being inhospitable. You've come a long way. Would you like anything to eat or drink?"

Taelien offered a strained smile. "I wouldn't mind some water to start, and maybe some food after we finish discussing things."

Aayara nodded. "Scribe, be a darling and fetch some water? Not the swill from the well — go get some from my carriage."

Jonan frowned. This was a calculated way of getting him out of the room, if only briefly. "Of course. But before I forget, I have a little something for you."

Aayara put a hand over her chest in mock surprise. "A gift? For me? Whatever for?"

He reached into a pouch at his side, retrieving a pair of earrings. "Silk knew she wouldn't be able to see you for a while, so she asked me to help her make some gifts and to give them to you."

"Oh, how lovely!" Aayara accepted the earrings. "I love them. Which of you made which?"

Her question implied an immediate understanding of what he'd just handed her. That was useful, but also somewhat disturbing. As far as he was aware, they'd made something unique. "Left is from me, right from her."

"How wonderful. When you see Silk, please give her my best wishes. But we're being rude to our guests! The water?"

"Yes, of course."

Jonan left the room.

"And close the door behind you."

He did.

Then he slipped on an earring from his bag, matching the left one that he'd given Aayara.

She could easily dispel the sorcery inside, but he didn't think she would. He'd countered her movement, and she'd reward that.

He sent a spark of essence into the earring and activated it before exiting the building and heading to find the carriage outside.

"...Now then, it's much less crowded in here, now isn't it?"

The voice came from within his earring, but it wasn't audible to anyone else. That factor made it superior to most traditional listening enchantments.

He was able to bypass the normal limitation through a bit of stolen ingenuity. Traditional enchanted items were made with dominion bonds that tied them to a single dominion. That limited the variety of functions that were possible; an item bonded to the dominion of sound could copy or transfer sounds, but it had little other functionality.

These earrings were more complex, made through researching the dominion marks that Edon had used in Orlyn. Jonan had studied Edon's notes, and Velas had seen Edon work directly on a number of occasions. When he'd last seen her a few months ago, they'd worked on a couple enchanting projects together.

The pairs of earrings were a result of their combined efforts. They involved four runes enchanted with different functions; sound transference, silence covering the area around the ear to prevent the sound from escaping, an activation rune, and a final rune that could be used to make the earring invisible.

Jonan had only performed the fourth enchantment, but they agreed that it was integral to making the device useful; he could drop one of the paired earrings somewhere, make it invisible, and listen to the area remotely.

For now, he'd just turned on the function that would let him continue listening to the part of the conversation that originally Aayara had intended for him to miss.

He heard Taelien's voice next. "I didn't mind the company, but if you'd prefer to keep this to a smaller group, that's fine by me."

"Perhaps you'd be more worried about Jonan if you knew more about how his mind worked."

Jonan sighed, both at Aayara's way of turning suspicion toward him — which she'd later call "training" or something — and the distinct lack of a carriage outside.

He wandered over to one of the Thornguard and inquired about its location — predictably, the carriage was on the other side of the village.

Fortunately, that was only a few minutes away, given the size of the place.

Jonan headed toward the carriage.

Taelien spoke again. "I was aware he worked with the Thornguard, but until recently I wouldn't have believed he had as famous an employer as you."

"Oh, I wouldn't underestimate that one. But enough about my little Scribe. We have business to discuss, yes?"

"Of course."

"She sends us on an errand of death." Asphodel's voice. Apt as usual.

"Oh, let's not be quite so dramatic, darling," Aayara replied. "There's no need for there to be any killing on this assignment."

"But there will be." Asphodel again.

Jonan heard Aayara sigh audibly. "The future is far from fixed. You should know that better than anyone, don't you?"

Asphodel didn't respond.

One point to Aayara, then.

"Now, then," Aayara continued. "The task at hand. I require something simple of you, and offer something you would be quite interested in. I will not pretend that 'simple' will mean 'easy', in this case, but I am aware of your abilities and believe you will be up to the task. In fact, it's something you may quite enjoy."

Taelien shifted to a more even tone. "No need to dance around it, Aayara. What are you looking for?"

"I'd like for you to attend an auction on my behalf. One of the items available is something I would quite enjoy having in my collection of curios."

"An auction? I'm sure you have plenty of money to work with, and numerous Thornguard you could send. What's the catch?"

His mistake is assuming there's only one catch.

"Ah, the auctioneer is, shall we say, somewhat eccentric. We do not have the best relationship, and he is not fond of the Thornguard in general. Are you familiar with Lord Korus Kyestri?"

Jonan's heart sank when he heard that name.

This was, almost without a doubt, why he'd been sent out of the room. Even if he didn't say anything, he wouldn't have been able to avoid giving away his panic with body language.

He quickened his pace toward the carriage. It was in sight now. He might still have time to intervene.

"I've heard the name. One of the rethri prime lords. He's a recluse, lives virtually alone in the woods. They say he keeps a menagerie of monsters."

"Right on all counts, I'm pleased to say."

"And this auction item is...what, a monster? Looking to buy something dangerous?"

No, no, no, Taelien. You're thinking about this all wrong.

But he couldn't be blamed. He didn't know her.

And Jonan hadn't even tried to help him, not really.

Jonan reached the carriage. It was unattended, so he just threw open the doors. No water in the main seating area, so he went and searched the compartment in the back.

"Nothing so vulgar as that, I assure you. No, the prize is a curio from Lord Kyestri's collection. In addition to his menagerie, he maintains a large museum. He's decided to get rid of some of his item collection to make room for newer finds."

Everything about that sounded reasonable, but there was a serious problem that Taelien couldn't be aware of.

Jonan found several bottles of Liadran lake water in the back compartment. He grabbed four, holding them awkwardly, and started shuffling back toward the others as quickly as he could.

"That all sounds fine, but it doesn't explain why you want me in there. Couldn't you just hire a mercenary?"

"No, no. They'd need an invitation. You, however, would interest him keenly — he would be quite interested to meet you. He's a collector of artifacts, you see."

"Ah. The sword. Of course that's the reason." Taelien sounded somewhat disappointed. "Very well. War, you want to come with me?"

"I would be pleased to meet one who keeps monsters as pets," The Wandering War replied.

"I may have a better proposition for you, Harvester. But allow me to conclude this deal before making another."

"Of course."

Taelien spoke again. "Anything else I should be aware of?"

"He's unlikely to part with the object I want for mere money. You'd need to part with something significant. Perhaps an artifact, like that lovely sword of yours."

A moment of silence, then Taelien replied. "What is it that you're offering?"

Oh, he shouldn't have asked that so soon.

"Why, I'm offering what your friends have been wondering about for close to a year now. The identity and location of The Shrouded One."

Jonan tried to pick up his pace, but one of the bottles slipped. Fortunately, it didn't break — they were pretty resilient — but he had to stop to pick it back up.

He's going to agree before I can stop him.

But of course he is. There was never any other way this was going to end.

Taelien was more reserved in his reply than Jonan would have expected. "I would need to know more details. For example, if the Shrouded One is already dead and you point me at a graveyard, that's not useful. If the Shrouded One is a title used by multiple people, and you give me one that's completely unrelated to the one I'm looking for—"

"Reasonable objections. Very well, I will clarify. I will give you the current location and identity of the person who hired Sterling to kill the members of the Theas family. I also give you my assurance that this person is, to the best of my knowledge, alive and not imprisoned, and still actively leading their organization."

"That assurance is sufficient on that topic, thank you. What's the item you're looking for?"

"A silver half-face mask. It's a bit of an antique."

Jonan didn't recognize the description.

"You're talking about the Mask of Kishor." Taelien's tone was accusatory.

Aayara didn't respond for a moment. Jonan was mildly impressed — apparently she'd underestimated his knowledge. In truth, Jonan had as well, even if he knew Taelien had spent the last several months hunting for dominion bonded items for his order.

"Quite right. I commend you on your scholarly knowledge. It's a rarity to find someone who appreciates the antiquities these days."

"That's not a mere 'curio' or 'trinket'. It's an artifact from the world of Rendalir, before it was destroyed. I can see why you'd mention trading my sword for it; they're probably of similar value."

Aayara chuckled. "Oh, I wouldn't *actually* put it on quite the same scale as the Sae'kes. But you're not likely to have anything else of similar value, are you? Unless you're hiding Hartigan's Star somewhere?"

That was not a comforting answer for Jonan, and it probably wasn't for anyone else involved.

"You're asking a great deal."

"I'm also offering a great deal. The identity of the leader of a dangerous cult. Isn't that worth handing over something you barely even want?"

"I'll have to consider—'"

"We'll accept the deal." Asphodel's voice.

Jonan paused for a moment in his step. *What?*

"Oh, fascinating. I thought you would be the one to object, oracle?"

"No. What you offer is of greater value than a sword or mask. The Shrouded One must be stopped."

"You're sure about this?" Taelien's voice.

Silence.

The silence lingered too long.

It took Jonan a few moments to realize what had happened — Aayara had turned off the other earring.

When he made it back to the building, he brushed passed the guards without a word, then swung open the door to Aayara's room.

He found Taelien shaking Aayara's hand. "We have a deal."

"Excellent." Aayara turned her head to where Jonan stood helpless in the doorway. "Ah, Scribe. Just in time. Let's all enjoy a drink to celebrate our deal."

***

Hours later, Jonan stood alone with Aayara in her office. The others had been sent to lodgings nearby where they could enjoy a meal.

"Well, what do you think?" Aayara slipped a bottle of wine out from under the table, pouring glasses for them both.

"You shouldn't have dismissed me like that."

"Oh, but you countered so wonderfully! Wonderfully inadequately, but wonderfully nonetheless." She nudged one of the drinks without even bothering to slide it across to him, so he reached over and picked it up.

The wine was too sharp for his tastes, but he sipped it anyway. "Getting him killed isn't going to be good for any of us."

"Who?"

"Either of them."

"Bah, you're too soft. I'm not like my darling Jack, I don't revel in removing people. But there are cases when someone is sufficiently disruptive that sometimes it's the best option."

"And that applies to Taelien now, or to this 'prime lord'?"

"No need to take that tone with me, Jonan. It's rude." She stared at him, her eyes burrowing into his until he turned away.

She still had Luck's Touch at her hip, but he wasn't worried about that. She wouldn't physically harm him.

Not directly.

"Fine, I'll behave." He took another sip and sat down across from her. "But that doesn't mean I have to agree with you. And since I happen to be involved with *both* parties, I think it's fair to want some information."

Aayara sipped from her own drink, then smiled. "I suppose I could share a bit, for my favorite apprentice."

Jonan set his glass down. "Favorite? Wouldn't that be Silk? She's the one with the title, after all."

"Oh, are you jealous, dear?" She waved a hand dismissively. "You're both my favorites. I couldn't possibly choose between my children."

Children. Jonan shuddered in spite of himself. "You could have told me about her."

"What, and spoil the fun? I let you meet her when the two of you were old enough."

"I could have used a partner."

"For what? Oh, perhaps when you killed Lord Kyestri? Was that too difficult to manage on your own?"

The image of a wine glass tainted with poison flickered in his mind.

He lifted his current glass. Was it the same type, a Selyrian red?

Of course it was.

"That wasn't the hard part. Teaching his replacement was."

"It was excellent training for you. Even after all these years, I haven't heard the slightest hint of suspicion — and you know how broadly I listen."

Jonan grimaced. "Why set him up against Taelien, then?"

"What makes you think I'm doing that?"

Answering that was surprisingly easy. "Because I know him, and I know what I've reported to you. You're positioning them with the intent for the two to conflict, just like I did when I put him in Edon's periphery."

"A masterful bit of work. Enough that I don't even mind you comparing your work to mine, even if your plans still tend toward a little too direct for my tastes."

"Are you implying you have another goal, then?"

"My dear, I'm always implying everything you can't think of. You should know that by now."

"Of course." He sipped again. It wasn't poisoned, fortunately. The wine itself was just a reminder. "Okay, answer me this, then. That...thing you had me train to take Kyestri's place. What is he really? Why do this now?"

"I'm not going to give you those answers for free. You should have paid closer attention. Tell you what, though. I'll answer your questions if you get your own assignment done quickly enough."

"Oh? Need me to prepare a *third* Lord Kyestri for you?"

"What did I say about your tone? Manners, Jonan."

Jonan took a moment to phrase his response a bit more carefully. Upsetting Aayara, even in small ways, was always unwise. "My apologies. What is it that you require of me?"

Aayara gave him a smile that held all the fondness of a child playing with a toy that they would break within the month. "Now, that wasn't so hard, was it? As for your assignment, you're not going with them to meet with Kyestri. He'll be able to see through your illusions by now, and seeing you would put him on high alert. We can't have that. Instead, you'll be taking a bodyguard and going on a different assignment."

She was offering a good excuse, but there was another reason for it that she wasn't stating — if she sent him somewhere completely different, he couldn't intervene to protect either party from one another.

Not directly, at any rate.

She was offering him answers with the knowledge that he'd probably rush to finish his assignment quickly enough to try to get back and take action based on that information. Of course, she'd set it up to make that implausible, one way or another.

Implausible, never impossible. That was one way she used hope to her advantage.

Fine. I can play that way.

Jonan thought back to one unusual part of her last statement. "A bodyguard? That's atypical."

Aayara waved a hand. "It's an atypical assignment. We wouldn't want you to get hurt doing something dangerous, now would we?"

"Right, of course. Clearly, none of my previous work has been dangerous."

"Not like this. You'll need a very special bodyguard for a job on this scale."

"Who..." Jonan frowned, thinking back to the meeting. "Wait, I think I already know. And I'd ask if you were serious, but I know you always are. Fine. A 'bodyguard'. What sort of mission warrants assistance of that magnitude?"

"Haven't you figured that out yet? Your assignment is quite simple. Find the identity and current location of The Shrouded One. You must, of course, finish this before Taelien returns...if he returns at all. We wouldn't want to fail to deliver on our part of the bargain, would we?"

Jonan sighed, turning his head to the side.

How typical.

"No. Of course not."

A deal was a deal, after all.

CHAPTER V – LYDIA II – CROWNS

Lydia moved a single piece on the Crowns board. The spy wasn't the most powerful piece she had available, but it was in just the right position.

And, of course, it didn't look like a spy — it looked like a humble soldier, unless one identified it with another spy or a diviner. The only physical indication of which soldier was actually the spy was on the bottom of the piece.

It could move two squares to a soldier's one — and straight through enemy units. Doing so would, of course, reveal that it was the spy...

"Spy takes throne." She grinned, then reached up to fix her hair. A few strands of red had slipped out and gotten underneath her glasses. "You're getting slow in your old age."

Landen of the Twin Edges sighed and leaned back in his table. "Somehow, no matter how many times you play that trick, I still fall for it. Must have been just like that in Orlyn, hmm?"

"Not quite as simple as that, as much as I wished it was." She knew Landen was making a friendly joke, but she couldn't laugh. Infiltrating that city's government had not only been a harrowing experience, it had been one that challenged her morals.

"Perhaps the visit to Selyr will go better," she added with a hint more levity than she'd managed with her previous statement.

Landen picked up the wine glass next to the Crowns board and lifted it idly without drinking. "Less sneaking, I'd imagine, but similar risks. You sure you want to head into Thornguard territory? I suspect it won't be a particularly warm welcome."

She thought back to Jonan's last letter and the vague warning it contained. "No, most likely not. But I won't be going alone."

[I will accompany you.]

That wasn't quite what Lydia had meant, but she felt gratitude for Vendria's presence regardless.

The stone had grown progressively more coherent over the last few months, but Lydia expected Vendria to fall silent again soon. There seemed to be a pattern to Vendria's coherence; she was much more capable of communicating during some months than others. Lydia suspected that had something to do with the balance of the dominions in the world, but Vendria had offered no answers.

"You sure I can't convince you to take me along?" Landen finally stopped fiddling with his drink and took a sip, then set it back down. "House Theas has connections there. There may be some people that can help."

Lydia shook her head. "I'd like that, but there's a good chance we're going straight after Sterling if they have information on him."

"I don't see the problem."

Lydia folded her arms. "Don't be stubborn. Of course you do."

"He failed. I'm alive. Made it through that assassination better than most of you. No offense meant by that, of course." He took another draw from the cup. "And I wouldn't mind another round."

Lydia ignored the play on words. "That's just the problem. Even if he decided to break his contract, there's a good chance he'd see failing to kill you as a point of pride. You'd be a target. And, given that you survived last time, he'd be likely to approach you from a different angle this time. Like slipping something in your drink."

Landen set his drink down, crinkling his nose. "He'd have to get pretty close to do that."

"Wouldn't have to do it himself. Any innkeeper or barmaid could be one of his agents. We're all at risk, of course, but if you went after him directly you'd be inviting a confrontation."

"Is that really a bad thing? We want to catch him. Let me be bait."

A hand fell on Landen's shoulder from behind. "I would rather not risk my last remaining relative on revenge quite so soon, Larkin." Nakane Theas leaned over his shoulder. "Even if you are drinking all my wine."

"Please, Nakane. It's Landen. That other name and role never suited me. I never would have been happy as a noblewoman like you." Landen sighed. "You're too young for wine, anyway. And your father is alive."

"Is he? I hadn't noticed."

Nakane's father — the legendary immortal sorcerer, Edrick Theas — had visited after the deaths of his wife and son, and then quickly departed the city again. In spite of his advanced age, he still served as a military leader, apparently fighting in some sort of distant campaign against a last bastion of the Xixian Empire on an island off the coast of the continent.

In Edrick's absence, Landen had asked his paladin superiors to assign him to his cousin's protection. While they were now aware of Sterling's identity, the organization that had hired him was still largely a mystery. His period of guardianship would end when and if Lydia managed to discover and handle the source.

Lydia allowed the cousins to banter for a few more moments, lost in her thoughts until a woman in servant's garb brought word from the gate. "Miss Jaldin is here to see you, Lady Theas."

Lydia took a moment to peer curiously at the "servant", noting her unusual blue hair and the all-too-familiar aura of protection sorcery glimmering around her. The effect was virtually invisible to the naked eye, but as a protection sorcerer herself, Lydia could sense its presence like a pressure in the air.

Not just a servant, then. A sorcerer in a servant's uniform. Not unwise, given how ineffective the guards proved to be the last time Sterling paid House Theas a visit. I'll wager that if they hired one, there are probably more lurking somewhere just out of sight.

Nakane waved a hand. "Thank you, Emily. Send her in."

Landen's eyes followed Emily as she vanished back toward the gate, leaving Lydia with a few more questions to ask him the next time they had some privacy.

Velas arrived a few moments later, wearing a formal dress in House Jaldin's colors — white and gold — rather than her usual paladin garb. She bowed to Nakane. "Lady Theas, thank you for the invitation."

Nakane rose and returned the gesture. "The pleasure is always mine. Can I interest you in a game of Crowns before you get to business?"

Velas gave Lydia a quizzical glance. Lydia shrugged a shoulder. "May as well enjoy yourself, we haven't left yet."

Landen got out of his chair and walked over to Velas' side, looking her up and down. "You must have gotten awfully out of shape if you're wearing something like that to cover up your figure."

Velas sent a casual slap in his direction, but Landen stepped back and grinned. "Or maybe you just picked up a few new scars?"

Velas blurred, reappearing right in front of him, almost nose-to-nose. "I'll show you scars." She grabbed him and pulled him into a hug. "Missed you."

"Well, yes, you weren't aiming very carefully." Landen chuckled. "I missed you, too."

"I know, otherwise you wouldn't have been eyeing my dress." Velas released him from the hug, then sat down in his chair and picked up his glass of wine. "Now, about that game of Crowns..."

***

Later that evening, Lydia arrived at the entrance of another familiar home. In simpler times, it would have been a comforting sight.

At the moment, however, Lydia felt her heart beating rapidly as she continued to debate her current course of action.

She steeled herself and knocked on the door.

It was no servant or guard that answered the door, but one of the owners of the home — albeit not the one she'd expected.

Lydia blinked as she processed the ancient rethri, his black hair streaked with white. That factor alone was a peculiarity among his species, since they typically ceased having any outward signs of age after their coming of age ritual.

Ulandir Ta'thyriel was far from typical in a number of regards, however.

The white in his hair matched the paleness of his eyes, as well as the rune-like markings that stretched beyond them. The lack of color was not a sign of blindness, but rather an unusual eye color, even by rethri standards. Ulandir's dominion bond was a rare one, and his life-long exploration of its uses the cause of his atypical appearance.

Lydia bowed. "Lord Ta'thyriel, it's been too long. I wasn't aware you were back home."

The elderly rethri stared at her for an uncomfortable moment, and then he nodded. "Yes. I suppose I am, aren't I?"

"May I come inside?"

Another moment of silence, and then he replied, "I suspect you might." After a few more seconds, he stepped out of the doorway, shaking his head.

Lydia nodded. "Thank you." She stepped inside, closing the door behind her. "I'm looking for Aladir. Is he home?"

Ulandir shrugged a shoulder. "He's probably around somewhere." He raised a hand to his head, closing his eyes for a moment. "Ah, Lydia. Yes. Forgive me. My manners seem to have fled. Please, come in, and make yourself comfortable."

Lydia breathed a sigh of relief, following Ulandir to a sitting room. "Make yourself comfortable. I will prepare some tea."

Ulandir retreated from the room, still looking somewhat...*off*.

He's likely been overusing a sorcery type related to knowledge. I must be cautious, or I may end up much the same.

[Is that what happened to me?]

Lydia was surprised to hear the response from the stone. She knew Vendria *could* hear her thoughts, but she rarely responded to them without prompting.

I don't know, Vendria. I can try some more diagnostic spells on you again later, but I'm not a memory sorcerer. It's not my area of expertise.

[I understand. I believe I am beginning to remember more, but...it's all in fragments. I feel as if I was once something much more, but I don't know what that means.]

We'll work on it. You seem to be doing much better than usual.

[I believe the knowledge spells you have been casting on me have been helping...but I fear the effects may only be temporary. I sense my cognition waning with the changing of the seasons. I do not know why.]

Interesting. That lines up with some of my previous observations. I'll see what I can find. I have some additional spells we can test when we leave the city, including one that may be able to link our minds. Perhaps that could help me explore the problem more directly.

[Is linking our minds safe?]

It has risks. We'll try other spells first. I'll save that one for an emergency, or if we exhaust our other options.

[I see. Thank you, Lydia. I appreciate your efforts.]

Lydia didn't have long to wait. Aladir arrived in the sitting room a few minutes later, grinning brightly. "Lydia! It's so good to see you." His grin shifted to a conspiratorial look. "And a bit out of character for you to pay me a social visit."

Lydia laughed, standing from the couch where she'd been seated. "I've been away for nearly a year. Is it so strange that I'd visit my partner upon my return?"

Aladir laughed, walking closer and opening his arms. "Not at all, it's certain you've come up with a few ideas on how to make use of me by now."

In spite of the cheer of his demeanor, there was something worrisome about Aladir's message.

Still, she brushed it from her mind for the moment, stepping forward and accepting the offered hug. Aladir gave the best hugs. "I did miss you, and not just for your willingness to cooperate with my schemes."

"Of course, but that's always a part of it." Aladir released her. "Come, tell me what's on your mind."

The pair sat on the couch, and Lydia took a moment to collect her thoughts and determine her approach.

Direct is likely best with this, she decided.

"I've been invited to pay a visit to Selyr. I suspect Sterling is there, and I plan to apprehend him."

Aladir clasped his hands together. "You never think small, do you?"

"Rarely," she admitted, "But this is something that needs to be done. We need to know who hired him, and if they're a long-term threat to our order."

"I don't deny that, but I suspect your motivation may be somewhat more personal?" He gestured to her new ever-present companion — a walking cane, used to support the weight from her bad leg. She could move about without it from time to time, but it was difficult, even after Aladir's own life sorcery had been used and all this recovery time.

"I won't deny that I want some degree of closure, but less because of the leg. He killed one of us, and there needs to be justice for that."

Aladir waved a hand. "I agree, of course. I simply don't want you to do anything reckless."

"I won't. And I'd like to ask—"

Aladir interrupted her. "Give me a few days. I'll need to file the paperwork to take some leave, then be seen somewhere public on vacation."

She leaned over and hugged him again. "You know I wouldn't ask you if it wasn't important."

"Of course. And there must be a good reason you came here, instead of simply asking for backup through official channels."

He phrased it as a statement, but the query was obvious. "Velas is coming with me, and I don't know if I can trust her. I want you to come with us. I also want ideally at least one other paladin to tail us, off the books. Honestly, I wouldn't mind an entire squad. But I need them be careful; I don't want Velas knowing they're around."

"You're an officer, Lydia. You could get a squad assigned to this yourself."

Lydia shook her head. "After what happened with the paladin trials, I strongly suspect we have someone in a high position in our organization that's directly working with Sterling. A vae'kes and multiple Thornguard getting into the trials... that implies either a high degree of incompetence or deliberate sabotage."

"We investigated that pretty thoroughly while you were away. Vetted everyone even peripherally involved in the trials, as well as some other people with potentially suspicious backgrounds. All the former Thornguard members of the paladins were checked, as well as anyone connected with the Haven Knights. Poor Kestrel was under observation for months."

Lydia tried to place the name. "Kestrel? The girl with Aendaryn's gifts? Isn't she Rowan Makar's daughter?"

Aladir shook his head. "Makar adopted Kestrel as an adult. Kestrel's birth name is Kestrel Haven. She's been with us for years, but you can imagine why there were concerns. She went through extensive tests, though. Fires of purification, all that. I'm confident she's clear."

"That's comforting, but did you find anything in the search as a whole? There's a screening process to get into the trials. How could a vae'kes have gotten through that?"

"Void sorcery sounds like the most likely answer. We believe Sterling used void sorcery to prevent his own sorcery from being detected."

Lydia frowned. "Void sorcery doesn't do paperwork."

Aladir shrugged. "We looked into that, too. The Thornguard and Haven Knights had records for everyone we checked on. Someone must have prepared for this operation in advance, potentially years ahead of time."

"That doesn't make me feel any better."

Aladir shook his head. "It's more likely that preparation work was done from within those *other* organizations, not ours. But I understand your reasoning, and I'm not going to dismiss the idea we might still have Thornguard agents among us. Okay. I can find a way to make this work unofficially, but we're going to be a little lighter on resources that way. Who do you want me to bring?"

"Ideally, people I know and trust, and that have the kind of power we'd need to potentially fight a vae'kes. Taelien would be ideal, but I know he's assigned to something on the other side of the continent."

"You really shouldn't call him that until it's officially sanctioned. I don't really mind, but some of the other paladins find him using that title to be more than a little arrogant."

Lydia winced. "He has the sword, and he can use it. I think he can rightfully claim the title...but I won't make that argument right now. Either way, *Salaris*," she used his personal name with conscious effort, "is out of the picture, at least for now. What about Kestrel? You've mentioned she was vetted heavily. She has Aendaryn's gifts, so she might be able to cause a vae'kes harm. Can she be trusted?"

"Trusted in a fight, yes, and she wouldn't stab us in the back. The problem is that she's too trustworthy. She might have some difficulty with a mission that's off the books. We'd have to keep her far in the background. And I mean *far*."

"Very well, I'll keep that in mind. Aside from artifacts and divine gifts, there aren't a lot of things that can threaten someone like Sterling. I only know of one other person with Aendaryn's gifts, and I don't think bringing him is wise."

"There are two more, actually," Aladir noted.

Lydia blinked. "I know Keldyn Andys has them, but I was hoping to avoid bringing someone who was a candidate during those trials. Who else manifested the gifts? Could we bring them?"

Aladir laughed. "I'm sure Lucas would be thrilled to be invited, but there's a small problem with that."

"What sort of problem? Could we find a work around?"

"He's eleven years old."

Lydia paused, considering... "No, I think perhaps that's a bit too young."

"Obviously." Aladir rolled his eyes. "Have you paid a visit to Dyson yet?"

Lydia frowned, shaking her head. "No, why? Has he manifested gifts recently?"

"Because he's your *brother*, Lydia. You should visit him while you're in the city. And while he doesn't have any gifts that I'm aware of, he *is* an excellent swordsman. Remarkably fast."

"Landen and Velas are skilled and swift, and they couldn't put a scratch on Sterling." Lydia shook her head. "No, we need power, not just skill. And Dyson is young and reckless. He could..."

"He's not a child anymore, Lydia. You should visit him before you leave, even if you're not planning to take him. If nothing else, he's more social than either of us. He may have some ideas on who else we should bring."

"I'm not sure telling him would be wise... But you're right. Perhaps I should at least see him while I'm here."

Aladir smiled. "You should. I'll put together a list of potential candidates for your review, and we can discuss them tomorrow."

Lydia considered that, then nodded. "Very well."

A few years ago, I would have been writing that list myself. I've been away from home for too long.

Aladir stretched, relaxing back against the couch. "Excellent. I'm certain you'll be pleased to see some of the new talent we've acquired. In the meantime, how about you tell me about what you've been studying with Hartigan?"

Lydia relaxed, leaning back. This was a subject that she was much less stressed about, and much better prepared for. "Well, most of the focus was offensive sorcery, but he did teach me a bit of dominion marking theory that I think might interest you..."

She launched into an explanation, while Aladir stopped her from time to time to ask relevant questions.

It was the best evening Lydia could recall in ages.

Ulandir never did come back with tea.

***

The following morning, Lydia went in search of her brother.

Embarrassingly, she didn't know where he currently lived. He'd joined the Paladins of Tae'os during the two years she'd been in Orlyn.

She'd seen him when she'd returned to Velthryn after that, but he'd always been the one to visit her. He had an uncanny habit of being able to find her anywhere near the citadel, and sometimes just around town in general.

It wasn't sorcery, though. Dyson just had a better feel for people than she'd ever managed.

Lydia didn't like feeling predictable, but she supposed it was acceptable in her brother's case.

And, thinking in those terms, she still understood his drives relatively well, even if she hadn't made as much of an effort to contact him as she could have.

It was too early in the morning to be drinking, even for Dyson. So she crossed the local taverns off her mental list.

That left a few other options.

I could put together a tracking spell that finds anyone nearby that's related to me, Lydia considered. *It wouldn't be a difficult variant of my existing "Locate Person" spell.*

But it'll be more fun to puzzle this out manually, and see how difficult it is.

She checked the prayer fields at the citadel next, stopping to say a few words herself, but her brother was not among the many paladins saying their morning prayers. She did see a few people she recognized, though, and exchanged a few words with Makar before she left.

Makar hadn't seen Dyson that morning, but she did have some useful advice — there was a combat demonstration happening at the stadium in a few hours.

After another half hour of fruitlessly checking the grounds, Lydia had breakfast, then headed to the Korinval Coliseum and searched the area for anyone familiar.

She found Lieutenant Alaria Morwen near the entrance.

"You fighting today?" Lydia asked.

Morwen laughed. "You know I'd love to, but I'm just babysitting today. We getting you in there?"

Lydia shook her head, gesturing with her cane. "Afraid I'm still not quite ready for that yet."

"Shame. You were a real pain back in the day. Wouldn't mind seeing you teach the kids a thing or two."

"I'm sure you're doing plenty of that for both of us." She paused. "Do you know if Dyson is participating?"

"'Course he is. You think he'd miss a chance to show off?"

No, not in a thousand years. "Good, I've been looking for him."

"You want me to get you inside to talk to him?"

Lydia considered, then shook her head. "I'd rather not distract him before a fight. I'll get a spot in the stands and watch, then find him afterward."

"Your call, Hastings. Anything else I can do for you?"

"I wouldn't mind a primer on the rules for today's match."

Morwen nodded. "It's a barrier bout."

Lydia knew the term; it meant a fight where the combatants were protected by sorcerous barriers of equal strength. The match would end when one barrier broke, preventing any injuries.

At least in theory. Taelien had nearly lost a hand in his match with Velas, due to a number of complications.

Morwen continued explaining the particulars. "Only two fighters are allowed in the arena at a time, but as soon as one is eliminated, someone can step in from one of the other entrances and challenge the winner. Priority to whoever steps in first. The 'winner' is whoever lasts the most rounds in the arena, but there's no prize, aside from glory. It's mostly for entertaining the crowd."

Lydia frowned. "And there's a fee for outsiders to watch, I take it?"

"Got it in one." Morwen must have seen her expression change, because she added, "I don't like it, either, but we have to raise money somehow. It's not like we get a share of city taxes like the Thornguard."

"I know. It just feels awkward demonstrating the gifts of the gods for something as base as money." Lydia sighed. "But I suppose prayers don't feed the populace."

"Not unless we get a god of food added to the pantheon," Morwen chuckled. "Or maybe if Eratar adds that to his list of titles. I wouldn't be surprised."

"Neither would I."

"C'mon," Morwen waved, "If you won't let me sneak you in, at least let me find you a decent seat."

Lieutenant Morwen accompanied Lydia to a private box where a few other paladin officers were congregating, then headed back to...whatever she'd been doing near the entrance. Waiting for someone specific, maybe?

Or, based on the way Morwen had been searching the crowd with her gaze, maybe avoiding someone?

Her father, maybe, Lydia realized. *They weren't on great terms last time I checked.*

Satisfied with the hypothesis, Lydia found a seat and settled in to watch the fight.

Rather than having an external announcer, this match had paladins stationed at entrances on opposite sides of the colosseum.

At first, Lydia expected that they'd each call out the names of the people entering from their side, but it didn't turn out that way.

A paladin in full armor walked in from the left side, carrying a sword and shield. The guard waiting on that side of the arena made an announcement.

"On the blue side of the arena, we have Paladin Aiden Makar!"

Oh, one of Makar's kids. I wonder who he'll be up against.

A tall, brunette woman entered on the opposite side. She carried a spear. Lydia didn't recognize her.

The same paladin that had spoken before concentrated for a moment, then announced, "On the red side, we have Squire Cassidy Ventra!"

The two fighters saluted each other and began to cross the arena. Lydia had a moment of surprise at the term 'squire' — it was unusual for a squire to participate in a demonstration like this — but she was more interested in the announcer.

Did he recognize Cassidy, or did he somehow learn her name during that brief pause?

She frowned, focusing on the announcer. He was wearing scale mail and Sytrian colors. A knowledge sorcerer, perhaps?

If he has a spell for identifying names at a distance, I really need to learn that. I should ask him about it later.

And he's using sound sorcery to amplify his voice, too... That's an excellent combination.

Cassidy closed the distance with speed, then slowed when she got close to striking distance. She took a tentative jab, but Aiden side-stepped it easily and stepped forward to try to close the distance.

As soon as Aiden pushed forward, Cassidy swept low, managing a glancing strike against one of Aiden's knees. The impact wouldn't have done any real harm, but it did activate Aiden's barrier, showing a small crack.

Cassidy hopped backward, dodging a slash that probably would have fallen short anyway, and smacked Aiden a second time.

Those hits wouldn't do a thing to Aiden under that armor, but they're still triggering the barrier spell, Lydia realized. *The squire knows she can't actually hurt him, so she's just taking advantage of her superior mobility and chipping at the barrier.*

Aiden must have realized it, too, because he backed off instead of pressing his charge. He lowered his stance, blocking one of Cassidy's strikes with his shield, and then stomped the ground.

Stone spikes shot up from the ground right beneath Cassidy. She danced backward, but one of them scraped along her leg, making a crack in her shield.

She let out a groan, then reoriented herself and charged back in, swinging at Aiden's legs again.

Aiden was ready this time. He stepped in rather than blocking, swinging down, and cut the tip right off her spear.

In that close, a sword typically had an advantage, but Cassidy flipped the back of the spear upward and slammed it into Aiden's helmet. While he stumbled backward, she stepped in closer and kicked the back of his leg.

He didn't fall like she'd obviously hoped, though. Both impacts did damage to his shield, but she lacked the force to topple him. He smacked Cassidy with his shield, then took a swing with his sword. She managed to get the spear up in time to block, then dropped it entirely.

While Aiden raised the sword to swing again, Cassidy slipped past him and kicked him in the back. He stumbled forward — and tripped over the stone spikes he'd created, falling right on top of them.

Numerous cracks appeared in his barrier when he landed.

"Winner, Cassidy Ventra!" The Sytiran paladin announced.

The first series of cheers came from the stands.

Cassidy helped Aiden to his feet, then he saluted her and exited the arena.

Cassidy looked absolutely thrilled. She waved to the crowd, then looked around, clearly searching to see if someone specific had been watching.

Lydia leaned over to the paladin on her left. "Who's the announcer?"

"That's Durias Moss. One of the latest batch of graduates."

Lydia nodded her thanks, then reached into her bag for a notepad and wrote down "Durias Moss".

Durias announced the next fighter a few moments later. "Now entering from the blue side, Paladin Terras!"

The new contestant was an orange-eyed rethri woman that Lydia had seen during Taelien's paladin trials. From what she could recall, Terras was skilled at Heat sorcery, as well as...

Terras pointed a hand at Cassidy and a blast of lightning crossed the arena, crashing into the squire's shields and leaving a tremendous crack.

Cassidy staggered, but righted herself quickly and began to charge.

Terras remained right near the entrance, casually calling down more bolts of lightning. Cassidy dodged and wove as she ran, managing to avoid one blast simply by throwing off Terras' aim, but she couldn't close the distance fast enough.

A second lightning bolt smashed into Cassidy, then a third. Her barrier crumpled.

"That's enough," came Durias' voice. "Winner, Paladin Terras!"

Another cheer from the crowd, but more muted this time. Everyone could see that it hadn't been a fair exchange.

But battle was rarely fair.

Lydia wrote "Terras" on her list. She wasn't sure Sterling could absorb lightning sorcery quickly enough to prevent it from harming him, and even if he could, it would be a significant distraction.

"Entering, from the red side, Paladin Gladio Gath!"

A human swordsman with dark brown hair entered the arena, resting a sheathed greatsword against his arm like a polearm.

He pointed his free hand toward the ground, then began to charge.

Terras pointed her hand toward the newcomer and called another blast of lightning. It flashed toward him, crossing the battlefield in a moment, then veered off to his side.

The electrical charge moved too fast for Lydia's eyes to follow completely, but as Gladio pointed toward another spot on the ground, Lydia began to understand.

Terras called another blast of lightning; again, it veered off as it approached. This time, Lydia managed to see the electrical charge strike something small on the ground, then flicker, and then dissipate.

He's a metal caller, she realized. *And he's making lightning rods.*

Gladio continued to close the distance, now half-way across the arena.

Terras must have realized that her strategy wasn't working. She waved a hand and the air in front of her rippled, expanding forward like a wave across the arena. When the distortion hit Gladio, he winced, but didn't slow.

Heat sorcery. And the barrier didn't activate to help block it. Whatever type of defensive spell they're using, it doesn't treat a change in temperature as attack sorcery. Meaning that Paladin is cooking in his armor, and the barrier isn't going to help.

The heat extended from Terras' position all the way to the midpoint of the arena. It wasn't just a momentary attack; the spell was persisting in that area. Gladio would have to continue moving through it to reach her, or find another way around.

Gladio's face visibly reddened, but he continued to close the distance.

Terras took an uncertain step back, conjuring a handful of balls of lightning that swirled around her in a circular pattern. She pointed, shooting one of the spheres forward.

Gladio countered with another lightning rod, but with noticeable difficulty. He slowed his charge, taking a breath, and then moved his hand in front of him, extending two fingers upward.

A glowing blue aura appeared across his body, then gradually pushed outward into a spherical shape.

The sphere appeared to push back the heated air around him, giving him a protected bubble of ordinary air. From the way he slowed his steps after casting it, however, it was clearly taking a lot out of him.

A Sphere of Exclusion spell. High-end protection sorcery designed for inhospitable areas. From the looks of it, he maintains the spell with a gesture using his left hand. That could be trouble if he's using a two-handed weapon.

Gladio continued to march slowly toward his opponent, looking more comfortable now that the heat had been pushed away, but sweat was still flowing down his face. His hand trembled with the effort of maintaining the barrier.

He was close to reaching Terras when she bolted right past him, hurling a pair of lightning spheres as she ran.

Lydia anticipated that he'd continue to block using the same pattern as before. His opponent must have counted on that, too.

Instead, Gladio pointed his right hand at the ground in front of Terras herself.

The two spheres of lightning crashed into Gladio's Sphere of Exclusion, breaking through it and cracking the barrier beneath. He was back in the heat now.

Terras, however, failed to avoid the metal block that appeared in front of her. The moment she collided with it, her remaining lightning sphere jumped to the metal and electrocuted her.

She fell backward at the jolt, her shield cracking, and began to push herself to her feet.

Gladio unsheathed his sword, swaying on his feet. He looked like he could barely stand in the heat.

When she pointed to call another blast of lightning, Gladio threw his sword at her.

That sword...

Lydia's eyes narrowed as she recognized the black blade with gleaming runes on the surface. *Arcane Hold. It's a teleportation anchor, preventing any use of travel sorcery in the area near it. Not applicable in this fight, but potentially useful.*

Apparently, Gladio didn't quite have Taelien's talent at sword throwing. The sword missed badly, but it did attract the lightning from Terras' latest attack.

Terras stumbled backward and shivered, clearly feeling the toll of all her attack spells.

Before she could cast another spell, Gladio pulled a dagger off his belt and hurled it at her. It flipped around and hit her pommel-first, but that still cracked her barrier.

She fell backward, groaned, and raised both hands. "I give up."

"Winner! Paladin, Gladio Gath!"

Gladio marched forward drunkenly, clearly barely able to stand, and offered his opponent a hand.

Terras grinned and accepted, and he dragged her to her feet.

The crowd cheered.

Terras snapped her fingers, ending the heat spell on the arena, and began to make her way out.

Gladio found his sword, wiped his face, and sat down.

For a few moments, no challengers approached.

Lydia wrote the name, "Gladio Gath" on her list with a plus sign next to it.

A man in a black and white suit with no obvious weapons and a ludicrously tall hat entered the arena.

Durias began to announce him with a clear note of exasperation in his tone. "Now announcing...Paladin...Bob—"

The newcomer clapped his hands, making a thunderous noise, and birds appeared around him, flapping toward the skies. "Behold! I am Bobax, sorcerer extraordinaire! Witness now, my latest performance!"

Gladio covered his eyes for a moment, although it wasn't clear if that was some sort of strategy or merely out of embarrassment.

A vast whirlwind of colors appeared around "Bobax", the newcomer. The rainbow of lights shot upward, then curved downward, landing near Gladio and impacting with what looked like a liquid splash.

From the pool of lights emerged a second version of Gladio himself, resplendent in golden armor and carrying a bright blue sword.

"The knight has shown his might, but how shall he fare against his own reflection?" Bobax clapped his hands again and vanished.

Gladio sighed, taking the handle of his sword and then pushing himself back to his feet.

This glowing duplicate lunged forward, swinging its glowing sword at his midsection.

Gladio stepped back, avoiding the swing, and then turned and swung his own sword at the seemingly empty air behind him.

"Hah!" The voice came from somewhere to Gladio's right side. "You didn't think I'd be that close by, did you? Why would I bother appearing so close to—"

Gladio punched to his left.

Bobax appeared, stumbling backward and holding his nose. Cracks were visible in his shield. A crossbow clattered to the ground at his feet.

Gladio spun toward Bobax, taking a hit from his golden duplicate in the process. His shield cracked further, but didn't break.

Bobax recovered and swung a hand downward. A shadowy duplicate of Bobax stepped forward and mirrored the swing, but Gladio sidestepped it and shoved the golden copy of himself in the way.

The shadows and light met. Both vanished.

Then Gladio closed the distance and smashed Bobax with the flat of his sword.

Bobax's shield cracked, not quite breaking. Bobax stepped back, raising both hands. "Bah. This is why I never fight in arenas." He bowed at the waist. "The match is yours, sir."

A cheer went up from the crowd as Bobax's form turned to shadows, then to birds that flew out of the arena.

"Winner, Paladin Gladio Gath!"

Gladio raised a hand to his chest and lowered his sword, breathing heavily.

That Bobax was a showoff, but a spectacularly talented one. We don't usually recruit people with that type of personality...but perhaps there's more to him than what I see on the surface. I should investigate him further. Invisibility is always useful.

Lydia wrote the name, "Bobax?" on her list.

The next to enter was a short, stout woman in heavy armor. Only her head was left exposed. She carried no weapons, but her bracers glowed with blue-white light.

"Now entering from the blue side, Paladin Finn Pine."

The woman waved to Gladio amiably. "Hey, 'dio. You look overheated. Figured maybe I'd give you a hand with that."

She clasped her hands together briefly, and a second suit of armor formed around her body — this one made entirely of ice.

Gladio straightened himself, then concentrated. The cracks in his barrier began to mend themselves. "Nice of you to offer, Finn, but I'm just getting warmed up."

Finn slowly advanced across the arena, fists raised.

Gladio assumed a defensive stance, waiting patiently, taking deep breaths. He'd successfully repaired a lot of the damage to his shield, but he was clearly in bad shape.

Under ordinary circumstances, the right answer when someone swings a greatsword at you is "don't be in the way."

When Gladio swung at Finn, however, she opted for a different route.

She charged straight into the swing, which chipped her ice armor and sent Gladio's arm wide.

Then she crashed right into him, shoulder first, and punched him with her other hand when he fell backward.

To his credit, Gladio maintained his footing, simply sliding back from the impact of the attacks.

He raised his hand to begin repairing the damage to his shield again.

"Sorry about the cold shoulder," Finn said with a grin.

Gladio sighed. "Did you plan your entire attack around making that terrible joke?"

"It was worth it. I have simple needs." She flicked her wrist forward, firing a spike of ice. Gladio was too distracted — either by the joke or his attempts to recharge his shield — to dodge it properly. It glanced across his side, making another crack in his shield.

Finn took advantage of the opening, stepping forward and swinging again.

Gladio backed off, pointing at the ground. Finn stumbled as metallic wires rose from the ground at her ankles, then ducked and jumped forward faster than seemed natural, slamming a punch into Gladio's chest.

With that, his shield finally cracked apart.

"Winner, Paladin Finn Pine!"

Gladio stepped forward, giving Finn a slap on the shoulder. "Luck to you."

"And you, brother." Finn gave him a wink. "Good fight." She leaned close to him and whispered something, then he laughed and walked out of the ring.

More cheering from the crowd.

The next opponent entered. "From the red side of the arena, Paladin Keldyn Andys!"

Finn cracked her neck, turning toward the other entrance.

Keldyn strode forward, casting an arm out to the left, then the other to the right, with obvious flourish.

As he did, four glowing golden swords appeared on each side of him, hovering in mid-air.

That's...considerably more than I remembered him being able to make, Lydia remembered. *He's clearly been practicing.*

With no further discussion, Keldyn pointed his right hand and those four swords flew forward, leaving a gleaming trail in their wake.

Finn dropped and punched the ground. A wall of ice shot up in front of her. The three swords embedded into it, but Keldyn moved his hand at the last moment and one of the four diverged from the path, flying around it.

Finn blocked the first swing of the remaining sword with her bracers, sending white and gold sparks into the air, then jumped on top of it.

Lydia blinked. That was...not how she would have approached the situation.

Finn dragged the glowing sword to the ground, punching it repeatedly, until the sword cracked and vanished.

She stood back up just in time for the next wave of four swords to approach. At that point, she fell back on the defensive, blocking with her glowing bracers as best she could.

At first, the four swords came at the same trajectory, allowing Finn to side-step and parry the group with moderate difficulty. As Keldyn came closer, however, he folded his arms and the swords flew apart.

Then he closed his eyes — and each of the four swords floated to a different side of Finn, slightly changing their positions and elevation.

They still struck at the same time, but from four different locations.

Finn blocked the two closest to the front of her, but took two glancing hits from behind. Her ice armor stopped most of the damage, but began to break apart.

Her barrier didn't seem to have taken any damage yet; apparently, the ice armor was the outer layer of her defenses, and damaging it didn't trigger the protection spell. That was good for Finn, especially if she was capable of renewing it.

Unfortunately, she didn't seem to have the time.

The four swords attacked relentlessly, and Finn had few opportunities to counter. She tried to freeze one of them with a blast of ice, but it flew right through the attack before the ice could take hold.

When she tried to grapple another sword to the ground, it flew back out of range, breaking from the attack formation the other three were using. That was particularly interesting, because Lydia had not been aware that Keldyn had sufficient control for that kind of maneuvering of the weapons.

Her ice armor continued to chip and break. Finally, she waved a hand across the ground, creating any icy path leading straight to her opponent. Then she broke into a run, the ice appearing to accelerate her travel, without any signs that the slippery surface impeded her.

She might have made it if the three swords embedded in the ice wall hadn't broken free.

They flew straight in front of her, slashing simultaneously, and caught her straight in the chest.

The attacks didn't just break her armor — they broke her momentum. She slipped and fell backward off the path. She recovered quickly, but then the other four swords had caught up behind her.

The seven remaining swords began to circle her.

Finn glanced from side-to-side, then threw a blast of ice straight at Keldyn.

Two more swords appeared in front of him seemingly instantly, blocking the attack.

Then Finn was struck seven times, breaking her armor and barrier in a moment.

"Winner, Keldyn Andys!"

Finn took a breath as the swords flew away to circle around their caster. Then she smiled, walked over, and gave him a light punch in a shoulder. "Hell of a trick you've got there, Andys. Maybe teach it to the rest of us sometime?"

"Would if I could," Keldyn replied. "But only a pair of us are blessed with Aendaryn's gifts."

"Now entering from the blue side, Kestrel Makar!"

Keldyn nodded to Finn, then turned toward his new opponent. "And there's the other one."

"I'd better get to the stands so I can watch this. Luck to ya, Andys." Finn rushed out of the arena to the sound of cheers.

Lydia made a mental note to write her down as well, but she didn't want to miss a moment of what happened next.

Kestrel was a tall, athletic blonde, much like Andys himself. The hair color and their light complexion was common for Valeria, where they'd both originally come from.

And the center of power for House Haven, which Kestrel was born into, Lydia recalled. *I wonder what happened there that made her join the paladins and change her name.*

Kestrel gazed out at the crowd briefly, showing a combination of nervousness and excitement, before she refocused on her opponent.

"This is a poor match for you, Kestrel. You would have been wiser to wait for others to wear me down, then taken the victory over the tournament as a whole." Keldyn walked forward, his conjured swords spinning around him in a circular pattern.

"I don't like to do things like that," Kestrel replied. "Doesn't seem very fair."

Keldyn blinked. "You don't think using strategy is fair?"

"It's not that, I just wanted to see how I'd do against you. We've sparred and stuff, but you're the only one like me. I mean, aside from Lucas, and he's too little. I just wanted to—"

Keldyn's swords launched forward before she could finish, faster than Lydia had seen them move before.

Kestrel was in the middle of talking, which generally was a good time for a surprise attack, but she just paused with what she was saying, flicking her sword from side to side, and deflected the attacking blades without seeming like she'd been caught off guard at all.

"—see what it would be like to fight someone else with his gifts, you know?" She finished what she'd been saying as if she'd never been interrupted, and without any sign that the swords had even been a distraction.

Keldyn's swords circled around her, adjusting their heights and angles. "I understand quite well." He bowed his head. "Aendaryn be with you, then."

"You too." She shifted her stance, then ducked as a single sword flew at her from behind. Lydia hadn't seen any tells, and the sword had been outside of Kestrel's field of vision.

There was a blur as the other blades flashed inward, all at once.

Kestrel simply stepped in between and around them, never once being cut.

She paused to stare at one of them afterward, raising a free hand to reach out and try to touch it. The sword flew out of her reach before she had a chance.

"Strange," Kestrel said simply. "It works so differently for you."

Another series of attacks, these a bit faster. Kestrel was forced to block a trio of them with her sword, and they began to burn through the mundane blade. Another clipped her shoulder, finally damaging her barrier for the first time.

She's not impossible to hit, but her defensive abilities are almost as good as Asphodel's. Does she have a similar form of precognition, or something else entirely?

Lydia leaned forward, but whatever Kestrel's abilities were, they weren't visible to the naked eye.

After the attacks abated, Kestrel stepped back a few steps, noticed the state of her blade, and then raised it toward the sky.

Kestrel's sword began to gleam brighter and brighter, until it was almost blinding.

A sword hit her straight in the back a moment later, cracks forming in her barrier. She stumbled forward, losing her concentration.

But her sword never lost its glow.

As the next wave of swords approached, Kestrel swung her blade to meet them. The conjured blades didn't deflect or break on impact as Lydia had expected.

They glowed brighter for just a moment, then vanished.

And her own sword grew brighter still.

Keldyn glowered, waving a hand and repositioning his swords, pulling them out of her reach.

Kestrel's sword was not only glowing now, but the aura around it had grown longer, extending her reach. She turned toward Keldyn and began to walk toward him.

Keldyn conjured a pair of additional swords to replace the ones he'd lost, then drew the metal sword at his hip.

When Kestrel was almost close enough to strike, Keldyn drew his left hand downward. The remaining swords in the distance flew at Kestrel from behind. Immediately thereafter, he stepped forward and swung with his real weapon, his two newly-conjured swords mirroring his strike.

Kestrel slammed her greatsword into his smaller one, batting it aside, and absorbed one of the two conjured swords into her weapon in the process. Then she charged past him, putting him in the way of his own swords before they could hit her.

Keldyn froze for an instant, then stopped his swords with what seemed like little more than force of will.

That instant was all Kestrel needed. She pulled her sword back behind her shoulder, and then when Keldyn turned to meet her, she swung right through his one remaining conjured sword and into his chest.

He fell backward, his barrier shattering apart in a single blow.

"Winner, Paladin Kestrel Makar!"

The next opponent entered — another Paladin of Aendaryn, but lacking his gifts. Kestrel beat him easily.

The next opponent was a flame sorcerer. Kestrel had more difficulty with him, but managed to cut through most of his spells and land a victory, at a cost of some of her shield.

She beat the next six opponents after that.

Lydia made one important observation during that time; Kestrel wasn't dodging anyone else's attacks with the same degree of ease that she'd avoided Keldyn's swords. After some consideration, she surmised the cause.

Keldyn's skill is almost entirely blade calling. He conjures weapons, then uses some degree of shaping to make them move. Kestrel is the reverse. She can't seem to conjure remote weapons like he can, she just makes a blade-like aura around her sword. Then she shaped it to make it longer, or shaped Keldyn's swords on contact to absorb them into her own weapon.

Shapers have a degree of perception linked to their dominion. She must have some kind of enhanced perception of the energy that is used to conjure blades. That's unusual, because there is no single dominion that these weapons are made from; they're a combination of multiple types of energy.

Her gifts are completely different from his. Less ranged power, but perhaps some useful applications we haven't even considered yet.

The crowd roared more and more with each victory, and Lydia found herself cheering right along with them.

She was so excited that she didn't even see the last challenger enter.

"Entering from the blue side, Paladin Dyson Hastings!"

Lydia's heart hammered in her chest.

She'd forgotten about him entirely.

Her eyes turned to her little brother, not so little now. He was in his twenties, his brown hair taking after his own father, rather than their mother. He was mostly shaven, save for a goatee that Lydia might have interpreted as rakish, but that he probably would have insisted was simply a mark of style.

His light blue and flowing garb marked his allegiance to Eratar, though she had never known him to display any of the gods' gifts.

He had a pair of curved swords and, and as far as Lydia could tell, no chance at all against Kestrel Makar.

"Hey, Kestrel!" Dyson shouted, waving with one of his swords.

"Oh, no! Why'd it have to be you?" She paused, looking flushed, though Lydia couldn't tell if she was simply overexerted or if she'd embarrassed herself. "I mean, uh, hi, Dyson!"

"You look tired, you need a few moments?" He walked over toward her, lowering his weapons.

She lowered her sword as well. The weapon was still glowing, but only faintly now. Her lips contorted as she seemed to consider the offer. "No, I think I'm good. Might as well get this over with."

Dyson raised his right sword in a lazy salute. "Let's do this."

Kestrel didn't hesitate. She swung at him immediately, a clean diagonal cut aimed at his chest.

Dyson wasn't there.

Kestrel barely managed to spin around and raise her sword in time to parry a hit, then took a cut to her leg from his other sword.

Lydia blinked, then Dyson was in another position, this time on Kestrel's right.

Kestrel let out a growl, stepping back and raising her sword into a defensive stance. Dyson darted in, swinging both blades from opposite sides. Kestrel stepped out his reach, attempting a jab, but he hopped easily out of the way.

Lydia caught a blur as Dyson repositioned, then hit Kestrel with a glancing blow to her right arm.

"Ugh! I can *never* hit you!" Her sword swept out at chest level, and Dyson simply danced out of the way.

Dyson moved backward a few more paces, stretching his arms. "It's fine, you're just tired. I think I'm the last one, by the way. If you want to give up, we can—"

Kestrel charged him, swinging wide. It seemed wild and uncontrolled at first, easy for Dyson to dodge, but she turned the attack into a spin and jammed her sword into the ground right where he was going.

The stone floor of the arena cracked apart, sending bits of rock blasting upward along with beams of concussive light.

Dyson jumped backward, but the stone beneath him continued to tremble.

For just a moment, he lost his footing. Kestrel dragged her sword *through* the ground, streaming light as the stone cracked, and swept it upward.

Dyson managed to raise a sword in a successful parry. Kestrel's glowing blade snapped his sword in half.

He was moving backward, then, in the sliver of a moment while his weapon slowed hers down.

Her sword cut cloth.

His second sword caught her across the chest.

Her barrier, already weakened from nine other battles, finally broke apart.

The crowd froze.

"And the winner of our final round is...Paladin Dyson Hastings!"

Lydia's brother raised his swords, broken and unbroken, to tremendous applause.

And Lydia raised her pen, stared at the page, and hesitated to write a name.

***

"Lydia!" Dyson's eyes brightened as he sighted her on the way out of the coliseum. He ran over and threw his arms around her, pulling her tight against him. "You're back home!"

Lydia smiled, sinking into the hug. "I am indeed, though only briefly. You did very well in the arena."

"I know, right?" Dyson laughed, then jerked his head toward the blonde woman who had exited to his right side. "I owe Kestrel a drink for breaking her win streak. You want to come with us?"

Kestrel had frozen upon seeing Lydia and raised her hand to her chest in a salute.

Lydia blinked at Kestrel. "At ease, Kestrel. I'm not even in uniform."

Kestrel nodded. "Yes, ma'am." After a moment of hesitation, she lowered her hand and moved to a *slightly* more relaxed posture.

After a moment of evaluation, Lydia shook her head to Dyson, then finally slipped free from his embrace. "No, I think it's a little too early in the day for me. You and Kestrel go on ahead, you've both earned a drink or two."

"Aww." Dyson nudged her. "You never join in the fun. At least walk us there?"

Lydia glanced to Kestrel. The young woman still was looking at Lydia with a mix of respect and almost childlike awe.

It was discomforting.

I haven't done anything to earn that kind of reaction.
Not yet, at least.

Still, as awkward as that made her feel, a look back into her brother's hopeful expression dictated her decision. "I suppose I can handle a walk."

"You're the best!" Dyson looped one of his arms under Lydia's. "C'mon, it's this way."

Lydia allowed herself to be led, and, for the moment, swayed a bit by her brother's enthusiasm. A smile managed to break its way across the surface of her face. "Lead on."

Kestrel silently fell into step on Dyson's other side.

"So," Dyson turned his head toward Lydia, "How long are you in town?"

***

"You set me up." Lydia folded her arms, leaning back against Aladir's couch.

Aladir fluttered his eyelashes, holding a hand to his chest with a look of faux innocence. "Me? Whatever do you mean?"

Lydia's eyes shifted into a glare. "You knew that when I looked for Dyson, I'd end up watching him fight, and that he'd win. You're trying to convince me to bring him."

"That's quite a leap." Aladir gave her a playful grin. "Did it work?"

Lydia rolled her eyes. "I should have known better than to expect anything with a Ta'thyriel to be straightforward. Aside from Lana, perhaps. You're always playing games." She shook her head. "I'll...think about it. He's clearly more capable than I gave him credit for, and I'm proud of him. But I don't feel right willingly putting my brother in such a dangerous situation."

"He's a paladin, Lydia," Aladir had a hint of warning in his otherwise friendly tone, "You can't play favorites."

"I'm not pulling strings for an early promotion here, Aladir. I'm simply saying that I don't want to put him directly in harm's way."

"Did you see him in that arena? Most types of harm would never get close to him."

Lydia glowered at Aladir, but he wasn't wrong. "Yes, I saw him. You were right — he has preternatural speed. A tremendous talent for motion sorcery, or breath sorcery like yours. But that isn't invulnerability. Someone could catch him unawares, or use a wide area of effect spell he can't avoid. Or even teleport next to him, now that Sterling has—"

She hesitated, recalling the memory of how Sterling had stolen Garrick Torrent's sorcery. And, of course, how he'd killed Torrent immediately thereafter. "—travel sorcery."

Aladir nodded, replying in a wistful tone. "Perhaps if this mission is so dangerous that you won't even consider including your brother, you should be concerned that the assignment itself has flaws."

Lydia paused, unable to object. After a breath, she asked, "...What alternative do you propose?"

"You could simply turn down the invitation. It would be a missed opportunity, but there will always be others."

Lydia shook her head. "Can't pass on this. We need information."

"What about sending a completely different group of paladins in your stead? You know that you, Landen, and Velas are the most likely to be Sterling's targets. Perhaps if you sent a completely unrelated group, he would have no motivation to attack."

"You're missing the point. I *want* Sterling to attack. Or, at least, to play his hand openly in a way that we can discover his location." Lydia shook her head. "...But you're right, there are many things that could go wrong. Perhaps I'm too emotionally invested in this. I haven't been able to look at the situation objectively. What do you think we should do?"

"I think," Aladir gave her a devious grin, "we've been letting the Thornguard and the vae'kes dictate the terms of engagement for too long. We need to set a trap of our own for a change."

CHAPTER VI – TAELIEN II – RELICS OF THE PAST

It was late in the evening when Taelien and Asphodel arrived back at The Perfect Stranger tavern. War was no longer accompanying them, having stayed behind to have a "private talk" with Aayara.

I don't like that in the slightest, but War was right. I have no authority over him, and he's free to make his own decisions.

Taelien paused before they headed in, turning to Asphodel. "You sure going back here is wise?"

"It is the most efficient course. You will need the prime lady's help before this is done, and she will need yours." As usual, Asphodel was infuriatingly vague, but her future knowledge was still too useful to ignore.

Taelien raised an eyebrow. "Does that mean you can see my future now?"

"No. But I can see hints about her, and if you're near her, I know you'll help each other." She smiled softly.

"But...couldn't you just tell me about what I'm going to need to do? Or, if there's something happening where we're going to need help, couldn't you, maybe, prevent that?"

Asphodel shook her head. "I will not needlessly oppose the forces of fate. We've discussed this before."

If I had her skills...but I don't, I suppose. And I know she had something bad happen to her when she tried to mess with fate in the past, even if she won't tell me what it was. I suppose I shouldn't push too much. As infuriating as this is for me, it must be worse for her.

Taelien resigned himself to the present course and opened the door.

"Back so soon?" Wrynn set an empty mug down on the counter of the bar and headed over to the doorway. She didn't actually sound surprised. "Boots off, cloak on the rack."

Taelien nodded, following her instructions. Asphodel did the same.

"We'll be staying the night, if you have room." Taelien glanced around the tavern, noting that it was practically empty now. It was late enough that everyone could have just gone to sleep, though.

Wrynn looked like she'd been working on cleaning the tavern before they arrived. She had her sleeves rolled up, exposing those strange tattoos on her forearms. Her forehead was matted with sweat, and strands of dark hair were stuck to it, drawing Taelien's vision toward her pitch-black eyes.

If she noticed his gaze, she didn't mention it. She just grinned and lifted an arm to wipe her forehead. "Think I can manage that. Two silver regals per room for the evening. And one more per person if you want me to heat up some leftovers."

Taelien glanced at Asphodel. "Hungry?"

She nodded in silence.

Taelien reached into his coin pouch and offered Wrynn four coins. "One room is fine for the two of us, but we could use some food."

"Have a seat, I'll be back in a bit."

Taelien and Asphodel took a seat at an empty table, as far from the few remaining patrons as possible.

Taelien glanced to Wrynn, then back to Asphodel. "Your oracular insights telling you anything useful?"

"The Prime Lady of Shadow will be of great use to us. You will need to talk to her privately, however. She will not trust me."

Taelien groaned. Any sort of subterfuge and bargaining wasn't his area of expertise. That was probably part of the reason Aayara had set him upon this path in the first place.

Going to Wrynn was a part of how he planned to get ahead of that, but her fees were so high that allowing the Lady of Thieves to rob him might have left him with more.

And that was *with* the discount of being one of Wrynn's "favorite customers".

Wrynn smiled brightly as she came by, setting down two plates of food. The dish was *kavatkas*, a form of pastry with meat baked with garlic and onions inside. "What can I get you to drink?"

Asphodel replied before Taelien had a chance. "I'll have the blueberry cordial. Taelien will have an apple juice."

Wrynn glanced to Taelien. "...Apple juice? What are you, five?"

Taelien frowned. "It's delicious."

Wrynn laughed. "I think I still have some. I'll be back."

***

Asphodel went to sleep after eating, but a few of the other late night patrons stayed down by the fire.

Taelien steeled himself and found a moment to pull Wrynn to the side. "Do you have somewhere more private we can go?"

Wrynn gave him a wry look. "You ought to buy a girl a drink before you ask something like that."

Taelien raised an eyebrow. "Don't you own the tavern?"

"Sure, but that doesn't mean my time is free." She winked at him. "C'mon, I'll take you home."

Taelien blinked. "...Home?"

Wrynn took his hand and led him into a back room. Then, from there, she lifted up a carpet and uncovered a hatch.

Taelien watched as Wrynn pulled a thin metal object out of her hair, sticking it into a mechanism on the side of the hatch and jiggling it around.

"...Are you picking the lock on your own cellar?"

Wrynn shrugged. "Keys are such a hassle to keep track of."

There was a click, then Wrynn grunted, tapped three times on the surface of the hatch, and lifted a handle on the left side.

The hatch swung open, revealing a ladder leading down.

Wrynn led the way. "Close the hatch above you."

Taelien followed, complying with her instructions.

The ladder didn't make it all the way to the bottom.

Instead, it stopped at a rocky shelf, lit by a single glowing crystal embedded in the wall. Wrynn ducked down at the edge of the outcropping and felt around for a bit. "Rest of the way is down this rope."

"What *is* this place?" Taelien looked down beyond Wrynn, and he could see another pinpoint of light further on, but the floor was still out of sight.

"Like I said, it's home. Keep up." Wrynn slipped off the platform and began to climb down the rope.

Taelien followed right behind her, regretting his life choices more by the minute.

They climbed for minutes before reaching the bottom of the shaft. More glowing crystals lit a thin corridor.

Wrynn raised a hand for him to wait. "Need to disarm a few things before we go any further."

She moved to the left side of the passage, ducking down and pressing her hand against one of the walls. Taelien didn't see anything change, but he heard a click.

Wrynn took a few steps forward, hopped, and then ducked down. It took him a moment to realize that she'd bypassed some kind of tripwire, and that she was pressing something into a mechanism in the nearest wall.

After a moment, the wire retracted into the wall.

"One more." Wrynn walked a bit further, pausing at what looked like a slate. She withdrew a piece of chalk from her bag and drew an intricate figure, which began to glow. Then she wiped the slate clean.

"All good. Head down the passage into the open room. You'll know what I mean. I need to reset these behind us."

"Is that necessary? I don't think we'll be here long."

Wrynn folded her arms. "You wanted to talk. We're going to do it on my terms or not at all."

Taelien raised his hands in a conciliatory gesture. "Understood."

There were obvious risks to walking ahead of Wrynn in an area that was clearly riddled with traps. He knew her well enough to know that he couldn't trust her.

But excessive caution wasn't really his style. He headed the rest of the way down the tunnel.

The hall opened up into what looked like a large (but otherwise unremarkable) wine cellar. He paused near the entrance, looking for other traps, but he didn't see any.

Taelien waited for Wrynn regardless. It was better to be safe.

She brushed past him a few minutes later, walking deeper into the cellar...then straight through the rear wall, as if it wasn't there.

Taelien followed her, passing a hand through the illusory wall before he tried to step through it. He didn't feel anything unusual on the other side. It was a little cold, but not remarkably so.

He stepped through.

That led into another tunnel, where Wrynn was already running a finger across the wall as she moved.

The architecture was different here; it was worked stone rather than looking like a natural cavern, and lit torches lined the walls.

The particular grey color of the stone was uncomfortably familiar.

When they reached the end of the hallway, it opened up into a tremendous chamber, hundreds of feet across and at least fifty feet high.

Everything within the chamber was familiar. The tall support pillars, the bright red carpeting leading straight through the room, and the depression in the ground that led to a pair of colossal metal doorways.

It wasn't the entrance to the Paths of Ascension, but it was very nearly identical.

Taelien stopped at the entrance to the chamber. "Your 'home' is outside a Xixian Vault?"

Wrynn paused, shaking her head. "Obviously not. Nowhere near secure enough that way. My home is *inside* the Xixian Vault." With that, she resumed her walk, leading him to the double doors. "We can stop here for now. You haven't impressed me enough to earn a tour of the interior just yet."

Taelien glanced at the double doors, remembering his last experience with one of the vaults, and felt a bit of gratitude that she'd chosen to stop. While the Paths of Ascension had been exciting, he hadn't exactly enjoyed the aftermath. He looked to Wrynn, then back to the path they'd come from. "The tavern is just to hide this place?"

"Hm? Oh, no. The tavern's one of my businesses. Not that I need the money from selling rooms and ales, of course."

Taelien nodded. "I take it this is a place where you deal with business that can't be handled in Selyr? Maybe trading goods that you wouldn't want to be seen in the city, or information you wouldn't want to talk about in a public locale?"

"I'm glad you've been paying at least some attention." Wrynn smiled, leaning up against the ancient vault doors. "Besides, sometimes it's nice to just have a place to stay outside of the big city."

"There's a huge distance between your businesses, though." Taelien eyed the vault doors. "Did you find a teleportation gate inside the vault, perhaps?"

"Please, Sal. You *know* I'm not going to answer that. What is it that you always say? 'It's a trade secret?'" Wrynn rolled her eyes. "Let's focus on the important things, like the present you got me."

Taelien smiled. "You're going to like this." He slipped his backpack off his shoulders, opened the top, and rummaged through it until he found what he was looking for.

He pulled out a peculiar looking box. It was currently closed and empty, but several runes glowed softly on the surface. He reached out and extended the box toward her.

Wrynn snatched it out of his hands and cradled it against her chest. "Box! You found my box! Oh, I've *missed you*!" She lifted it to her lips and kissed the top. "You've been away for far too long." She glanced up at Taelien. "Where'd you find her?"

"Sitting on a table in the middle of a ruined village in the center of a swamp. Whole place had been torn apart, with signs of a ritual gone wrong."

Wrynn tightened her jaw. "Someone tried to summon something they shouldn't have."

Taelien nodded. "I concur. I suspect it was one of Daes—"

"Don't even say that name here."

"I didn't take you for superstitious." Taelien blinked. "But sure, I'll be careful."

"I'm not being superstitious. This is literally a summoning device, remember?"

Taelien shrugged. "It's currently empty. I checked."

"Including the extra dimensional space?" Wrynn wrinkled her nose.

"No." He shook his head. "Didn't know how to use it properly, nor did I want to risk opening it if something dangerous was still inside."

Wrynn set the box down. "That's wiser than you usually are. Might want to get yourself ready."

Taelien nodded, setting his hand on the hilt at his side.

Wrynn knelt down, put a hand on the box, and said, "Retrieve: All Items."

Dozens of objects appeared on the floor. Taelien tensed, but no monsters appeared, and none of the items reacted in any way that looked dangerous.

Wrynn frowned, appraising the items. "There are some key items missing, but this isn't as bad as it could be. And you can relax, there's nothing here that's going to be immediately dangerous."

"Your use of the word 'immediately' is concerning, Wrynn."

"It's fine, it's fine. There's nothing dangerous on its own. Some of these are pretty potent if they fall into the wrong hands...but I can make sure they don't, now." She looked up at him. "This'll take some time to sort through, but I can do that later. Thanks, Sal. I owe you big for this one."

He nodded. "As much as I'm sure the paladins would have wanted to keep the legendary Jaden Box, it's got your name on it. I couldn't justify keeping it."

"I'll compensate you fairly." She paused, considering. "Give me time to come up with something appropriate."

Taelien wasn't sure what she'd consider to be a fair trade for a legendary artifact like the Jaden Box, but he was curious what she'd come up with. "Thanks. For the moment, I could use some information to start with."

"Ah." She smirked. "One of my specialties. Is that why you're here? I figured you wouldn't be in the area just to see the local wildlife."

He'd considered how best to present his situation several times, but dancing around an issue never appealed to him. He'd decided on 'direct'. "Lady Aayara asked me to retrieve something. I'd like your help with that."

Wrynn's eyes narrowed. "You're working for Aayara...? I don't know if I should be laughing or crying right now."

Taelien raised a hand in a warding gesture. "I don't work for her. I work for the Paladins of Tae'os. But she's offered me information on someone who killed one of our members in exchange for an item."

Wrynn sighed, shaking her head. "Some sort of valuable artifact, I presume?"

"The Mask of Kishor. Apparently, the Prime Lord of Stone has it in his possession. As a prime lady yourself, I was hoping you might have some insight on how I could get him to relinquish it."

"Hmmm..." Wrynn made a contemplative expression. "Kyestri has the mask, eh?" She raised a hand to her chin, frowning. "No."

"...No?"

"This isn't about the mask. Aayara doesn't need it." Wrynn shifted some of the objects on the floor to the side, waving for Taelien to sit down.

Taelien sat across from her. "She did mention that Kyestri was hosting an auction. Maybe she's having me focus on the mask as a distraction, while her agents obtain something more valuable? Or maybe she just wants me to trade the Sae'kes to him, then she'll get my sword from Kyestri."

"Maybe..." Wrynn went silent for a moment, her gaze growing distant.

Taelien gave her a moment, considering possibilities.

Wrynn could be wrong. Aayara might want the mask even if she doesn't "need" it. Or maybe it has abilities Wrynn is unaware of.

It's also possible that she's right. If she is, I have to wonder if I'm being set up to fail. If the mask isn't her goal at all, she loses nothing by sending me on a fool's errand.

It's also possible that she wants the mask, but it's just a bonus, and something else is a higher priority for her.

Taelien loathed these sorts of situations. He couldn't afford to just ignore Aayara's request outright, but without a clearer idea of her motivations, he had no way of knowing if he was simply playing into a larger plot or wasting his time.

"I have some ideas." Wrynn gestured at his backpack. "What've you got to trade me?"

He folded his arms. "I did just return one of your favorite possessions."

"I'll get you something for that later. Trust me. Let me see what you've got. I can make you a good deal."

"I'm not in a position to offer you anything valuable for just 'ideas'. Can you help me get the mask, or get ahead of whatever Aayara is planning?"

"I can get you into the auction, at least, and I have some baubles that Kyestri might be willing to trade."

Taelien nodded. "You have some kind of disguise or false identity that I can use?"

Wrynn scoffed. "Oh, you're just precious. No, I have an *invitation*. You can come along as my escort. Provided you can afford my time." She looked him up and down. "And that you wear something a little nicer."

Taelien sighed. "I don't exactly have formal wear with me."

"I'll make arrangements. In the meantime, let me see those toys you've been hiding."

Taelien reached into the backpack again, and he felt a momentary sting from stretching the injury that War had given him. It still hadn't completely healed. "Give me a moment." He set his mundane supplies on his left side and then began to unload the dominion bonded items he'd been collecting on his right.

His shoulders tightened as he began setting the objects down. They represented nearly a year of his work, tracking down relics hidden in old ruins and buying curios with long-forgotten properties. He didn't like the idea of giving any of them up for a nebulous potential reward, but he had limited options.

Taelien laid down the first item, a sheathed dagger. He unsheathed it briefly, showing a silvery blade with a faint glow. "Silverbrand. Bonded to the Dominion of Radiance. Some people say it was blessed by the God of Swords himself."

Wrynn snorted. "Not likely. Probably just something a priest threw an enchantment on to pawn for a few extra gold."

"I don't think most priests do that sort of thing."

Wrynn shrugged. "Why not? I know I would."

Taelien sheathed the dagger, but kept it out. "I don't think most priests *can* do that sort of thing. Dominion bonding requires extensive knowledge, and radiance callers are rare. And regardless of the origin, it's useful. Well-balanced for both close combat and throwing, and the enchantment makes it effective against creatures of shadow."

Wrynn raised an eyebrow. "You do remember who you're talking to, right?"

"Of course. You're the 'Witch of a Thousand Shadows'. Very fancy. But you're a sorcerer, not an elemental. You can use things opposed to your dominions." He nudged the dagger closer. "And I know you like knives."

"Guilty, I admit it." She picked it up, testing the weight. "A little boring, but I'll think about it. Got anything juicier?"

Taelien removed two spheres from the bag, each just small enough to fit in a palm. The balls were filled with liquid, with a single object suspended within each — a metallic arrow, like the point of a compass.

"These are useful." Taelien lifted one, and the arrow swung to point toward the other orb. "Very simple. The arrows always point toward the location of the other orb."

"For tracking?" Wrynn twisted her lips. "Not bad, but a bit too big to plant on someone."

"They're built for giving to friends, so you can find each other at a distance, not tracking your enemies."

Wrynn shrugged. "Wouldn't be useful to me, then."

Taelien set the orb down. "Why?"

Wrynn set Silverbrand down, looking at the spheres. "Only had one person that was worth keeping an eye on, and she's already dead."

Taelien's heart sank. "I'm sorry to hear that."

Wrynn gave him a curious look. "Because it makes it harder for you to sell me an orb, or do you actually care?"

"Little bit of both, but mostly the latter. Must have been difficult to lose someone that close to you."

"More than you know." She sounded wistful. "Maybe I'll tell you about her at some point. She would have liked you. Or hated you. Maybe both." Wrynn nodded to herself. "But enough of that for now. Show me something interesting."

Taelien put Silverbrand away, then removed a lantern with a white metallic frame.

"Ooh, I think I know that one. Is that Ulandir's Ghost Lantern?"

Taelien nudged the lantern closer. "It is. Have a look."

Wrynn lifted the device, inspecting it. "Fascinating that he managed such a complex effect with a bonded item, rather than a marked one. Must be several different bonded components here. Have you tried it? Does it work?"

"It definitely illuminates spirits when it's lit, but I wasn't able to find any that I could interact with. Some of them looked at me, but I couldn't get any of them to talk." He frowned. "And now I'm seeing them even with the lantern off. Which is irritating."

Wrynn gave an appreciative hum. "That's quite impressive. Spirit dominion items aren't cheap or easy to come by. And it's probably *better* that the spirits didn't take an interest in you. I doubt you have any defenses against them if they proved hostile." She paused. "And those lingering effects are...odd. You're sure you're still seeing actual spirits? Maybe you just need to have your eyes checked."

Taelien shook his head. "I'm pretty sure. They're still there when I do turn the lantern on, and they seem to notice me if I use it, but not before."

"...That...definitely shouldn't work that way. But okay, you've got me somewhat interested, at least."

"So, you'll trade for that, then?" He tried not to sound too hopeful.

"Keep going." She set the lantern down. "I'll tell you what I want when I've seen the whole inventory."

Taelien laid out the next item.

"One spool of silk from a Lightweave Spider. Extremely resilient and inherently bonded to the Dominion of Light."

"Boring. Next?"

Taelien retrieved a smooth, oval-shaped white stone just a bit smaller than his palm. "A purestone. I know you do some travel, so you're probably familiar with them."

Wrynn nodded. "Water purification. Drop it into a water source, it'll eventually purify the whole thing. I've heard it even 'purifies' things like poisons. True?"

Taelien nodded. "Yeah, as far as I can tell, although it isn't exactly easy to slip it into something you think is poisoned before you drink it. Believe me, I've tried. Might even offer some protection against poison for whoever is carrying it, but I'm less sure on that part."

"Not something I need. I never get sick, and poison isn't a threat to me. Useful bauble to most, though, I'm certain."

This isn't going well.

"You're sure I can't convince you to take it in trade, perhaps? You could even sell it."

"Eh, maybe. But it's boring. I want something that *excites* me."

He wanted to argue, but he could tell that she wasn't likely to change her mind. He tucked the stone back in his bag.

At least I'll have it for myself if Aayara tries anything.

"What's next?"

Taelien hesitated. "I'm afraid this will be the last thing that's up for trade right now."

He only had one more item in his bag, but it was a good one. It was a necklace holding a teardrop-shaped blue crystal. "I'm sure you remember telling me where to find the Arturo's Amulet of Sanctuary."

Wrynn gave the necklace an appreciative look. "I'm impressed. The portal still worked?"

"The crystals powering it were long gone, but I bought replacements and got it up and running. Barely made it out of the pocket dimension in time, but I got the necklace. And what appears to be a map." He removed a piece of parchment from the bag, passing it to Wrynn. "I couldn't read it, though."

Wrynn's eyes sparkled as she unfolded the map and looked at it. "This is...Davorin, I think. The language, not the location." She closed the map. "Hold onto these. The map and the necklace. I don't need them, but they might be worth something. Did you manage to activate the necklace?"

"No, couldn't figure out how to work it. Maybe the map has the instructions." Taelien turned the necklace over in his hands. "You're sure you don't want them? We're both aware of the value of what the map might lead to."

"It also could lead to nothing." Wrynn's eyes remained focused on the necklace. "I'll think about it. For now, pass me Silverbrand. I can always use more pokey things."

Taelien nodded, retrieving the dagger again and packing away the necklace and map. He was a little sad to part with the weapon, but at least it was for a worthy cause. Wrynn *did* love daggers. She'd take good care of it.

Wrynn turned the dagger over in her hands. "I'll get you into that auction, and I'll give you something to trade with Kyestri."

"I appreciate it." He began to pack the other objects back into his backpack. "What've you got for me?"

Wrynn folded up the map, handed it back to Taelien, and pushed herself to her feet. "Hold on just a moment."

She turned, tapping on the metallic doors behind her.

Then she vanished in a puff of smoke.

Taelien blinked. Not because teleportation was a surprise to him at that point, but because it wasn't usually accompanied by any sort of visual effect. The smoke was both unusual and seemingly unnecessary.

Wrynn reappeared a few minutes later, accompanied by a similar swirl of soot.

Taelien was standing by that point, his hand sitting on the hilt of his sword. He wasn't expecting an ambush, but it was always best to be ready for one.

Wrynn was armed, too, but not for a fight. The dagger she was holding was sheathed, and she flipped it around to offer it to him. "A dagger for a dagger. Seems fair, although I'll miss this one. This is Sculptor."

Taelien raised an eyebrow, accepting the dagger. "Sculptor?" He immediately felt a familiar type of essence within it. "Ah, stone shaping?"

Wrynn nodded. "It cuts straight through stone. Most famously, it was used by a Xixian prince named Shosan Ver. Not for anything insidious; he literally used for sculpting."

Taelien unsheathed the dagger, feeling the aura of it. He had some level of stone shaping ability, but it was minimal. He'd always been much better at manipulating metal.

He could tell that the weapon's stone shaping aura was much stronger than what he could manage on his own, but that didn't make it particularly useful. His personal aura was able to burn straight through stone if he needed it to.

Still, he could see why she was offering it to him. "Kyestri is the Prime Lord of Stone. I take it he collects items connected to his dominion?"

"He collects dominion marked and bonded in general, but I suspect that a Xixian curio tied to his dominion would be an excellent fit for his collection." Wrynn smiled. "I have a few other things I can show you another time, but for the moment, that's what I'm offering."

Taelien nodded, sheathing the dagger. "Very well. I'd also like any personal information about Kyestri you're willing to share. Any interests he has, how he got the mask, and anything else he'd be willing to trade for it."

"I'll have to look through my notes first, but I can agree to that."

Taelien pondered for another moment. "Any chance we could get a meeting before the auction?"

"Not a bad plan. I'll send him a letter and see if I can arrange it. Is that satisfactory?"

Taelien reached out with a hand. "I believe we have a deal."

Wrynn smiled and clasped it. "As always, it's a pleasure doing business with you."

CHAPTER VII – VELAS II – FALSE FAMILIES

Velas sat up, brushing aside her bedsheets. There was something wrong.

It took her a moment to process the fact that she hadn't gone to sleep in a bed, and certainly not in this location.

The white walls and portraits on the walls were familiar, though. So was the bed, after a moment, though she hadn't seen it in many years.

Groaning, she dislodged herself from the bed entirely. This was also disorienting, because her standing height only reached the bottom of the picture frames.

She cautiously raised a hand. It was familiar, too, but entirely too small. After a moment of dysphoria, she grabbed a strand of hair and pulled it in front of her. It was all black, her natural color.

I must be awfully young if I haven't bleached it at all yet.

She scanned the rest of her surroundings, searching for anything that might be of use. Her closet was filled with a dozen identical white dresses. That, unlike the rest of the scenario, was *not* accurate to her childhood room.

She ignored the clothing, searching for a weapon, but there were none to be found. While breaking something for an improvised tool would have been possible as an adult, she didn't think she could manage much that would be useful with her child body.

I can find some knives in the kitchen, assuming everything is where it should be. Or maybe something in the training hall with more reach.

She opened the door, finding the hallway to be in the right place, and headed past her sister's room toward the training hall.

She slowly opened the door to the training hall, prepared to slam it shut if she detected any threats.

Velas did find someone already inside the hall. And she *was* a threat. But slamming the door on her would have served no purpose.

Velas stepped into the room, folding her arms. "Hello, Auntie Ess. Is this really necessary?"

Symphony was dressed just as she often had been when Velas was a child, in a traditional Velryan fencing uniform. Pants and a shirt, nothing loose for an enemy to grab onto, with a rapier on her hip. She smiled brightly as Velas entered. "Good morning, dear."

"Is it?" Velas glanced at the windows, seeing light streaming in, then back to Symphony. "I think I'm still asleep."

"Oh, you are." Symphony waved a hand. "But I'm sure it's morning somewhere."

"You didn't answer my earlier question. What's with all *this*?"

Symphony had a hurt expression. "You don't remember? It's Children's Day, dear. And the anniversary of when I first agreed to train you."

"Children's Day." Velas let out a sigh, then pointed to herself. "I think you might be taking the name a bit too literally."

Symphony laughed. "I know, I know. You've grown older. But you'll always be one of my—"

"Dolls? I remember you mentioning that you liked to play with those." She took a step closer, in spite of the danger that posed. "I imagine you also break the ones you're bored with."

Symphony gave her a considering look. "Admittedly, Lady Two-knot was eventually executed."

Velas took a step back in alarm, but Symphony waved a hand. "Oh, don't worry about that. She was a literal doll. You're not, dear, and I know that. I value your life and your autonomy."

"Do you? Because you didn't exactly warn me when you sent Sterling to kill my friends."

Symphony rolled her eyes. "I didn't have anything to do with that. Sterling can be...impertinent at times."

"He's an 'ess', Auntie. You had to be aware of what he was up to."

Symphony smiled. "Of course. But you asked me for autonomy. Would you deny others the same?"

"I'm not talking about pulling on puppet strings. I'm talking about keeping your agents from murdering people, especially your *other* agents."

"A valid point. I'm certain he wouldn't have killed you, though. He had specific targets." Symphony shrugged. "But do you really want to talk about that? I haven't seen you in ages, dear. We should celebrate!"

"I'm not even really here." Velas sighed. "And frankly, this setup is more than a little creepy."

"Is it?" Symphony frowned. "I've never been very good at judging that. I was hoping it would be a nice surprise."

"Sending someone flowers or baked goods is a nice surprise. And I mean baked goods in the literal sense, not in guild code. This," Velas waved at the building, "is putting me in a position that makes me feel vulnerable."

"Perhaps I overdid it a bit." Symphony flicked her wrist and a single white rose appeared in her hand. "Can you find it in your heart to forgive me?"

Velas rolled her eyes. "For the theatrics, perhaps. You're going to need to work on the Sterling part. And you've reminded me about something I've been meaning to ask you for some time."

"Oh?" Symphony raised an eyebrow.

"All this. Everything I grew up with. It was just as fake as this dream, wasn't it? Those people who raised me weren't my parents. I doubt if we were related at all. You certainly aren't my aunt."

"Was there a question in that, dear?"

"Why? Where did I come from?"

Symphony nodded. "Ah." She waved toward the ground, then sat. "Take a seat. I'll tell you a story."

"Fix my body first."

"Very well. It's irrelevant, though. This is just a dream." She snapped her fingers.

Velas felt her entire body *tremble*. There was an instant of pain after that, then it was done.

She had her adult body again. She breathed a sigh of relief and sat down. "Thank you."

"You're quite welcome. Now, let's see. Where should I begin?"

Velas narrowed her eyes. "The truth. I don't want some Tarren tale."

Symphony's eyelids fluttered. "Whatever do you mean, dear? Tarren *barely* figures into your childhood. Much less than some."

"Just talk. Start from the beginning."

"Well, when the old gods made the world—"

Velas folded her arms.

Symphony chuckled. "Fine, fine. Let's find a suitable beginning... Ah!" She snapped her fingers. The light in the room dimmed, then faded to near blackness. "Perhaps a demonstration would be better."

A curtained stage rose from the floor, stopping at four feet in height.

The curtains parted, revealing a scene. It was atop a mountain range dotted with tall trees, each of which was dusted in snow.

"In days long past, when I was but a girl, there were two great heroes."

Two puppets descended from the air, jerking to a halt as they landed atop the stage.

On the left was a woman in rune-etched white armor, carrying a sword that was wrought from white stone.

On the right was a man wearing an outfit of green formed from leaves and vines. He carried a two-handed sword with a handle that resembled living wood giving way to a golden blade. He wore a crown of leaves.

That one is Vaelien, most likely. I'm not so sure about the first one.

"Each was a legend, forged through the heat of many battles. They were, perhaps, the greatest warriors our world had seen. Each had triumphed over many terrible foes, and on occasion, they even had worked together against common threats.

The stage shifted briefly, showing a throne room. A third puppet descended, his body marked with obsidian scales, wearing a tall metal crown. In his hands he wielded a long spear that looked quite familiar.

Vyrek Sul, the Xixian Emperor, wielding the Heartlance...? No, that has to be Cessius, his legendary staff. But the Heartlance looks so similar. I suppose Symphony is showing me that Lydia's hypothesis about the Heartlance being a piece of Cessius is probably right.

The two hero puppets flew toward the emperor puppet.

There was no intricate fighting. They simply ran right into him repeatedly until the emperor puppet exploded in a shower of gore.

Velas wiped a splotch of blood off her face and sighed.

The scene changed back to the snow.

"But alas, in spite of time spent working together, they knew there could only ever be a single end to their journeys. The world had room for only a single hero, and long had they disagreed on who that should be."

The two hero puppets lunged at another. There was an exaggerated "slash" effect of white as they passed by each other, then the armored woman puppet fell into two pieces.

The stage darkened, and the two heroes vanished.

On the right corner of the stage, another puppet appeared. A dark haired woman, fallen to her knees in the snow. Tears poured down her face.

Velas turned to Symphony. "This is a good story, but what does it have to do with me?"

"Patience, girl. You'll see soon enough." Symphony waved her hand and the stage darkened again. "The death of a hero is never a simple thing. Some were struck with great fear, while others sought to rise to replace what had been lost."

A diagonal beam of light struck the center of the stage, showing a pair of new puppets. A younger-looking woman puppet wore the armor of the fallen hero — with a clear stitch in the center, where it had once been cut in half. Next to her stood a man in a blue tunic, who held a shining silver blade.

Velas frowned. "How long ago was this, exactly?"

"Not important." Symphony snapped her fingers. "The new generation trained hard, seeking to reach the great heights that their master once had."

The puppets ran around in a circle on the stage, chasing each other.

Eventually, their strings got tangled together...which brought the two puppets closer and closer, until they were face-to-face.

Most of this hasn't been very subtle, but that's not a bad metaphor.

"Soon, the apprentices of the fallen hero were inseparable. They grew strong, and in time, they challenged the one who had defeated their master."

There was a flash and the green-armored knight appeared.

The two other puppets rammed into him, then fell over.

"But he was too strong."

The green-armored puppet vanished.

"Still, they were young, and he was merciful. His rivalry had been with their master, not with them, and he saw no need to end the lives of ones with such youthful talent."

Velas raised a skeptical eyebrow at that, but didn't reply.

"They continued to train, occasionally challenging the superior hero, but each time he proved victorious. Eventually, they gave up, and decided to settle down."

The scene changed to a home, showing the two apprentices in a humble cabin, legendary sword and armor hung up on the wall.

The female doll had an obvious roundness to her belly.

"They made one final mistake, however. One final challenge. They trained another."

The scene changed.

A red-haired woman appeared on the stage, lifting a sword that glimmered with the light of dawn.

She stood in the center of a coliseum, opposite from a younger man in a green and gold tunic. His resemblance to the green-armored hero — almost undoubtedly Vaelien — was clear.

They charged at one another. A slash, and then the man in the green tunic fell to the ground. There was the sound of a cheer from the sides of the arena, though Symphony had not seen fit to fill it with any people.

The scene faded.

Velas understood immediately the "mistake" that had been made. Apparently, this red-haired woman had somehow hurt or killed one of Vaelien's children.

And, knowing Vaelien, that could not have ended well.

The scene shifted to a forest glade.

The red-haired woman was face-down in the dirt, a pool of blood collecting beneath her.

That scene faded immediately, going back to the cabin.

Both the male and the female "apprentices" were on the ground, with blood everywhere.

There was a small child puppet in the corner of the room, wrapped in swaddling cloth. But, oddly, the female puppet still had a round belly.

A continuity error, or were there two children involved?

The Vaelien puppet stood over the two blood-stained apprentice puppets, his sword in hand.

Then the scene went dark, and the curtains closed.

Symphony clapped her hands together. "And that's where you came from."

Velas put her hands to the sides of her head, rubbing her temples. "That was...completely unclear. Are you saying I'm the child that was in the corner of that room? Or the one that woman was pregnant with? Or was that all misdirection, and I'm the child of the red-haired woman, or one of Vaelien's replacements for the child he lost to her?"

"Oh, I'm sorry, dear. I don't have time for any questions. But happy Children's Day!" Symphony stretched her arms upward and smiled. "I hope you enjoyed the show."

Velas took a step forward. "You're really going to leave it at that? Giving me half-answers that only lead to more questions?"

Symphony stepped closer, raising a hand. "I think it'll be far more interesting if you figure things out on your own. Besides," she put a finger against Velas' forehead, "someone is about to wake you up."

***

Velas' eyes snapped open. Someone was looming over her in the dark.

She reached for the blade under her blanket, but the figure caught her arm.

"Take it easy." It was pitch black and they were in a confined space with minimal room for Velas to maneuver. She couldn't make out the figure's features, but after a moment, she recognized the voice and she relaxed.

"You were having a nightmare," Lydia explained. "One of the sorcerous variety."

Velas gritted her teeth. *That was real, then. Auntie Ess really was paying me a visit.* She took a couple breaths, closing her eyes and clearing her mind. Then she relaxed her arm and nodded to Lydia. "I'm better now. How'd you know?"

"I have a bit of a sense for dream sorcery. I could feel it." Lydia shifted her position, moving to sit at Velas' side. "Are you well? Any indication of who might have attacked you?"

Dream sorcery? That's right, Jonan mentioned that she'd knocked Edon out with a sleep spell. That's rather unusual for a paladin — dream sorcery is something of a taboo for them.

Velas groaned and sat up. "Nothing to worry about, Red. It wasn't an...attack, exactly. Just a visit from a nagging family member."

Lydia folded her arms. "Using dream sorcery to communicate is generally frowned upon. Are you certain you're all right?"

"I am. What time is it?" She felt a slight jolt as the wagon beneath them hit a bump in the road, tensing again for a moment, then taking a breath.

"Give me a moment." Lydia closed her eyes. "Identify Local Time of Day." There was no visible effect from Lydia's spell, but Velas was close enough that she could feel something subtle in the air. "Just past three bells. You still have another two hours to sleep before your watch shift."

Velas shook her head. "Forget it. I'm not going back to sleep after that." She paused. "Anything happen on your watch?"

"Nothing of note. I don't anticipate any danger until we get closer to Selyr."

"Right." Velas rubbed at her eyes. "And what's the plan once we get there?"

"We'll see if the Thornguard have any indication of Sterling's location."

Velas blinked. "You're just going to *ask*?"

"Selyr is under Thornguard jurisdiction. Sterling is in a position of authority there. There's a good chance he's not even hiding."

"Sure, he might not be now. But if we start asking questions about him, we're going to tip him off to our presence."

Lydia smiled. "Yes, that would be likely."

Velas paused, considering, then shook her head. "You want him to come to us. You're making us bait."

"That would be ideal. But if he's uncooperative, we have other angles to pursue. I might know a few Thornguard that would be sympathetic to our cause."

"Ah, you mean the paladins have spies in the Thornguard." Velas didn't know if she should find that impressive or depressing. The paladins certainly knew how to sound righteous, but when it came to tactics, they didn't seem to differ much from any other organization she'd worked with. "Why not talk to them first, rather than risking alerting Sterling?"

"I've tapped a few resources already. I'd rather not dig into that well too deeply unless we have to, since there's always a risk of exposing anyone we contact. I suspect the direct approach is actually more likely to give us useful information, and with less risk."

"I'll be the last person to turn down a fight, but you think alerting Sterling that we're looking for him is a low risk?"

"Ah, allow me to rephrase. When I said *we* are going to talk to the Thornguard, I really meant *you* are."

"Oh, lovely. I get to absorb all the personal risk."

"Not at all. After all, you'll be in disguise."

Velas frowned. "...Disguise?"

"Indeed. You'll be asking about Sterling while dressed as Silk, the legendary apprentice of Aayara, the Lady of Thieves." Lydia gave Velas a smile. "What reason would they have to deny information to Aayara's own protégé?"

For a dangerous moment, Velas froze.

Did Lydia *know*?

From the shape of her grin...yes, she definitely did.

The role was too specific for this to be a mere suspicion or a coincidence. In spite of Lydia's phrasing, Silk wasn't an everyday name like Aayara was.

There were plenty of people who knew the traditional title that Aayara's apprentices used, but there was no reason that Velas could see for Lydia to bring up that specific disguise in this context without knowledge of her identity. Any number of other disguises would be both easier to manage and more believable for an ordinary person.

A part of her screamed to draw steel and cut off this loose end. But she didn't know how much Lydia knew, or how. And such an action would be pointless if the information had already been broadly distributed.

Instead, she simply crossed her arms and asked, "How?"

"I have my sources of information, just as you do."

Velas glared at her. "That's infuriatingly vague. Sources..." Velas sighed. "Reshing Kestrian, wasn't it?"

Lydia raised a hand to adjust her glasses. "Mm, perhaps in a manner of speaking. But don't place any blame on him. It's not what you're thinking."

"Right. Of course." Velas sighed. She'd been trained to accept that betrayal could and would happen at any time. In cultivating her various roles, she'd lied to and manipulated many people herself.

It had given her an unlikely sort of happiness when she learned that Aayara had another secret apprentice — another person trained with skills that mirrored and complemented her own. She'd sensed a kinship in him that she'd never felt with her false family. She'd *liked* working with Jonan.

But if he'd broken her cover identity — deliberately or otherwise — he'd have to answer for that.

Velas felt her shoulders tighten. "Well," she took a breath, slowly and deliberately, "If I'm going to be bait, I suppose you'd better tell me where we're keeping the trap."

***

The city of Selyr originated as a Thornguard border fortress in the days of the Xixian Empire, one of the first bastions of human and rethri power in the region. In time, the fortress grounds expanded to house Thornguard family members, and enterprising merchants set up businesses to provide the residents with supplies.

Decades passed. As the power of the Xixian Empire waned, Selyr expanded further, with a town blossoming around the original fortifications and gradually growing into a city.

Though the Xixian Empire had ostensibly been wiped out, Selyr's layout and culture were a lasting reminder of the city's military roots.

The city had four layers of walls, each having been built as the city grew beyond the scope of its original fortifications. The innermost layer had never been breached by enemy forces.

All citizens participated in some degree of mandatory military training upon reaching adulthood — earlier in the cases of those who demonstrated any sorcerous talents.

And so, as Velas looked for a likely source of information from the Thornguard, she realized that practically every adult citizen was an option. Those in her age range were either currently in the service or would have finished relatively recently, and the younger and older generations would still have family members and friends that were currently enlisted or in training.

As Velas Jaldin, she might have simply listened for gossip at a tavern or bought drinks for someone who looked both useful and easy to twist to her purposes. Maybe a lower-ranked officer, important enough to have sources of information but not important enough that making contact would involve a high degree of risk.

As Myros, she'd have probably gone straight to the closest military base — the city apparently had several, for various different branches of service — and demanded to speak to someone in charge.

That approach might have gotten her answers, but the risk factors were severe. It would have been a political issue if things got back to the *other* Myros in Orlyn. She'd always been the muscle for the role, but not the public face. And of course, showing up in the guise of a "god" of a foreign religion was very likely to come across as hostile, and she'd be inviting a fight.

That's basically what Taelien did in Orlyn, even if he didn't realize it at the time.

I've never gotten to pick a fight with a whole government like that. Lucky bastard.

Taking that approach was *extremely* tempting, but it wasn't what she was there for.

She'd agreed to play a different role, and sadly Silk wasn't there to bash any heads. At least not immediately.

Who's on my contact list for Selyr? Let's see... Stranger wouldn't be a good fit for this, Star is too eccentric, Scribe obviously is already involved... Hm. Stillness might be useful, if I can track her down.

I guess there's always Scullery and Scone. They're hilarious, but probably not in a way that would be useful.

Might be easiest to go straight to someone associated with the Thornguard.

She wished she had a physical list. It would have been a lot more convenient than relying on memory, but the security problems with that approach were obvious.

Before getting too deep into her plans, she checked her mirror to see if she had any new letters.

Silk,
Symphony moving pieces toward "Kyestri". Avoid.
-Scribe

Velas wrinkled her nose at the message. She didn't write a reply.

Quotes around Kyestri, huh? Was he on the replacement list? Hm. That'll be useful to know if I do get tangled up in that business, but...

She shook her head. It didn't concern her, at least for now.

After a few more minutes of deliberation, she settled on an option and got to work.

She'd worked in Selyr before, but not much. Fortunately, Lydia had a map, and it was recent enough to point her toward the area she wanted — Fort Kaldri, the base of operations for the Thornguard's Bladebreaker division.

Cassius Morn had been a member of that division before "disappearing", which meant that Sterling probably had contacts there. It was possible that Sterling's connection with Cassius was of a personal nature rather than going through standard channels, but it seemed like a good place to start.

Unlike in most cities, starting at the front gate and actually identifying herself was an option here. She didn't have any formal rank in the Thornguard, but their whole organization was pledged to the service of the vae'kes, and that meant extending help to the servants of those vae'kes as well. She could have just told them that she was Silk and gone through the "proper" channels to verify her identity.

But that was both slow and boring, so she found herself breaking into the fortress in the middle of the night instead.

Fort Kaldri was built to resist a conventional assault, but she judged it one of the easier bases to infiltrate. It was built at the top of a hill with a very traditional moat-and-drawbridge setup, with the drawbridge being up for the night. Beyond that, the fortress' high stone walls, with a few patrolling guards atop them. There were five watchtowers — four on the corners, and one just above the center in the front, overlooking the drawbridge.

There was forest cover on the way up the hill, which kept her relatively concealed. If she ran into any patrolling guards at this stage, she'd have raised alarms, but she didn't see any.

From there, she circled around to the back of the fortress, staying within the forest cover as long as possible.

A quick glance didn't show her any obvious figures on the parapets. She judged the dimensions of the fortress to be about eight hundred yards in each direction — large enough that she didn't think that someone in the corner watchtowers was likely to see her unless they were looking straight in her direction.

At that point, it was less about luck and more about speed.

She rushed out of the brush, jumped once, and concentrated.

Surge.

A blast of motion sorcery carried her across the moat and toward the wall.

Surge.

A second blast altered her trajectory, carrying her upward at an angle toward the top of the wall.

The arc of the blast took her a little too high. Rather than use a third motion calling spell, she concentrated. Motion shaping was a more recent skill development for her, but after the Wandering War had used it to pull her out of the air, she'd realized how useful it could be and begun to practice.

She felt the essence propelling her, then subtly shifted the direction and level of force. Just prior to landing, she wove a different type of shape.

Silence.

She landed on the parapets without a sound, ducked, and looked from side-to-side.

No patrols nearby. Good. Lights are on in the towers, but I doubt they saw me.

From there, it would have been a simple thing to hop over the opposite side of the wall into the courtyard below, but she took a moment to orient herself first.

Her target was in an officer's quarters in one of the six buildings on the northeast side of the facility. She took a moment to find it — the layout was a little different from her map, due to the addition of new buildings — and then jumped in that direction.

Surge.

A little bit more force, this time directed downward, and then a similar application of shaping took her down into a copse of trees not far from her destination.

There *were* patrols out in the base itself, but fortunately none of them seemed to be looking up. She took a mental note of the locations of the ones she saw during her descent, and then cautiously made her way toward her destination.

The door was locked. She fished out a bit of metal from her hair, trying to pick it, but without success.

Must be one of those ones where you have to hit multiple pins at the same time, she grumbled to herself. Lockpicking was never her area of expertise. Maybe she could have sorted it out eventually, but she didn't have the patience for it.

She located a nearby window instead, pressing her hand against the bottom.

The window was on the second floor of the building, without any sort of balcony or platform for her to stand on. That made for an interesting shaping exercise.

Surge.

She blasted herself upward from the ground, then shaped the force below her to stop her movement just at the level of the door.

Then she *held* the remaining kinetic energy in place, leaving herself floating in mid-air. It wouldn't last more than a few moments, though.

Silence.

Push.

She shaped the burst of motion at the bottom of the window frame, successfully flipping the latch on the inside of the window. Then, with it unlatched, it was trivial to lift.

The spell holding her airborne failed, so she used another, bursting herself back upward as she fell and throwing herself into the window.

Her body was beginning to ache from the expenditure of sorcery, but that wasn't her biggest problem.

Silk's legendary veils covered her face and much of her body, thoroughly obscuring her identity. If they weren't enchanted, she would have been virtually blind. Fortunately, they were enchanted, and that meant the only problem she had to deal with was constantly getting snagged on...well, everything.

In this case, she managed to catch on a stray nail on the inside of the window frame.

The jolt of getting caught pulled her backward, and she landed gracelessly — but fortunately, still soundlessly — in a pile on the floor of the room.

The enchantments on the veils ensured they didn't tear easily, but that just made it harder to dislodge. She tried to stand, failing and getting caught even worse. It took her a few awkward moments before she decided to pull that veil free, adjust the other ones, and then try to unwind the veil that was caught.

Ugh. I wonder how many previous Silks this outfit has killed.

She finally ended up pulling the entire nail out of the wall to free herself, then righted herself and examined where she'd ended up.

She was in someone's bedroom. From the pile of clothes on the floor, there were two...no, three people in there. Only one of them was an officer.

She gave the unconscious figures an amused smirk.

None of them appeared to be who she was looking for, unfortunately, or it would have made a great entrance once she'd fixed her outfit.

She closed the window — still under the veil of her silence spell — and slipped out the door.

That led into a larger living room. She crossed it without much concern for the contents. She wasn't here to rifle through a random Thornguard officer's things, as fun as that might be.

The next door took her into a hallway. She closed it behind her, then headed down the hall toward her destination.

When she rounded a corner, she nearly ran face-first into a patrolling guard.

"Wha?" He stammered, his hand fumbling for a sword on his belt.

Velas was faster, as usual. She wasn't carrying the Heartlance — that wasn't Silk's weapon of choice — but she had a knife at the guard's throat a moment later. "Sssh."

"Ahh!" He managed, stumbling backward. Silk followed his movement, keeping her knife in place. And then, after a beat, he said, "Ohh! Silk, it's just you."

Velas blinked. Fortunately, she knew he couldn't see her perplexed expression behind the veils.

The guard shook his head, raising his hands. "Okay, you got me. I'll be faster next time."

...What?

Velas didn't recognize this man in the slightest. Did she know him? She wracked her memory, but he didn't look familiar.

She wasn't an expert at sight sorcery, but she could feel it if she concentrated. She didn't sense any on him. Not Jonan in disguise, then.

Velas pulled the knife away. "You'd better be."

She had no idea why he recognized her, but she also knew how to play along. "Is Captain Nolan still in this building?"

The guard nodded. "Yeah, just around the corner. Think he's still up." He turned his back on her — a horrible idea, given how they'd encountered each other — and walked to a doorway. She followed. "Right here. I'll leave you two alone."

The guard *saluted* her, and then headed further down the hall.

She stared after him for a moment, pondering.

Captain Nolan is an Ess, so maybe the guard on his floor is, too. That wouldn't be a bad security precaution...but that still wouldn't explain his utter lack of surprise and ease of recognizing me.

Were they warned that I was coming?

Jonan knew I was on the way, and he's the one who gave me some of the names on my list for Selyr. Maybe he was thinking far enough ahead to warn Nolan that I might stop by, as frustrating as that might be. But he wouldn't have told some random guard, would he?

Aayara is the only other one who keeps close enough of an eye on me to guess where I was going, and she's similarly not inclined to chat with random guards.

The other explanation, then, is that I'm expected for an entirely different reason. That could be good or bad.

She didn't bother trying to break into the captain's room.

If she was right, then...

She knocked on the door.

A few moments later, an older man in a full Thornguard officer uniform opened it. He took a look at her and gave her a friendly smile. "Ah, Silk! Back so soon?"

CHAPTER VIII – TAELIEN III – PRIME NOBILITY

"Breakfast is ready!"

Taelien woke to Wrynn's voice at the door of his room. Asphodel was reading on her bed on the opposite side of the room. She looked like she'd already been awake for some time.

After groggily dislodging himself from bed, Taelien dressed and headed down to eat. Breakfast consisted of some kind of eggs, sausage, and a heavily spiced porridge.

Wrynn set down a pitcher of apple juice next to it with a wry grin.

Taelien was too famished to bother with a retort. After tearing through his meal, he checked with Wrynn about heading to the auction.

"You've got a few days before the auction starts. I arranged for a meeting with Kyestri before the auction like you wanted, but I'm not sure he'll be keen to sell the item early."

"I'd like to beat the competition to it if possible, even if that means an added expense. Can we leave now?"

Wrynn shook her head. "I've got other customers to deal with. Let me get them squared away. Should be gone by mid-day, then we go pay Kyestri a visit."

"Are we going to be able to make it there before nightfall?" Taelien had a general idea of where they were going, but he hadn't been to the Prime Lord of Stone's lands before.

"Won't be an issue. We can get there and back here by evening, so you can leave your things behind if you want."

"I'll think about it. For the moment, I'm going to spend some time outside."

Wrynn gave him a wave and he headed out the door.

Asphodel followed him outside shortly thereafter. She'd been upstairs and too far away to hear the conversation, but he was long past being surprised by her predictive abilities, even if he wasn't exactly certain how they all worked.

"She mourns for one who should never have fallen." Asphodel turned her gaze downward. "We must be cautious not to remind her of what she has lost."

Taelien raised an eyebrow. "Why? Was Kyestri involved somehow?"

Asphodel slowly shook her head. "No. But she has long sought revenge against a force that cannot be contested. And we cannot afford the cost of helping her."

"A force that cannot be contested? You mean one of the gods, then?"

"I have said too much." Asphodel bowed at the waist. "May I join you?"

Taelien started to mention that he'd come outside to train, then he realized what she'd just offered. "I'd like that. It's been too long since I've had a sparring partner."

Asphodel smiled softly. "I know."

"How are we doing this?" Taelien glanced Asphodel over. She wasn't carrying any obvious weapons. This was no surprise, since she typically fought unarmed. A portion of her crystalline hair was still gray and lifeless from her battle with Susan Crimson, but he couldn't see any visible signs that she'd used her delaren transformations to change her body since they'd last met.

"You may fight however you choose."

"I'll figure that out as we go, then."

Asphodel nodded, assuming a basic defensive fighting stance.

Taelien responded in kind, debating how to approach. He left his sword on his belt, undrawn. His control over the Sae'kes had improved significantly, but he still wasn't comfortable using it while sparring, especially against an unarmed opponent.

Without the Sae'kes, though, he was at a terrible disadvantage.

He did have other weapons — a pair of knives on his belt, as well as the newly acquired Sculptor, currently sheathed and tucked into his right boot. He left those weapons alone for the moment as well. If he was going to use them, he'd want to surprise her with them.

Asphodel couldn't gaze deeply into his fate like she could with most, but her altered form of perception still allowed her to see and hear things seconds ahead of time. That worked against him just like it did with anyone else.

I could try to hit her too quickly for her to dodge, even if she can see it coming. Or I could try to use flame sorcery on such a broad area—

Asphodel came at him swinging before he had a chance to collect his thoughts. He side-stepped her first punch easily, but she was already swinging a kick into the direction he was moving. He raised an arm to block.

He felt a jolt of agony as her kick smashed into his arm. He stepped backward rapidly, half out of pain and half out of surprise. It had been years since an unarmed attack had hurt him that much, and it wasn't because he was out of shape. He was the toughest he'd ever been, his body continuously reinforced from years of both physical training and constant sorcery use.

Asphodel simply hit harder than anyone he'd ever fought against, aside from maybe the ten-ton golem they'd used to simulate a Xixian prince in his paladin tests. Others had been faster or more skilled, but no ordinary human he'd encountered could match his own physical strength.

It was easy to forget that Asphodel was neither human nor ordinary.

And that meant that, for the first time in a long time, he could actually put some effort into fighting back.

Asphodel's next attack came almost immediately, another straight punch aimed at his chest. Rather than blocking, he snapped a kick at her, hoping his speed might be enough to catch her off-guard.

It was a vain hope. She hopped out of the way effortlessly, then danced to the side and threw another kick of her own.

He stepped backward and avoided the kick, but stumbled over a rock. He didn't fall, but he did stagger for long enough for Asphodel to close in and throw another punch, catching him in the ribs.

Taelien grunted and withstood the pain of the impact. Asphodel threw another punch.

Body of Stone.

The spell flooded his body with stone essence, temporarily increasing his strength and resilience at the cost of speed. He had a similar spell called Body of Iron that utilized metal essence, but he couldn't afford the larger toll it would take on his body against an opponent like Asphodel.

Normally, he wouldn't have used *either* spell in an actual fight. The speed cost usually wasn't worth the benefits to his strength and resilience, except for brief moments and emergencies, like when he'd desperately used it to reduce the damage he'd taken from War's swords.

In this case, though, Asphodel's prescience meant that a small change in his speed was unlikely to change the outcome of any given attack, and he needed all the extra durability he could get to survive the beating she was giving him.

Asphodel's next punch still connected, but the impact didn't rattle him as much. He reacted immediately, grabbing for her arm while it was still extended. If he could get her into a grapple, that would nullify the advantage of her foresight almost entirely.

She jumped back, of course. Even if he hadn't just slowed himself, he doubted he could have managed to catch her. But as she moved backward, he opened his palm and concentrated again.

Flame Arc.

It was one of the simplest flame calling spells, conjuring a fan-shaped wave of fire to burn everything within several feet in front of him. He felt a chill as the spell extracted its cost, but the effect was worthwhile.

Asphodel anticipated it, of course, but the fire came out too quickly for her to simply jump back. Instead, she hit the floor, dropping below the fire.

That bought Taelien valuable moments to act before she closed back in to strike.

Taelien pulled a knife from his belt, shaped it with a pair of thoughts, and hurled it. Asphodel regained her footing just in time to leap aside, then rushed to close back the distance.

He threw another one. Asphodel dodged that as well.

Then she was back in reach, swinging a punch at his jaw.

Her eyes widened and she pulled away just at the last moment, hurling herself to the side.

She just barely avoided the knives as they boomeranged back to Taelien, and then stopped just in front of his chest.

He pointed his hand. The daggers flew toward Asphodel again.

She caught the first one by the blade, then used it to smack the other one downward. It didn't quite work — the second knife wobbled, then continued forward, scraping across her side.

It might have drawn blood under normal circumstances, but the second shape Taelien had applied to the weapon had dulled the blade. It wasn't truly harmless — it was still metal — but Asphodel wasn't easy to hurt, either.

Asphodel threw his first knife back at him. He caught it, then flipped it in his hand, dropping into a lower stance to use it in close range.

Asphodel didn't approach like he'd expected. She frowned, glancing at the knife on the ground, then looking back to him. "You're not taking this seriously."

"We're just sparring, Asphodel. I'm not supposed to be trying to kill you." He felt his fist tightening around the knife's hilt, Asphodel's statement reminding him of similar arguments with Velas.

"You misunderstand. I was not objecting to your role. I was simply realizing my own weakness." She looked down at the knife again. "If I had been fighting you seriously, I would have been badly injured by a simple trick. *Again.*"

"You know you landed more hits on me than I did on you, right?"

"It doesn't matter." Asphodel shook her head. "You shouldn't have hit me at all. I... I don't mean to sound arrogant. But I have to be better. I can't afford to let people touch me. Not even once."

"Why...oh." Taelien nodded. "You're thinking about what happened with Susan, and how she got away."

"I told myself that it was a fluke. That she'd caught me off-guard with that void potion. I practiced. I can see things further ahead now. I'm stronger and faster than I was then. But in just a few moments of a sparring session, you realized that I still had an exploitable weakness — I'm still only seeing in front of me."

"You still avoided the knives without even seeing them. That's nothing to scoff at."

She shook her head. "Only barely, by noticing that you weren't trying to avoid me, even in the future. I knew something was wrong and got out of the way, but I didn't know what it was. And then you hit me with the second throw. If that knife had been covered with void essence, or even just poison..."

"You're overthinking this. If you're going to be fighting people, you're going to get hit. You can plan for that, train for that. I saw you sparring with Kolask and Teshvol dozens of times. I'm sure getting hit isn't new to you."

"You're right, of course. I've prepared for being injured against conventional opponents. I've even picked up some emergency supplies." She opened her belt and pulled out a couple vials. One of them was dark red, which he recognized as being a healing potion of some kind. Such potions were rare and expensive, but he'd seen his friend Arkhen brewing them many years before. "It just feels...insufficient."

Wish I could afford some of those. And that they didn't expire so quickly. Maybe she got one of the longer lasting ones from Wrynn, but I think those require supplies from other continents. I can't imagine having enough money for something like that, she must have dug deep to afford it...or maybe traded Wrynn a favor.

The other potions were pitch black, and he wasn't sure what they were. Poison, maybe, or void essence? That seemed a little odd for a paladin to use, but he didn't want to put her in a worse mood by questioning the choice. "Well, your movements have definitely improved. We can keep sparring and getting you some more practice if you've got the time."

"No, it's just..." Asphodel shook her head, tucking the potions away. "Last time I made a mistake, I failed. Susan got away. And if Sterling had taken the time to fight me..." She reached up a hand to touch the crystals that streamed from her head in the place of hair. "One touch would be all it would take."

Taelien paused, processing. "He could drain your essence. And that would..."

"...Kill me within a matter of seconds, potentially."

"Okay. And you were using me as a sort of test to see if you could avoid someone like Sterling getting their hands on you?"

She shook her head. "Not exactly, but something like that. I'm sorry."

"No need to be. Anyone in their right mind would be afraid of fighting a vae'kes, and you have more reasons than most. But why'd that thought strike you now? Because we're looking for information on the

Shrouded One? I can see that being connected, since Sterling worked for the Shrouded One for a while, but..."

"I'm sorry. I've said too much already." Asphodel took a deep breath. "I... You know I'm not supposed to change events that I see in the future."

"So, running into Sterling is in our future?" Taelien found his hand slipping to the sword on his side. "Good. I never got a match against him last time. And I've been wondering how I'd do."

"No, no. It's not like..." Asphodel winced, then she started shivering. "I'm sorry. I've said too much." She glanced from side-to-side. "I need some time. I'm sorry. I can't go with you today. Just... ah, be careful, okay?"

"I will be." Taelien wasn't really certain that was true, and his tone reflected that.

Asphodel just nodded, bowed for some reason, and headed back inside the tavern.

Taelien sighed, picked up his other knife, and sheathed it.

Well, he considered, *that wasn't foreboding or anything.*

***

Taelien spent the next hour practicing with some of the dominion bonded items he'd picked up.

He started with Sculptor, holding the knife out and closing his eyes. His hand was tight against the metallic grip, letting him feel the metal more effectively. Through that, he could feel where the hilt connected to the blade, and the fainter sense of the stone essence that imbued the weapon.

He reached for that stone essence. Stone had never been his specialty, but the knife's aura felt easier for him to connect to than an ordinary piece of rock. He wasn't sure if that was because of his practice with using enchanted weapons, or because the stone was connected to a piece of metal, or some other reason entirely.

In any case, it was an opportunity for practice he had no intention of ignoring.

Body of Stone.

He felt the familiar sensation of stone essence flooding his body, but in greater quantities than usual. Some portion of it was from the

Dominion of Stone itself, but he was also drawing directly from the knife, just as he'd hoped.

Release Body of Stone.

The spell ended, and he sensed no ill effects on his body from the increased amount of stone essence he'd been using. Taelien smiled, stretched, and did it again.

Body of Stone.

With the spell active again, he began his standard workout routine.

He'd been taught to use Body of Stone as a part of his workout routine when he'd been doing his mandatory military training many years before. Res'vaye, his instructor, had taught him that years of practicing with the spell active would gradually build up the amount of stone essence that his body generated, permanently increasing his strength and resilience. That natural buildup of essence wouldn't slow him down the way the spell itself did, since it occurred slowly enough for his body to acclimate and compensate.

After about a half hour of using the knife, Taelien was feeling uncharacteristically exhausted.

Must be putting more strain on me, since the spell is stronger than usual.

He kept practicing anyway, hoping that exhausting himself would encourage his body to work even harder to build up his strength.

After another half hour, exhaustion was turning into pain, and he decided it was time to stop.

He slipped Sculptor away, switching to simply sitting down with Ulandir's Ghost Lantern lit next to him instead. He wasn't sure if it would provide him with any benefit, but he needed to rest regardless. The enchanted lantern's light cast the entire area with a strange grey glow, but Taelien was used to it.

Once again, he closed his eyes and concentrated, trying to sense the source of the lantern's power. He thought he felt *something*, but not enough that he could make use of it directly.

Another mark against my supposed heritage. If I really was Aendaryn's child, this should be one of my strongest dominions. He was a master of spirit sorcery, if the legends are true.

That didn't mean that learning to use it would be impossible. Day by day, his sense of the lantern's aura grew stronger, as long as he used it for at least a little while. That seemed consistent with what was happening with the Sae'kes, even if he still didn't understand *why* that was happening.

Sometimes someone could learn a new type of sorcery by practicing with an object, but it generally took a significant period of time and effort. He hadn't heard of other sorcerers picking up new types of abilities simply through exposure, and certainly not in just a few months.

If I've got a talent for picking up sorcery from items, I need to make use of it. Maybe I can buy some other dominion bonded items when I'm done with this assignment and see if I can pick up some other sorcery types. Motion would be nice.

An hour later, Taelien finished his morning exercises and went back inside the tavern. He found Wrynn shortly thereafter. "You don't happen to have anywhere I can wash off, do you?"

"We've got a tub in one of the upstairs rooms, and I've got one of those water calling things to fill and empty it, but it isn't heated."

"That's good enough for me."

"That'll be two silver, or one if you empty the bath out and clean it yourself."

After sighing and paying the lower fee for the bath, Taelien went and washed himself, emptied and cleaned the tub, then redressed and prepared to leave.

"You ready to get moving?" He asked Wrynn.

"Sure thing. But did you want me to stow those dominion bonded items of yours somewhere safe first? No need to lug them around for our trip, unless you're planning to try to trade them to Kyestri. I don't think he'll want anything aside from Sculptor."

Taelien considered, then shook his head. "I'll deal with the extra weight. I trust that you're right, but I could run into someone else that wants to trade something. I'm sure we're not the only ones visiting for an early look at the auction goods."

More importantly, I might actually need some of these if things go poorly. Especially the purestone.

"Fair." Wrynn nodded. "Shall we go, then?"

***

Wrynn wove her way through the woods, and Taelien followed.

There were no roads this deep in the forest, but Taelien was able to judge their general direction from the Dawnfire's location in the sky. It wasn't what he'd expected. "I thought Lord Kyestri lived in Xelxen Reach. Isn't that to the south of here?"

"That city is on his lands, but he doesn't live there. Hasn't in years." Wrynn smirked. "You've been away from home for too long."

Taelien shrugged. "I've been busy."

"You visit your parents yet?"

She was talking about his adoptive parents, of course. He still hadn't figured out how he'd been born. That was business he'd have to ask Erik Tarren about eventually. "As I said, I've been busy."

"I had that excuse, too, back when my parents were alive. Make the time. You'll regret it if you don't."

"I'm sorry to hear about your parents. I didn't realize..."

Wrynn shook her head. "Don't worry about it. That was a long time ago."

"Right. It's easy to forget how old you are."

"I don't think I've ever *told* you how old I am." Wrynn snorted. "And you'd be wrong if you guessed."

"Sure. It's tough with rethri in general. And you're a prime lady, so..."

Wrynn paused, turning to look at him. "What makes you think I'm rethri?"

"Uh, the eyes? Definitely the eyes." He waved a hand. "And prime lady is a rethri title?"

"Lots of things can make someone's eyes look different. Even your eyes look a little different from when we first met, you know. More gray in them. Or silver, maybe."

Taelien blinked. "Really?"

"Yep. Take a close look in the mirror sometime, you'll see it. Subtle, but it's there."

"Okay, sure, but the title..."

"Anyone can challenge for a prime lord or lady position, it's just that rethri usually win. Age and experience and all that. But I'll wager Hartigan could handle being Prime Lord of Fire if he wanted the job."

Taelien shook his head. "That'd be a huge scandal."

"With Hartigan? Sure. He's high profile. But if no one knew you weren't rethri..."

"You're saying you're a human in disguise? An immortal sorcerer, like Haritgan or Theas?"

"I'm not *saying* anything of the sort. I might be implying a few things, but let's not get caught up on that too much. We're almost there." Wrynn resumed her walk, quickening her pace.

Taelien followed behind her, pondering her motivations behind the odd turn in the conversation. Wrynn was notoriously strange in general, but he liked to think he had a good grasp on her motivations after knowing her for years. Admittedly, he'd been wrong before.

It wasn't much longer before they reached their destination — a manor house wrought from dark wood in the midst of a clearing of similarly dark trees.

Ravenoak, most likely, with the growth accelerated by the use of wood sorcery. Someone really wanted to go for the 'haunted house' aesthetic.

Wood sorcery wasn't the same as stone sorcery, but they were connected, much like stone was connected with metal. As the Prime Lord of Stone, it made sense that Kyestri might have some mastery over wood as well. Or perhaps he'd simply hired someone else to handle the décor.

There were no gates around the building, just a rectangular wall of trees with a single gap to mark the entrance. As they passed through that section, it led them into a statuary garden, with human-sized statues of ancient heroes — and villains — lining the path to the building's doors.

These are very lifelike. Almost disconcertingly so.

Taelien paused to inspect one particular statue of a muscular gladiator with his sword raised to strike. His expression wasn't one of anger or determination as one would have traditionally expected, but of horror.

Lord Kyestri apparently has a taste for the macabre.

They reached the door a moment later, with Wrynn still taking the lead. "Let me do most of the talking. Don't interrupt either of us. And don't do anything rash if you see someone or something you don't approve of."

Taelien folded his arms. "What do you know that you're not telling me?"

"A whole lot of things. Be more careful with your questions next time. For the moment, we're out of time." She smiled and knocked on the door.

The door opened a few moments later, revealing a tall gentleman in a grey and white suit. His outfit matched the color of both his hair and his eyes, but he was clean shaven. "Prime Lady Jaden, it's always a pleasure." He bowed at the waist, then turned to Taelien. "Ah, and you must be Prime Lady Jaden's guest. I'm Frederick Conway, Prime Lord Kyestri's manservant."

Taelien nodded. "Pleased to meet you, sir. May we come in?"

"Of course, of course." He took a few steps back, clearing the entrance, then paused. "I'm afraid you'll need to leave your sword here, however. No swords inside the house. I'm sure you understand."

Taelien's mouth opened and then closed again.

That's...eminently reasonable, actually. But I can't take the risk that it'll be stolen.

While he was pondering how to reply, Wrynn shook her head. "I'm sure you can make an exception for a sacred relic?"

"Hm. That does put me in a difficult position, Prime Lady Jaden. I'm sure your friend understands the necessity to disarm our guests, especially if you'd like a tour of the auction goods. While I'm certain neither of you would ever think to initiate anything untoward, there are certain precautions that must be taken for the safety of my master."

Taelien unslung the bag from his shoulder. "That's perfectly understandable, but I'm afraid I can't take my eyes off of it. I can't go in without it. I'm sorry. Lady Jaden," he used her title to maintain the appearance of formality, "Would you be kind enough to handle any trading with Lord Kyestri for me?"

Wrynn waved a hand at him. "Don't be ridiculous. You can make your own deals." She turned back to the manservant. "And besides, he has no business confiscating anything. That isn't Frederick."

The manservant raised an eyebrow. "Pardon?"

"You can drop the act, Lord Karheart. Taelien is with me, and as entertaining as you might find it to run off with his sword, we don't have the time for your games."

The false Frederick rolled his eyes, then his image shifted, revealing a much younger-seeming rethri man wearing shades of purple. He smirked. "What gave me away?"

"Your performance was exemplary, but after a moment, I recalled that Frederick is vacationing with his family in Tesri Rethil. And you're likely the only person brazen enough to try to steal something from another one of the prime lord's guests." Wrynn sighed. "Taelien, may I introduce Lord Karheart, the Prime Lord of Deception and Crown Prince of Keldris."

Oh, lovely.

Taelien bowed just slightly, his jaw tightening. He loathed dealing with these sorts of tricks. Having Jonan as something resembling a friend was bad enough. "Crown Prince, it's an honor."

"Please, no need to be so formal. You can just call me 'Prime Lord'. Anyway, I'm on the way out. Without your sword, sadly, at least for today. I'm sure we'll meet again."

I most certainly hope not.

Taelien moved out of the way — far out of the way — as Lord Karheart walked out of the house and past them. "Always a pleasure, Lady Jaden. You should visit me at my own manse sometime. I believe you'd enjoy it."

"I believe that you believe that." Wrynn stepped into the manor. "Come on, Taelien. We'd best get moving. He won't be the last shark you have to deal with today. Best to move before too many of them scent the blood in the water."

"I'm not entirely sure I like that image."

"You shouldn't. Come along."

Taelien followed Wrynn into the house and shut the door behind him.

I thought I was prepared for this, but apparently, I need to study the prime nobility more closely. Everyone has an angle here.

Fortunately, the servants they encountered within the manor didn't make any further uncomfortable demands, and one of them swiftly led the pair deeper within. After traveling up two flights of stairs and down a hallway lined with yet more statues, they reached a large door.

The servant who had led them there knocked once on the door, then retreated.

The door opened a few moments later, but without anyone standing directly behind it. Instead, it simply revealed a large chamber where a tall, broad-shouldered man stood in front of an incomplete statue.

The room was ringed with more statues, all of whom appeared to be large animals and fantastical monsters. The central one that he appeared to be working on was some kind of large bird, almost human sized, but with three heads, each from a different type of animal.

At present, the room's resident had his hands inside the midst of the central statue's chest. The surface of the statue glimmered briefly, then shifted in color and texture, changing from a mud-like consistency into something more like marble. The man withdrew his hand a moment later, turning toward the entrance.

"Ah, my guests have arrived!" The man turned toward them. Now that he was facing them directly, it was clear that he was wearing a mask — one that covered his entire face, and made of stone.

Not the mask I'm looking for, Taelien noted. *The one I need is made of metal and only covers the upper half of the face.*

"Prime Lord Kyestri, Titan of the Northern Reaches," Wrynn bowed. "Thank you for allowing our visit on such short notice. I hope we're not interrupting you."

Kyestri bowed in return. "Prime Lady Wrynn Jaden, Witch of a Thousand Shadows. I have to admit, I've always rather liked your title more than mine. Did you bring any shadows today?"

Wrynn snorted. "Just one. Or two, really." She jerked a thumb at Taelien. "He's a little more solid than the type you're thinking of, though."

"Excellent, excellent. I'm thrilled you're here. Just allow me to clean up for a moment."

He raised his hands, and some mud-like residue flowed off, floating into the air and settling into a tub near the statue. Similar stains pulled themselves free from his otherwise immaculate garments a moment later, then moved to the same container.

After that, he dipped his hands into a barrel of water at the side, dried his hands with a nearby towel, and then turned back toward them.

"Apologies for the mess. I should have stopped some time ago, but I always find it difficult to judge the time when I'm working. Please, come in, and feel free to look around."

Wrynn walked into the room, offering her hand, which Lord Kyestri took and pressed to his chest. "It's been far too long, my dear."

"I suppose it has, at least from your side."

"Ah. I always forget how your...condition tends to influence your perception of time. Have you been well?"

Condition?

Wrynn shrugged a shoulder. "As good as can be expected, thank you." She pulled her hand away a moment later, looking a bit awkward. "I'd rather not talk about it."

"Of course. Forgive me. And I've been terribly rude; please introduce me to your friend. Is this the swordsman I've heard so much about?"

The masked man walked toward Taelien, extending a hand. Taelien pressed it against his chest in acceptance of the greeting, much as Kyestri had with Wrynn. It was a common rethri gesture, meaning, "I trust you with my heart."

Taelien *didn't* trust this man, of course, but he also wasn't going to insult him by ignoring tradition upon their first meeting.

"He is indeed," Wrynn explained. "This is Taelien Salaris, and he's an old friend of mine. We met just after he'd gotten out of his Thornguard training, and we've kept in touch on occasion ever since."

"A pleasure to meet you, Prime Lord Kyestri, Titan of the Northern Reaches."

I hope he doesn't expect me to keep repeating that. Formality has never been my strength.

Taelien released the other man's hand, and fortunately, the prime lord took a few steps back and smiled.

"How wonderful! And you actually go by Taelien? That's marvelous. It's been too long since those Tae'os followers actually had a symbol that their gods are still paying attention. It might actually make Vaelien pay attention for a change, too."

"And you think that's a good thing?" Wrynn walked to Kyestri's side. "I'm surprised. I figured the gods would be bad for your business."

"Nonsense." Kyestri slipped off his mask, revealing a handsome man with stark white hair. He tossed the mask and it floated to sit on a nearby pedestal. "They're the ones who built many of the treasures in my collection, after all. A bit of competition between them might lead to more opportunities."

Taelien concealed a bit of surprise at seeing the mask come off, having expected the mask to be a part of the theatricality of the prime lord's appearance, but it was possible it was just an item for enhancing his stone sorcery. Or maybe he was just comfortable enough in Wynn's presence that he didn't feel the need for it.

Oddly, his eyes weren't the dark brown or grey that Taelien would have expected from a stone-using rethri — they were bright green. That indicated a connection with the Dominion of Life, rather than stone. His particular shade was a tinge darker than Aladir's, but similar.

Rethri could learn spells outside of the dominions they were born with the strongest bond to, but it was generally much more difficult. Being the Prime Lord of Stone without an inherent connection to the dominion implied a tremendous degree of talent and focus, even beyond what a prime lord would be expected to possess.

Perhaps items were a large source of Kyestri's stone shaping abilities — if so, that explained why Wrynn thought that Sculptor would be an appealing tool.

Kyestri turned toward Taelien. "Speaking of my collection, I understand that you're interested in making some early offers, prior to my coming auction. Given some of the people I've invited have been known to make grand offers for the types of antiquities that I collect, I'm skeptical you can offer enough to make it worthwhile for me to skip the public display, but I'm willing to entertain the notion."

"Thank you, Lord Kyestri. I've brought a few trinkets that I think might interest you."

The lord raised an eyebrow. "Mere trinkets and curiosities aren't likely to be worth much to me."

Taelien mentally winced at his poor phrasing. "Ah, perhaps I phrased that badly. I'd like to think the quality of the items will be sufficient to change your mind, however."

"Very well. Is there anything in particular you're here to look at?"

Be careful, he told himself. *Can't give too much away and drive the price up.*

"I've heard you have a shield that once belonged to one of my paladin mentors, Herod Morwen." The statement was true, even if it wasn't his primary objective.

"Ah, yes, of course. It was found on a battlefield near the old capitol of Xixis, some twenty-odd years ago. I understand that he was taken wounded, and forced to leave it behind." Kyestri shook his head. "Unfortunately, I've already sold it."

Taelien raised an eyebrow. "Someone else came here before the auction?"

"A few people, actually." Kyestri nodded. "I have many valuable items, and you're not the only one who wished to beat the competiton."

Taelien nodded. "I don't suppose I could ask you who bought the shield? Perhaps I could offer them a deal for it."

Kyestri hesitated. "I'm afraid that won't be possible. I could ask them to speak to you, perhaps...? Or offer you another shield. Did you want a shield in general, or was this more of a gift for your old mentor?"

"The latter. I've never been much for shields myself, truth be told."

Kyestri waved his hand toward the Sae'kes. "With a sword like that, I'm not surprised to hear it. I don't suppose that's up for trade...?"

Taelien shook his head. "Apologies, but no."

"Of course. I had to ask. Well, could I interest you in some other gifts? I have a few other items from the same battle."

"That would be excellent, thank you." Taelien nodded.

Kyestri turned toward Wrynn. "I suppose you'll probably have a few things you're interested in trading for as well?"

"The Lady's Hour," Wrynn replied. "If you still have it, of course."

"Ah, the time saver. Of course. How appropriate for you. I'll have to give that some extra consideration just because of how poetic it might be." He nodded. "Very well, then. Follow me to the gallery."

***

Lord Kyestri led the pair down a series of hallways to another portion of the manor, pausing on occasion to point at a particular statue and relate a story about its origins. Taelien tuned most of them out, having never had much interest in history, but he did appreciate the attention to detail in the craftsmanship.

At the end of a hall, Kyestri knocked on a wall. It slid down into the floor, revealing a hidden passageway. "A minor precaution, you understand, and one of many. I don't show the gallery to just anyone, but Lady Jaden is a colleague, and I am most interested in hearing what the wielder of the Sae'kes is interested in as well."

The secret passage led down another similar looking hallway to a door that looked largely ordinary, save for a huge and intricate lock around the handle. It had no less than six keyholes, as well as three runes near the center.

Kyestri pressed a thumb against each of the runes, then reached into a pocket in his coat and retrieved just one key. He placed the key in the leftmost of the six holes, turned it, and pressed a thumb against the rightmost rune.

After that, he retrieved the key, slipped it in his pocket, and opened the door.

"This way." Beyond the doorway was a stairway. They headed down it, then at the bottom, Kyestri repeated his arcane process at yet another door.

Beyond that door was another path, no longer wrought from wood, but rather made from rough and uneven stone, like the interior of a cave. As the path led downward, Taelien realized they were heading underground.

Could this be the entrance to yet another Xixian Vault?

It wasn't as unlikely as it sounded. The Xixian Empire had controlled this entire area of the region only a few hundred years before, and the capitol — Xixis itself — had supposedly been not far from their current location.

If there was a vault, however, Taelien didn't see one. Instead, the rough path opened into a massive underground chamber.

When he'd been told about a "gallery", he'd pictured something like a museum.

Instead, this area was a damp underground lair — and "lair" was the only word Taelien could think to properly describe an area housing so many monsters.

The chamber was hundreds of feet across, but the majority of it was dominated by cages. Within those cages were the largest variety of monsters Taelien had seen in a single location. Monstrous animals of colossal size, essence devourers, flamebirds, and even some foreign monsters he couldn't recognize. The monsters didn't seem happy to see them, either. Most of them hurled themselves against the bars of their cages the moment the visitors arrived, snapping their jaws and thrashing around.

Taelien's hand didn't drift to his sword like it usually would when he sensed danger. His response wasn't to feel threatened, but a sense of pity.

"Ah, forgive me for the ruckus. The beasts haven't yet been fed today." Kyestri smiled. "Do any of them catch your eye, or are you more interested in the items?"

"The items." Taelien said hastily, not trusting himself to say anything else. His instinct was to free the caged creatures immediately, but he knew that would be disastrous.

Remember the esharen. You can't just rush in and free everything you see.

The argument felt unconvincing, but he checked himself, at least for the moment.

"Of course. This way, please."

Kyestri led them to the far right side of the chamber, on the opposite side from the caged monsters. In doing so, they passed through a circular marked area in the center of the room.

A fighting ring, most likely. Probably for pitting the monsters against one another, or against human opponents.

Taelien wrinkled his nose in disgust. He was no stranger to violence, but keeping creatures in cages to fight for the amusement of others was something he couldn't condone.

Did Aayara send me here with the knowledge that I'd be bothered, in hopes I'd do something about it? Either to get me into trouble with Kyestri, or possibly to remove him as an obstacle to her?

Considering the motivations of his enemies — and grudging temporary allies — wasn't something that came as naturally to him as it seemed to for Lydia and Jonan, but he was working on it. He had to; the world would never stop using him as a game piece if he didn't stop himself from being played.

I need to focus on completing my objective, even if Aayara expects me to deviate from it. I can alert someone to the problems here, or handle them personally, after I've provided Lydia with the identity of the Shrouded One.

The section of the "gallery" dedicated to displaying items was closer to what he'd been expecting. Small crystalline cases on pedestals held small individual objects, each of which had a plaque describing the contents.

Two larger crystal sections held full exhibits of themed items. One of them held full suits of armor and the other held a broad variety of weapons.

Taelien drifted to the weapon case. Not because it was what he was there for, but because it was expected that he'd be interested in weapons, and he hoped to deliver on that expectation. If he showed too much immediate interest on what he was actually there to see, he knew that would drive up the owner's perception of its value.

And besides that, he did *actually* want to see the weapons. He liked swords.

There was a distinct lack of swords, sadly, at least by Taelien's estimation. There were only four in the case, and only one of them had the kind of reach he preferred.

The first sword was a rapier with a thin enough blade that it looked to be built for dueling or display rather than actual combat. Taelien inspected the plaque below it.

Sliver of Iron Rain
A relic of the Talisian order, enchanted with protection spells to assist in the wielder's role of defending the queen of Fallowden.
Created Est. 2464 VF

The current year was 3123VF, and thus, that made the sword over six hundred years old. Protection enchantments might have been useful for most, but they'd never worked quite properly on him. And he'd never had much reason to be interested in the Talisian Order, so he wasn't particularly interested in it just for collector's purposes.

"May I?" Taelien asked, gesturing toward the sword.

"With that one, yes." Kyestri nodded, then moved to open the case. He reached inside, retrieving the sword, and handing it to Taelien.

Taelien lifted the sword, flicking it in the air and giving an appreciative look. "Very light."

"Is that something you look for in a sword?"

Taelien shrugged. "The Sae'kes is light, but no, not typically. I actually tend to enjoy heavier weapons more, for the most part."

"Ah, the next one is perfect, then. Although I can't allow you to hold that, sadly."

Taelien had to admit, Kyestri was right. The next one *was* perfect for him.

He concentrated for a moment, closing his eyes, then handed the Sliver of Iron Rain back to Kyestri and turned to the next sword in the case.

It was a crimson-bladed greatsword that was almost six feet in length, close to Taelien's full height. The crossguard curved upward on both sides, and the top of it was sharpened to be used as an additional cutting surface.

Impractical, given the length, Taelien considered, *but I do like the aesthetic of it.*

Given that and the weapon's size, Taelien expected it was designed to be used by someone with great enough strength to wield it as a crushing implement against armored foes, rather than just as a traditional slashing and cutting sword.

The most interesting part was the pommel, which contained a large red crystal, not dissimilar from the blue one in Taelien's own weapon. Gems like that were often the power sources for ancient sorcerous weapons, but he'd rarely encountered ones other than his own.

World Cutter

A dominion marked greatsword once used by Vanden Kaye, one of the supposed "gods" of the continent of Tyrenia. According to legend, it was forged with the heart of a star from metal in the depths of the elemental planes. It is considered the most successful attempt to replicate the Dominion Breaker, the sword crafted by the worldmakers to protect our world from outside threats.

Like the Dominion Breaker, the World Cutter has abilities designed to combat divine opponents, though they function differently. While the Dominion Breaker utilizes a single unknown dominion to detonate essence, the World Cutter channels the power of dozens of different dominions simultaneously. This unique mixing of energies causes it to shimmer like a rainbow and allows it to exploit the vulnerabilities of nearly any opponent. Unfortunately, it is so heavy that no ordinary human or rethri can even lift it.

Creation Date Unknown

Taelien tilted his head to the side.

I bet I could pick that up. And it's built for fighting divine enemies...

He shook his head at himself. Dominion marked swords were, unfortunately, not what he was actually there for, as much as he might have been interested in them.

"I can see you like that one, and with good cause. It's one of the three most valuable items in my entire collection. Sadly, due to the risks, I can't allow you to pick it up. It's quite volatile and powerful, not unlike your own sword, from what I'm given to understand."

That makes it even more interesting. Still, I don't really need another sword that's difficult to wield.

Taelien gave Kyestri a nod, then turned to the next sword. It was a gold-hilted saber, with the blade visibly glowing with matching golden light.

The Descent of Twilight

A weapon said to have been once wielded by Vaelien himself, long before his acquisition of his more famous greatsword. The Descent of Twilight is enchanted with both light and shadow, possessing capabilities related to both. With light, it can strike at distant foes with blinding speed. With shadow, it can conceal the wearer, or ebb the strength of enemies.

Creation Date Unknown

Kyestri reached into the case and removed it, allowing Taelien to test it in the air.

Once again, Taelien felt the weight of the weapon, giving it a considerate nod. "Not bad. I somehow doubt Vaelien would approve of a paladin carrying it, though."

"I won't tell him if you don't," Kyestri said with a wink.

Taelien laughed. He concentrated on the sword for another moment, then handed it back to Kyestri.

He moved on to the last sword, which had a broad and curved blade. More interestingly, the blade was black, with such an intensity that he couldn't tell if that was a property of the material or some sort of sorcerous effect.

Void Branch

The sword of a Xixian princess, recovered after her defeat in the siege of Velthryn in 2730VF. After being retrieved by a Thornguard captain who helped force the princess into retreat, the Void Branch was passed down through his family for several generations, before eventually being sold to cover the family's gambling debts. From there, it passed into the hands of a master thief, who was not masterful enough to steal from Lord Kyestri's vault. The weapon nullifies all nearby sorcery and cleaves through both sorcerous and physical defenses with ease.

Creation Date Unknown

That was an intriguing weapon, potentially even more useful than the World Cutter. While the World Cutter sounded more impressive, the functions and legends of the weapon had likely been greatly exaggerated. In the case of the Void Branch, however, the visible aura of sorcery around the weapon was enough confirmation that it had at least some of the functions described.

Void sorcery was extraordinarily rare and difficult to use, and from the sound of it, it also had some sort of secondary enchantments for cutting through armor. Ruin sorcery, perhaps, or maybe even metal sorcery like his own. While he didn't think he'd enjoy wielding the weapon in its present form, perhaps he could reshape it...

"See something you like?" Lord Kyestri asked.

Taelien pointed at Void Branch. "I always appreciate enchanted weapons, and this one looks fascinating. May I test it?"

"Not that one. My sincerest apologies. Ah, I should have expected you to gravitate straight to the swords. Of course. I do have a few more that aren't on display, if that's what you're here for...?"

That's sorely tempting.

Taelien turned to Kyestri. "I haven't made up my mind about anything specific, but swords are always of interest to me. I'd be thrilled to see any other weapons of note in your collection, but we'll have to see if I have anything left to trade you after I've perused what you already have on display."

Kyestri smiled. "Of course. Forgive me for interrupting. Take your time and look around."

"Thank you."

Taelien turned back to the weapon display, focusing on the next best thing after swords — polearms and spears.

The first was a broad-bladed halberd.

Valerian Legion Halberd

A halberd used by Lieutenant Commander Kori Wolfe of the Fourth Valerian Legion during the final battles outside the capitol of Xixis. The weapon has been preserved in the condition in which it was found.

Forged Est. 3055VF

"That one's not dominion marked," Kyestri explained. "But perhaps something of sentimental value to many. Perhaps a good replacement for your old friend's shield?"

Taelien nodded at the logic. "Definitely worth considering. I'd like to bring him back something if I can, but my priority is on enchanted goods."

"Of course. I would expect nothing less."

After that, Taelien examined a massive two-handed hammer with a head that was constructed entirely out of glimmering white crystal.

En-Vamir, the Hammer that Broke the Spine of the World
This weapon requires little introduction, for it is well known in myth and legend. En-Vamir was the weapon wielded by Koranir, the God of Strength and Stone, as a mortal man. The weapon's title comes from his use of the hammer to collapse an entire mountain range, preventing the escape of the Buried from their prison deep underground. The shaft was broken in the process of this great feat, and the current shaft is a replacement. The hammerhead, however, is the original.

Upon ascending to godhood, Koranir gifted the weapon to his high priest. It was passed down throughout the priesthood until the final battle against Xixis, at which point the weapon was lost in the siege.

Taelien's eyes widened at the description, and for a moment, his gaze shifting to the intricate golden pommel in the shape of a lion's head, then moving upward to examine the four glowing runes on each side of the hammer. It certainly met the description of Koranir's legendary weapon, but of course, he knew it was more likely to be a replica.

...Is this how everyone feels when they see the Sae'kes? The same skepticism, mixed with awe?

"Something of a personal favorite, that one," Kyestri explained. "One of the few that can be very directly traced to being used by a member of the Tae'os Pantheon, much like your own weapon. Normally, I wouldn't consider parting with it, but I was hoping that perhaps you'd be interested in trading a sword for a hammer..."

Taelien shook his head. "While I appreciate the offer, my sword has a bit too much sentimental value."

"A pity." Kyestri shook his head. "Ah, well. There are plenty of other things to look at."

The next item looked something like a spear or glaive, but with something more like a pointed crossguard near the bladed portion at the top of the shaft. The two additional points on the guard made it almost resemble a trident, but they weren't quite long enough to call it that.

The Three-Thorned Rose

A spirit-imbued glaive from Artinia Dyer Tal. In spite of our best efforts, the exact functions have not been able to be identified. According to the traveling merchant who sold it, the weapon is a relic of House Diamond, once used in many battles in their legendary tournaments.

Forging Date Unknown

Wrynn looked at that weapon with interest. "That's not a glaive. It's a yari."

"Ah, I'd forgotten. You spent a bit of time in Artinia, did you not?" Kyestri smiled. "Perhaps you could help me discern the function? I confess, it's proven all but impervious to conventional identification spells."

Wrynn narrowed her eyes at the object. "You don't want anything to do with that weapon. And it's not a House Diamond relic. It's of the Buried."

"The Buried?" Kyestri frowned. "You're certain of that?"

Wrynn stared at the item for another moment, then gave a soft nod. "I'd get rid of it as quickly as possible. Honestly, you might wish to have Taelien here destroy it for you."

Taelien turned to Wrynn. "Wait, are the Buried still a threat? I thought the gods handled that thousands of years ago."

"Nothing to worry about right now." Wrynn took a breath. "I'll explain some other time."

"I'll have to consider this...problem." Kyestri sighed. "Perhaps I could get you to take a look at my other Artinian purchase? It's so hard to get anything from there that I just bought everything I could."

Wrynn nodded. "That's because selling spirit-imbued items to foreign nations is almost entirely illegal. The 'traveling merchant' you spoke to was more than likely someone on the run from the empire. You're fortunate that the presence of these things hasn't brought you any Artinian interest."

"My, that *would* be troubling. What about this?" Kyestri pointed to one of the object cases nearby, and Taelien tore his attention away from the weapons to follow Kyestri's gesture and look.

Artinian Soul Diamond
This diamond is said to be imbued with great spiritual power. If properly utilized, it can increase the strength of the spirit of the one who uses it.
Creation Date Unknown

Wrynn looked at the object intently again, then nodded. "It's real. I'm a bit surprised; that's a valuable find."

"Could you, um, perhaps, give me an estimate of the value? Purely as a favor to a colleague?" Kyestri seemed abashed.

Wrynn chuckled. "Open the glass. I'll need to touch it to evaluate the amount of spirit inside."

"I suppose that would be acceptable..." He reached forward, touching a rune on the glass and whispering a word. A section opened, allowing Wrynn to reach inside.

"Not bad." She pulled her hand back. "It's nearly a tenth full, which given the size and the cut... In Artinia, something like this would be worth a small fortune. Unfortunately, it's very nearly worthless here, save for symbolic value. The Authority can't be invoked properly here, so you can't make use of the spirit inside." Wrynn wrinkled her nose. "Maybe with a powerful spirit sorcerer, you could do *something* with it?"

Kyestri folded his arms. "I seem to recall that *you* are a powerful spirit sorcerer, Lady Jaden."

"Guilty." A wry grin crossed her face. "But I don't offer my services lightly. Especially considering the risks of making a mistake when working with an item like that. It could tear my spirit to pieces."

"You can spare me the theatrics. I'd be interested in moving the spiritual essence in there into someone, perhaps myself. What would you charge for such a service?"

Wrynn winked at him. "I haven't found anything I like that much here yet. We'll see."

Kyestri grunted, leaning toward Taelien. "Be careful with that one. Feed her too much and she'll bite your hand right off."

"Now, that's hardly fair of you, Korus. Hands are one of my *least* favorite foods." Wrynn turned to examine the other miscellaneous items, and Taelien moved back to the weapons.

There were a few more in the case, but none of them were quite as tempting as the World Cutter or the Void Branch. There was a dagger with a lightning enchantment that the plaque claimed to originate from Rendalir, a fire-imbued axe said to have once been used by a Xixian general, and a single arrow said to have once been fired by one of the old gods that predated the Tae'os Pantheon.

There were three full suits of armor in the armor case, but Taelien was less interested in those, at least at first. He did see one particular item in the case that caught his eye, however.

Silverweave Tunic
This shirt is woven from silverweave, a form of metallic thread woven by the silverweave spiders of Kaldwyn. While metallic, it is nearly as light as conventional cloth, and nearly impossible to pierce or cut with ordinary weapons. It is not enchanted, but offers better protection than many enchanted suits.
Creation Date Unknown

"How much for the tunic?" Taelien asked.

"Ah, you have an eye for quality, I see." Kyestri grinned. "I'm afraid you'll have to be the one that makes an offer, however. You're going to need to give me more than what I could expect to make at the auction, otherwise it would be foolish to sell it now."

Taelien nodded. "I'll think about what I'm willing to offer. I don't suppose you'd be willing to compensate me or offer me a discount if I help you dispose of the Three-Thorned Rose?"

"I'll consider that at some point, but not today. It hasn't caused me any trouble in the months that I've had it, so I don't believe I have any need to hurry." Kyestri gave Wrynn a questioning look.

"You're right, it isn't that urgent." Wrynn frowned. "But I wouldn't wait forever, either. The yari will attract attention eventually, and not of a kind you'd like."

Kyestri nodded seriously. "Very well. Have you found anything you're interested in, Lady Jaden?"

Wrynn pointed at a case. "Maybe. Could I trade you something for this?"

Taelien looked over and realized Wrynn was pointing at the case containing the item he'd come to look for. It was a silvery mask that covered the upper half of the face with a single clear rune on the forehead.

The Mask of Kishor
Once the mask worn by Kishor the Artisan, one of the gods of the destroyed world of Rendalir. It is one of very few artifacts that escaped the destruction of that planet, most likely due to its enchantments, which assist the wearer in avoiding detection sorcery and identification. The mask is also notably resilient to damage.

Taelien watched the conversation, hoping that Wrynn was asking for his sake and not in an effort to buy it out from under him. He doubted she would make that kind of move, but he couldn't be certain.

"Ah, that one might be a bit of a problem." Kyestri shook his head. "I'm afraid I wasn't planning to put that up for auction. I don't trade items from Rendalir for anything but other items from Rendalir, since they're so rare. In truth, part of the reason for the auction is so I can purchase more items from there."

Wrynn leaned a little closer to the box. "Interesting. Don't think I have any toys from Rendalir to trade." She turned to Taelien. "What about you? Maybe we could do a two-part trade. If you have something he wants, you could trade me the mask for one of the swords you liked in my collection."

She hadn't offered him any swords, so the intent behind her remark was clear.

Taelien reached into his bag, retrieving the crystalline necklace that he'd shown Wrynn earlier. "Arturo's Amulet of Sanctuary. You've heard of it, I assume?"

Kyestri's eyes widened momentarily. "...That..." He regained his composure after a moment, shaking his head. "Was anything else with it? Any *people*, perhaps?"

Taelien hesitated. Kyestri seemed a little *too* interested, far more than he should be for something that was an ancient relic from a ruined world.

"Nothing else," Wrynn said for him. He didn't correct her. If she didn't think it was wise to mention the map, she probably knew more than he did. "I'm the one who told him where to find it, you know."

Kyestri looked noticeably flustered now. "And where was that, may I ask?"

"I think we'll trade that to you along with the necklace." Wrynn smiled. "For the mask?"

Kyestri raised a hand and ran it through his hair, turning away. "I'll...need some time to think about that." He frowned. "I don't suppose I could trade you the Lady's Hour instead? I know you had an interest in it before."

"Definitely still want it, but not as much as the mask. Hm." Wrynn lifted a finger to her lips.

"Perhaps I could trade you this dagger for The Lady's Hour, and the amulet for the mask?" Taelien retrieved Sculptor from his belt, offering it to Kyestri.

Kyestri accepted the weapon, turning it over in his hands, then unsheathing it. "A stone shaping dagger? Ah, interesting. This is of Xixian make, no?"

Taelien nodded. "A tool that once belonged to the Xixian prince Shosan Ver. It's called Sculptor. I thought it'd be useful in your line of work."

"How fascinating." Kyestri sheathed it, then handed it back to Taelien. "Unfortunately, while I do appreciate the concept of the item, it's of limited actual use to me. I would trade it for another weapon, perhaps, but not something on the scale of The Lady's Hour or the Mask of Kishor."

Taelien nodded. "I'd like to discuss a weapon trade later, then."

"Of course." Kyestri turned back to Wrynn. "Did you have a better offer for me?"

"I do think I know about one more item from Rendalir. Maybe we could trade you items from Rendalir for the mask and the Lady's Hour?"

"That would depend on the item in question, but I'd be willing to entertain it." Kyestri's gaze showed a great deal more interest now. "What sort of item?"

"It's a crystal," Wrynn smiled. "An intelligent item with powerful sorcery. I'm sure you've heard of them."

Taelien turned his head toward Wrynn in alarm. *He* knew about one of those crystals, too, and it was currently in Lydia's possession.

"Yes." Kyestri smiled brightly. "Good. *Very* good. If you truly can find one of those crystals and bring it to me, I will give you exactly what you need."

"Excellent." Wrynn grabbed Taelien by the arm. "Let's go, Taelien. We have some exploring to do."

CHAPTER IX – JONAN III – HINTS OF THINGS TO COME

Opening his eyes did nothing to bring him vision.

The darkness around him was immutable, at least at first. Until the fires came.

There was a moment of panic as the air reddened and he began to smell the smoke. He tried to move, but he was constrained by wood on all sides.

A coffin?

No, there's a crack in the middle. I can almost see through it.

And then he knew where he was.

An all too familiar cabinet, where he'd hidden in a thousand nightmares before this one.

But usually, he wasn't quite this aware.

His hands clenched.

Wake up. Just wake up! I'm so tired of this.

He pulled his arm back, ready to smash a fist into the cabinet door. Maybe he'd alert the woman outside who was murdering his family, but it didn't matter.

It was just another nightmare.

She couldn't hurt him more than she already had, could she?

The cabinet doors swung open before he could throw his punch, revealing his childhood home, ablaze with the flames that consumed his family.

A woman stood in front of the cabinet, grinning brightly. She looked just the way that she had on that day.

But she wasn't the one who had butchered his family.

"Happy Children's Day!"

She was the one who had saved him.

Or, "saved", at least.

Jonan lowered his fist, shuddering with rage. "Aayara."

His mentor winked at him, then gazed around. "Dreaming about our first meeting? How appropriate! I was going to visit you either way, but you've already set the scene so perfectly."

Jonan took a deep breath to center himself, but that forced him to inhale smoke. He let out a hacking cough, then wiped his face to clear the water from his eyes.

"...Change...it," he managed before breaking into another cough.

"Change? Oh, this?" She glanced around. "I suppose I am here a bit early. Did you want to play out the bit with Lavender first?"

He almost swung at her, as futile as that would have been. "Get us *out* of here."

"Oh, I suppose I can rescue you a little bit early. Come along, then." He winced as she grabbed onto his shoulder, then after a moment of vertigo, they were elsewhere. "Better?"

They were in a simple circular bedchamber now. It was the one where he'd spent his next several years sleeping, high in an obsidian tower in the forests near Liadra.

Jonan stumbled back. It was in part because he was still nauseated from the smoke and the rapid movement, but the greater part was simply to get him some distance. "Much better." He coughed again, then added, "Thank you."

Aayara bowed theatrically. "Of course, my dear."

Jonan groaned and rubbed at his eyes. They were still burning from exposure to the smoke. "You had something you needed that couldn't wait for me to wake up?"

"Can't I just want to celebrate a simple holiday with my child?"

Jonan folded his arms. "You could, but it would be completely out of character for you."

"How rude. You're just as bad as the other one."

The other one?

"...You did this to Velas, too?" He processed belatedly. "I don't know if that makes me feel better or worse."

"Oh, dear, don't be jealous that I visited her first. You should be jealous for completely different reasons, like that I took your hard earned artifact away and gave it to her."

Jonan let out one more cough, then managed to look up and roll his eyes. "Is that what this is really about?" He paused, considering. "You want me to compete with her. This whole thing with discovering the identity of the Shrouded One is a test to see which of us manages it first."

"That's within the dominion of possibility." Aayara shrugged. "Or perhaps I truly need that information before the paladins get it. And since Velas is currently wearing a paladin hat, she counts as a paladin for this discussion."

"No," he shook his head, "Things are never that simple with you. There's another layer to this. Maybe you're trying to use competition to make us stronger. Maybe you've decided that you only need one of us, and this will determine which. Or maybe it's something entirely different, unrelated to the two of us, so far into your chains of schemes that I can't see it."

"I'm flattered you think so highly of my planning abilities, Jonan." She clasped her hands together. "You certainly know how to make me feel proud."

"That wasn't flattery. I'm just trying to figure out your current game so I have the highest chance of keeping my head on my shoulders."

"Should you really be telling me what you think, then, dear?" Aayara went and sat down on the nearby bed. It had seemed massive and luxurious to his childhood self, who had shared something half the size with his siblings before being taken here.

"I'm tired. So tired, in fact, that I am *literally* asleep right now. I'm not exactly planning ten steps ahead of anyone." He sat down on the floor. "So, Happy Children's Day. You can give me a present in the form of some straight answers."

"Straight...answers?" Aayara frowned. "I'm afraid I don't have any of those. All out of stock at the local stores, too. Must be in short supply due to the holiday."

Jonan put his hands over his eyes. "Fine. Give me some of your usual cryptic clues, then."

"I already have, dear, if only you'd pay attention."

That got him listening. He put his hands down, turning his gaze to focus on Aayara directly. "Care to repeat them?"

"No, you're obviously already irritated. I suppose I'll give you something different, however, since I'm feeling generous. It would be a good time to pay attention to prophecies and portents."

Jonan wrinkled his nose in distaste. "Prophecies are nonsense. You made me write one and spread it as one of my earliest exercises in learning about rumors and belief."

Aayara smiled. "Ah, yes. The trials of the Fateless Eight. You were nearly hanged for heresy for that one."

He managed a chuckle. "Ironic, considering who I work for. But it was effective at demonstrating a lesson — drop a few 'ancient' seeming documents in locations for them to be discovered, spread a few rumors in taverns....oh."

"It seems you've had a revelation. A message from the gods, perhaps?" Aayara bowed her head, as if in prayer. "Praise be to the Fateless Eight, saviors of us all."

"Praise be to the Fateless Eight, 'til one by one they fall."

Aayara tilted her head back upward. "That was a rather dark prophecy, wasn't it?"

Jonan shrugged a shoulder. "You should have seen the earlier drafts. At least some of the children survived in the final version."

***

"I'd like to access the restricted section," Jonan explained. "I have the proper clearance." He slid a card across the table. It read:

Jonan Kestrian
Scribe in the Service of Aayara, Lady of Thieves
No Permanent Address

Beneath the description was a single rune, etched with a mark corresponding to the Dominion of Sound.

Such objects were *exceedingly* rare. Dominion Marks were still the stuff of legends, and the idea of using them on something as mundane as a business card was almost unthinkable.

But Aayara did the unthinkable often, and on this rare occasion, that worked to Jonan's advantage.

Most people believed that only deities could make dominion marks — and thus, a forgery would be even less plausible than the card itself.

The Thornguard librarian raised an eyebrow. "What's this here?"

Jonan pointed at the rune. "Touch your thumb to that to activate it."

The librarian frowned in obvious distrust. That was a good instinct, but fortunately for Jonan, curiosity won the battle. The librarian touched the rune.

A moment later, a woman's voice rang out. "The owner of this card is my dear disciple, Jonan Kestrian. Or someone who killed him, I suppose. In either case, please afford them the same courtesy you would to me. Love and kisses, Aayara."

The librarian paled, the card slipping out of his fingers. "What did you say you were here for?"

Jonan folded his hands and leaned closer. "I'm doing a bit of research on a cult called the Disciples of the First. Nothing to be overly concerned about. Unless you're a cultist."

The librarian's frown deepened. He bent down to find the card, then lifted it again carefully, as if afraid it might bite him. "I'll need to verify this, of course."

"Of course." Jonan smiled. "I'll wait here."

He could have simply told them his name and waited for someone to look him up in the directory the old fashioned way, or even called in a favor from a Thornguard agent he knew at the base.

But this was much funnier, and a good way of testing his latest trinket with minimal risk. After all, all the information on the card was true, even if the voice wasn't *actually* Aayara's.

For the first few minutes of waiting, Jonan was simply bored.

For the next several minutes, he was beginning to grow concerned.

Within a half hour, he had several different exit strategies in mind, depending on who they sent to ambush him.

It's possible I should have brought my 'bodyguard', rather than leaving him at home. He stands out so much that he might have made things worse, though.

They didn't send a whole squad, at least.

When the librarian finally returned, he was following behind an athletic gentleman with dark hair and a short goatee that gave him a somewhat wolfish appearance. His build and the longsword on his hip said military, but he wasn't wearing a uniform. Instead, he wore black garb that lacked any distinguishing markings. Beneath it, Jonan saw the lines of both heavy musculature and what looked like it might be a concealed shirt of chain armor.

The librarian looked nervous, but the man ahead of him was confident, walking with a straight back and an affable expression.

The swordsman spoke first. "Didn't mean to keep you waiting. We don't have visitors like you very often." He turned to the librarian. "Remove any remaining library visitors, then leave and lock the door behind you. You're closed for the day."

The librarian swallowed hard, then nodded. He looked like he was about to raise an arm to salute, then stopped himself. "Of course."

The other man turned away from the librarian, toward Jonan. "This way." Without another word, he headed down another hallway.

An officer, then. Extremely unusual to see one giving orders while out of uniform. And from the librarian's expression, this isn't exactly a standard social visit.

If I die here, I'm going to haunt Velas for her poor Aayara impression.

Jonan frowned and followed behind the swordsman, watching for anyone else in the library that could have been a threat. He tried to keep at least blade-length away, although he doubted this would turn into a physical altercation without significant warning first. He might have been skirting the rules a little bit, but the Thornguard weren't in the business of executing people in the middle of libraries.

Not typically, at least.

"I didn't catch your name," Jonan tried.

The swordsman just turned his head, smiled, and lifted a single finger to his lips. "Ssh. We're in a library."

Jonan narrowed his eyes, continuing to follow until they reached the library's back wall.

The swordsman knocked on a section of the wall, paused, and then let out a low whistle.

There was a brief grinding sound as a section of the wall shuddered, then lowered into the floor, revealing a hidden room. It was pitch black inside.

The swordsman turned to Jonan, and then made an "after you" gesture.

Jonan tapped the side of his head as he walked forward, activating a dark vision spell. He wasn't going into a dark room blind if he could avoid it.

As it turned out, he couldn't. There was nothing but complete blackness ahead of him, even with the spell active.

Void sorcery, probably. That's...about half my contingency plans down, if it's saturating the whole room. Only a few of them down if it's just the doorway, though, which it probably is.

He walked ahead, straight into the dark.

As he expected, he was through it in a moment, like walking through a curtain. The room ahead was a well-lit sitting room, with a table and two chairs. On the table were two teacups and a decanter of some kind.

There was a single row of bookshelves along the back wall. As unimpressive as the collection appeared, Jonan knew they contained some of the most dangerous secrets the Thornguard had ever uncovered.

In front of those shelves, there were a set of crystalline cases, like a much more fortified version of a display case for a jewelry store. The objects inside those cases were individually labeled with a name, description, and reference number. Those numbers corresponded to one of the shelves behind, which had a series of journals containing notes.

In front of the shelves and cases was a line of runes visibly etched into the floor. Defensive runes, either as an extra precaution to keep things out — or, potentially, to keep things that were truly dangerous trapped inside.

Looks like someone has been using this room as a place to research some dominion marked items of the more dangerous variety.

Jonan eyed the crystal cases warily. He'd have to be cautious if he decided to examine anything inside — but they weren't what he was there for. Not immediately, at least.

There were no people visible inside, but he immediately blinked his eyes and activated a spell to detect for invisible ones. No one appeared, nor did he detect any sight sorcery when he scanned for that.

He stepped in further, and the swordsman followed just behind him.

The swordsman whistled and the section of the wall moved upward behind them, closing the way. There were no other doors or windows in the room.

The swordsman extended a hand. "Taer'vys Ironthorn. I've been eager to talk to you, but we needed somewhere with sufficient security."

Jonan shook the man's hand in the classic way, clasping at the wrist. It was usually done that way to confirm that the other person didn't have a weapon in their sleeve.

Taer'vys Ironthorn definitely *did* have a weapon in his sleeve.

Jonan found himself smiling at the sheer audacity of that kind of performance. "Jonan Kestrian."

"So I've heard." Taer'vys made a toothy grin that only added to Jonan's existing "wolf-like" impression. "And you're here on Aayara's business."

It was posed as a statement, not a question.

Ironthorn... Where do I know that name from?

Taer'vys waved to the chairs. "Let's have a seat."

Ironthorn...

Taer'vys moved to a chair, sitting down and grabbing the decanter. "Tea?"

Jonan sat opposite him. "Yes, please."

"It's poisoned." Taer'vys poured for both of them, not changing his expression. "Only mildly, though."

Jonan nodded, picking up the cup. "Is it any good?"

Taer'vys picked up his cup, sniffed, and then took a sip. His expression shifted to pondering, then he nodded softly. "A little tart, but poison will do that."

Jonan sniffed at it as well.

He wasn't an expert on poisons. He did use them, though, and he was familiar enough to recognize some of the more common ones.

What he sensed was a minty herbal blend, mixed with one of the uncommon ones. But fortunately, it was an uncommon one that he did recognize.

"Lysen's Tears usually are, yes." He took a sip. "You're looking to extract some sort of confession?"

Taer'vys' grin returned, and he waved a hand dismissively. "Nothing like that. Mostly interested in your business. I might even be able to help you, depending on your angle."

Jonan sipped again, feeling coolness wash over his mind. Memory came along with it. "I'm surprised to see military intelligence taking an interest in an...issue that does not have clear connections to the Thornguard." He had initially intended to say 'small matter', but the poison was already kicking in. It had been years since he'd last taken the Lysen's Tears, and longer since he'd practiced trying to resist or work around the effects.

He wondered how long it had been since Taer'vys had taken them, and if he'd be similarly affected. Drinking the same tea certainly gave an *illusion* that they'd both be operating under the same restrictions, but reality was often different.

Fortunately, Jonan was quite familiar with illusions, and he had some ideas on how this one worked.

Taer'vys most likely either had some resistance to the poison or a way to cure it at will.

Or, alternatively, he simply thought he was good enough at concealing his motives in a conversation that he could operate at peak proficiency even while under the effects. That was a far more arrogant approach, but one that somehow already suited Jonan's first impressions of the man.

"If you're not aware of our reasons for being interested, you must be early in your investigation. I find that surprising, given that you foiled one of their plans nearly a year ago." Taer'vys leaned back in his chair, lifting his cup and very deliberately taking another sip.

"I wasn't aware of their involvement prior to that," Jonan admitted. "And afterward, I had other responsibilities that took priority."

Taer'vys nodded, then gestured toward Jonan's cup.

Jonan sighed and took another sip. "Would you care to share why you're so interested, then?"

"In time, perhaps. I'm still getting to know you. Files can be quite dry."

Jonan gave a forced smile and took another sip. "I'm afraid you have the advantage of having a file at all. Tell me, are you still working under Highguard Res'vaye Fayne?"

Taer'vys shook his head, turning serious. "No, it's Bloodsworn Fayne now. I'm taking care of many of the things he had to leave behind."

That was significant news, to the extent that Jonan would have ordinarily been quite skeptical. If it was true, it had to be recent.

"Bloodsworn" was a position indicating that a member of the Thornguard military had been tapped to serve as the personal voice of one of the vae'kes. There were, so far as he was aware, only two other Bloodsworn currently alive. Each of them ran an entire branch of the Thornguard.

It was a tremendous honor, the pinnacle of what a human could hope to earn. It was what ambitious Thornguard strived for their entire lives.

And it was, in essence, a similar fate to what Jonan had been doomed to when he'd been plucked from his burning home by Aayara's hand. Ordinary soldiers were generally beneath a vae'kes' notice. A Bloodsworn was someone who would never live another day without having their every decision weighed by one or more capricious demigods who could eliminate them with little more than a stray thought.

At least they had a level of authority that Jonan lacked, but Jonan didn't envy them.

Bloodsworn were prone to dying even more rapidly than people with the title "Silk".

"I suppose I should be congratulating you on the position of Highguard, then. You must be pleased."

Taer'vys took another sip, staring at Jonan unnervingly. "It's a start."

A few things clicked together in Jonan's mind at that time.

There were, in general, three types of ways of reacting when someone found out he worked for Aayara.

Most people reacted the way the librarian did, meaning with a combination of terror and the immediate urge to pass off the responsibility of dealing with him onto someone else.

The next category included people like the guards outside of Aayara's temporary home, the kind that would give him knowing looks and occasionally exchange stories about her strange urges and demands. They'd learned to try to *manage* Aayara, with long years of exposure having driven fear so deep into them that a layer of faux amusement was required to retain their sanity.

Jonan liked to think he fell into that category himself.

The third category was people like Taer'vys.

The type of people who heard the name of the Lady of Thieves and saw it as an opportunity. A ladder standing just out of reach, waiting to be climbed toward the heights of power.

Most failed to realize that the ladder wasn't a ladder at all, but just a series of snakes tied together and painted to look like one.

From their brief encounter, Jonan had a different impression of Taer'vys.

He saw the snakes.

He'd just decided that he could handle a little bit of poison in his veins.

Well, Jonan considered, *if he decides to work against me, I'll just have to make sure that there's more than a little poison on my particular rung.*

"Well," Jonan took one more sip, then set his tea cup down. "If you believe I'm under-informed about the situation, I'd like to hear what you have to offer."

Taer'vys nodded slowly, seeming to consider his words, then took another sip of his tea. "The Disciples of the First have infiltrated a number of organizations, including our own. I do not work for them. Do you?"

"No."

Taer'vys nodded. "And you do, in fact, work for Aayara? The Lady of Thieves in specific, not just some random person calling herself that?"

That was a good clarification to make, and Jonan appreciated it as such. "Yes. I actually work for the Lady of Thieves."

"Good. What's her interest in this subject?"

Jonan shook his head. "It's not my place to say."

Taer'vys gave just the barest hint of a frown. "Of course. Well, if you're working for Aayara, I believe I may be able to assist you." He waved at the shelf. "If you're doing research, you can do it here."

"And those books are..."

"The types of things that were too dangerous to put in something as lightly guarded as the restricted section." Taer'vys set his cup down, leaning forward. "The types of things we're not supposed to know about. Blood shaping, void calling. And, more relevant to you, copies of the 'holy' scriptures used by the cult you're looking for."

Jonan raised an eyebrow. "What's so dangerous about a 'holy book'?"

Taer'vys gave him another grin. "Read and find out."

Jonan nodded, then began to stand.

Taer'vys leaned forward, putting a hand on his arm before he could get very far. "One more thing. You'll be doing your reading here, under my observation. You will not remove any of those books from this room. Is that clear?"

"That...seems like a very inefficient use of your time."

The grip on his arm tightened.

"But yes, of course. I understand perfectly."

Taer'vys released Jonan's arm, then gave it a pat. "Good." Taer'vys stood up. "I'll show you the right books, then get to some reading of my own."

"What will you be reading?"

Taer'vys glanced at the shelf, then back to Jonan. "The types of things that I wouldn't have the authority to read, unless I had a reason to be in here to observe you. So, feel free to take your time."

Jonan smiled softly. "Ah. I believe we understand each other now."

"You're getting there." Taer'vys walked over to the line of runes, bending down, and ran his finger across one of them. The runes flickered and died, then he stood up and pointed a finger at one aged tome. "You'll want to start with this."

Jonan approached cautiously, then took the selected tome. "The compiled works of Erik Tarren." He frowned. "This is a forbidden holy book? Erik Tarren writes all sorts of things."

"He does. Read for a bit. You'll understand."

Jonan took the book and moved back to his chair, sitting down and flipping it open.

He skimmed through the table of contents, seeing a list of historical events that he'd read about dozens of times. It was organized by year.

2950 AR – Hartigan and Theas Turn the Tides of War
3090 AR – The End of the Xixian Empire
3110 AR – The Creation of the Kalsiris Fortress
3121 AR – King Byron Ascends to Orlyn's Throne
3122 AR – The Deaths of House Theas
3125 AR – The Fall of Velthryn

He paused after reading the last line.

It was dated two years in the future.

CHAPTER X – LYDIA III – EYES EVERYWHERE

Lydia stood in front of a map, running her finger slowly across the surface. The map was the most recent she could find, and it was presently laid out atop the surface of a table inside the rented house that she was using as a base of operations.

Her eyes were closed. Her vision was elsewhere.

She saw the city from above. Not like a bird — she moved too slowly, too meticulously for that comparison, and her focus was too close to the ground.

It was more like she was simply hovering just above the buildings, gazing downward along the streets. Rather than flying along, she had a moment of disorientation every time she moved her finger, moving her view to a different location.

The spell was simple in theory, but rare in execution. It required a combination of knowledge sorcery and sight sorcery, which were rarely found in the same individual. She hadn't had the capability to cast it even a few years ago, before she'd experienced Jonan's sight sorcery and comprehended a fraction of how it worked.

She'd figured out how to use a basic sight spell in Orlyn, when she'd needed to look inside wagons from outside.

Since then, she'd had a considerable amount of practice. She still didn't have nearly Jonan's level of capability for illusion, but she'd found it much more intuitive to use sorcery to modify her own sense of sight. This spell was one of the most advanced applications she'd managed thus far.

It would be taxing on her eyes for days, but it was worth it. She could not be idle while sending Velas into harm's way.

While Lydia had been training with Blake Hartigan, she'd made sure that the paladins in her branch were exhausting every basic option to try to find Sterling through sorcery. They'd tracked down some of the clothing Sterling had worn, as well as the vial of poison that Velas had tricked Sterling into drinking, and used those items to try to track him.

Every spell they attempted was met with failure. They believed that was either due to the inherent spell absorbing properties of being a vae'kes or that Sterling had simply cloaked himself in void sorcery, which he was known to be able to use.

Repeated attempts were made over time, testing to see if he let down his defenses, but there hadn't been any luck. If they had some of his blood, they would have had a much better shot at bypassing his defenses, but they had never found any.

That was disappointing, but it didn't mean sorcery couldn't be used to help find him. It just required a bit more active problem solving.

Now that Lydia was in Selyr, she was looking for him directly. She didn't expect to physically see Sterling walking through the streets — although that was possible, given that it was territory where he might be safe enough to walk openly.

No, she was looking for something else — blind spots. If someone was using void sorcery or another form of concealment, she'd see a person shaped void — or area of void, depending on how the specific spell worked — while she attempted to use sorcery to look at the location.

There was no guarantee Sterling was still in Selyr at all, of course, and there also could be other people or places with defenses against sorcerous viewing of their location. In fact, it was almost a guarantee.

But it was a place to start, and she was tired of being idle.

She lingered for a few moments each time she moved her finger, searching for the telltale marks of inky blackness that would indicate a gap in her sorcerous surveillance. Over the course of a few hours of meticulous searching, she had found eighteen of them.

Most of these are in Thornguard military bases. That's not surprising — even we have a few areas like that at the citadel. The vault, the rooms of the Arbiters, that sort of thing.

Sterling absolutely could be on a military base, but investigating those will be difficult. Jonan might have more luck than I would in that regard, but I certainly can't expect him to help with something like this. The military facilities will have to wait until I've checked the easier to access spots.

She moved her finger back to a place that she'd marked with a dot of ink.

This isn't military... looks like people are leaving with money? A shame I can't adjust the angle of the divination. Oh! It's probably a bank or a moneylender. Possibly a pawn shop, but I don't see people carrying items in for trade.

Lydia shifted her finger again.

There's a spot of void inside this library. That probably isn't Sterling's hiding place, but I'd love to find out what's inside.

She blinked as she saw someone walk out of the void — and that someone was definitely, unquestionably Jonan. He looked haggard, like he hadn't slept in a while.

...of course Jonan was in the secret void library. Where else would he be?

I'm definitely going to ask him about that later, but for now...

She slid her finger one more time, finding another spot of ink. *This looks like the most likely area to start with. A single house. Not too big, not too small.*

Lydia lifted her finger, blinking as her eyes re-adjusted, and then lifted a cloth to wipe the ink off of it.

Aladir was sitting across from her on the opposite side of the table. He'd been quiet enough that she'd almost forgotten his presence, but she was grateful for it. He shut his book and set it down. "Find anything?"

Lydia nodded. "Dark spots, but nothing conclusive. We'll need to take it manually from here."

"Very well." He stood up and stretched. "I'll go prepare the team."

Lydia frowned. "Make sure they're inconspicuous and keep a good distance behind us. I don't want whoever we're dropping in on to see them until it's too late."

"Understood. I'll tell them to be cautious..." Aladir chuckled, "But you know, we may have picked the wrong group for that."

"I know." Lydia sighed. "But that's a risk we'll have to take."

Lydia reached into a pouch on her belt and felt the comforting presence of the green crystal. "You ready, Vendria?"

[I...]

Lydia gave the crystal a concerned look. *Are you well, Vendria?*

[...Fading. Season.]

She reached into the pouch and put her hand on the crystal. "Dominion of Knowledge, identify present essence composition."

Numbers flashed through her mind. Lydia winced as a throbbing pain ignited in the back of her head as the spell extracted a cost.

Vendria, your knowledge and stability dominion essence are significantly lower than when we last left the city. Have you been casting any spells?

[I...don't think...so?]

Something was draining the crystal's power, then, or preventing her from regaining it properly over time.

If it was a seasonal change, perhaps nothing can be done...but why would her sorcery be structured in such a way?

Vendria, I'm going to loan you a bit of essence.

Lydia closed her eyes, focusing on the crystal. "Knowledge Shaping: Transfer."

She felt a wave of vertigo overtake her, but steadied herself swiftly.

Taking in a few sharp breaths, Lydia rubbed her head and concentrated.

Did that help?

[...Grateful. Feel better...a bit.]

Lydia nodded.

I'm afraid that's all I can do for now.

[I think...I'm fine. Remembering something...quiet for a time.]

Lydia nodded.

I'll ask you more about that later.

For now, I've got work to do.

INTERLUDE I — VENORA — RENDALIR REMEMBERED

Venora remembered Rendalir.

She remembered the towering spires of Davorin, shimmering with arcane power. She remembered the students in their universities, the paladins of the Kingmaker, and the bickering of their politicians.

She remembered the vast trees of the Fiachna forest, and the people who lived sheltered beneath — or within — their branches.

She remembered the zealous piety of the Monteaque, with their white walls and their purification ceremonies.

And she remembered when the world burned to ashes.

***

She stood in the midst of a battlefield, walking among the wounded. She would kneel amongst them, Monteaque or Qin, and offer them healing — or, if their wounds were too severe, a few moments of comfort before the end.

This battle had a disconcertingly large number of the latter. One of the Sun Eater's generals, Akadi, had been here. The wounds inflicted by his scythe wracked the body and spirit with an infectious disease, making healing nearly impossible. It was a terrible weapon, among the worst she'd encountered.

She wore the robes and distinctive gauntlets of a Silver Gauntlet healer, a group dedicated to treating the injured regardless of their origin. They were mostly followers of Lyrielle, a goddess of spirits and dreams.

Venora wasn't one of them, but she admired Lyrielle and her followers. And blending in was important. She had many enemies she couldn't afford to run into while she was in her current state.

Not until the seasons changed, and she changed along with them.

As she knelt by a wounded warrior's side, she smiled in spite of the pain ravaging her mind. With a gesture, his wounds began to knit together. The physical ones, at least. War would leave scars beyond the ability of any mere sorcery to mend.

She worked for hours, long past the point where exhaustion had set in. How could she not? Mere mortals were pressing themselves just as hard beside her. Harder, perhaps. The toll on her body from the use of spells had always been milder, less permanent than what humans dealt with.

It was only after night had long fallen and her hands began to spasm from overuse that she finally ended her shift and told the others she needed to rest. They asked no questions, even those that likely knew that she did not belong to their order.

And with that, she wandered away into the night.

Soon, she realized. *The change will come to me soon. Just one last night...a few more hours...then I'll be able to strike back.*

Or she will, at least.

In a few hours, she would cease to be her current aspect — Venora, the Heart of Spring — and she would take on the aspect of Venshara, the Fire of Summer. Then, later, Venshara would give way to their third aspect — Venlyra, the Deep of Winter.

Together, the three were called Vendria. But while the three shared a single existence, they shared little else.

With the change of the seasons, she would be changed in mind, body, and spirit. She would lose her nurturing aspect and persona. Her memories of Venora's life would be buried, like those of a fading dream.

In early years, she resented these changes. She resisted them with force of body, mind, and power.

In truth, now she welcomed this particular change.

She had never before felt so powerless.

Venora was a creature of empathy, of healing. She would bring rains to nurture crops, or sit as a midwife for a mother who could not afford a doctor and help bring new life into the world. She would bring bread to feed to orphaned children and sing songs to ease their grief.

But all around her, the world was dying.

Crops burned. Mothers wept at the loss of their children, born and unborn. And there were more starving orphans than she could ever hope to feed.

The world didn't need nurturing. It needed someone to fight on its behalf.

And Venshara, with her sword, her shield, and her fire, would fight that war.

There was only one thing she would miss about her current form—

She found him sitting on a nearby hillside, his gaze turned upward toward the stars. Always looking toward something greater.

Her heart leapt every time she saw him with her current eyes.

When she saw him with Venshara's eyes, he would be little more than a stranger.

"Tysus!" She called out to him as she approached.

He turned his head downward, smiling that soft, beautiful smile of his. "Vendria. I've been waiting for you."

She ran to him. How could she not? She had only minutes left. "You're back so soon! I was worried I wouldn't get to see you before..."

He shook his head. "Nothing to fear, love. I couldn't miss the chance to see you one last time. Sit with me?"

She nodded eagerly, moving to his side. Her hand moved to his.

He slipped his fingers into hers, holding them tight.

Cold, she thought. *Strangely cold.*

And his scent...

"Is something wrong?" He asked.

"It's just...how'd you get back here so quickly, love?"

He smiled, reaching up to run a hand down her face. "Anything is possible with enough determination."

Tysus sounded so certain...so heroic.

But his answer was a little bit too evasive. "Was it Arturo, then? Teleporting you here?"

"An excellent guess, my love. You know me entirely too well."

She nodded slowly. "I do."

Arturo is the most talented of the warriors among them, but he is no sorcerer.

And Tysus would call me Venora, not Vendria.

Slowly, she began to extract her fingers from his.

...But he wouldn't let her go.

His eyes turned to focus on hers, looking hurt. "Leaving so soon?"

She drew in a breath, yanking her hand away. "I—"

Something sharp pierced her chest.

He'd drawn the knife so quickly that she hadn't even processed it.

Her eyes widened, and she stumbled back, hands going to the bleeding wound.

Blood spread far too rapidly, and something else was spreading along with it.

She grasped the hilt, hissing as a feeling of cold spread across her. Cold like the hands that she'd touched.

"What gave me away?" The impostor asked, stepping over to her as she scrambled backward on the dirty ground.

"You..." She couldn't focus on him. Something was wrong. A mere blade shouldn't be causing her this kind of pain. Shouldn't have harmed her at all.

But she'd been wounded before, and she was far from defenseless.

She wasn't a warrior, but she was still a god.

Body of Diamond.

Her strength multiplied in an instant as the power of three stars flowed into her. She tore the weapon free from her chest, hurling it to the side.

Divine healing, she commanded. The wound rapidly closed, but it left a trace of inky blackness within her.

She smashed a fist into the ground.

A fissure opened where she struck. The impostor jumped backward in shock, avoiding the gap, but stumbling when he landed.

Venora pushed herself to her feet. No dust or dirt clung to her form; she did not will it to.

She waved a hand. The would-be assassin flew backward, smashed by an invisible wave of force. He crashed into the nearby mountainside, leaving a crater on impact.

Venora floated over to him, flexing her hands in the air. "You dared to—"

She coughed, choking on a black substance that flowed out of her throat. Her eyes widened as pain once again blossomed in her chest.

The assassin coughed, too. He was on the ground below where he'd been smashed against the mountainside, his left arm snapped in twain, and his entire body ragged and worn.

Venora was pained to see Tysus' body in such a way, even if it was a mere fake. But it was only a brief concern; the false form of Tysus melted away a moment later.

Flesh, muscle, and bone rebuilt itself as she watched in horror. The resulting creature was neither human nor god, but a vestige of a time long gone. With dark blue skin below bits of armored black carapace, it stood half-again as tall as a human, with vast eight-fingered claws on each hand.

"Karna," she spat, before breaking into another cough. Her wound had reopened. How?

Heal, she commanded.

The wound closed again, but only for a moment.

"...What have you done?"

The shapeshifter walked toward her in the strange, erratic movements that their kind favored in their natural form. It reminded her less of a human and more of some sort of insect, moving briefly, then freezing in place.

"It was a human idea, in fact."

In spite of the creature's shark-like jaws, it still spoke with Tysus' voice. Venora shuddered at the sound of his voice coming from that, and horror filled her at the possible implications.

"They sought to forge weapons capable of fighting against the gods. And so, when we infiltrated their little group, we stole their ideas. And, some of their bodies, of course."

Venora pushed herself forward, through the pain of the reopening wound and the substance that still seemed to be spreading throughout her body. "What have you done with Tysus?"

"Nothing but observe him, dear. Attacking him now would only have worsened things. But you—" The creature raised a clawed hand. "You would have been a problem if you were allowed to change."

"I will not be killed so easily, even in this form." She wiped her mouth with a hand. "Your plan has failed."

The creature scoffed. "Killed? No, no. I couldn't possibly kill you, even with the knife." It reached out with a hand, and the weapon floated into the air. "And Ionel never would have approved of such a thing."

Ionel?

One of the other gods. Ionel, the Preserver. The great librarian, lover of history. Lover of her winter aspect. But he was...

She got a better look at the blade, dripping with black ichor, for the first time. She saw the runes on the surface, and with horror, she recognized and understood what she was seeing.

"No. He wouldn't..."

The karna shrugged. "Deals were made. Apparently, your shifting nature was not a good match for his—"

Venora struck. She wasn't fast in her current form, but she was strong. Strong enough to punch the air and smash the shapeshifter deeper into the mountainside.

She heard its bones crack on the impact.

She didn't care. The pawn didn't matter.

She rushed for the knife. She tore into stone to find it, crushing rocks to powder.

She found it just as the sun's rays began to chase away the night.

No, no. It's too soon. I won't—

And then she was gone.

And winter, not summer, came in her place.

***

The memories that followed were still too disjointed for her to parse properly, even with the help of Lydia's spell.

But she remembered much of what had come before, and fragments of what had happened after.

There were so many memories to sort through. Times of joy with Tysus at her side. Her hero, her champion. A mortal that hoped to lead humanity against the Sun Eater, once a creator of Rendalir, now turned toward its destruction.

Tysus had failed, and so had Vendria.

The Sun Eater's followers had spread across the world like a plague. Creatures of shadow and spirit — ruinshades — had sundered the souls of humans and gods alike, then taken their bodies and worn them like suits.

She hadn't seen the end herself. She'd only felt it.

She'd been trapped in that form, her winter aspect. She'd been tricked, chained, and bound.

And she'd been shattered apart, just as Rendalir itself had been.

I was a goddess once, Vendria remembered.

But that was long ago. Her world was gone. Her people long dead.

Her champion...

She didn't know. But she had to assume that Tysus had been lost along with all the rest of the mortals of her world.

The Sun Eater reigned triumphant and she...now, she was nothing but a stone. A sorcerous curio in a world that was not her own.

A mere fragment of her former self.

And of the other fragments...

...She didn't even know where she could begin to look or how.

She didn't have eyes to see.

She didn't have eyes to weep, either.

But she did have her mind. And thanks to Lydia, she remembered who she once was. She knew what she had to do.

I've failed one world already.

I won't fail another.

I'll be ready when the Sun Eater arrives.

CHAPTER XI – LYDIA IV – THE SCHOLAR

Lydia and Aladir walked side by side, trying not to look too conspicuous as they scanned the streets of Selyr for any potential threats.

It was a slow walk. Even after nearly a year of recovery, Lydia still relied heavily on her cane for walks of any significant distance. She could walk without one, but only with great difficulty.

The back of Lydia's mind still burned from loaning Vendria essence, but the fresh air was helping. She couldn't recall ever wandering a city that felt this pure before. Velthryn was a lovely place, but walking the streets of Selyr felt more like being in the midst of the wilderness.

She could smell the scents of pine and blooming flowers, and, more distant, the scents of spiced meat and vegetables cooking in many of the city's famed outdoor restaurants. Her stomach grumbled, but now was not the time for food.

It was a city of greens and browns, with bushes and trees lining every road and many homes painted with forest tones to match. She wished she could have simply taken the time to stroll peacefully through, but Lydia saw a place for a hidden assassin in every tree and large patch of shrubs.

She reassured herself with the fact that concealing assassins was hardly necessary — if Sterling wanted to get rid of her here, he could simply have her arrested. The vae'kes had near absolute authority in the entirety of the region.

Lydia was the one that had to act with subtlety here, not him. Extracting a vae'kes from one of their strongholds would be a complicated affair. She had plans, but even those plans had variables she couldn't account for. She needed more information.

The house they arrived at was easy to identify purely through contrast to the surrounding area. It was built in an old fashioned style, the paint a mix of grays and whites, but with only blackness visible within the windows. Civilians seemed to be avoiding the side of the street where it stood, but they weren't going so far out of their way that she suspected an immediate threat. There were enough side streets that if the house had a reputation for being terribly dangerous people could have just gone around it entirely.

There was a waist-high wall and a gate outside the house, but the gate was unlocked. Lydia swung it open and headed for the front door.

"You certain this is wise?" Aladir clenched and unclenched his hands, obviously nervous.

"No, but it's the most expedient approach. I need answers. And we have contingencies if things go badly."

Aladir gave her a curt nod, but looked unconvinced. "Ready when you are."

[I am also ready, Lydia.]

Thank you, Vendria. Don't exert yourself unless you need to.

[You needn't worry about me. I will protect you and myself.]

Something about Vendria's response was different from usual. A bit more coherent, and tinged with something else. Determination, perhaps?

That was a positive sign, if it was so. Most of the time, the stone merely seemed confused. Lonely. She'd investigate further when she didn't have more pressing matters to attend to. Perhaps she'd found a good memory to latch onto.

Perhaps that mind-linking spell that she'd found could help, but it had risks. She'd plan to try a few more options before resorting to that.

Lydia reached the door, raising a hand to knock. The door opened before she had a chance.

"Good day, Miss Hastings." The man in the doorway wore white robes, belted by a knotted rope. He had no visible weapons. A white blindfold covered his eyes. He offered a slight bow, then stepped out of the way of the door and beckoned to the house within. "The Scholar has been expecting you."

The way he emphasized the first two words made them sound like a title, rather than a mere occupation. That gave a specific implication.

Lydia froze, momentarily stymied. "The Scholar? Meaning Erik Tarren? Isn't he supposed to live at Winterspire Mountain?"

"Not in this season, I'm afraid. The Scholar travels extensively, and he has a number of different homes. I'm certain he can provide you with more context himself."

Lydia glanced at Aladir, who simply shrugged in response.

Lydia turned back to the blindfolded man. "May I—"

"You may check me for sorcery and weapons, yes. Also, you may take your weapons inside."

Without any further hesitation, Lydia stepped forward, putting a hand on the blindfolded man's shoulder. "Dominion of Knowledge, I invoke you."

A familiar stream of information flowed into her mind, with information translating into letters.

Dominion of Knowledge.
Dominion of Air.
Dominion of Motion.
Dominion of Destiny.

"You're..."

"A seer, yes. Though not quite in the same way as the Crystal Oracle that you are familiar with."

He knows about Asphodel, and has similar sorcery to her own.

Lydia stepped back. "Are you the Shrouded One?"

"Ah. I can understand the presumption, but no. I have no connection with that organization. I serve largely the same forces that you do, albeit in a different way."

He clearly could have been lying, but even if he was, this was definitely a new source of information. She had to pursue it. "Very well, we'll come inside."

Lydia stepped through the doorway, passing the blindfolded man. She could only see a few feet beyond; the rest was obscured by some sort of sorcerous darkness effect, most likely the same void sorcery she'd detected with her earlier spell.

The blindfolded man stepped into the doorway a moment later. "I'm afraid The Emerald Knight will need to wait outside."

The Emerald Knight? That's an interesting title for Aladir. Is this oracle merely being theatrical with the use of all these titles?

Aladir reached for his sword, but didn't draw. "I go where my partner goes."

"Apologies, but that will not be possible. The Scholar was quite clear. No disrespect was intended, but bringing you inside would complicate matters intensely. We will return The Cryptographer to you, unharmed, within less than an hour."

Well, it would seem my title is even stranger than Aladir's.

More importantly, an hour is more than enough time to kill someone and move the body to an inaccessible location. Lydia wrinkled her nose. *But I'm not your average someone. I'm aware of the dangers here, and I'm not a novice.*

Lydia snapped her fingers. "Comprehensive Barrier." The physical gesture was entirely unnecessary; it was a clear signal that she was preparing for trouble. With that, she turned back toward Aladir. "I'll be out soon."

He gave her a grim nod, then settled his hand on his weapon. "If you're not out in an hour, I'm coming in."

"Of course." The blindfolded man smiled, then shut the door. "Shall we?"

He clapped his hands. The darkness ahead of them dispersed, giving way to a perfectly ordinary looking hallway. The walls were lined with paintings and — Lydia noted with greater interest — more than the necessary number of mirrors.

The blindfolded man slipped past her, leading the way down the hall. "Apologies for the rudeness to your friend. It is too soon for The Scholar to meet with The Emerald Knight."

Lydia raised an eyebrow. "Why do you use that title for Aladir? I haven't heard it before."

"You will. Come."

Apparently it's not just Asphodel. Oracles are universally frustrating.

Nevertheless, Lydia followed him down the hall. "I didn't catch your name."

"Ah. Sometimes I forget basic niceties. Forgive me. I'm Estan."

She'd been expecting another strange title, so something as simple as "Estan" was a pleasant surprise. "Good to meet you, Estan."

"Yes." He nodded absently. "You may sit in the room ahead. The Scholar will be with you shortly."

The hall terminated in a large sitting room with a low table in the center. A pot of liquid — presumably tea — sat on the table, with teacups already laid out on both sides. There was a back exit to the house on the opposite side, leading toward a sunlit garden, and other rooms to the left and right.

Estan wordlessly departed through the door on the right, then closed it behind him.

Lydia examined the room further, searching at first for traps or other dangers. There were a few rugs on the floor, but nothing obviously between them.

"Dominion of Knowledge, illuminate that which is touched by your cousins."

One of the mirrors on a nearby wall glowed faintly, surprising her not in the least. Aside from that, however, the room was conspicuously lacking sorcerous auras.

She dismissed that spell and cast another immediately.

"Dominion of Knowledge, illuminate the hidden."

The spell was designed to show anyone or anything that was currently under a form of invisibility. Like the previous spell, it did not detect anything amiss. She dismissed it, but she wasn't quite finished.

"Dominion of Knowledge, illuminate all illusion effects."

Again, nothing. But she kept this one active; it would be useful to see if "Estan" or "Erik Tarren" were under the effects of any illusion spells when they next appeared, and she didn't want to cast the spell right in front of them.

With that done, she continued inspecting the more mundane elements of the room.

Beyond the tea, there were a few baskets of bread on the table. It looked — and smelled — delightfully fresh.

There were two chairs by the table, and a lower table nearby that contained a board for Crowns. There were a number of pieces on each side of the board, as well as a few to each side. The owner, it seemed, had a game that was already in progress. It was unclear whether or not he was winning, since there was nothing to indicate who was playing each side.

The factions in play were the Paladins of Tae'os and the Thornguard. The symbolism there did not escape her.

But that wasn't what drew her attention the most.

The walls were lined with dozens of bookshelves. Lydia ignored the obvious place she was supposed to sit and drifted toward the inexorable pull of the books.

Her eyes scanned the shelves, noting many familiar titles —— *Elements of Sorcery* and so on — and a handful of others that were less familiar.

The Gifts of the Stars: Kelryssia's Legacy in the Modern Age, The First Four: Gods of the Ancient World, Understanding Immortality: Rethri and Delaren, Advanced Principles of Planar Movement, The Lies of Lovers: Aayara and Jacinth's Eternal Dance...

...is that last one some sort of...romance novel?

Lydia reached forward, intrigued in spite of herself. Her interest was purely academic, of course.

"I should have expected you'd have a hard time resisting the call of further knowledge."

Lydia spun around, briefly embarrassed by her failure of decorum and its apparent predictability. Then she stopped worrying about that, because there were books, and books were always a good reason to be distracted.

The speaker appeared largely the way she'd expected. He was an older gentleman, but with few wrinkles aside from smile marks. His hair was the greatest tell of his age, long and silvery, and marked with a matching goatee. He wore a gray pointed hat with a single white feather, though the traveler's garb that Taelien had described had been replaced by something slightly more formal. He wore flowing robes of white, embroidered with a blue pattern that wrapped all around it, resembling a snake with horns and wings.

His resemblance to Taelien's description did not, of course, actually mean this was Erik Tarren. Jonan could have managed an illusion with basic details like these, as could any number of other sorcerers.

Her Detect Illusions spell didn't actually show any illusion effects active on him, but there were ways around that. Sufficiently powerful void sorcery could block her detection abilities, or he could have permanently shapeshifted rather than using an illusion. The latter was a costly tactic, since shapeshifting had serious medical risks, but it was not unprecedented. And she wasn't going to be caught unawares just because she believed her spells to be infallible.

Lydia dismissed the Detect Illusions spell, since it didn't seem to be picking anything up. She could always recast it later if she decided something seemed suspicious, but keeping it active at this point was an unnecessary drain on her mind.

She smiled, but kept her distance. If there was any chance that this was Sterling playing a trick, she wasn't about to let him get in arm's reach. Not again.

And if somehow he did, she'd have a few new surprises.

For the moment, she decided the wisest course was to play along and evaluate the situation further. Erik Tarren or Sterling would both have information that interested her, and thus, she thought this could be a worthwhile encounter in either case — provided she was cautious enough to survive it. "Master Tarren, I presume? Forgive me for the lack of decorum; I was quite enthralled by your collection."

"No, no, by all means. My old teacher always said that knowledge was meant to be shared, and I firmly agree with her. I'll try to give you some time to peruse the books after our discussion, if our schedules permit it."

"That is quite kind of you." She bowed lightly. "You seemed to be expecting me?"

"Ah, yes. Not today in specific, mind you, but Estan has a way of making everything sound like it was long foretold and recorded in prophecy." The older man grinned, showing the source of his smile lines.

"Oh? Should I beware of any other prophetic elements, then? Old crones with riddles and young farm boys toting dominion marked swords?"

Erik Tarren chuckled and took one of the nearby seats. "I do believe you've already stumbled upon the latter, though he wasn't precisely a farmer."

Lydia sighed. "Indeed. And that seems to have been your work. You dropped him off as a baby, if I recall? Along with a legendary sorcerous relic? Tell me, have you ever written anything in your many books about the ethics of distributing swords to children?"

Tarren sighed and shook his head. "I was only honoring the wishes of a dying friend. But enough of that. You're not here to talk about the swordsman. He can come visit me himself if he wants answers. I'm somewhat surprised he hasn't already."

"He's been quite busy with work." Lydia took the seat across from Tarren. "And I do believe you gave him a different location."

"I move about frequently. It's in my nature. You can tell him I'm here right now. You may be seeing him soon enough."

Lydia raised an eyebrow. "Oh?"

"We'll get to that." Tarren raised a hand. "What did you really want to ask me?"

"Ah, business, then. What can you tell me about the identity of the Shrouded One?"

"Very little, I'm afraid. She has powerful friends that I would rather not agitate."

Lydia wrinkled her nose. "She?"

Tarren smirked. "A slip of the tongue. Think nothing of it."

Was that a deliberate hint, or an actual slip? Hm.

"What sort of person would an immortal sorcerer find intimidating, Master Tarren?"

The older man leaned forward. Lydia tensed briefly, but he was only reaching for the teapot. He poured a cup for himself, and then for her. "I'd rather not go into any details, but I'm certain you're aware that there are beings that even I would not dare face alone. The Xixian Emperor and Empress, for example, were among them in the past."

"But they're long gone, and you helped with that. There are few with that degree of power, save the gods themselves..." Lydia frowned. "Really? Is that what you're implying? This Shrouded One has a *god* backing them?"

"You can draw what conclusions you will." He took a sip from the cup. "Mmm. Excellent. The teapot is mildly enchanted, you see. Keeps the liquid inside at just the right temperature."

Lydia took a glance at the steaming liquid he'd poured, evaluated the slim chance of poisoning against the discourtesy of refusing hospitality...and chose discourtesy. She was taking more than enough risks just by being in here by herself, and she knew that Sterling used poison. "I'm not thirsty, thank you."

Tarren shrugged. "I'm sorry I can't help you with that particular issue. Perhaps something else?"

"Sterling."

"Hm? What about a Sterling?"

She'd said the name by itself to gauge his reaction. Sometimes you could get someone in disguise to break character if you called them by their name.

But since he didn't react that way, she simply used that to segue into a different conversation. "Jonathan Sterling. Do you know anything about him?"

"Ah, the one who was responsible for those poisonings during your paladin exams. You have my sincere condolences for the losses to your order."

"Thank you." Lydia frowned. "Did you know that you were sending a group of paladins to his location?"

"What do you mean?" Tarren frowned, setting down his cup.

"You teleported a group of paladins directly to Sterling's location during the exam, did you not?"

"Ah, that." He shook his head. "I'm afraid I sent them to a cave they showed me on the map. I wasn't aware that anyone was there at the time. I do feel responsible to a degree, since I did not go along with them, but I had no way of knowing your paladin trials would be unsafe. As I'm sure you know, I've helped with some other trials in the past, and there have never been incidents on that scale."

That's consistent with how the paladin candidates described their meeting with Tarren on the road, implying he at least has knowledge of the event. That still doesn't rule out the possibility that this is Sterling — since Sterling may have also had someone watching the path and reporting to him — but it does make it less likely.

Should I try to tease out more details of that prior encounter for clarity?... no, that's not the priority right now.

"Very well. I appreciate the assistance you've provided our organization in the past." She took a breath. "Now, do you know anything else about this Sterling? His whereabouts? His goals?"

Tarren straightened up. "If you're looking to catch and stop him, I'd urge you to reconsider."

"I appreciate the concern. Will you please answer my question?"

Tarren raised a hand to cover his eyes. "I have an idea of what he is up to, yes. He is still working with this Shrouded One you mentioned. For that reason, I still can tell you little."

"Anything. Please. A nudge in the right direction, without any way of tracing it back to you."

Tarren reached up and fiddled with his goatee. "Hmm... I suppose I can give you a bump toward him. But you may not appreciate the method or the results. Are you certain that's what you wish?"

"No, absolutely not, I want exact details before I agree to something like that. None of this vagueness." Lydia folded her arms. "Honestly, who would agree to something like that?"

"You'd be surprised." He sounded chagrined. "Fine. When we conclude this discussion, I will offer to teleport you to someone who will help guide you to Sterling's location. But I will be sending you alone, without any of the reinforcements you have outside."

"How—"

He waved a hand. "Estan may have a hint of theatricality about him, but his foresight is matched by only a handful of others. Your friend Asphodel is among them, as is the Shrouded One."

Which all but confirms that Asphodel is not the Shrouded One, if this man can be believed.

Drawing from that, I can determine that the Shrouded One is female, not Asphodel, and has actual divinatory capabilities. I don't know anyone who fits that profile perfectly. Morella was specialized in Memory Sorcery, which is related, but the opposite direction... Hm.

"Why can't you send me with anyone else?"

"Too conspicuous. I can't move too many pieces at once without being noticed. And I would require you to take a message."

"What sort of message?"

"When you see Taelien, give him this address. We have important matters to discuss."

"What sort of important matters?"

He shook his head. "I'm afraid it's too early in the game to explain all that to you. And, you're out of questions."

Lydia's frown deepened. "I do not like playing *games* of this kind, Master Tarren."

"Perhaps I would offer you a friendly game of Crowns instead, but alas, I already have one in progress. And I would hate to disrupt the pieces."

Lydia sighed, standing up. "This has been quite enlightening, Master Tarren. Thank you."

"You're refusing my deal, then? Even with such a simple price?"

Lydia peered down at him. "Your 'deal' is ludicrous. Why would I consent to be teleported to talk to an unknown person, at an unknown location, trusting only your word that it might somehow be helpful? I would rather trust in my own skills and those of my fellows."

Tarren groaned, looking down. After a moment, he let out a sigh. "...You have a great deal of her stubbornness in you, more than I'd realized."

An image flickered in her mind. A book given to her by her mother, written by Erik Tarren. She'd never forgotten about it, of course, but it had been a lower priority than business. "Who are you talking about?"

"My niece. She was quite precious to me. She still is, though we haven't spoken in quite some time."

Lydia blinked. "Your niece?" *Stop hesitating, Lydia. Just ask the question.* "Is that my mother, by any chance? Or are you perchance my father?"

Tarren didn't laugh, or sigh again, or give her any of the responses she'd expected. Nor did he give her the answer she'd so often dreamed of.

He simply looked up, catching her gaze in his, and said, "Perhaps in another life." Then he shook his head, suddenly looking very old. "But not in this one. Not in the way you mean."

"Then—"

"We are, in fact, family. The truth of that is complicated and not my place to share. No, your mother is not the niece I referred to, either. But yes, I gave your mother a book a long time ago. I hope you found it of some use."

Lydia froze, clenching her hands together. "...Do you know who my father is, then?"

"Ah. It's...no, that's not my place to say, either. I'm sorry. If your mother did not share that with you, it would not be—"

"Coward." The word came out without any conscious decision on her part. That was a rarity, and she regretted it almost immediately.

The response was even more surprising. "Yes. I am, in more ways than you could imagine. I will not ask you to trust me. And I cannot possibly ask you to forgive me. But please, do know that I have tried. That I am trying... That it's... it's difficult."

He sounded heartbroken in a way that Lydia was entirely unprepared for. Lydia's mouth opened and closed without any words emerging.

Erik Tarren steeled himself, taking a deep breath. "I'm sorry. I didn't mean for our meeting to go like this."

Lydia sat back down. "You can still help me. If you can't give me certain answers, fine. But if we're family, if that's really true...then please. Please help me *solve* this. There's a murderer that is still roaming free, and if he's working with this Shrouded One, there could be more deaths before he's caught."

"There will be." Tarren sounded certain. "I do not wish for you to be one of them."

"That's not your choice to make. You're not in any position to give me orders."

Erik shrugged at that. "Perhaps you're right. Perhaps...no, I've said too much already."

Lydia tightened her jaw. "There's something you're not telling me."

"There are many things I'm not telling you. A lack of knowledge is ever the scholar's frustration, but often also our delight. There is always more to learn. I've given you the few pieces I can, at least for now. Perhaps there will come a time when I..."

Lydia waved a hand. "Don't worry about platitudes or giving me false hopes. I'll work this problem out."

"You really do remind me of her. For better and for worse." Tarren stood up. "I believe we've taken all the time we can. Now, would you like me to send you a step further on your journey, as we discussed?"

"No," Lydia replied. "No teleportation. But I would very much appreciate a map."

Tarren rubbed his temples. "You're going to be the death of me, Lydia Hastings."

"Well, if you're going to die, you may as well tell me what you know."

Tarren chuckled. "You won't change my mind quite so easily, I'm afraid. But I'll do this much, at least." Tarren snapped his fingers, and a scroll appeared in his other hand. "You shall have a map." He extended the scroll to her.

Lydia accepted it, breaking the seal and opening it immediately. She frowned. "This is just a single scribbled arrow with the name 'Wrynn Jaden' written on the other side of it."

"It's important to maintain a sense of humor at my age." Erik Tarren laughed. "And to remember the art of a good distraction."

"Distra—"

Superior Teleportation, her Comprehensive Barrier reported helpfully, sending details of how the spell worked into her mind just before it smashed through the shield.

CHAPTER XII – VELAS III – DUAL IDENTITIES

Velas narrowed her eyes at Captain Nolan. Fortunately, he wouldn't be able to see her expression through the veils she was wearing. After a moment of deliberation, she moved straight to the issue at hand. "I'm looking for Sterling."

"Ah." The Thornguard captain showed a hint of disappointment in his face. "I was hoping you might have...never mind. Business it is, then."

She folded her arms, leaning against the doorway. She didn't say anything further. It was better to let him fill in the blanks, rather than make a mistake by asking something she should already know or offering information that might contradict what he'd already heard.

"Last I heard, he was planning to go to some sort of auction. You'd probably know more about it than I do."

"Kyestri is having one." She offered the hint of information as a hook for more.

"The prime lord? Hm. I suppose that would explain why he'd be interested — Lord Kyestri has a few rare relics that a vae'kes might enjoy getting their hands on." Nolan frowned. "This isn't some internal problem I'm dealing with, is it? I can't afford to get drawn into another conflict between the children, Silk. I have enough on my plate."

Velas shook her head. "It shouldn't concern you. I'll handle everything from here."

"That's what you always say." He sighed. "Do you want to come in for a drink, at least? It's a cold night, and I wouldn't mind the company while you're here..."

"Can't." She tried to sound apologetic, while inwardly suppressing her irritation. "Business to attend to. Night."

Nolan let out an exhausted sigh. "Good night, then."

Velas slipped out the door, gently shutting it.

She left the fortress the same way she came in. There were no further encounters with guards. The only frustration came from the questions still running through her mind.

***

Velas ran.

She was absolutely certain she was being followed.

She'd noticed it after she'd made her way out of the fort, jumping from the walls to the trees below. Nothing visible, but an aberrant sound a good fifty feet behind her.

Whoever it was could keep up with her, at least for now.

Unfortunately, when she glanced back toward the source of the sound, she didn't see anyone there

A sight sorcerer, or someone with another form of invisibility. Shadow or deception, maybe.

As she landed in the trees behind the fortress, she reached into a pouch on her side and threw down a handful of spiked balls — caltrops.

Vanish.

Her own practice at sight sorcery with Jonan hadn't gotten very far. She couldn't make a convincing illusion of a person in motion, so she couldn't disguise herself. Making herself invisible was even further from her abilities.

Making a few tiny stationary objects invisible, however, was something she could just barely manage.

She didn't wait to see if her pursuer ran over the trap. She just kept moving, dodging through trees at a steady pace.

The sounds behind her gradually faded, but she never heard her pursuer grunt or scream. Unfortunate, but caltrops were easily replaced.

Velas tapped the side of her head.

See invisibility.

She scanned the forest again, but she still couldn't see any sign of a pursuer. That didn't mean much, though. More powerful sight sorcerers could still easily conceal themselves from her, including Jonan.

It's not him, though. He couldn't have even kept up with me as long as they did.

Probably.

She wrinkled her nose and ran back into the city.

Well, I'm compromised. This is wonderful.

Once she was back in the city proper, she found an alley and pulled off her veils and wig and stuffed them in her pack.

Wish I'd practiced sight calling with Jonan just a little more. Changing my appearance further would be extremely useful right about now.

If it had been earlier in the day, she might have taken a quick detour into a shop for an alternate outfit. She'd stopped carrying extra disguises a long time ago, when her combat skills had gotten to the point where she could generally fight her way out of her problems.

Invisible enemies made that approach much trickier.

Can't go back to Lydia right now. I'm not dragging her into this until I have a better idea of what I'm dealing with.

Jonan is probably a better option, but I don't know exactly where he is.

She made for the city gates, then slipped out into the forest. Once there, she was reasonably confident she was no longer being pursued.

Velas pulled out her mirror, hastily sketching a note.

Ran into trouble. Need to talk. Earrings at soonest convenience.

With that, she pinned on one of her earrings from her bag — the one that corresponded to one Jonan kept in his possession. They'd made a few pairs while working together. Jonan had handed a pair connected to each of them to Aayara, too, but she wasn't interested in talking to Aayara just yet.

She headed down the road a bit, stopping outside a roadside inn beyond the city proper. Not Wrynn Jaden's place — that was considerably further out. Just a nice, ordinary inn.

Depending on Jonan's answers, she knew she might be spending the night there. As much as she wanted to get further from town, she hadn't brought any gear for camping.

It took about an hour before she heard anything.

"...Hello? Testing?" Jonan's voice sounded in her ear.

"I'm here." Velas replied. "Can you hear me?"

"Yeah. You in a secure position?"

Velas scanned from side-to-side again. Her vision was oddly blurry.

Oh, resh.

She tapped the side of her head, disabling the invisibility detection spell. She used them so infrequently that she'd forgotten to turn it off.

Velas sighed. "I think I'm good. You?"

"About as good as I'm going to be in this city."

"Fair." She grunted, looking around again. "We need to talk."

"We're talking. We are literally talking right now."

"Not a good time for teasing, Scribe. I'm in a bit of a bind."

There was a pause. "That doesn't sound like you."

"Thanks for saying so." Velas took a breath, collecting her thoughts. "Fair warning that this chat might get both of us killed."

"Lovely. Now *that* sounds more like you."

"Okay. Let me fill you in. You know how Silk is a hereditary title for Aayara's apprentices?"

"Of course. When one of them dies, she replaces them with a new one."

Velas nodded, then felt a little silly, since he couldn't actually see her. Probably.

She wouldn't have been surprised if Jonan did have a way of seeing her. He was creepy like that.

"Yeah. Well, there's a new Silk in town."

Jonan paused. "And you didn't even invite me to your funeral?"

Velas snorted. "Okay, that was a good one. But seriously, help me out. What do you think the odds are that Auntie Ess is responsible for this new one, versus them being a pawn for another vae'kes trying to tweak her nose?"

"Difficult to say. Could also be some amateur trying to exploit your reputation."

"If we were in a small town, sure. In Selyr, I'd think most people would know better."

"Never underestimate the depths of human stupidity."

Velas leaned against the side of the inn, rubbing her temples. "Fair. But let's assume the more likely cases here. Either Auntie is prepping a replacement — meaning I'm on the way out — or someone else is making a serious move. This other Silk has been interacting with Thornguard in high places."

"In what way?"

Velas sighed. "Sleeping with at least some of them, from what I can gather. Or at least leading them on."

"Ooh. You've had an awkward day, haven't you?"

"Yeah, no kidding. But you're still not giving me any answers, here."

"I'm thinking." Jonan paused. "Okay, done thinking. Either of your scenarios is eminently plausible. But."

"But?"

"But it's also possible this is a test."

Velas wanted to scream. "You're reshing right. This could be one of her tests. I thought I was *done* with that garbage years ago."

"Welcome to being employed by a psychopathic demigod."

Velas lowered her head. "Okay. Where does that put us?"

"Well, we're obviously going to need to figure out who this other Silk is."

"Obviously."

"I can probably help with that."

"Yes, that's why we're talking."

"A 'thank you' would be nice."

Velas snorted again. "You'll get your pat on the back when you find me some answers. Not before."

"Fine, fine. Such high standards for praise. I can see who you take after." She heard Jonan sigh. "Okay. Is there anything else I need to be worry about?"

"Oh, right. I'm outside the city. Someone was chasing me. Invisible, fast. Not good at concealing their sounds, though. Basically like you, but better."

"As always, your compliments are the highlight of my day."

Velas smirked. "Any ideas?"

"Well, if they weren't concealing sounds, Aayara is out of the question. Unless she was allowing you to hear her deliberately."

"You think it was just her trying to scare me?"

"Not impossible, if she's testing you. But I should stop focusing on my favorite hypothesis. Other options: Sterling if he absorbed any sight sorcery, which he easily could have. Any random 'ess' or Thornguard with invisibility sorcery. Oh, or Rialla."

"You're supposed to call her Shiver when we're using code names."

"Oops. So, it could be Rialla."

Velas sighed. "She uses deception, but I don't think she's that good. And wouldn't she have just talked to me?"

"That's presuming she isn't the new Silk candidate."

Velas fell silent. "...Resh. That's...not impossible, I guess."

"It's really not. She's an ess with a broad skill set similar to the type that Aayara would be looking for. But I don't think it's likely."

"Then don't scare me like that!"

"Sorry, sorry." Jonan didn't sound very apologetic. "Just considering all of the options. Do you need a place to lie low for a while?"

"Yes."

"Give me an hour to change locations. If there's a good chance that Aayara might be the one sending someone after you — for a test or otherwise — we can't use the usual spots."

"We?"

"Obviously. If you have a sight sorcerer after you, someone is going to need to watch out for you for a while."

Velas paused. "...You'd do that for me?"

"We're having this conversation, aren't we?"

"...Thanks." Velas paused. "You're not the one that's supposed to be replacing me, are you?"

"You think I'd fit into that outfit? With my hips? Please." Jonan chuckled, then his voice turned serious. "No, it's not me. This is the first I've heard of any of that. I do have one more possible idea...but I'm going to need to do a bit of digging before I say too much. Don't want to give you the wrong notion and waste your time."

"Sounds interesting."

"It is." Jonan took a breath. "It's also horrifying."

"Hm."

"Hm?"

Velas smirked. "Think I might have read you wrong when we got started."

"Maybe. But don't stop reading yet. You're still in the prologue."

CHAPTER XIII – TAELIEN IV – SOUL SURVIVOR

"So," Taelien began as Wrynn led the way back toward her tavern, "why didn't you want to tell him about the map?"

Wrynn glanced back at him. "Because he was too interested in items from Rendalir. That means there's a chance he could read the language on it, and if so, he might have figured out where it was leading just at a glance. At that point, the map would lose its value. I'd rather find someone else to translate it first."

"We could have told him we had a map without actually showing it to him."

Wrynn shrugged. "Sure, but I'd rather not play my hand that openly. There's…ugh." She paused, bending over and clutching her chest.

Taelien rushed closer. "You okay?"

"It's…ah. No, but I will be. I need to get back to the vault, fast." Her expression shifted from pained to apologetic. "If I collapse, you may need to carry me for a while."

"Is it that bad? I can carry you now, if you need me to."

She hesitated for a moment, then nodded. "Please. I'm going to meditate. Wake me when we get back to the tavern."

Taelien knelt down and lifted her up, then continued walking. She was light enough that she barely burdened him at all.

She closed her eyes immediately after he lifted her, a look of strain on her face.

For a moment, he thought he saw one of the tattoos on her arm *move*.

When they reached the outside of the tavern, he spoke quietly in her ear. "We're here."

Her eyes fluttered open. "Mm. Thanks. You can set me down."

She wobbled a little on her feet when he lowered her to the ground, and he continued supporting her as they walked inside.

"Help me down the stairs, please."

She switched to linking arms with him, putting on a cheerful expression and waving at customers as they passed through the main room into the back. Her expression shifted again immediately when they made it to the back room. From there, she led the way slowly down to the vault entrance he'd seen before.

When she pressed her hand against the gigantic metal doors of the vault, they swung open immediately. "This way."

Taelien's last experience inside a Xixian vault wasn't exactly a pleasant one, but he certainly wasn't going to abandon Wrynn, either.

Fortunately, there was no flood of water or click of a deadly trap being triggered as they stepped inside. Instead, the opening of the vault was a virtually empty stone room, about twenty feet in each direction. There were a set of four ordinary stone doors on the opposite wall.

"Far left," Wrynn explained. She was sweating profusely.

He helped her walk to the door, then reached for the handle.

"Wait." She stopped his hand, then reached into a pouch on her belt. She removed a small stone, pressing it into a gap on the stone wall next to the doorframe. There was a click, then she reached for the knob. "I've disarmed most of this place, but I keep a few things active for my personal use."

Wrynn pulled the door open, and it led into a small room the size of a closet. There was a small gap between the larger chamber and the small room, and the smaller room was constructed of metal, rather than stone. It appeared empty. "In."

They stepped inside.

Wrynn said something in Xixian. Taelien understood only a bit of the language, but he thought it sounded like 'sixteen'.

The entire room began to move.

Taelien suppressed his instinct to react at the sudden movement. The doorframe to exit the chamber disappeared, quickly replaced by another, and then another, as the room they stood within continued to shift.

After a breath, he processed what was happening. *It's not a trap, it's just a mechanical lift, like one of the ones they have in some of those fancy sorcerer towers.*

The room ceased moving after a time, then the door in front of them opened, leading into a circular chamber of white stone.

In the center of the chamber was a circular pool of crystal-clear fluid. It looked like an exceptionally large spa bath, complete with steps leading partway down into it.

"I need to get inside." She moved toward the pool. "I'll be in there for about a day. If you go back to the lift, just say 'sholver' and it will take you back to the entrance floor."

"You look like you're about ready to faint. Do you need me to stay here to make sure you don't lose consciousness? I don't want you to drown."

She shook her head. "The fluid in there won't drown me. I often spend...long periods of time in there. I'll explain later." She began stepping into the pool without bothering to slip off her clothes. She turned back briefly before submerging herself completely. "I owe you one. Go get some rest, I'll see you tomorrow."

Taelien nodded absently. "You're certain you'll be okay here?"

"Positive." Wrynn nodded with a determined expression. "This is...unfortunately, somewhat routine. I'll explain more soon, but for now, I need the pool. I can't delay any longer."

"Got it. I'll be back to check on you tomorrow if you don't come to me."

With that, he headed to the lift, said the word, and made his way back to the tavern.

***

Taelien found Asphodel serving food and drinks to the customers. He blinked at her.

She turned and smiled to him. "Miss Jaden will be unavailable this evening, so I am taking care of things. She has been most hospitable to us, and thus, I am ensuring that her business continues to operate smoothly."

"Did she—"

"No, she didn't ask," Asphodel interrupted. "But I know she'll be grateful for the help tomorrow."

"Your predictive abilities seem to have grown considerably more precise over the last year."

She nodded. "If I had taken the time to hone my abilities sooner, our encounter with Sterling might have gone much differently."

"I thought you were firmly opposed to any form of intervening with fate?"

"I am. But Sterling's patron *is* interfering with fate, and thus, I have concluded that using my own foreknowledge against them is a valid way to ensure the proper path is taken."

Taelien paused, considering. "Wait. Sterling's patron — the Shrouded One? Can you divine what they're up to?"

Asphodel shook her head sadly. "No. Other oracles are impossible for me to see properly, much like you and Velas are."

"Wait. Hold on. Velas is like me?"

Asphodel shrugged. "No. Gazing into your destiny shows me that of another. Seeing into her fate shows me nothing but a void."

"...Could she be the Shrouded One, then? Blocking your vision?"

Asphodel seemed to consider that, then shook her head. "I don't think so. Looking at Velas doesn't feel like I'm being blocked by sorcery similar to my own. It's more like there's simply...nothing there."

"That sounds like void sorcery to me. Couldn't the Shrouded One have access to that?"

"Yes. But I do not think it is the same. I have encountered those with void sorcery, and that is like staring at a pitch-black wall. This is more like looking into a box, only to find the box is empty."

"That's...creepy."

Asphodel nodded. "It is."

More questions about Velas for the future. I still know so little about her.

Taelien shook his head, then dismissed the thought to focus on the present. "Okay. But if you're predicting that Wrynn needs help in the kitchen today, isn't that messing with fate?"

"No, no. If that was the case, I wouldn't be able to do anything at all. My restrictions relate to things that would change major events. Lives and deaths. Declarations of war. Political decisions. Simple things like this," she pointed toward the tray of mugs she was carrying, "Aren't significant enough to count as interfering with fate. I am not changing the course of any lives, merely lending a bit of comfort."

That seemed like an odd distinction to make, but he wasn't going to complain. He'd never agreed with her non-intervention policy in the first place.

It was almost equally odd that she was being more verbose than usual, but he didn't mind that, either.

He sat and ate the food that Asphodel brought him. And he worried.

What am I doing here?

He could have been training, or searching for more items of myth and legend. He would have been most comfortable seeking a battle. Perhaps practicing for a tournament, or hunting a dangerous monster that threatened a village.

Dealing with politics, manipulation, and lies — that wasn't his skill set. And as much as he was trying to adapt to it, he was still far from comfortable.

Everyone seemed to have so many layers of secrets.

How could he combat that without secrets of his own? Should he even be trying?

This kind of brooding doesn't suit me.

He finished his food and headed outside to train.

Body of Stone.

His hands moved in a familiar pattern, striking at opponents he envisioned in his mind.

In this practice, his questions and concerns faded to the back of his mind, and he found the tranquility that he needed.

***

When Taelien found Wrynn the next morning, she was outside the Xixian Vault, sitting in a chair and knitting. The sight of it was so utterly mundane that he barely even recognized her.

He was somewhat comforted when he realized that whatever she was knitting wasn't made of ordinary cloth; it was black as ink and rippled and shifted in her hands like liquid. The needle she was using to weave it was a glowing point of silver, and as she turned to look at Taelien, it vanished entirely.

Wrynn stood up, wobbly on her feet, and draped the incomplete garment over the back of her chair. "You're up early."

Taelien walked closer, his expression concerned. "Asphodel woke me. You feeling better?"

"As good as can be expected, given the circumstances." She grunted. "I'm used to it by now."

"Is it something I can help with?"

Wrynn stared at him for a moment, appraising. "In theory, yes. But you wouldn't like it."

Taelien folded his arms and leaned against a nearby wall. "What's that mean?"

Wrynn set the garment she was working on down. "First, let me show you something." She stood up, turned around, and lifted up her shirt, displaying her back.

While Wrynn had tattoo-like marks across much of her body, the design on her back was on a completely different scale. There was a single, huge mark between her shoulder blades that spread outward into numerous tendrils, reaching toward each section of her body. Dozens of other tiny markings were etched into the spaces between and around the blackness, glowing bright with a variety of colors. They were a beautiful contrast to the ink-black of the central mark.

That's the epicenter of her markings, he realized. And, as he watched, the central sigil *moved*. It shifted like liquid, just slightly changing in shape. When the writhing blackness made contact with one of the other sigils, Taelien saw *sparks* flash from the point of contact, and Wrynn visibly winced. "What *is* that?"

Taelien took a step closer, raising a hand toward the central mark.

"Don't!" Wrynn pulled her shirt back down, turning around. "You don't want to touch that. Certainly not while it's *active*."

"I'd thought those tattoos might be dominion marks, but that's something different, isn't it? What is that?"

Wrynn leaned up against the nearby wall. "A seal. One that *must* not be broken."

"A seal? As in, it's preventing something from getting out of...what, your body?"

Wrynn shook her head. "No, not...well, sort of. My body would be a potential medium for it to escape, but it's not sealed inside me. Rather, it's trapped somewhere far away, and my body is one of the locks on its prison. If that lock breaks, my body becomes a gate through which it can flee."

Taelien blinked. "And I take it this thing is something terrible?"

"That's an understatement if I ever heard one." Wrynn rubbed at her temples. "It has an awful sense of taste. It's one of the beings that made our world, after all."

"No." Taelien shook his head. "There's no way. You're joking."

"I wish I was." Her voice lowered to a whisper. "My life would be very different if it was."

Taelien held up a hand in a pausing gesture. "You want me to believe you have a *worldmaker* sealed away somewhere? I know you're a prime lady, but that should be a few orders of magnitude too difficult, even for you. And they're supposed to be long dead."

"Ah. You've got more than a few misconceptions there. There are plenty of dead worldmakers, but I assure you, the ones that made *our* world are unfortunately quite alive. Some of them, at least." She sighed. "I can't believe I'm getting you involved in this. Your parents would never approve."

Taelien drew in a breath. "You knew my parents? Wait, *which* parents?"

Wrynn waved a hand. "Ah, sorry, sorry. Didn't mean to alarm you. I mean the Seven-Branched Sword Deity and the Impervious Forest Goddess. I don't actually *know* if you're their kid. Not definitively. I'm afraid I wasn't around when you were born."

Seven-Branched Sword Deity? I've never heard that one. That must be the Artinian name for Aendaryn?

Taelien frowned, bothered by how little he knew about his supposed parents. "But...you knew them?"

Wrynn snorted. "Better than most. The Seven-Branched Sword Deity practically adopted me as a teenager."

"And you think I might be..."

Wrynn shrugged. "Maybe. I understand the gods often have difficulty bearing children through conventional means, but your parents were a clever sort. They may have figured something out. Or maybe you're an ordinary child they found and invested some power in — that can happen. I don't know that for sure."

"Can you tell me about them?" Taelien felt a surge of hope. He'd *desperately* wanted answers for so long, it was surreal to finally be getting even a hint of them.

"Can't tell you much in regards to recent years, but I can share some stories, sure. Probably once we get on the road...but I'm going to need a few days to recover here, first." She shifted awkwardly. "In fact, I think I need you to walk me back to that pool now."

Taelien approached and offered his arm. "Sure, let's go. But what's it for?"

Wrynn took his arm and they began to limp back toward the vault. "How old do you think I am?"

Taelien tilted his head to the side at the odd question. "...Several hundred? It's obviously hard to tell with rethri, but if you were adopted by Aendaryn..."

"I'm probably a bit shy of thirty, at least as far as life lived." She laughed. "And that's what the pool is for."

"You mean it de-ages you?" Taelien asked.

"No, no." She opened the vault doors, and they headed toward the same area they'd used the night before. "It's a stasis pool."

Taelien paused, processing that. "A stasis pool? Wait, you mean something that permanently makes a stasis effect? I know stability sorcery can accomplish very short-term stasis, but...is long-term stasis even possible?"

She dragged him forward. "Fortunately for me, it is. It's the only way I've found to successfully keep this guy," she jerked a thumb at her back, "contained for any significant length of time. The longer I'm out in the world, the more he acts up, and the longer I need to put myself into stasis next time to recover."

They reached the lift, heading back up to the area with the pool. "So, you put yourself in stasis, and during that time the seal stabilizes?"

"Exactly. While I'm in stasis, the worldmaker has no way of breaking through, so it sleeps. And during that time, the seal's integrity recovers a bit. In order to maintain the seal properly, I sometimes have to sleep for years at a time. Occasionally, even decades."

"Decades? ...Is that how you lost your box?"

Wrynn nodded as the lift arrived at the appropriate floor, then headed toward the pool. "Exactly. I've always tried to find secure locations for my valuables before I need to sleep, but sometimes I don't have time. Or, places that are 'secure' when I go to sleep are less so when empires rise and fall during my slumber."

"That sounds...intensely difficult." Taelien winced. "Is there no other way?"

They arrived at the pool. "There's always another way. I've tried hundreds of them, and some have helped. The most effective, however, is reinforcing my spirit." She raised a hand, displaying one of the markings. "You see these smaller marks, the ones that are separate from the seal?"

"Yeah. Dominion marks to reinforce your spirit, I take it?"

She sighed. "I wish. You're close, but an ordinary dominion mark just draws energy without form. I've tried them — and I do have a couple. But they barely help. These ones here that look a little swirlier are more like containers."

"For...what, exactly? What do they contain?" Taelien had a feeling he might know the answer, but he was hoping he was wrong.

"Well, the first set of them are dedications and spirit arts that I've acquired over the years. You'd probably call them spirit marks in your nomenclature. They hold pieces of my spirit. The rest...they hold *other* souls."

Taelien's eyes narrowed. "You—"

She raised her hands in a warding gesture. "I don't steal any. They're given freely, and they're not complete souls. Just pieces. Whatever someone can spare."

Taelien drew in a deep breath. "That's still..."

"I know, I know. It's not the kind of sorcery that most people approve of. But it's in service of an important cause. One that may be necessary to keep the entire world from being destroyed."

"Why? Did the worldmakers plan to destroy their own creation, like what happened with Rendalir?"

"No, nothing like that. We were more fortunate than they, at least." Wrynn shook her head. "Instead, our makers chose to war with each other, both directly and through proxies — great armies of their creation. Humans, monsters, and colossal machines. Their last war left empires in ruins and divine corpses strewn across the planet."

She sounded pained as she continued. "I wasn't one of the ones that sealed them away — that was before even the time of your parents. It was the firstborn children of the makers, the ones you'd call the first generation of gods, that turned on the makers and caged them deep within the world. On my continent, the firstborn trained our people to serve as living seals for the maker sealed there, as well as the terrible beasts that served him. I trained for many years with your father to become one of the seals."

"Why not gather the strongest people we can and release it so we can defeat it more permanently?" Taelien's hand drifted to his hilt subconsciously. "I'd help you fight him."

Wrynn snorted. "Of course you would. I'm sure you'd love that. I would, too, in concept. But none of us would stand even the slightest chance. Last time a seal broke on one of the children of this maker, I fought it for a time to hold it at bay while it could be re-sealed. Your father and mother were with me, as well as your father's first apprentice, and dozens of others of similar strength. It nearly obliterated us all in a matter of minutes."

"But...my parents did survive that, didn't they?"

"Sure, but only just." She shook her head. "If it had been a maker, I don't think any of us would have. It's easy to assume that you're strong when your only competition is what you see here on Mythralis. There are some truly powerful people here, like Aayara or Jacinth, but they don't exactly go show off in fighting tournaments. If you want to grow strong enough to face threats like what I'm telling you about, you need to leave here and see the rest of the world. Learn the things that have been hidden from you."

Wrynn shuddered again. "I'm sorry. I need to get into the pool and rest for a time. We can discuss this more in a few days, when I've recovered enough."

"Wait." Taelien reached out with his hand. "Exactly how much of my spirit would you need to buy yourself a few more weeks out here? I'm sort of on a tight schedule right now."

Wrynn took a breath and stepped away from the pool. "Not much. Just a small section. But you should know that as long as I have a portion of your spirit, we'd be connected."

"I'm not worried about that. I'm more worried about how much it might diminish my combat abilities, or if it would make me vulnerable to forms of spiritual attacks. Creatures like Daesmodin, for instance."

"You're right to be concerned about things like that." She took a sharp breath. "I'll have to be brief, I'm running out of time. Minimal loss of combat performance. You'll be weak to possession and such, but only briefly. Your spirit will heal itself within a few weeks."

Taelien nodded. "Do it."

Wrynn's eyes narrowed, scrutinizing. "You're certain?"

"I don't think we can wait a few more days to get started on finding that crystal you mentioned. And, I'd like to help you bear your burden, even if it's in a small way."

Wrynn sighed. "You're just like someone I used to know." She shook her head. "Fine. I'll do it. But you should know...this is going to hurt."

CHAPTER XIV – LYDIA V – IMMORTAL SORCERER

As the teleportation spell broke through Lydia's Comprehensive Barrier, her second barrier — the green, shimmering shield generated by Vendria — manifested beneath it.

Even then, Tarren's single spell left wide cracks in the second barrier, threatening to break through.

The next instant, Lydia flooded that remaining shield with additional power.

"Repair." A year before, when her incantations were slower and more focused, she wouldn't have managed such a quick response.

A heartbeat after that, she was lifting her cane.

Tarren blinked, taking a step back. "Unexpected. You'll have to forgive—"

Lydia twisted the top of her cane and pulled upward, drawing the steel blade within and stepping forward. She whispered as she moved. "Sorcerous Shield."

An additional barrier fell into place around her, replacing the Comprehensive Barrier that had broken.

[Be cautious, Lydia. That is no ordinary opponent.] Vendria's voice rang more clearly in her mind than usual, tinged with more than a little worry.

"Erik Tarren, I'm placing you under arrest." Lydia leveled her blade at his chest, but didn't strike.

Tarren snorted. "I think not. Do you realize who you're talking to? And where we are?"

"I'll take my chances with filing the paperwork with the Thornguard. You're clearly up to something."

"I'm always up to something, my dear. Several somethings, in fact. And I truly was just trying to help expedite your travel."

Lydia narrowed her eyes. "I'll take my chances with moving the old fashioned way. The last people I remember you teleporting ended up seriously hurt, and *I* still have the scars from my part in the rescue."

"Ah." Tarren winced. "I truly regret my part in that. I didn't intend...but it doesn't matter. I understand your reticence to accept. Fine. Don't trust me. But I'm not going—"

Lydia reached into a pocket at her side, then hurled a handful of dust at Tarren. He didn't react fast enough to get out of the way.

He didn't need to.

The dust passed right through him.

Lydia grit her teeth. "Detect Illusion."

The image of Erik Tarren in front of her began to glow, and she swung her head around, looking for the original. He must have swapped places with an illusionary duplicate just moments before, while they'd been talking — an illusion couldn't have handed her the objects just before that. Not unless it had been a solid illusion, which this wasn't, since her dust had passed through it.

She found another Tarren standing in a corner nearby, watching her. He also was glowing, indicating that there was an illusionary effect over him as well. He could have been another fake, or simply disguised; her Detect Illusions spell wasn't that specific.

I should have kept that spell active earlier, but it doesn't matter now.

She ignored the Tarren she'd been talking to and marched toward the second one.

He frowned. "You're not going to take me by force, either. I can keep this up longer than you can."

"I'll go get my squad, then, and we'll make this complicated. Is that what you want?"

Tarren raised his hands in surrender. "Fine, fine. I'm not going with you, but I'll answer *one* question for you that I shouldn't. Any one question. Be careful what you ask for."

"You're distracting me again. You could flee the area and leave illusory duplicates while I ponder."

Her Detect Illusion spell might identify such duplicates, but she couldn't be certain. Sufficiently advanced tricks could fool her spells.

Tarren shrugged. "False on the first, true on the second. I could be doing that, but I admit you've actually put me in a bad position. I do not want you to bring your squad in here."

Lydia was about to ask "why", then realized that might have counted as her one question.

Then, she realized that even asking if it counted as her one question could also count as one question.

What is it with old sages and their ludicrous riddles and games?

[That's the same in any world, believe me. We had our share of them on Rendalir, too. Including a whole deity dedicated to that sort of thing...no, several deities, really. The Fateweaver was particularly obnoxious, but he also had his children, and there's also the Apparition, and the Jester...]

Rendalir? Is that where you're from?

[Ah, yes. Forgive me. I have remembered much. I will share the pertinent details with you soon.]

Lydia took a moment to think, never taking her eyes off Tarren.

Any insights?

[The obvious question is 'Who is the Shrouded One?'.]

True, but he already said he didn't know that. It might be a waste of a question if he was being honest before. Maybe I could go with something less direct, however.

[You could also dig deeper on personal information, like 'What do you know about my father?' or 'What do you know about Taelien's past?']

Both tempting, but I'd like to stay focused here.

"You seem to be concentrating very hard, Miss Hastings."

I could take my chances with trying to capture him and interrogate him at my leisure, but the chances of success are low, and the chances of actually holding him for any significant period of time are even lower.

But if he's going to play this game, I don't have to accept it on his initial terms.

Lydia wrinkled her nose. "Five questions."

Tarren gave her a strained smile. "Three questions. And that is my final offer, I'm in no mood to barter."

She nodded. She would have accepted two. "Very well. If I sense any hint that you are deceiving me, however, our deal is off."

"Understood." Tarren leaned up against the nearby wall. "Shall I give you some time to consider?"

"Just a moment. Detect Truth."

Lydia didn't actually have a truth detection spell. She'd spent months attempting to get one to work, but she'd run into many obstacles. Knowledge sorcery didn't seem to have a clear way to discern objective truth, at least as far as she'd been able to find through her experiments and researching previous attempts at similar spells.

That left attempting to determine if the target thought they were telling the truth, which was possible, but generally required casting something on the other person that would give a signal if they were being deceptive. The flames used in the court of Xerasilis were an example.

She *did* have a spell for making people glow when they were knowingly attempting to deceive someone, but she would have to touch Tarren to execute it, and he almost certainly could fool it with illusions. Deceptions and sight spells were the bane of knowledge sorcerers everywhere, which was what made people like Tarren — and Jonan — so irritating to counter.

Sensory-enhancement spells used to pick up verbal and physical tics were also possible, but generally involved other types of sorcery, rather than knowledge.

So, in short, she didn't cast a truth detection spell at all. She simply acted like she was casting one and hoped Tarren wouldn't notice.

Meanwhile, the *actual* spell she was casting took effect.

A line appeared between the paper that Tarren had given her and the current Tarren she was speaking to.

It was a tracking spell — one that drew from the dominion of knowledge to trace the caster of an active spell effect, like the one on the piece of paper Tarren had given her. The glowing arrow that she could see overlaying her vision would show her the location of the real Tarren, which meant that she'd be able to tell immediately if he'd teleported away in the middle of the conversation and left a duplicate behind.

Tarren raised an eyebrow, presumably reacting to her saying "Detect Truth". He was a famous scholar of sorcery, and there was a high chance that he'd know how difficult and unreliable truth sensing spells were. That was fine. All she needed was to sow some seeds of doubt in his mind. If he thought there was *any* chance she'd detect a fabrication, he'd be less likely to attempt to deceive her.

Probably.

She didn't have a complete model of his personality. Perhaps he'd be the type to try to test if he could lie to her...but she didn't think so. He seemed to sincerely want to avoid any further conflict or investigation, and she was counting on that.

"What are your questions?"

"Give me a moment." Lydia folded the paper he'd given her, tucked it in her bag, and withdrew a blank page and a pen. Then she began to write.

"Let me stop you right there. If you're trying the 'what are the answers to all the questions on this page list' trick, I'm not going to answer that." Tarren laughed. "I do appreciate the effort to squeeze as much information out of me as you can, I'm not some elemental being bound by a sorcerous pact. Your three questions are three questions, don't try to artificially extend them."

Lydia folded the note she'd been writing, then tucked it back away. "Very well, then. I will be more direct."

Well, it was worth a try.

[It would be a good strategy for dealing with a Gatherer of Knowledge. Many of them are quite literal with the terms of their agreements.]

Three questions.

I'll need to prioritize the ones that give me the broadest information to act on.

Tarren was probably expecting them all to be broadly related to her current investigation, but he'd never said that they had to be. There were plenty of options to ask about.

Events in the ancient past. His current goals, and why he was hiding them.

Those were all intriguing and potentially important. But she had something to ask that had far greater significance in the grand scheme of things.

I don't want to scare him off with my first question, though, so I should keep that simple and within his expectations.

"Who is the powerful backer for the Shrouded One that you were concerned about?"

Tarren sighed. "You can't make this easy for me, can you? Fine. To the best of my knowledge, the Shrouded One is being supported by the Blackstone Assassin."

Lydia felt a shiver run down her spine. She was about to ask if he was certain, then she recalled that would count as a separate question.

Jacinth, the Blackstone Assassin. Once he set his eyes on a target, their fate was sealed. Even gods could not escape his judgment.

That certainly explains why Tarren wouldn't want to antagonize him. And why Aayara might be willing to provide Taelien with the name of the Shrouded One — she may be playing us against her legendary rival. They're always looking for ways to earn advantages against one another.

Tarren gave her a strained smile. "I can see you understand the implications of that knowledge. Do us both a favor and do not spread it further. You will only put more people at risk."

Lydia tightened her jaw. "I will take that into consideration."

I don't like keeping information like that to myself, but...

[Is this Blackstone Assassin truly that dangerous?]

If the legends are true, you could make a pantheon out of the gods he's put in their graves. And in terms of mortals, you could probably fill a city with his victims.

[Can you stop him?]

I don't know.

Honestly, I'm not even sure I should try.

The Shrouded One is the priority. She's the one who orchestrated the attacks against my own people...unless she was acting on his orders.

That would complicate matters significantly.

"Next question?" Tarren asked, sounding impatient.

"Right. Allow me a moment." She unconsciously tightened her hands, then released them.

"What methods do you know for humans to achieve immortality?"

Tarren gave her an appraising look, then broke into a deep laugh. "I'm impressed. Most people would have focused on their immediate investigation, but you thought about broader questions."

"There will be other ways for me to gain information on the Shrouded One and her patron. Now that I'm aware of who we're dealing with, I need to take the opportunity to ask you about things that might benefit humanity as a whole."

"You're just like her." Tarren smiled. "Very well, then. Since you asked for 'methods', I'll tell you a bit about a few. Not all the details. Neither of us has the time for that."

Lydia nodded curtly. "Go on, then."

"First, in all cases, I should note that what most call immortality is a misnomer. None of us have truly solved eternal life. We have, however, discovered methods for addressing the problem of aging. I could get hit by a carriage, just like anyone else."

"Understood. Your methods are effectively similar to the rethri, then."

"Some are, some are not. Pausing aging like the rethri most closely resembles Edrick's method."

Lydia perked up at that. "You are aware of the methods used by the other immortal sorcerers, then." She was careful to phrase it as a statement, not a question.

"Yes. Edrick preserves his life through the use of a dominion bond, similar to the 'coming of age' ritual undergone by the rethri. Obviously many humans have tried that method; he's simply the one who managed to make it work. But his method, like every other, has flaws. Edrick *is* aging, just very slowly."

Lydia nodded. "Go on."

"Hartigan would be next, then. I suppose you already know his methods?"

Lydia smiled. "Perhaps."

"Ah. Seeking to use this as confirmation that I am speaking the truth, perhaps? Very well. Blake began with attempting to find an alchemical solution, much like the people of Tyrenia. He succeeded for a time, but found the results...unsatisfying. His modern method is actually quite brave — he isn't immortal at all, in the conventional sense."

Tarren looked wistful for a moment. "You have heard of Kelryssia, yes?"

Lydia raised an eyebrow at the surprising shift in tone. "Of course. She was one of the worldmakers. An ancient goddess of destiny, long dead."

"Indeed. And, notably, the ancient deity most strongly associated with sorcery itself. She wove rituals without equal. When she learned of her own coming death, they say she wove a ritual into the stars themselves."

The stars? Does he mean that literally or figuratively?

"Go on."

Tarren sighed. "The goal of her ritual was to ensure her own resurrection. The full details of the ritual are unknown, even to me, but her intent seemed to be to revive herself with the fullness of her power and knowledge. If she could not prevent her end, she sought to circumvent it. A clever strategy, but ultimately, it did not work as planned." He sighed. "The details of that story go well beyond the scope of your question. But I have studied what Kelryssia sought to accomplish, as have many others. And Hartigan made it the foundation of his immortality strategy."

Lydia raised an eyebrow at that.

"Hartigan has learned to control his own cycle of reincarnation. Each time he is reborn, he retains his full memories. A member of his family who is aware of his secret finds where the child version of him is born, then retrieves him. He lives in seclusion until he is able to present himself as an adult."

"That is...interesting, thank you." The story confirmed bits and pieces of what Hartigan had told her, but it provided additional context that she was missing. Hartigan had not entrusted her with the entirety of the secret, but she had gathered enough to believe Tarren's explanation contained large portions of truth. "Please, continue."

"There are other methods besides those. As I mentioned, Tyrenia has a method of alchemical life extension, but some call it unsettling. And then there's the Xixian method of reanimating corpses...one might call that a form of immortality, in a certain sense. Artinans extend their lives through some method of empowering their body with the strength of their spirit, but I confess I do not understand the full details of how that works. House Theas and House Ta'thyriel have also experimented with using spirit sorcery. Of course, there's also godhood. The Tae'os Pantheon was reportedly mortal, once."

"You're not going to tell me your own method."

"Am I not?" Tarren shrugged. "I believe I have said enough. I have no desire to give you insight into my personal strengths and vulnerabilities. That concludes my answer on this subject."

He's implying he's using one of the methods he already explained, then? Hm.

Interesting, but not worth a follow up question.

In truth, he's already given me more than what some Sytirans have discovered in a career worth of study. I need to report this.

But first, the most important question of them all.

"What is the current location of each of the gods of the Tae'os Pantheon?"

Tarren reached up and rubbed his forehead. "You really want to make this difficult for me, don't you?"

"You must understand that as a Paladin of Tae'os, the current status of my gods is of the utmost importance. They have been absent from world affairs for too long."

Tarren sighed. "Perhaps they have a good reason for such behavior."

"I suspect so. But if you know something, I would like to hear it. I need to draw my own conclusions."

"That may be true...and perhaps it is time." He turned away for a moment, then back to her. "You will not like the answer."

"I need to hear it, regardless."

He waved toward the nearby table. "Sit down, please. I won't flee, I promise. Not before I've answered this question, at least."

Lydia narrowed her eyes at him. "Don't teleport me anywhere else, either. No tricks."

Tarren gave a sad-sounding laugh. "Ah. Of course."

[He sounds sincere to me.]

Agreed.

With that feeble assurance, Lydia moved to take a seat near the table, and Tarren sat across from her.

He leaned forward, tapping his fingers against the weathered wood. "There is no Tae'os Pantheon. Not anymore."

Lydia froze.

Tarren gave her a sad smile. "I told you that you wouldn't like the answer."

She leaned forward. "What do you mean, *there is no Tae'os Pantheon?*"

"They lost." He drew in a deep breath. "And they scattered. The survivors, that is."

Lydia's hands clenched tight. "The sword..."

"Aendaryn could no longer wield it. Not without his right arm."

Lydia winced. "But is he..."

"I spoke truthfully when I told young Taelien that I did not know Aendaryn's fate. Perhaps he lived, terribly injured. But the day he gave me the child and the blade marked an end. In truth, it was only one ending of many, however. Others had fled long before."

"Fled? Where and why?"

Tarren turned his head away. "Two left for other continents. One to hide, and another to raise an army to continue a doomed war. Three chose to change their allegiance, or to simply abandon the battle entirely. And of the last..."

Lydia gave him a faint smile. "He remained, biding his time, with the flimsiest of all portmanteaus as his name."

"It really is obvious, isn't it?" Tarren laughed. "When the others picked 'god names', they went with things they found fancy. I just used a nickname. At that point, I had no reason to hide my mortal identity. I was the oldest, and I had quite a reputation even before we ascended. Ironically, that was what made me the most naïve. I never believed I would have a reason to hide."

Tarren leaned back in his chair after that, his expression distant.

So, it's true, then.

One of the gods that she had worshipped since childhood sat in front of her, a being of legendary power and grace.

And he looked *old*. Exhausted.

Like there was too little of him left to live a human life, much less a divine one.

He had been right. This was not a revelation she welcomed.

Her next words were wistful, as she reminisced.

"When I was at the university, we'd joke about the similarities between 'Erik Tarren' and 'Eratar'. Since you were both legendary figures, there were always a few people who thought you might be one and the same. Of course, most people thought you were simply named after him, like how Keldyn Andys is named after Aendaryn. I know a priestess who named all of her children with variants of Tae'os names, it's not uncommon."

Tarren closed his eyes. "I would prefer that people continue to believe the latter, at least for the moment. It is easier for me to operate in silence, as much as it displeases me. I enjoy tricks and games less than I let on. They are, at this point, an unfortunate necessity."

"*Why*? Why must you hide?" Lydia felt her usual stoicism crack. "What happened? Even if you are the last, why can't you..."

"I'm not a fighter, Lydia. I never was." Tarren rested his hand on the table, scratching the wood. "I wandered the world. I saw things of great beauty and wonder. And I wrote books, hoping to spread my knowledge and joy with others." He shook his head. "Hiding the truth is the furthest thing from what I want. It is antithetical to everything I stood for...but, god or not, I am powerless. There are things that even my knowledge cannot change on my own."

"But you are not alone!" Lydia leaned forward, reaching out. "Please, allow me to help you. Your paladins and priests, we can—"

Tarren winced, pulling away. "You cannot help me, child. Not yet. There may be a time when you have that strength...but not now." He shook his head. "I am sorry, Lydia. There is a time and a place to fight, and it is not now. Not for me."

"But you have a plan, yes?"

And in that old man's tired eyes, she saw the slightest hint of a spark. "Oh, yes, Lydia." His lips curled. "I have *many* plans."

***

Lydia left Erik Tarren's home with a mix of emotions whirling within her.

Pain was the first and foremost among them.

The Tae'os Pantheon is no more.

She had already known that there was a chance that Aendaryn might have died. This conversation had not changed that, but it had told her something far worse.

Some of them switched sides.

There was no question in her mind what "sides" meant. Vaelien was the only one that could have injured — and potentially killed — Aendaryn. Unless some foreign god from another world had gotten involved, and Tarren had given no hint of such a thing.

He hadn't explicitly said that any of the gods had gone to work with Vaelien directly, but it would have explained a great deal. How Aendaryn had lost, why others had fled, and why Tarren himself was so cautious about revealing information.

Perhaps the deity that she herself worshipped — Sytira — was a traitor. If so, then Tarren's reticence to share anything with her made a high degree of sense.

But he *had* helped her. Ultimately, he'd told her a great deal, and she sensed that he'd wished to say more.

Erik Tarren — no, Eratar, God of Travel and Freedom — had told her just a hint of his plans.

She hadn't liked them in the slightest. But she *had* understood them.

He was right about one thing, even if she might have disagreed about certain details.

I need to find Taelien.

And so, she lifted the comical piece of paper he'd handed to her with an arrow and "Wrynn Jaden" written on it.

And as she turned, the arrow moved. It was a tracking spell etched into the paper.

She might have taken him up on his offer to simply be teleported there, now that she had a better idea of who she was dealing with...but she still disagreed with his methods.

Unlike Eratar, she had not given up on her friends.

Aladir awaited her outside the building. "Everything go okay in there? I was about ready to order the others to raid the place."

Lydia wasn't sure how to answer.

The pain had cut her deeply, but there was something else in what he'd told her.

A hint of hope. That spark within his eyes that hadn't quite burned away.

She'd fan that flame in any way she could, or she would make her own fire.

She'd save this world with or without the gods.

Lydia smiled at her partner. "It was awful. But I've learned a great deal. And we have a lot of work to do."

CHAPTER XV – JONAN IV – BRANCHES

Jonan rapped once on the house's door.

Moments passed, then he heard two knocks and a scratching sound from the other side.

He knocked once, paused, then three more times.

The door opened. Velas stood behind it. "Could have just used the earring."

"I'm a traditionalist." Jonan definitely was not a traditionalist, but he hadn't been thinking about the earrings, and it was as good an excuse as any.

Velas moved out of the way and Jonan stepped inside the house. He closed the door behind him.

"Everything secure?" Velas asked.

He nodded. "As far as I can tell. This place is equipped with a sight-blocking enchantment, but it won't stop Aayara if she's the one looking."

"If Auntie Ess is the one who wants my shrouds to switch to the funeral variety, I'm going to be wearing that outfit pretty quickly either way." Velas grimaced. "Still, I appreciate you looking out for me. More than I can say."

Jonan shrugged. "You'd do the same for me."

She probably wouldn't, but he felt obligated to pretend.

"Right. You find anything of interest at that spooky secret library of yours?"

"Plenty." He walked by her and sat on the nearby couch. This house wasn't the nicest one he had access to, but it *did* have a decent couch. And, more importantly, it was purchased under one of his more obscure alternate identities. He hoped that might delay anyone looking for him (or Velas) that was familiar with their more typical disguises. "Nothing that seems immediately relevant to your situation, however. Plenty of references to Silks over the years — and by years, I mean centuries — but nothing that seems applicable to your situation."

"I'll take what I can get." Velas flopped down on the other side of the couch, then sprawled out to take up all the empty space. "What about in that weird future part?"

"There are a few Silk references in there, but nothing that mentions two Silks being around at the same time."

"Well, out with it. What's it say?"

"There's a reference to a failed heist on Hartigan's Star in which both Symphony and Silk were involved."

Velas raised an eyebrow. "Auntie Ess failing a heist? I know Hartigan has to have some impressive security for his most valued possession, but..."

"Yeah. It also says something about how Symphony and Silk 'changed' after that, but not a lot of details. It's toward the end of that particular book's timeline. I couldn't find any 'history' books that go any later."

"Hm."

"Hm, indeed." Jonan turned away. "Sorry I couldn't be of more help."

"No, you're good. Just giving me a place that's a little more obscure to hunker down is useful. Most of my safe houses are back in Orlyn and Valeria. I haven't worked in Selyr in ages; you know the lay of the land better." She took a breath, then coughed. "Mite dusty in here, though."

"Sorry. Haven't cleaned the place in...uh, three or four years. I could hire someone?"

"I'll take care of fixing the place up." She waved a hand. "Least I can do. Aside from the books, you got any other angles to chase down this other Silk?"

"Problem is that Aayara has a colossal reach. She's got a whole city named after her. This other Silk could be a veteran Thornguard, a promoted agent of the Orchestra, an orphan she plucked off the street...or someone else operating with that name that she has nothing to do with."

"What are the odds that Aayara would permit someone to use that name — even briefly — without her permission?"

"She's not omniscient." Jonan tapped on the couch. "But it'd be a terrible risk for whoever is playing that game. I suppose Jacinth could be dangling bait for her. I've heard...very little about him lately. And given their famous rivalry, it's long past time he makes some sort of move."

"Fair point." Velas sniffled, then rubbed at her nose. "Ugh. Going to have to do something about that dust soon." She paused. "Okay. Can I beg you to look into this through some more traditional means?"

Jonan sighed. "I have some Thornguard contacts I can ask. But the more I dig, the more likely we end up in a direct conflict."

"Good."

Jonan blinked. "Good?"

"I don't want to die after sipping wine from a glass. I don't want to die choking on a cloud of gas. But a fight?" She gestured toward the Heartlance, lying up against a nearby wall. "I'll take my chances against any other Silk in a fight. I just need to get her in front of me."

Jonan narrowed his gaze. "I'll see what I can do."

***

The invasion occurred without the slightest warning. The city council building exploded in an inferno, followed by much of the palace district. Velthryn responded to the disaster promptly, but incorrectly. Fire brigades were sent to the sites of the disasters, and of course some of the local guard went to investigate...but not a full military response.

No one had the slightest hint of what was truly happening until it was too late.

As rescue forces reached the scenes, they were promptly slaughtered. Only a small contingent of off-duty paladins who had been near the scene managed to survive and escape. Without their warning, Velthryn may have fallen without even putting up a proper fight.

But even that alert came far too late. They did not have the slightest hint of who they faced.

Botheas. His sorcery was on a scale that had not been seen since the vanishing of the gods, and he leveled it against the people of Velthryn without the slightest hint of restraint.

Within days, it was clear that the battle against him was a lost cause. From there, efforts turned away from triumph and toward an effort that once might have been unimaginable — evacuating the most powerful city in the known world.

Jonan closed his book and set it down on the table to his side, then yawned and rubbed at weary eyes. It had been another long night.

He was reading the third book he'd discovered that dealt with this time period — the "Fall of Velthryn", which supposedly took place two years in the future.

In all cases, details were vague, but they mentioned someone — "Botheas" — who destroyed the city with unparalleled sorcerous power.

Jonan had never heard of a Botheas before.

A pseudonym, then? Or a title, rather than a name? Or maybe a name from a non-Velthryn language?

Xixian, maybe? There could still be remnants of the Xixian Empire on other continents, or even just a small contingent here. There was that one esharen we found in Orlyn...

"More poison?" Taer'vys asked, lowering his own book just enough to examine Jonan. His soft tone didn't betray a hint of humor, but the corner of his mouth was just slightly askew.

Jonan waved a hand at him. "No, thank you." He took a deep breath. "What are you reading today?"

Taer'vys lowered his book again. The writing on the cover was in a language Jonan didn't recognize, which was a rarity.

"A primer on the Edrian Empire on the continent of Kaldwyn."

Jonan raised an eyebrow. "That's quite the jump from your usual perusal of forbidden arts and ancient secrets."

Taer'vys gave him a fuller grin. "Call it a personal research project."

"Hm." Jonan sighed, slipping the next book off his pile and into his lap. He didn't open it. "Isn't that something you could read when you're not in the restricted archives?"

"You'd be surprised how much *isn't* out there." Taer'vys waved to the doorway back to the library proper. "And how rare it is to get a chance to peruse these things. I'd advise you to make the best of it. Maybe spend a few extra weeks on 'researching the Shrouded One'."

"Meaning I should spend a few extra weeks so that you can have access to this place longer without having to request it for your own personal use."

"Precisely." Taer'vys paused. "But for your own benefit as well, of course."

Well, at least he's honest about his goals. Or some of them, anyway.

"I don't think I have that long. This is a somewhat time sensitive matter."

"Unfortunate, but I suppose we must all do what we can with the time we're given."

Jonan raised an eyebrow at that. "Is that supposed to be as foreboding as it sounds?"

Taer'vys just smiled. "You never know."

"Ugh. Fine. Be like that." Jonan sighed. "Unrelated question. One of my compatriots, Silk, is supposed to be in the city." He had to calculate his next words carefully — even if he hadn't been drinking tea that was doused with a truth-forcing poison, he trusted that Taer'vys seemed like the type to be able to evaluate obvious lies. "Have you heard anything about her whereabouts or recent activities?"

Taer'vys raised an eyebrow. "Isn't she another one of Aayara's agents? I'd trust that you'd know more about her than I do."

"Things are...complicated when you work for Aayara. She plays a lot of games. One of her favorites is 'deprive my own agents of information and see how they handle it'. I have other ways of reaching out to Silk, but simply asking someone who might know is often the easiest route."

"Is this the sort of 'game' that ends poorly for uninvited participants?"

Jonan smiled. "Ah. I don't think a simple request like this would involve you too heavily. This is more of a time saving measure on my part."

"I note you didn't answer my question."

Jonan smiled. "Correct."

Taer'vys leaned back. "I want in."

Jonan blinked. "You...excuse me?"

"The game. I'm not looking to *avoid* whatever Aayara is playing. I want an introduction."

After a moment of consideration, Jonan responded with, "I can make some arrangements...if what you provide is sufficiently useful."

"Excellent. I'll have something for you within a week. Unless you need something sooner?"

Jonan hesitated, then shook his head. "No. A week is fine." He trusted that he could keep Velas from running off and doing something foolish for that long, but not much longer. "That reminds me. Did you set up the meeting that I requested?"

Taer'vys nodded. "My adjutant, Mairead Caelan, will accompany you to a meeting place for the Disciples of the First in three days. She'll provide you — or rather, your new identity — with an introduction. From there, you'll need to establish yourself with the local branch."

"What did you end up going with?"

"Thornguard working for Velthryn's division. You're here to meet with the Shrouded One and report...something. You can come up with the details. You've been to Velthryn more frequently."

Jonan grunted. "What Thornguard Division?"

"Blackstones." He watched Jonan as he said it, clearly evaluating his reaction.

Jonan sighed. "*Really*? You're making me an assassin?"

"You looked like the type with some experience with wet work. I figured you could manage it if you need to." Taer'vys' tone was as soft and even as always, but his eyes showed a hint of amusement.

"You know they're going to want me to...ugh, fine." He rubbed at his temples. "I'll make it work."

"I'll be interested to hear the results." Taer'vys set his book down. "You *will* be reporting back to me on your findings, won't you?"

Jonan shrugged. "We'll see."

Taer'vys eyes narrowed for just a moment. "I suppose we will." Then he went back to reading his book.

***

Three days came and went.

Jonan sent some important messages to some of the mirrors he'd left behind in Velthryn. The first was to a private residence, the second was to a Thornguard base.

Need you to get out of town quickly and quietly. Stay gone until I contact you again. Can't explain the details right now. It's going to be a little messy for a while, sorry. Will update soon.

Scour,

Going to need you to do some clean up and information control. Details will be sent shortly. High priority work related to Symphony. Will need a report as soon as it is completed.

-Scribe

After each of those brief notes, he sent a list of instructions.

This is going to cost me some favors, but it's a necessary precaution. I hope they can get things done soon. For now, more reading.

His studies continued throughout that time, focusing on the unusual "historical" records that the Disciples of the First used, but with some time dedicated to his own personal studies as well.

He was simply too curious about the items in the crystalline cases not to give them a look at least.

There were a total of eight compartments, but only four of them currently appeared to be occupied.

With a moment of concentration, Jonan's vision changed, and he realized there was a fifth occupied case — the item inside and identification card were simply both invisible.

Every single compartment had runes carved into the sides, making them dominion marked items in their own right.

Jonan examined the contents of each box.

The first contained what looked like a simple metal rod.

Xixian Artifact Remnant

This scepter was found heavily guarded within a Xixian Vault, but with no indication of its purpose. It radiates tremendously potent chaos sorcery. It is believed to potentially be one portion of Cessius, the Staff of Dissonance, an artifact once wielded by the Xixian emperor.

Currently under research to authenticate its abilities, activation methods, dangers, and potential relationship with Cessius.

Jonan pondered that for a moment.

They say the Heartlance might be a part of Cessius, too. If this thing is another component, maybe they could be combined somehow...

He shook his head. He could look into getting it as a gift for Velas later, if he decided he wanted to risk looting this entire place at some point. At the moment, that was an unnecessary risk.

The next was a black-bladed dagger with a crossguard that looked like a stylized blue rose.

The Wilting Flower

This dagger is believed to originate from the world of Rendalir. It is one of the most complex dominion marked items known, possessing travel, ruin, shade, knowledge, spirit, and deception sorcery. It appears to shift to different locations inside its box when unattended. Our agents have reported disturbing feelings while carrying and studying the object, as well as unusual desires to remove it from its container.

Observe with extreme caution.

Jonan re-read the description, then decided he would absolutely not be opening that case.

The last thing I need is a potentially sapient dagger from another planet to worry about.

He shook his head, then turned toward the next case.

The third was a simple silver ring with a large red crystal.

Hartigan's Star Replica

This replica of Hartigan's Star was forged by the Blackstone Assassin as a "gift" for Symphony. As a reproduction of Hartigan's Star, it possesses deadly flame sorcery abilities. It can also be utilized to enhance the abilities of an existing flame sorcerer. The command word for activation is "Ignition".

At Symphony's request, the library is currently attempting to discern if the ring had hidden enchantments intended to be traps for the wearer.

Jonan snorted at the second line. That definitely seemed like the type of gift Jacinth would give Aayara, and he would be shocked if it *didn't* have some kind of deadly tricks built into it.

The fourth was a blue hat with a white feather.

The Hat of Tricks

This hat appears to be linked to an extra dimensional space that can be used to store and retrieve items, similar to the legendary Jaden Box. One can simply reach inside the hat and concentrate to attempt to pull out a stored object, or place a new object inside the hat to store it. When storing an object, one must think of a word that corresponds to that object in order to store it for later.

There does not appear to be a function that tells the user what objects are already inside, nor have we found a function for emptying it out entirely. As such, we have been asked to research what objects the hat already contains. Dozens of objects have already been found inside.

We currently have no indication of what the hat's maximum capacity may be, if any.

Do not attempt to wear the Hat of Tricks.

And finally, the invisible item. It was an amulet containing a single, heart-shaped crystal. The note read:

Amulet of the Unfaltering Spirit
Once one of Vaelien's personal possessions, this amulet was said to strengthen the connection between the wearer's body, essence, and spirit, bolstering all three. It provides near immunity to offensive death and spirit sorcery, as well as resistance to other effects which interfere with the wearer's essence.

This object is stored for research by vae'kes Saffron. No unauthorized research is permitted.

Jonan considered each, then made a choice that he knew would come with significant risks.

"Can we open these safely?" Jonan asked.

"Sure. I've got the code phrases. You can study them while you're in here, but you can't take them across the line." He gestured to the line in the floor. "You'd need specific permission for that, and given what you seem to be here for, I don't think either one of us is getting it."

Jonan nodded. "That won't be a problem."

After getting that explanation, Jonan dove into reading a bit in the journal entries about each item. From there, he had Taer'vys open the cases for the ones he wanted to look at in more detail, inspected the runes on each item, and took some of his own notes.

"I heard you'd done some research on dominion marks. Going to try to make copies of those items?" Taer'vys asked.

Jonan smiled. "Not exactly."

Working without letting Taer'vys know what he was doing would be tricky, but he wasn't going to squander a rare opportunity.

The void shield on the library will make anything I do in here virtually undetectable, hopefully even to someone like the Shrouded One. I need to make every moment in here count.

And so, while Taer'vys was distracted with his own books, Jonan did some subtle work. His arms and eyes burned in the aftermath, but that was a cost he was glad to pay.

Beyond examining the items in the case, he spent some time simply reading a few of the more obscure books he wouldn't ordinarily have access to. There was no reason *not* to study time sorcery while he had a chance, after all.

It would take much more than a few days of practice to learn to utilize it, but he had a foundation in the theory behind it now, and a smattering of knowledge about other obscure sorcerous disciplines the restricted section had offered.

I can see why Taer'vys likes this place so much. I'm going to miss it.

On the fourth day, he received instructions — and paperwork — for his latest persona, as well as a meeting point for his new contact.

At least a Blackstone doesn't have to wear full armor, he considered, *but I look ridiculous.*

Jonan was dressed in black utilitarian clothes, with a longsword on his left hip and a pouch containing a mask and supplies on his right. This wasn't an unusual outfit by Selyr's standards. It was quite similar to what Taer'vys had worn when they'd first met, in fact, although Jonan was missing the chain armor beneath the blacks...and, admittedly, he was also lacking Taer'vys' muscular physique.

It wasn't that Jonan was out of shape, exactly. Being out of shape implied he'd ever been *in* shape in the first place.

Regardless, the outfit served its purpose.

He looked exactly like the archetype of what one might *expect* a Blackstone to look like, with a few minor details to prevent it from being an obvious costume. A locket around his neck added some degree of personalization, as well as a well-worn pair of bracers. He'd picked up a sword that looked worn, but well-maintained. His boots contained two daggers, concealed just badly enough that someone *might* notice them.

Once he was as ready as he could be, he headed to the designated meeting point. It wasn't a sketchy tavern or a rooftop like he might have expected for a covert mission. Instead, he knocked on the door of an old blacksmith's shop.

"I'm here about the last-minute order," he said after knocking. The door slid open.

The woman on the other side was wearing a heavy apron and thick gloves. She had a wide, muscular build that looked suitable for the blacksmithing hammer she was carrying in her left hand. She didn't bother to set it down. "Mr. Calloway?" She shifted her weight as she asked, casually enough that it didn't appear too threatening, but Jonan recognized someone who was ready to swing a weapon.

He nodded. "And Miss...Caelan, was it?"

The woman relaxed just slightly. "Come in and close the door behind you. I'll get cleaned up."

Jonan stepped in, shutting the door. "I wasn't aware you did *actual* work here."

The woman snorted. "Taer'vys says that making weapons helps you learn to use them more intuitively. Really, I think he just wants me to pick up his family business."

Jonan nodded. "His father was a blacksmith, yes?"

"Yep. And he was, too, for quite a while. Both before the Thornguard and during a portion of his service." She set down the hammer, then moved about the shop rapidly, picking up tools and supplies and moving them into cabinets. Jonan waited patiently until she finished, then slipped off the apron and gloves. "You probably already know, but I'm Mairead Caelan, his adjutant."

Jonan reached out and clasped her wrist in a traditional greeting. "Vincent Calloway, Blackstone Division."

"Right. Sure you are." Mairead winked at him. "How much have you been briefed on?"

"Their holy scriptures. Very little about their numbers, organization, leadership structure, specific personnel, resources..."

"Ugh," Mairead grunted. "Leaving all the hard work to me, as usual. Fine. I'll walk you through it. It's going to have to be quick, though, if we're going to make it to tonight's meeting."

"Tonight's meeting?"

"Listen carefully. And when we're there, just follow my lead."

***

After speeding through a bit of explanation about the organization, Mairead led Jonan to an unexpected place to meet with the Disciples of the First.

Jonan was more than familiar with the structure — the Crescent Thorn was one of the oldest places in the city. It was an eight-story tower of dark green stone with a slight curve to the shape, giving Jonan the impression of a claw. The shape of it always made him nervous; it didn't look at all structurally sound. Sorcery was likely involved in the construction, but that didn't make him much less nervous. Sorcery was just as fallible as stone if you hit it in the right place.

That was not the part that truly made him cautious, though.

"This is a *temple of Vaelien*. What are they thinking, using a place like this?"

"I presume they're thinking they can get away with whatever they want, given their connections and supposed visions of the future." Mairead pointed at the top of the tower. "The Shrouded One lives up there, at least supposedly. I've never actually seen her."

Her? Interesting choice of words, there.

Jonan paused. "Does that imply she's someone involved with the Order of Vaelien? A high ranking priest or official?"

"Don't know. Haven't been able to get close enough to identify her yet. Only people who get to meet her are the ones that are performing tasks to insure the 'integrity of the future'."

"Hm."

"Hm?"

"I can work with that. Let's go to this meeting first, though."

She led him to the temple gates, but rather than bringing him in through the front door, they moved around the side of the building toward the back and then into a garden.

That garden gave way into an area with high walls of plants, causing Jonan to groan again.

A hedge maze. Of course there's a hedge maze.

"The meeting will be at the center. Stay close to me."

Jonan did stay close to her, but not where she expected.

A simple gesture while she wasn't looking created an image of Jonan — or rather "Vincent" — a few feet away from his actual location. He then made himself invisible.

He didn't expect to be backstabbed here, but precautions were important.

A few minutes of walking took them to the center of the hedge maze. Jonan tried his best to memorize the route so he could return without Mairead if necessary.

The center of the maze had a fountain with two statues above it. One represented Vaelien, raising his namesake sword skyward. To his left was a statue of a rethri woman holding a harp. Stories about her identity varied significantly, and Vaelien himself refused to address the topic. Jonan's personal theory was that she was Vaelien's queen back when he had been a mortal king, but historical records of that time period were notoriously unreliable.

He didn't have much time to think about religious theory. There were five people around the statue, all wearing the most stereotypical cult hooded robes he'd ever seen. Each of them also wore a blank-face mask, but with a slightly different symbol on the forehead of each: A gem, a sword, a flower, a shield, and a musical note.

That last one was particularly interesting; musical notes were generally used as code by the Orchestra, Aayara's organization of thieves. The particular note on this mask signified "doctor".

The use of that note might have been a coincidence — Aayara wasn't the only one who used musical symbols, of course — but it was worth noting.

Jonan mentally labeled all of the robed figures based on their mask symbols and resolved to look them up later.

Flower Mask stepped forward. "This is the newcomer?"

"Not a newcomer, exactly." Mairead waved for Jonan to step forward, and he did. "Vincent is visiting from our division in Velthryn."

"Here to beg for more support?" Sword Mask asked.

Jonan shook his head. "Not at all. I'm here to report something important. Something that needs to go to the top of the chain."

"We'll determine if that is necessary," Gem Mask replied. "What can you tell us?"

"Precious little." He had to measure his words carefully. "You're aware of the failures about ten months ago?"

The hooded figures looked at each other, then looked back to him. "Your division reported that as a success."

He shrugged. "Political talk. It was a *limited* success. Some pieces remained on the board."

"This is the first I've heard of such a thing." Sword Mask folded his arms. "Are you meaning to imply that we were given inadequate information before?"

Jonan shrugged. "I don't know exactly what you were told, but the fact of the matter is that we lost agents and left a mission incomplete. I have an important update to deliver on that subject. Given how pressing certain issues are with Velthryn in the coming months," he left that line to linger for a moment, "I'm sure you understand the need for everything to be *perfect*."

There was a moment of silence. Some of the figures leaned in to whisper to each other.

Jonan heard them anyway.

Velas hadn't managed to teach him *much* sound sorcery, but amplifying and focusing his hearing was among the easiest spells possible.

"This is likely about the Theas incident," Gem Mask whispered. "I was under the impression that was being dealt with by a third party."

"Some random underling shouldn't know about that. And I've never heard of this 'Vincent' before." Sword Mask replied.

Flower Mask replied. "He's probably one of Sterling's. That man is awful about keeping secrets. I don't know why he'd be coming back here, but we need to know what he knows."

Mairead smiled and raised a hand. "Can we head in and deliver the report directly?"

"What's your connection with this, Miss Caelan? I wasn't under the impression you had contacts with the Velthryn branch."

Jonan waved a hand. "I approached her. My superior listed her as a first-layer contact for this city. I wasn't just going to show up here and talk to you without an introduction."

Mairead shot him a questioning look. That wasn't *quite* what they'd discussed before, but now based on the whispered contacts, he wanted to create an impression that he was already well-established in their organization.

Fortunately, she adapted quickly. "He followed proper protocol. He hasn't reported anything to me directly, but he made it clear that this is a correction, and that needs to be addressed by a proper authority."

"A correction...?" Gem Mask folded his hands. "Of what nature?"

"I am pleased to report a successful historical correction. Two, in fact." Jonan smiled. "I am, of course, required to deliver the evidence of something of this magnitude directly."

"Evidence? What exactly do you have to deliver?"

Jonan grinned. "Two coffins. Occupied."

CHAPTER XVI – VELAS IV – A VARIETY OF SILKS

Velas had a variety of skills, but waiting patiently was not among them.

It might have been the safer option to lie low and wait for Jonan to bring her the answers she needed, but that simply was not her style. And beyond that, she had certain obligations and loose ends to take care of.

As Aladir and Lydia made their way out of the city, she stepped out from behind a tree and into the center of the road. They both reacted quickly, reaching for weapons before they realized who they were looking at.

"Velas." Lydia lowered her cane, shifting back to a neutral stance. "Where have you been? Rialla has been looking everywhere for you."

I bet she has. Especially given she's currently the most likely suspect for another Silk trying to replace me.

"Been a bit busy." Velas gave a strained smile. "Things went bad with my little investigation. I asked our mutual friend to send you a message."

"He did, but it was painfully vague." Lydia folded her arms. "You could have at least written a note yourself. Would have helped verify that you were actually safe. A message from him might have just been buying time to hide a body."

"Please. You think that scrawny boy could handle me?" Velas laughed.

Lydia wrinkled her nose. "Poison doesn't care how strong you are. As I'm certain you know from experience."

Velas had plenty of ways to deal with poison, but she didn't need to let Lydia in on that.

Instead, she simply nodded and tried unsuccessfully to look apologetic. "Fine, fine. I'll be more careful. The important part is that I'm here now, checking in." She patted her arms. "See? Fully intact."

Aladir took a few steps forward and poked her. "Seems like it."

"Hey!" Velas smacked his hand aside. "What was that for?"

"Checking if you're actually here." Aladir smiled. "That's easy enough to fake."

"True enough." She sighed. "Look, I'm sorry I vanished for a while. But I'm going to have to do it again."

"Reason?" Lydia asked.

"I'm being hunted by someone dangerous."

"All the more reason you should come with us." Aladir gestured toward the road. "Harder to find you out there, and we'll have considerable protection."

Lydia shot him a look and Aladir went silent.

"Protection?" Velas snorted. "I don't need protection. I need to find the person who is looking for me before they find me."

"That's reckless." Lydia frowned. "And if it's tracking that you need, I'm the one who should be doing it."

"Thought of that. I don't have anything for one of your tracking spells to hook into. Not yet. Maybe I'll come to you if I find something and my leads dry up before you get back to town."

"We could be gone quite some time," Aladir noted. "You'll be on your own."

"No, I won't be." Velas shook her head. "I have backup."

"The 'scrawny lad' you dismissed a moment ago?" Lydia adjusted her glasses.

Velas gave a shrug. "I'm not asking him to fight someone for me. He's good at what he does. And I think we have a lead on the location of the Shrouded One."

"And you were going to tell us about this when?" Lydia took a step forward. "That's pretty important."

"Easy, there. We just found out, and I need to verify it. I'm going to do it soon. But, in the spirit of cooperation, I'll tell you what I know. Rumor is that she — and they said 'she' — is on the top floor of the Crescent Thorn, at least some of the time."

Aladir looked at Lydia. "That's a holy site. She must have considerable influence if she's up there."

"Noted." Lydia turned to Aladir. "Perhaps we should all head there before we leave? This seems like an important enough opportunity to delay our other task."

"Let me handle it. As Aladir said, it's a holy site. I can get in. A couple of paladins aren't going to make it through the front gates without causing suspicions. If you spook her, she might flee."

"That's a fair objection, but we could lay a trap for her. You could lure her outside, perhaps, or flee to us if you get in trouble or injured."

"If you set up anywhere nearby, you'll be noticed. I honestly don't think this is worth your time. My lead could turn up nothing."

Lydia glanced between the two of them, then nodded, mostly to herself. "Aladir. Stay here. Coordinate with Velas. Velas, try to lure the Shrouded One back to Aladir so that you can confront her as a team."

"That's going to make this more difficult for me, not less." Velas sighed. "But I suppose having a healer on-hand in case things go badly isn't terrible. Fine. I'll handle it. But you're going to have to be cautious, Aladir. If you're caught looking suspicious right outside, it's going to make things much messier for me."

"I'm rethri. If I throw on some dark clothes, no one in the city is going to give me a second look."

He had a point.

"Okay. We'll make it work." She turned to Lydia. "Where are you headed?"

"Wrynn Jaden. She supposedly has information that might help us. And Taelien is with her."

Velas felt an unexpected tightness in her chest. "Wait. Sal? I knew he was in the region, but…"

"He's on an unrelated assignment. Or, one that we thought was unrelated, at least. Aladir can fill you in on the details. I'm going to get going."

"You going to be safe on your own?" Velas asked.

"As I said, I'm going straight to where Taelien is located. And Asphodel should be there, too."

Velas hesitated for a moment.

Lydia must have caught something in her expression. "You look like you have something you want to say."

"Mm... Lissari keep you healthy."

"You too." Lydia raised an eyebrow, but said nothing further. "Take care of her, Aladir. And yourself."

"Always." Aladir gave Lydia a nudge. "See you soon."

***

"Let me send Jonan a message to inform him we're going to have company. Then we'll get you some new clothes."

"No need, I already have a civilian outfit." Aladir motioned to the backpack on his back.

"In dark colors?" Velas raised an eyebrow. "You don't seem like the type."

"Black is one of the Tae'os Pantheon's colors, you know. Blue and silver are more prominent, but it's still one of them."

"Sure, but you worship Lissari. I'd expect more green."

Aladir laughed. "I'm a paladin, not a divine fashion model."

"Is that an actual occupation?"

"It could be."

Velas snorted. "That's quite an image. Anyway, give me a minute."

She wrote Jonan a note, then used the mirror to send it.

"That's quite a useful device." Aladir motioned to the mirror. "Have you considered making one that conveys sound?"

"Yeah, but it's not the best medium for it." She thought about her earrings, but managed to avoid reaching up toward one of them. She wasn't sure how much she wanted Aladir to know. "You sure you want to be with me and not with Lydia?"

"The mission is what matters. And frankly, you're much more likely to need healing."

"I'm pretty sure I'm offended by that."

Aladir shook his head. "Don't be. You're simply on a more dangerous assignment. It's not a reflection of your abilities."

"Fair enough, I suppose. Wait, was that a mirror pun?"

"You're bright to have noticed."

"Ugh."

The puns continued until she found a suitable place to hide.

***

Velas introduced Aladir to Jonan, but it wasn't necessary — they'd met before, if only briefly.

Jonan kept giving Aladir strange looks, but that wasn't out-of-character for Jonan, so Velas tried to ignore it and focus on the plan.

"I'll hit the Crescent Thorn tonight. Aladir, you'll be waiting a few blocks away, inside this blacksmith shop." She pointed to the map. "You may want to check it in advance. Jonan, can you introduce him to that adjutant?"

Jonan ran a hand through his hair, then took off his glasses to wipe them with a rag. "Yes, but please be cautious about including Mairead or Taer'vys in this. We don't really know their angle."

"But they're definitely investigating the Shrouded One?"

"Sure, at least on the surface. But if the Shrouded One turns out to be a ranking official in the Thornguard — which seems highly likely — Mairead might take the Shrouded One's side."

"And what about you? Wouldn't you do the same?" Aladir asked.

Jonan paused to consider the question. "Depends."

"On?" Velas asked.

"Who they work for. Keep in mind, I'm not actually a Thornguard. I simply work for someone connected with them."

"That's an understatement, but I'll forgive it." Velas sighed. "Fine. You don't even have to be at the shop, if you need deniability."

"Actually, I was considering going up with you." Jonan cracked his knuckles. "I can help keep us concealed while we go through the building."

Maybe, but...

She shook her head. "I'm not planning to go *through* the building."

"Ah." Jonan nodded in understanding. "Yes, I suppose that would be a more expedient route. And I couldn't keep up. Should we try to do some long-distance scrying on the place before you head over there?"

"It's a black spot for scrying," Aladir explained. "Lydia had it on her list of places to look at for signs of Sterling."

Jonan frowned. "That means they have someone with void sorcery. Or at least a void enchantment. That's going to make this considerably more dangerous. Sterling could be there himself."

While the other two looked nervous about that prospect, Velas found herself smiling.

Maybe I'll get another shot at him soon, then.

"Perhaps this is a bad idea, if there's any chance of Sterling." Aladir glanced off to the side. "We could wait for the others to return."

"Not a chance. Every day we wait is one more day they have to search for us. Proactivity is important here. Besides, Sterling isn't infallible. Now that I know who I'm dealing with, I can prepare for him." Velas glanced at the Heartlance, then toward Jonan.

"No." Jonan shook his head. "It's a bad idea."

Velas rolled her eyes. "I'll just bring it as a precaution. I won't go straight after him. Promise."

"Do you know if that weapon will work against a vae'kes?" Aladir gestured to the spear.

"Only one way to find out."

She got a pair of disapproving looks for that line, so she raised her hands in a warding gesture. "Fine, fine. We can be smart about it." She waved at Jonan. "You can throw an invisibility spell on me right before I leave then wait at the shop with Aladir."

"The invisibility won't last long if I'm not there to maintain it. I'm much more of a sight shaper than a caller, and I need to be near you to keep reapplying the effect."

"I think I might be able to extend it myself, if it comes to that. But I don't anticipate this taking long. This should just be a quick jaunt, in and out. I don't plan to engage the enemy."

"Void sorcery could wipe out the invisibility," Jonan pointed out.

"It's probably not covering the whole building. And if it is, I'll get out fast. Very fast."

"Even if you see the Shrouded One?" Aladir asked.

Velas hesitated. "Depends on the situation. I don't expect her to be wearing an identifying badge. I might not even know if I've seen her. But I'll plan to disengage if I'm attacked, and I'll be prepared for a fight if I have to. Just in case."

"Sounds safe enough. I don't think we have to be overly worried about anything." Aladir nodded.

Velas and Jonan exchanged looks, then Velas looked back to Aladir.

"Never say that."

***

The stylistic slope of the Crescent Thorn made it easier to climb, at least for a motion sorcerer.

Velas approached in the middle of the night, wearing the garb of her Silk identity. Unlike when she'd approached the Thornguard fortress, however, she'd brought the Heartlance with her. If there was any chance at all that Sterling was present, she wanted to be ready for him.

I've practiced for this. I can handle him.

"Eru volar proter taris." A defensive field of essence surrounded her, powered by the dominion mark Jonan had helped her link to her old armor. She found using it a little frustrating, given her bad memories of the armor, but it had worked well enough against Susan Crimson. She wouldn't turn down an extra bit of protection against whoever she was up against now.

Surge.

She blasted herself upward, along the side of the sloped tower wall. While driving the Heartlance into the side of the building like a climbing spike might have made the ascent easier, she decided against it. She didn't want to trigger any defensive spells on the building or alert anyone that she was present.

She landed on a ledge, then jumped again. Fortunately, there were outcroppings with standing space for each floor.

I don't know how anyone could live in a building with a slope like this. Must get absolutely nauseating.

Surge.

She boosted herself upward again and again, until she reached the top floor.

No windows or exterior doors on this level. They must have been at least somewhat concerned about someone using this method of entry.

She blasted herself upward to the roof, landing atop it. From there, she planned to search for a hatch.

When she landed, she discovered she was not alone.

Across the rooftop, Velas saw something uncanny. The woman wore silken veils covering her face and upper body and carried an oaken staff. The remainder of her garb was simple blacks, with a pouch and a few knives visible on her belt. Two more knives were sheathed in her tall leather boots.

The build, the outfit, and even the woman's casual stance were almost identical to her own.

Even the oak staff looks like when I had the Heartlance concealed, she realized. *She's an excellent reproduction.*

Velas took a few steps closer, remaining cautious. She kept the Heartlance ready. "Silk, I presume?"

The other woman stepped closer, but she was still a good thirty feet away. It was a large rooftop, and a precarious one, due to the building's awkward design. An obvious doorway leading to a stairwell was visible on the opposite end of the roof, near where the other Silk was standing.

"You're looking at her." She rested her staff against the ground. Velas couldn't see through her veils; they seemed to have the same one-way obscuring enchantments that her own veils did, or at least similar ones.

If I can get close enough to tear them off...

"I'm afraid that's my title at the moment, unless you haven't heard." Velas inched closer warily, searching for any signs of other possible attackers.

Sharpsight.

She couldn't quite manage a full invisibility detection spell yet, but Jonan's lessons had given her enough of a foundation to enhance her vision somewhat. The basic spell would help her catch the telltale distortion waves in the air that often signified the presence of an invisible opponent.

The other woman remained still, at least for the moment. "That's where you're wrong, little pet. I've had that title for a long time. Someone else just keeps trying to give it away."

Velas paused, frowning. "You're not intended to replace me, then?"

"Oh, gods forgive me, no. No, that isn't it at all." The other woman broke into hysterical laughter, bending double at the waist. "...Is that what you thought? You poor child. She hasn't told you anything, has she?"

Velas wrinkled her nose, understanding reaching her. "You're a previous Silk, not a new one."

"Is this truly news to you?" The other Silk lowered her staff, then began to walk closer. "She didn't send you for me?"

"No. Not directly, at least. I'm not here for you...or maybe I am."

Velas frowned. "Are you also the Shrouded One?"

The other Silk kept walking, pausing just about ten feet away. "Oh, yes. That's one of my newer titles. It was just 'Shroud' at first."

"Why Shroud?"

"Well, I'd very nearly died, you see. Terrible fire, I won't bore you with the details. After I recovered, I discovered that our mutual master had replaced me with a new Silk. Rather than going back to Aayara immediately, I spent some time trying to discover who had masterminded the attempt to kill me. As I'm sure you know, returning to Symphony in failure would not have endeared her to me."

Velas nodded curtly.

"Imagine my surprise when I learned that my dear mentor was the one who had orchestrated my demise. And so," the other Silk tugged at her veils, "I allowed her to believe that she'd succeeded. And this became my burial shroud."

"Poetic. I like it. But what was her motive?"

"Paranoia, I presume. She doesn't like it when her dear 'children', as she calls us, begin to get close enough to her skill level to threaten her. Jealousy, maybe. Her lover's eyes wandered toward me from time to time. Or perhaps just sheer boredom." She sighed. "I wish I knew. But it's far too late for justifications at this point. She betrayed me, and now I'm repaying her for it."

Velas shifted the grip on her spear. "With this...can I say 'cult'? I feel like that's rude, but you have a cult."

The Shrouded One laughed. "Now, now. We're not a cult. We have a book. Several, in fact. I'd inform you of the details, but alas, we're running short on time."

"Time?" Velas tilted her head. "What do you mean?"

"There are places I need to be. And, sadly, I can't have you interfering with things." Silk lifted her quarterstaff. "I'd say there's nothing personal, but that would be a lie. You're wearing my old outfit and name."

"I could change outfits, if it'd get you to share more of your plan." Velas grinned.

"I'd like that, but I'm afraid not. I'm probably going to kill you here, but I won't make the same mistake my mentor did. If you happen to escape, or if those glimmering earrings of yours are actively sending a message..."

They were, in fact, active and sending the sounds of their conversation to Jonan.

"...I can't allow whoever is on the other end to know any more details."

Velas took a step back. "No comradery for another Silk, then? Not going to offer me a chance to join you?"

"Distrust is the first and the last lesson that Aayara ever taught me. Perhaps if I'd reached you sooner, we could have come to some arrangement. But things are too delicate now to allow you to interfere. I can't have more variables in play."

"You're presuming an awful lot about how easily you're going to beat me."

The Shrouded One raised a hand. "Let me explain one more thing, then, just so you understand. I'm not just *a* previous Silk. I'm the very first to bear the title, aside from Aayara herself. You won't be the first Silk I've killed."

Black flames formed around the Shrouded One's outstretched hand. "You won't even be the first *Velas Jaldin* that I've killed."

Velas had always prided herself on her speed. Even when fighting against Sterling, she'd managed to follow his movements — it was his strength and impervious body that had been the main problem.

When the Shrouded One moved, she couldn't see it. Not because the Shrouded One had gone invisible; her enhanced vision would have noted the blur.

No, her opponent was simply so fast that she didn't process the movement, even when she'd been looking straight at her.

Something cracked in her chest, and then she was flying backward from the force of the impact.

Her veils were on fire.

She screamed, even as she flew backward to near the edge of the roof. With one hand, she drove the Heartlance into the stone, arresting her movement. With the other, she tore the burning veils off her face.

She'd never liked them, anyway.

The Shrouded One appeared right in front of her, putting a finger under Velas' chin. "Sorry to end it so quickly. I know you—"

Velas slammed her forehead toward the Shrouded One's face. She couldn't see exactly where she was aiming, but she hoped to break the woman's nose.

The Shrouded One moved again, appearing twenty feet away. She was still far too fast to follow. "My, my. Still have some fight in you?" The Shrouded One discarded her staff, which was now broken in the center. "No matter. It'll be over soon enough."

Velas coughed, clutching at her chest. She'd been hit hard, but the armor spell from her dominion mark had absorbed some of the force of the blow. Without it, she suspected a blow with that amount of power would have crushed her ribcage.

Even with the protection, she was hurting bad. She mentally thanked whatever gods that were listening that her opponent was, apparently, the monologuing type.

Then she flipped the Heartlance over and tapped the bottom of it against the ground. Golden lines began to flow up the surface of the spear, then onto her hands.

Her mind and body quickened.

When the Shrouded One moved again, this time she could see it. But she *still* wasn't fast enough to get out of the way.

Not without sorcery, at least.

Surge.

A blast of force carried her out of the trajectory of the Shrouded One's strike. As she landed, she thrust at the Shrouded One's side. Her opponent batted the jab out of the way with ease.

"I've always wanted one of those." The Shrouded One stepped in, grabbing the shaft of the spear with her right hand. "I think I'll keep it."

Velas yanked on the weapon. It didn't move.

The Shrouded One raised her *other* hand, this one still swirling with black fire. Then she pointed her palm at Velas' chest.

Jump.

Velas shot into the air, still gripping the Heartlance, and narrowly avoided the jet of black flame that shot into the space where she'd been standing.

She didn't let go of her weapon. Neither did the Shrouded One. A moment later, Velas felt herself torn from the sky as the Shrouded One pulled with absurd force.

Velas directed her fall.

Surge. She blasted herself feet first into the Shrouded One's chest.

The Shrouded One took a step back at the impact, but otherwise barely reacted. Velas braced against her opponent with both legs, pushing, but she *still* couldn't wrench the spear free.

She's as strong as Sterling or Taelien. Maybe stronger.

Velas kicked upward with one foot, but the Shrouded One grabbed her ankle.

The Shrouded One's hand was, of course, still on fire.

Velas screamed again, then shifted tactics.

She released her grip on the Heartlance, still screaming in agony, and moved her hand in front of the Shrouded One's face.

Burst.

A blast of kinetic energy rippled out of her hand with enough strength to shatter stone.

The grip on her ankle released.

Velas dropped to the ground, rolled, and concentrated on the black fire that was spreading up her pant leg.

Push.

The flames separated from her clothing and body, then dissipated in the air.

When she grabbed for the Heartlance, however, she found it missing.

She looked up just in time to find the Shrouded One looming over her. "Now, that's interesting. I rarely see motion sorcery powerful enough to move other spells these days. You have quite a talent."

Velas began to push herself to her feet, only to find the tip of the Heartlance at her throat.

"Ah, no. Don't think my curiosity is going to permit you to leave."

Sound. Form. Behind.

"I won't be permitting *you* to leave either, my dear. Your long years of running are at an end." Aayara's voice echoed behind the Shrouded One. It was, in Velas' opinion, one of the best impressions she'd ever managed.

"Sorry, little Silk. I can sense sound sorcery — Aayara teaches all her apprentices that. You don't have any friends here. And, if you're anything like me, you probably never had any true friends at all."

The Heartlance moved — but not toward her.

It vanished entirely.

The Shrouded One did spin, then, but not toward the sound of Aayara. She growled and hurled a blast of black fire toward someone or something that Velas couldn't see, save for a distant blur.

Jonan?

Velas' heart pounded in her chest as she searched the area. Had her rescuer just been obliterated? She couldn't see them in the wake of the blast.

So, she did what came naturally and threw a punch at her now-unarmed opponent.

Burst.

She enhanced her punch with motion sorcery, adding to the force of the impact. It hit the Shrouded One hard enough to knock her back a step, but otherwise didn't seem to cause any damage.

Except to her fist. Her knuckles cracked and bled from the force of the impact...and that was with her armor spell still active.

The distraction of the punch was all she needed, though.

The Shrouded One had stopped commanding the black fire and turned back toward her.

Velas made a rude gesture with her right hand and smiled. "Bye, now."

Surge.

She carried herself backward with a blast of force and off the edge of the building. As she flew backward, she pulled a knife off her belt and hurled it.

The Shrouded One flew after her, hesitating only a moment to deflect the thrown knife. That moment was just long enough for a wall of ice to appear in the Shrouded One's path.

Ice? That means...

Velas made it off the roof and began to fall.

The Shrouded One blasted through the wall of ice and jumped off the building to follow her.

There were no further taunts, then. The Shrouded One blasted herself in front of Velas with a surge of motion sorcery of her own, then threw a mid-air punch.

Velas didn't have the Heartlance, but she did still have the enhanced speed it provided. That allowed her to follow the swing and grab her opponent's arm.

"Now!" Velas yelled. The Shrouded One began to slip away almost immediately, but Velas held tight as long as she could.

A blast of ice hit the Shrouded One from behind, just as Velas had hoped. The ice began to spread rapidly, encasing her opponent's arms around the shoulders.

Got her.

Velas used her free hand grab for a knife, then jammed it into her opponent's chest.

The knife didn't break her opponent's skin.

Then the Shrouded One snapped the ice around one arm and touched a hand to it. "Useless. You still haven't figured out what you're up against, have you?"

The ice vanished. Not burned by flame, not teleported away...it vanished as it was absorbed by the Shrouded One's touch, serving to further fuel her strength.

And then Velas understood, too late, the nature of her foe.

Surge.

Velas tried to blast herself away, but the Shrouded One grabbed her with her left hand, arresting her movement.

Another blast of ice hit her from behind, but the Shrouded One absorbed it again, and faster this time.

Velas still couldn't see her ally, but she knew who was trying to help her. "Shiver! No more ice! She's a vae'kes!"

"Shiver, hm?" The Shrouded One pulled her close. "I'll remember that."

A moment later, their arms still intertwined, they hit the ground.

Surge.

Velas used motion sorcery to slow their descent just before the impact, but she still hit the ground hard. Her already injured leg buckled, and she fell backward, the Shrouded One on top of her.

"That motion sorcery of yours is quite useful. I suppose I shouldn't let it go to waste." The Shrouded One put her hand around her throat, pinning her to the ground. "Mine now."

The Shrouded One's hand flickered, and Velas felt something spread into her, reaching into her essence...

No! I won't let you!

There was a *crack* in the air as the foreign essence met something inside Velas' body, the same power that she'd always used to expel poison and sorcery. The dominion within her that she'd never understood.

The Shrouded One pulled her hand back suddenly, then let out a *scream* of agony.

Huh.

Well, that changes things.

Then Velas punched the Shrouded One again.

Expulse.

She'd never been able to push that strange dominion out of her body without a medium. Fortunately, her knuckles were bleeding, and that was enough. Essence flowed through the injuries as her fist crunched into the Shrouded One's face.

The Shrouded One screamed again, falling backward, and Velas rolled on top of her.

Expulse! Expulse! Expulse!

Velas slammed her bleeding fist into the Shrouded One as fast as she could. On the last punch, though, her enemy managed to grab her wrist. The Shrouded One twisted hard.

Then Velas was screaming again as bones shattered and her strength faltered.

A hand grabbed her shoulder from behind.

"Teleport."

Velas found herself on the ground several feet away, with Rialla standing where she'd been a moment before. As she'd expected, Rialla was holding the Heartlance in her other hand. She'd teleported it out of the Shrouded One's grip earlier.

Rialla turned toward her and yelled, "Run!"

Without another moment of hesitation, Velas turned and started to flee.

...And fell immediately, as her injured leg failed her.

Rialla appeared next to her, then raised a wall of ice behind them. "I'm still awful at teleporting, sorry! I only think I have enough essence left to get one of us out of here."

"The spear." Velas gestured at the Heartlance, which Rialla was still carrying. "Please."

Rialla handed it to her. "You can't beat her."

"No, you're right." Velas tapped the spear against the ground, once again activating the Heartlance's speed-enhancing effect. "But I can make her bleed. Get going. Warn the others."

"No." Rialla shook her head. "You're too injured. I'm sorry. You need to go. I can hold her off and teleport when I'm recovered."

The ice vanished, absorbed by the Shrouded One. Then a knife cut through the air — the same one that Velas had thrown at the Shrouded One earlier.

It hit Rialla right in the chest.

"Oh." Rialla looked down at the weapon embedded in her chest. "Well...I guess that settles that."

"Ri—"

Rialla's hand settled on Velas' shoulder. "Take care of my brother."

And then the world blurred and Velas was gone.

CHAPTER XVII – TAELIEN V – BLIGHTED WOODS

Taelien absently rubbed at his left shoulder. There was little purpose to it; no amount of massaging the muscle and skin could restore the feeling that he'd lost.

A fraction of his spirit was gone.

It would regrow, true. Perhaps stronger than before. But for the moment, Taelien couldn't help but feel the absence of something ephemeral, something beyond ordinary senses.

He'd felt it when she'd *torn* that piece from him, and she'd been honest. It had not been pleasant.

When he'd told her that he could see the piece she'd removed in the moments before she sealed it into her own body, she's been only mildly surprised. "That's a good sign. Seems you've developed a hint of spiritual awareness yourself."

"Spiritual awareness?"

She nodded. "In my home back in Artinia, we strengthen the spirit throughout lifetimes of training. Our sorcery works somewhat differently there. The Seven-Branched Sword Deity and the Impervious Forest Goddess were quite talented at it. Perhaps you've inherited a hint of their spark."

"The lantern, I think." Taelien rubbed at his chin. "I've been noticing things more ever since I started testing it."

"I suppose practicing with items can help, but most people can't develop entirely new skills from it." Wrynn gave him a skeptical look. "You must have already had some talent beforehand."

Taelien shrugged. "Not that I noticed, but I suppose it's always possible. Can you teach me to do more with it? Maybe starting with how to resist other people tearing out bits of my spirit?"

Wrynn laughed. "Don't think you'll have to worry about that much, but sure. I can give you some basic lessons sometime, when we have a few weeks free." She took a breath. "Thank you, by the way. I feel much better already. Your spirit composition is different enough that it should help hold for a while."

"Different?"

Wrynn nodded. "You can see each of my spirit marks as being like a combination lock that the worldmaker has to crack if it wants to break out. The essence composition of each mark is the combination; the worldmaker needs to push opposing essence through to counter it properly. Your spiritual essence is sufficiently...odd...that I suspect it'll take some time to negate."

"If it's like a lock, does that imply it's useless if the worldmaker figures it out once?"

Wrynn shook her head. "Not exactly. The seals recover while I rest in stasis, as I mentioned before. Then the worldmaker has to spend the essence necessary to force their way through each and every seal to make progress. That means that every seal I add makes the process more difficult for the maker, but as long as they remember the necessary essence types for each seal, they can bypass the old seals relatively quickly."

Taelien rubbed at his shoulder more. "What keeps you from just adding a whole bunch of seals at once?"

"I need variety in terms of essence types. To go back to the combination example, adding two locks with the exact same combination would add a bit of protection, but much less than an entirely different lock. Ordinary people only represent the same few hundred sets of locks, based on the types of sorcery they have available. Powerful sorcerers offer me the most value, but as I'm sure you understand, they also tend to be the most reticent to offer up a piece of their spirit to another powerful sorcerer."

"Couldn't you explain the severity of the problem to a sorcerer's college or something?"

"I have." She shook her head. "It usually doesn't go over well, but I've succeeded from time to time. That's why I do have *hundreds* of seals already."

"The 'Witch of a Thousand Shadows'. They should have called you the Witch of a Thousand Souls." Taelien grinned.

"It's seven hundred and eighty eight now. But close enough." Wrynn stood and stretched. "Ready to go find a magic rock?"

"You bet. I love magic rocks." Taelien stood as well. "Where are we headed?"

"The Blighted Woods."

Taelien wrinkled his nose and began to head back to the tavern proper. "Isn't that place...uh, blighted?"

"I can shield us from the disease. We'll need to be cautious and get in and out quickly, though. There are things there that aren't going to be pleasant to deal with, and even with your contribution to my spirit, I'm going to have to be cautious. Every time I use a spirit art, this thing," she jerked a thumb at her back, "tends to struggle to break free."

"Spirit arts? Are those what your spells are called?"

Wrynn nodded. "That's about right. They're a little more complicated and flexible than what you'd call a spell, but sure, go with that. I have a lot of spirit arts I've picked up over the years, but most of them are inaccessible, because I need to use them to maintain the seal. More recently acquired spirit arts aren't as risky for me to use, since they're further from the center of the seal structure, but most of my strongest arts are the old ones near the center."

"Meaning you're at a significant combat disadvantage right now. That's...unfortunate. Could I help you acquire more of these...spirit arts?" Taelien asked.

Wrynn shook her head. "The piece of spirit you gave me serves a similar function, but broader. I could probably leverage a hint of your abilities, but given how...odd they feel, I don't think it's a good idea. And as I mentioned, your spirit piece is a useful lock. I shouldn't discard it."

Taelien nodded. "Do you know where the thing we're looking for is located?"

"No," Wrynn shook her head. "Not exactly. But I think I know who can help us find it."

They emerged from the vault and headed back into the tavern.

Upon exiting the back room, Taelien spotted someone, stopped, and stared.

"....Lydia?"

***

It had been close to a year since Taelien had seen Lydia last. She'd left for Hartigan's tower after the disastrous fight with Sterling, and he'd been assigned to his own tasks far from her. He'd wanted to visit, to see how her injuries had been healing, but...

Lydia lifted a single hand, the one that wasn't currently resting on her cane, and offered him a wave. "It's good to see you, Taelien."

He rushed closer, wrapping her in a hug. "Hey."

There was a brief pause, then she lowered her head to rest it against his shoulder. "...Hey."

He pulled her a little tighter.

"You're crushing me a little."

He released her, backing away. "Sorry, sorry. You okay?"

Lydia laughed. "I'm fine. Better, now that I can see you're actually here."

Taelien raised an eyebrow. "You're here for me?"

"In part." She adjusted her glasses, straightening her back and turning toward Wrynn. "Prime Lady Jaden, I presume?"

"Ay-yep." Wrynn flashed her a grin. "You can just call me Wrynn, though. I take it you're the famous Lydia Hastings?"

Lydia's grin slipped a bit. "I'm not certain what you mean by *famous*, but yes."

Wrynn walked closer and gave Taelien a nudge. "You didn't tell me she was a redhead. And cute! You and your dad have the same type."

Taelien and Lydia's jaws both dropped just a little.

Wrynn snorted. "You should see your faces." She slapped Taelien on the back, then whispered in his ear, "It's definitely true, though."

Taelien let out an exasperated sigh. "It's not like that, she's my commanding officer."

"Uh-huh. Nice salute when she showed up."

Taelien glared. "...And can you *please* never bring up my supposed father's preferences again? I *really* didn't need to know that."

"Oh, foo. Don't be such a baby. It's well known that the Impervious Forest Goddess had red hair." Wrynn folded her arms. "And, you know, his other—"

"Don't. Want. To. Hear. It." He put a finger over her lips.

Wrynn tried to bite him, but he pulled his finger back in time to avoid it.

"Well, you two seem quite familiar." Lydia reached up and adjusted her glasses again. They'd looked fine beforehand, so Taelien was pretty sure it was just a nervous habit. "If you wouldn't mind, is there somewhere I can sit?"

"Oh, of course! I didn't mean to be inhospitable. Please." Wrynn waved at the nearest table. "Where's Asphodel? I figured she was still helping out up here."

Lydia frowned. "She was supposed to be here, but I haven't seen her. Admittedly, I haven't been here long, though. Perhaps she's just sleeping?"

"Or maybe she knows something we don't and she's chosen to go off and do something secret. *Again*." Taelien sighed.

Lydia raised an eyebrow. "Has that been a particularly large problem of late, Taelien?"

"She's being even more vague than usual. Something's bothering her, I can tell. Something serious. I think she's afraid."

"Any idea what of?" Lydia tilted her head to the side. "Sterling, perhaps?"

"Seems likely, but I get the feeling it's more than just that." Taelien shook his head. "I don't know. But what I do know is that it's fortunate that you're here. Assuming you're staying?"

"For the moment, I believe I am. A certain irritating old sage directed me to Miss Jaden here."

"Old sage...?" Wrynn frowned. "Tarren? That old coot sent you to me?"

Lydia nodded. "Indeed."

"Wait, Erik Tarren? Did he tell you anything about..."

"Not much in regards to your background, I'm afraid. Some interesting revelations in the grander scale of things, but nothing I should talk about in the open. He did, however, tell me to inform you that he's in Selyr right now if you'd like to visit after your business is concluded."

Taelien took a breath. "Got it. Do you have an address?"

She passed him a note card. He slipped it in the pouch at his side. "Thanks."

Wrynn sat down on the top of a nearby table. "Well, if Tarren wanted you to come see me, we're in for something big. And probably not in a fun way. You got any ideas on what that might be?"

"I do, but...can we talk somewhere a bit more secure, if we're getting to business?"

Wrynn looked around the tavern, then sighed. "Fine, fine. Back to the back room. Follow me."

***

"Is this..." Lydia gestured at the door.

"Yep," Wrynn replied. "It's a Xixian vault. Or, it was, at least. I've repurposed it."

Lydia seemed to look at Wrynn with a new appreciation. "That is...quite an impressive boast, Miss Jaden."

"Wrynn, please. Miss Jaden was my sister." She gave a wink, as if making a joke that neither Taelien nor Lydia understood.

"Apologies if I offended." Lydia frowned. "Wrynn, then. You can open this place?"

Wrynn opened the vault door. "And there you have it. Please, step inside. It's secure."

Lydia glanced at Taelien.

"It's true. I've been inside a couple times."

They all stepped in. Wrynn whispered a few words and the vault doors closed behind them.

"Okay. Secure, from both physical and sorcerous threats."

Lydia nodded. "May I check a few things?"

"Be my guest," Wrynn waved around the huge empty entrance room. "My vault is your vault. Except, you know, that it isn't. Don't touch anything."

Lydia nodded absently. "Dominion of Knowledge, illuminate your sources. Dominion of Knowledge, detect the presence of void. Dominion of knowledge, detect the presence of sight..."

She continued mumbling spells for several more moments before nodding to Wrynn.

"It is satisfactory."

"Glad my place meets your approval. Now, what was all that about?"

Lydia sat down on the floor, then let out a deep sigh. "We were being scryed on. I detected multiple different spells watching us while we were outside. Potent ones."

Wrynn let out a string of curses. "You're certain?"

"Absolutely. At least one source from the direction of Selyr, another from..." She frowned, then pointed up and to the side, "This way. And a third I couldn't trace. I wasn't able to determine the specific person scrying in any of the cases. They all had countermeasures."

"Ordinarily, I'd have spirit arts active to detect that, but right now..." Wrynn sighed, shaking her head. "Your Mythralian magic is always so bothersome."

"Mythralian? Then, you're..."

Wrynn shrugged a shoulder and sat down across from Lydia. "Artinian, originally."

Taelien sat as well. "You were going to tell me about some of your background at some point."

"Sure, sure. Now's not the time, though. If your friend here is up for it, we should be getting on the road as soon as possible."

"The road? Where precisely are you headed, then?" Lydia winced, stretching out her bad leg.

"The Blighted Woods," Taelien explained. "We're looking for a crystal. One very similar to one you're already familiar with."

Lydia's eyes widened. "You found another one?"

"Wait, hold on. *Another* one? What haven't you told me, Sal?" Wrynn turned to Taelien.

"Ah, sorry." Taelien gave her an apologetic look. "I think Lydia would probably explain better." He turned to Lydia.

"I'm not entirely certain I'm comfortable discussing this matter, Taelien. She is not a paladin, or even a follower of our faith. And, meaning no disrespect, Prime Lady Jaden, but you are a somewhat infamous broker of information."

Wrynn waved a hand dismissively. "Why'd I be offended by that? 'Course I am. Still, tell me all about your rock. I'm dying to know."

"We can trust her, Lydia. At least on this matter. Her interests are aligned with ours and, well...she knew my family. Or, I mean, the gods that supposedly sired me."

Lydia blinked. "Pardon?"

"Yeah, yeah. Knew the Seven-Branched Sword Deity and the Impervious Forest Goddess. I'll catch you up on all that later. Honestly, don't need to know much about your rock unless it can help lead us to the other ones."

"Ones?" Taelien frowned. "There are more than two?"

"Should be three total," Wrynn explained. "Maybe four. We don't need them all right now, but I have a feeling that we're going to want as much information on these as we can before we leave."

"Why?" Taelien asked.

"Because, given that we were being scryed on, I'm pretty sure we're about to walk into a trap."

Lydia nodded. "I concur. I'll trade you some information. I need to know everything I've missed that Taelien is already aware of, and then, I'd like some insight on whoever you believe might have an interest in watching us. Their strength, disposition, location, allies, assets, enemies, weaknesses..."

"Excellent." Wrynn rubbed her hands together. "I love trades. And then?"

"And then," Lydia sat up a little straighter, turning her gaze to Wrynn, then to Taelien. "We set a trap of our own."

***

Hm. One part of a seasonal goddess, eh?

Taelien pondered what Lydia had explained to them about the stones as he walked.

Maybe we could put her back together. Not sure the Tae'os Pantheon would appreciate more competition, though.

...Assuming they're still around at all.

It was only mid-day, but the forest grew darker as they marched. There was nothing sorcerous about it; they were simply getting into an area where the tree cover was so heavy that minimal light managed to break through.

That did make it even harder to notice the shadows following behind them.

One of these days, I need to take a vacation and just fight in a tournament or something. None of this subterfuge, just someone in front of me I can swing a sword at.

Instead, he turned his attention toward Lydia. She was still walking with a cane, but she didn't seem to have much difficulty keeping up with them. He could sense a metal core inside the cane, too, indicating a concealed blade.

I approve.

She had an ordinary dagger on her hip, too, but he wasn't going to complain about someone having an excessive number of weapons. Wrynn had them both beaten in that regard; he could sense over a dozen knives in various parts of her clothing. And that wasn't even counting whatever she had in her newly-reclaimed box.

"How'd your training with Hartigan go?" He asked her.

"It was quite productive. I've learned the foundation of a couple new sorcery types and improved my existing skills substantially."

Taelien nodded. "Any new tricks you want to show off?"

"Perhaps when we're not on a time commitment. I have a feeling I may need all of my strength for the Blighted Woods."

"That's wise," Wrynn cut in. "We should all conserve our strength. The Blighted Woods are dangerous, even without other *concerns*."

They caught her meaning. "What can you tell me about the dangers in the Blighted Woods? The barrier around them has been up for centuries — do you know what's actually in there?"

Wrynn nodded. "In generalities, at least. I wasn't there for much of what happened, but I'm familiar with the origins of the blight itself."

Lydia gave Wrynn an appraising look. "There's been a great deal of scholarly debate about that over the years. I would be appreciative if you could lend some insight."

"Sure, sure." Wrynn paused, seeming to consider something. "Okay. Vendria told you about Rendalir a bit. Did she explain much about what happened there?"

Lydia slowed her steps, giving Wrynn an odd look, "A bit. Are you implying Vendria is connected to the Blighted Woods?"

Wrynn shook her head. "No, no. I mean, probably not? You probably know more about Vendria's history than I do. But the Blighted Woods is a Rendalir-related problem."

Lydia made an odd expression, then nodded. "How so?"

"Maybe start from the beginning, for my benefit?" Taelien asked. "I know Rendalir was another world, and that it was destroyed by one of its worldmakers. I know Vendria is from there. I don't know a lot beyond that."

Wrynn nodded. "Right. So, Rendalir was destroyed, but some people managed to escape — and a number of those people ended up right here on Mythralis. That didn't mean they were safe, however."

"They were followed," Lydia added. "The Sun Eater came after them."

Wrynn turned toward Taelien. "So, the Sun Eater was the worldmaker that was directly responsible for Rendalir's destruction — but he also had followers. Some were humans who simply chose to serve him to save themselves. Others, however, were entirely different species. The karna are body-consuming shapeshifters, for example. And most importantly for our destination, there were two related types of creatures — ruinshades and vek."

"Vendria mentioned ruinshades, though only briefly." Lydia winced, bending over briefly to rub her leg. "A blend of a ruin elemental and a spirit, essentially?"

"More or less. More shade than spirit, but some of both. They served as the bulk of the Sun Eater's forces. They're essentially shadow copies of individual people, but entirely under the Sun Eater's control."

"Shadow copies of people. Lovely. And what were those other ones, then? Vek?" Taelien asked.

"Vek are worse. At first, the people of Rendalir believed Vek were caused by a disease — they called it the 'vek taint'. It manifested as strange symbols appearing across a person's body, spreading across them over time."

Lydia wrinkled her nose. "Like those tattoos of yours?"

"No, not like that." Wrynn smiled. "Nice try, though. The vek taint was facial markings, and they didn't look as lovely or organized as my tattoos. Anyway, they're not actually a disease; they're more like a form of possession. Vek are what happens when a ruinshade manages to claw its way inside a living human's body, gradually taking them over. Stronger ruinshades don't even need to inhabit the body directly; they just break off a small piece of themselves, and that piece is used to take over a person's body."

Taelien's eyes narrowed. "That sounds horrific. Is there a way to counter it? Banishment sorcery?"

"Only if you catch it fast." She drew in a breath. "And that was the problem with the Blighted Woods. You see, when people from Rendalir fled here, ruinshades followed — and *our* people had no idea what they were. And, when the ruinshades began to infect people, we made the same mistakes that the people of Rendalir did at first. We thought it was a disease."

Wrynn shook her head, sighing. "Several small towns had been entirely taken over before any help arrived. The first people who went to help were also taken over, and they began to spread it further, much like it *was* a disease. It took ages before we actually had enough information to act."

"You say 'we' — were you physically there?" Lydia asked.

"No, no. I'm using 'we' in the general sense of people from Mythralis. I'm not *quite* that old." She grinned. "Ultimately, it was one of the gods that intervened. Karasalia, the Impervious Forest Goddess. She saved those that were still capable of being saved. Rather than slaughter the others, she created a vast barrier around the area, sealing them inside, like one might quarantine a disease. She returned time and time again, trying to find a way to save those within...but she never succeeded."

Karasalia? My supposed mother?

He'd heard very little of her, given that she wasn't a member of the Tae'os Pantheon or associated with Vaelien. It was refreshing to hear a story that included her, even if it hadn't ended well.

"So, what about the trees?" Lydia asked. "I've heard the trees beyond the barrier are stark white and give off some kind of strange powder. Are they possessed by the ruinshades as well?"

"No, but it's a consequence of their presence. Vek don't require the same kind of sustenance that ordinary humans do; they absorb life energy from the environment. The trees were most likely altered to serve as long-term life sources, either deliberately or accidentally. I don't know the types of sorcery that were used, but I do know that the powder the trees emit is poisonous to ordinary humans. I have defensive spells that should help."

"Wait, hold on. Are you implying there are still vek living in there? After centuries?" Taelien asked.

"Oh, no." Wrynn shook her head. "It's only ruinshades we'll have to worry about."

Taelien frowned. "...How intelligent are these ruinshades? Do they have emotions? Societies?"

"Nothing to worry about in that regard. The average ruinshade is more like an insect, if even that. Maybe a golem would be a better comparison; they can follow instructions with some degree of intelligence, but they have no motivations of their own. Their instructions are implanted with a seed of dream sorcery, which was one of the Sun Eater's specialties."

Lydia made an odd expression at that, seemingly considering something.

Wrynn continued to explain. "Most vek are no more intelligent than ruinshades. They're little more than puppets. Vek made from ruinshades possessing beings other than humans are much smarter and more dangerous — but they're not something we're likely to run into. They're pretty rare."

Taelien gave a slow nod. "Back to the ruinshades, then. Wouldn't they be harmless, if nothing is controlling them presently?"

"No, they most likely still have a persistent instruction to kill or take over anyone they see. That order will continue until something changes it."

Lydia raised a hand to her lips. She had an expression of deep contemplation.

Taelien raised an eyebrow at her. "You're plotting something."

She raised a hand to her chest in mock offense. "Plotting? Me? You're mistaking me for Kestrian, I think."

Taelien snorted. "You were doing plenty of plotting of your own back in Orlyn, long before he got involved. But that's not an insult. I may prefer the more direct approach, but I can still respect using strategy. What are you thinking?"

"Please don't do anything foolish," Wrynn pleaded. "We do not want another vek outbreak. That wouldn't be good for anyone."

Lydia shook her head. "No, no, nothing like that. Merely considering possibilities."

Wrynn folded her arms. "Just don't let them out of the barrier."

Lydia nodded absently. "Of course. Now, how do we detect them? I imagine that the vek taint would not have been an issue if they're visible under ordinary conditions."

Wrynn nodded. "Yep, they're invisible to normal sight. I have the ability to sense shades and spirits, and it seems like Sal has been acquiring something like it, but you'll need to have detection spells active."

"Or just use Ulandir's Ghost Lantern." Taelien patted his backpack. "If they're spiritual entities, it should work, correct?"

"That's...not exactly right. They're shades, which refers to a different plane, but they do have spiritual energy. The lantern might work." Wrynn nodded. "We should use it. It won't hurt to try. I can detect them without it and warn us. But Lydia?"

"Hm?" Lydia was still wearing a thoughtful expression.

"*Please* don't let them out of the barrier?"

Lydia sighed. "Fine, fine. I just...haven't had a chance for field work in some time, and I was getting a bit excited. I will be cautious. If nothing else, this resource will be likely to remain here for future study long after we're done."

"I'm not sure I like the sound of that, either, but we'll talk about it another time. I'm going to try to make us invisible to them when we arrive, but just in case, be ready to fight."

A smile crossed Taelien's face. "Always."

***

Hours passed before they reached the barrier. Taelien spent a little bit of time chatting with Lydia as they walked, but he remained nervous about the shadows trailing them. That also limited the scope of what they could discuss.

Wrynn and Lydia spent some time discussing sorcerous theory, as well as varying categories and classifications of ruinshades and vek.

Taelien contented himself with anticipating the possibility of fighting a tremendous number of highly dangerous monsters, which he hadn't had a chance to do in a while.

The barrier itself was much more visually impressive than he'd expected. He'd been picturing some sort of ritual markings etched on the ground and a subtle field that couldn't be crossed by spiritual entities.

The actual barrier was a glowing dome of translucent blue energy that seemed to stretch for miles. He caught sight of the glimmer in the distance long before he approached, but seeing it up close was nothing short of awe-inspiring.

The power that it must have taken to weave something like this...

He ducked down to the ground, searching for the telltale markings of enchantment runes like those on Velthryn's city walls. He found nothing of the sort.

"How has this stayed intact for so long?" He wondered aloud. "Are there objects generating or securing it?"

Lydia approached, leaning heavily on her cane as she settled next to him. "You're not usually so interested in such things."

"Aww, are you interested because your mommy made it?" Wrynn poked him in the side. "You're adorable."

Taelien groaned. She wasn't entirely wrong, but he certainly wasn't going to admit that. "I'm *interested* because of the scale. I could see someone like Hartigan or Tarren managing something of this size for an instant, but how is it still here? Spells naturally disperse over time. I don't have to be a scholar to know that something is off about this."

Lydia winced as she knelt down, pressing a hand against the forest floor and whispering a few words. She'd apparently broken her habit for long, loud incantations.

"You're correct, Taelien. There's an intense concentration of essence underground in this area, but it's too deep for me to get any significant information. I can also sense that it's connected to something within the barrier, but I can't discern any details. The barrier itself is blocking me."

Taelien nodded, then offered Lydia a hand to get back to her feet. She accepted it without complaint.

"You two need a few minutes to catch your breath before we go in there?" Wrynn asked.

Taelien shook his head.

Lydia took a breath. "Just a few moments, if you please. I confess I haven't walked this distance in some time."

Taelien gave her a worried look, but she shook her head. "I'll be fine, just give me a few more moments."

She leaned up against a nearby tree.

Taelien gazed beyond the barrier, looking in at the strange, bleached white trees and grass within. He could see the powder that Wrynn discussed in the air; it looked almost like snow.

They rested for a few minutes before Lydia finally pulled herself away from the tree, walking to the side of the barrier. "I am ready."

Taelien came over next, resting his hand on his hilt. "Should I open it up, then?"

"Woah, woah, slow down there Mr. Swordy." Wrynn put a hand on his arm. "You probably *could* cut through this, but it's a bad idea. Ritual backlash. And you might end up collapsing the whole thing — we don't want that."

Taelien moved his hand away. "What's the plan, then? Dig a hole?"

Wrynn wrinkled her nose. "That might work, but I'd really rather not. No, we'll sorcery it right open. I was planning to do it myself, but with Miss Hastings here, it'll be even easier. Protection sorceress, yeah?"

Lydia winced, then nodded. "Not as much as I used to be, but yes. I believe I could reshape a section of the barrier to make a temporary hole, if that's your intention."

"Good. Be ready to open her up. First, protective measures. We don't want to breathe whatever is in there."

Wrynn reached into a bag at her side. "Retrieve: Purification Elixir." A bottle appeared in her hand, and she handed it to Taelien. Then she repeated the process twice more, handing a bottle to Lydia and holding one herself. "Drink up. These will help if we do end up inhaling anything from in there, or if any poisonous monsters attack us. They're not foolproof, but we're not going in there unprotected."

Taelien nodded, popping open the blue-green vial and downing it. It tasted like blueberries — far from the worst strange elixir he'd tasted over the years.

It brought back a memory of an old alchemist friend, one he'd hurt. But he brushed that memory aside to focus.

The other two downed their elixirs. "Okay. Get close." Wrynn instructed, and the other two followed her instructions. "Spirit Art: Eight-Part Barrier."

A shimmering field surrounded the group in the shape of an eight-sided polyhedron, which glimmered and rotated around them.

"This'll hold up against most spiritual threats, including shades. I'm going to have to expend a considerable amount of energy to maintain it, however." Wrynn took a breath. "Lydia, if you have any protection spells of your own..."

Lydia nodded. "Redundancy is important. Your spell seems similar to a Sphere of Exclusion, so I won't make another. I'll make an individual barrier for each of us, in case something gets through your field."

As Lydia tapped each of them and generated a field of glimmering energy of her own, Taelien raised a finger. "Problem. You do remember that my aura destroys protection spells, right?"

"Ah. That's...awkward," Wrynn admitted. "That's going to make this more difficult. We'll have limited time to work with."

"Should I wait here?" Taelien asked.

"No, there's a good chance we'll need muscle in there. We're just going to have to hurry." Wrynn waved to Lydia. "Open the barrier up, if you would."

Lydia nodded, approaching the titanic divine shield. "I hope we don't regret this."

"Don't be such a worrier, Lydia." Wrynn grinned. "If things go badly, I'm sure none of us will live long enough to regret anything!"

And on that note, Lydia waved a hand at the barrier, opening a hole in the field.

Taelien's hand rested on his sword as the trio walked inside.

***

The first thing that struck Taelien was the cold.

The sorcerous barriers that wrapped around the group did little to shelter them from the oppressive chill of the air and the wind that whipped against their skin. Fortunately, the snow-like powder stopped as soon as it blew against the rotating panes of Wrynn's shield. At least he didn't have to worry about inhaling some kind of death pollen.

As long as the barrier held, anyway.

Lydia tossed a pebble out of Wrynn's barrier, frowning as it flashed blue, then green.

Taelien raised an eyebrow, but kept walking. There was a clear path ahead, one unobstructed by debris even after what should have been centuries of disuse. That was suspicious, but there were few ideas Taelien hated more than breathing in death pollen, so he headed straight down the path.

As he walked, he unslung his backpack and opened it and reached inside, withdrawing a lantern. Then, after fastening his backpack back on, he closed his eyes and concentrated a spark of his essence into the device.

The crystal in the center of the device flickered, then brightened, shedding a grey-white illumination around the group. The light was heatless, giving it an unnatural feel, but it served two important functions.

First, it staved off the growing darkness of the wood, allowing them to see as they walked beyond sight of the shimmering blue barrier.

And second, with the lantern active, Taelien could more clearly perceive the shadowy figures that were beginning to amass among the nearby trees.

They were wispy figments of darkness, human-shaped but elongated and disproportionate. While at first he might have assumed the skewed proportions were a reaction to the light, much like a traditional shadow, more careful observation showed that some digits remained skewed regardless of the angle or intensity of the light shining upon them. Fingers and toes stretched and curved, seeming to end in vicious points.

In simpler terms, the shadows had claws.

Lydia took a step back after the lantern first illuminated them, drawing in a sharp breath. "They're everywhere."

"Just keep walking," Wrynn advised. "They're not likely to bother us if we don't bother them."

"Why?" Taelien asked. "Aren't they supposed to kill and possess humans?"

"My barrier is keeping them from sensing us properly. As long as it holds, they can probably tell something is here, but can't sense what it is. It's like we're holding up a sheet in front of ourselves, and they're not smart enough to know what is on the other side."

Taelien took an uneasy breath.

Given my previous experiences, the barrier is probably going to break at the worst possible time. Then it's death pollen and ruinshades for everyone.

He kept his other hand floating by the Sae'kes on his hip, just in case.

The shadows were utterly silent as they followed the group, but as they moved deeper into the woods, Taelien could hear sound up ahead.

It wasn't the simple noise of a surviving animal or monster, though.

It was the unmistakable cadence of a mournful song.

The words were in a foreign tongue, one Taelien had never heard spoken. But as the song carried through the woods, he felt something within them. A weight, like the burden of a lost world was carried within those sounds.

<Come to me, sing with me. You're too far away...>

Taelien's eyes scanned the woods, searching for the source. He still couldn't understand the words, but he could feel the intent behind them.

"It's a compulsion spell," Lydia hissed. "They're using dream sorcery to send messages directly into our minds. Try to ignore it. It's subtle enough that our barriers aren't stopping it."

"Can you do something about it?" Taelien asked.

"It occurs too quickly for me to reshape the individual messages and stop them. I could make a barrier that's completely impermeable to sorcery, but it wouldn't let anything else in, either — like sound or air. I can do that if it grows urgent, but we'll gradually suffocate, and we wouldn't be able to hear each other talk."

"Right. Lovely. Are we...heading toward the creepy singing voice?"

Lydia nodded. "Yes. I believe the crystal is in that direction."

"Good, good." Taelien sighed. "Only thing I like more than death pollen forests are *singing* death pollen forests."

"Don't forget frozen," Wrynn added. "Frozen singing death pollen forest."

"Right. How could I miss the most important part?"

They walked on, the voice growing stronger by the minute.

<Come to me, sing with me, sing the end of days...>

"I don't like it." Wrynn's expression darkened.

"I mean, I've heard worse. She sounds like she might be a bit out of practice, but—"

"Not the *quality* of the creepy death song, Sal. There shouldn't be anything here alive enough to sing like that. And ruinshades aren't exactly known for their musical genius."

"Hey, maybe one of them has been practicing. They've had centuries to do it, and everyone needs a hobby."

That didn't seem to cheer Wrynn up any. Instead, as he watched, the irises of her eyes seemed to twist briefly and change in shape from circles to a multi-faceted polyhedron.

"Um."

Wrynn winced, blinked, and her eyes went back to normal. "Hmm."

"Uh, what exactly—"

"Duck!"

Taelien ducked just in time to avoid a spear of ice that lanced out from the darkness ahead of them. His sword was in his hand a moment later, the destructive essence around the Sae'kes making a tearing noise as it crackled against the barriers around them.

He heard what sounded like a giggle from the forest ahead.

<Come on, come closer, just a little bit further...>

"Okay, nope. Done with games." Taelien walked ahead of the group. "Can you hear me, singer? You want to talk, you come to us. No more bewitching music, no more cowardly attacks from the shadows."

The music stopped in an instant.

<Cowardly, is it?>

The temperature around them dropped rapidly.

<A **game**, was it?>

Taelien heard a crack as the trees around them froze. Then, a moment later, the ones closest to them shattered like glass.

"Uh, Sal, I think you might have upset her."

"Yeah, thinking that might be the case, Wrynn, thanks." His grip on the Sae'kes tightened. "But I'm absolutely *done* with subtlety and tricks. That's never been my style, and I'm tired of it. Sometimes, when you're in an evil forest, there's only one thing to do about it."

Burn.

A burst of flame emanated from his right hand, surging up and mingling with aura around the Sae'kes. As the auras intermingled, the destructive aura shifted, taking on the properties of the flame.

His sword blazed with silver fire as he walked forward. "You want to sing? Fine. Come sing with us. We're right here."

A white blur descended from the sky, crashing into the ground in the middle of the path ahead like a meteor. As the blur landed, the stone path froze and cracked on contact, and the air around it fell still.

<You dare bring fire into my domain?>

As the blur shifted closer, the wind itself seemed to freeze in its wake.

It stopped a mere dozen feet away, solidifying into the form of a tall, blue-skinned woman. Her hair was a flowing sheet of ice, and her skin was translucent crystal, showing something white shimmering within.

In her right hand she held a halberd wrought from frost, and in her left hand she held a gleaming blue crystal. Strange dark markings were visible on her forehead, a stark contrast to the brightness of the remainder of her form.

She whipped her arm to the right, and a tendril of shadow erupted from it, lashing out into the shades that flanked the group. Where the shadow touched, the ruinshades changed, shifting in color to a blue-white and solidifying.

Then she moved her hand to the left, shadow striking out again — but Taelien was faster this time.

As he swung downward, a wave of flame shot forward, cutting the shadowy tendrils in two.

The icy figure hissed, stepping back.

<Go forward my children. Dance. Break them.>

The now-solid shadows on the right side of the group began to slowly advance from the trees, lifting their frozen claws.

Taelien smiled for the first time in days.

Finally, something I can actually fight. This is better.

He took a few steps forward. "I've got the big one. Handle the ice shadows."

"Uh, Sal, love you but no." Wrynn stepped up next to him. "You're not fighting her by yourself."

"Why not? I've got fire, and she seems to *hate* that."

Wrynn raised a figure. "Yeah, that's good. But remember when I said that ruinshades could *occasionally* possess things other than humans?"

The frozen woman floated closer, raising her halberd.

"Sure."

"Well," Wrynn winced. "I'm pretty sure *she's* what happens when a ruinshade possesses a god."

CHAPTER XVIII – LYDIA VI – WINTER

Vendria gasped in Lydia's mind.
[No, no, no. She can't be here.]
Please, be calm, Vendria. We are strong. We will handle this fight together.
[I...don't...]
Lydia couldn't focus on Vendria entirely. The frozen woman was striding forward, and the icy shades had begun to circle them.

Taelien ignored Wrynn's warning and charged straight at the angry possessed deity. This was, in Lydia's assessment, the least surprising thing that had happened in days.

The goddess didn't bother moving. Instead, the air around Taelien shimmered for an instant, then froze.

In a moment, he was encased in a solid block of ice.

Only then did the goddess raise her hand, pointing at Taelien's chest. A glimmering blue field appeared around her finger, growing larger by the moment.

"Taelien!" Lydia dropped her cane, reaching for a belt pouch at her side. She didn't have long to panic.

The ice around Taelien cracked. A moment later, it shattered into a thousand shards.

The goddess released her attack — a blast of focused darkness that seemed to warp the air around it.

Taelien cut the beam in half. The split blast streaked past him, careening into a nearby tree.

The tree withered where it struck. In moments, it was naught but white dust.

Taelien glanced back, saw the effect of the beam, then turned back toward the goddess and let out an appreciative whistle. "Nice. Wouldn't want to be hit with that." Next, he cracked his neck and stretched. "I can tell you're going to be fun."

Wrynn grabbed his arm. "Don't antagonize her. She's just warming up."

Taelien snorted at the pun. "Fine, fine. We'll end this quickly." He took another step forward, and again, his sword ignited with fire. "You want to go left, or..."

Lydia finished opening her bag and emptied it out. "Wind, rise."

A burst of wind carried the dust inside the bag across the battlefield, and with her mind, she controlled where it moved. If Wrynn was right, she'd need to do some subtler work to ensure the fight went the way they wanted.

Wrynn blurred forward, toward the left as Taelien had indicated. She smashed a fist into the frozen woman's form, sending the goddess staggering back a step. A glyph flashed in the air on the impact, but Lydia didn't have a chance to identify the strange symbol.

Taelien rushed to the goddess' right, swinging the Sae'kes.

The blade sliced through her halberd, then the center of her body, seemingly without resistance.

She slid into two halves. And, as the halves fell, her top half *screamed*.

Her body vanished entirely, leaving Taelien looking horrified. "That... shouldn't have happened. I was restraining the cutting aura, I wouldn't have..."

Lydia spun around, finding the goddess right behind her.

She barely managed to put her arms up and think "shield" before a frozen blast slammed into her.

Infectious permafrost, her Comprehensive Barrier reported.

She let out a gasp as she processed that, and noted the ice spreading further along the shield. She whipped a hand upward, blasting much of the ice clinging to the shield away with wind, but the few fragments remaining began to rapidly spread.

Then the frozen shades were upon them. Wrynn jumped in front of Lydia, smashing one apart with a bare fist. Again, a glyph flashed in the air on impact. Her movements that followed were a blur that was too fast for Lydia to follow, with individual strikes annihilating frozen creatures without difficulty.

Taelien rushed straight back for the goddess.

Again, his sword rose and fell, but this time she vanished before he even struck.

She reappeared right behind him, stretching out an already-glowing hand.

He spun, but not in time.

Lydia waved her hand. A gust of wind blasted Taelien out of the way.

That left the goddess to throw the blast of withering energy straight at Lydia instead.

Her barrier, already half-frozen, shattered the instant the beam came in contact with it.

Accelerated decay, her barrier reported as it failed.

Vendria's secondary shield flickered into existence just in time. The green, shell-like structure seemed to hold better against the blast, but still began to crack almost immediately.

It might have failed a moment later if the goddess wouldn't have stopped, tilting her head to the side in confusion.

<You...>

The voice that invaded Lydia's mind wasn't Vendria's. It was frigid and cold, withered and decayed. But it was *almost* the same.

It was Vendria's voice that replied.

[That's...Lydia, she's...]

Lydia's eyes shifted to the gemstone in the woman's hands, and she understood. "You're her winter aspect, aren't you? Venlyra, the Cold of Winter."

She stepped forward, reaching out with a hand. "It's okay. We're not here to hurt you. We can—"

<Stop.>

The world around them froze.

Taelien and Wrynn ceased to move, and the remaining shades froze along with them.

The air, the wind, even the flames around Taelien's sword stilled.

Lydia couldn't move. She couldn't even breathe.

<**Give her to me.**>

In a moment, she felt her breath come surging back, and she could move.

<I'm so...empty. I need her. I need...to eat...>

The others around her remained frozen, save for Venlyra. As Lydia watched, Venlyra slowly raised a hand in a beckoning gesture.

Lydia glanced around, processing what she was seeing.

...Is this...time sorcery?

She knew such things existed, but she'd never seen anything like it in person. It was truly remarkable, a power on a scale she couldn't possibly resist on her own.

But she wasn't alone.

A silver layer of energy appeared aroundCed energy appeared around Wrynn, then she snapped free of the spell effect. "Annoying."

Venlyra whipped her head toward Wrynn just in time to take a punch straight to the face.

Her frozen body flew backward, smashing into the ground and shattering to pieces.

Then it flashed and vanished, gem and all.

Taelien took a breath, spinning around, holding his sword defensively. "What...was that? It was like everything slowed, and then—"

"No time to talk. Now she's starting to get irritated. I—"

A frozen lance pierced Wrynn from behind without warning.

Wrynn looked down, groaned, and snapped it in half. Blood flowed from the wound. "That's...even more annoying." She fell to her knees.

"Wrynn!" Taelien rushed over to her, his eyes searching the area for the attacker without any success.

Lydia worked while Venlyra was gone. "Dreams, seek and bear my message," she whispered. The sand she'd spread flickered in the air, seeking targets. "Shield." A new barrier appeared around her.

"She's not here." Wrynn coughed, fingers going to the wound in her chest. "Those bodies we're fighting...they're just puppets."

The air around them grew colder.

"You're wrong."

Another form of the goddess appeared, speaking out loud for the first time. Hundreds of blades and spikes of ice flew in circles around her, obscuring her body. "They're not puppets. They're pieces. Precious pieces of me."

Venlyra's visage shifted to a scowl. "And you **broke** them. You'll pay—"

Taelien didn't give her a chance to finish talking, he just swung the Sae'kes and projected a cutting wave of fire in her direction. Her blades of ice flew in the way. A handful of them melted, but hundreds remained, and more began forming every moment.

Dozens of them flashed toward Taelien and Wrynn a moment later.

Taelien's blade moved in a flurry, his arms a blur beyond Lydia's ability to follow. His speed had increased vastly since she'd last seen him fight.

But he still wasn't fast enough. Tiny fragments of ice slipped through his defense. Many broke harmlessly against the defensive spell that Lydia had placed on him, and others shattered against his reinforced skin.

A few bits of ice glimmered brighter than the rest, leaving jagged cuts as they cut his skin like tiny knives.

He grunted, concentrating, and flames burst from his skin. No further ice would harm him; it melted before it came close.

She'd only seen him use that trick once before. It was an impressive technique, but one with a severe time limit.

She'd have to work fast.

"Eru volar shen taris." The ring on Lydia's right hand flashed, and a ball of blue-white flame appeared. She hurled it toward the goddess.

Frozen swords flew to intercept the sphere.

Lydia snapped her fingers. "Burst."

The sphere detonated in a thundering crack. Swords melted into rain, and the frozen air of the forest was momentarily replaced with a warm mist.

The bottom half of Venlyra's body had been melted away for a moment.

The ring's attack had been far stronger than she'd managed before. With Hartigan's training, she'd mastered it, preparing for a rematch with Sterling.

It still hadn't been enough to destroy the goddess.

...But it wasn't meant to. It just needed to make an opening.

As Venlyra raised a hand in the air to counterstrike, the ruinshades struck her from behind.

Venlyra screamed and spun in confusion as phantasmal claws raked the remainder of her body. She flickered backward, appearing on the ground, still missing her lower half. A barrier appeared around her. "What have you—"

The ruinshades pursued Venlyra, flying after her and clawing at her barrier. It held, but the goddess was struggling now. More ruinshades were emerging from the forest — dozens, hundreds of them.

Every time Venlyra blasted one, three more seemed to descend from the sky or emerge from the ground beneath her.

Venlyra howled, spinning toward Lydia. "You took my *children*."

The goddess raised her hands, darkness forming between them. Lydia recognized the spell as something similar to the withering beam she'd seen before, but this was on a much larger scale. "You'll wither and—"

Wrynn surged forward from the ground, grabbing the goddess by the neck. "**Stop.**"

Venlyra froze in place, her eyes wide. The sphere of blackness between her hands warbled dangerously.

Taelien made a running jump, swung the Sae'kes, and sliced the sphere of darkness in half.

Wrynn trembled. "The gem! Now!"

Taelien spun and raised the Sae'kes to strike.

"No, wait!" Lydia rushed forward and put her hand on his arm.

"It's her true—" Wrynn began, then broke into a cough.

Venlyra slowly began to move again.

"I know. Don't destroy her. I have a better answer." Lydia stepped forward, releasing Taelien and moving her hand to touch the blue gem. "Dominion of Knowledge, link our minds."

INTERLUDE II — VENLYRA — SEASONS

Venlyra remembered Rendalir.

She remembered the frozen tops of mountain peaks, the hidden palaces far below the surface of the oceans, and the seemingly endless books of Ionel's libraries.

Most of all, she remembered the cage.

She remembered waking in a prison of silver bars tinged with red. All around it was a void, seemingly without end.

She didn't remember how she'd gotten there, but she knew that something was wrong. There was a burning pain in her chest, and when she inspected it, she found the lingering traces of a wound. A scar that should have been impossible, for her body had been completely rebuilt as she changed to her current seasonal state.

Worse, she remembered the cracks.

The spiderweb-like veins of blackness spreading across her chest. It was a slow progression, but a horrifying one. She recognized it immediately.

She clutched her hand to her chest.

No, no, no. This isn't happening.

She trembled in her prison, sucking in a breath.

Stop panicking. Solve. You're intact, for now.

She balled her hands, but steeled herself. She was no powerless mortal to be consumed by a shade in mere moments. As long as she had her mind and her power, she could find a way forward.

Venlyra closed her eyes. She was not a healer, like her sister-self of spring, but she counted water among one of her dominions. True, her efforts to heal the so-called "vek taint" with water sorcery in the past had failed...but humans changed faster. She was more resilient. And she had ways of buying time to experiment further, didn't she?

She was the winter. She could freeze anything in place — an affliction was no exception. That had to be the first step.

She pressed a hand against the center of the spreading shadows and spoke. "Stop."

Nothing happened.

No flash of power, no cessation of the progression of the shadow.

Then pain shot through her body, seemingly striking every part of her at once.

>*You're awake, I see.*<

The voice was not one of sound; it was within the sharpness inside her body, digging into her very essence. And, somehow, it was also in the void beyond the cage. The infinite nothingness that stretched beyond even her comprehension.

She shivered as she recognized the tone. Not because she'd heard him speak before, but because every being on her world had been born with a primal fear of that voice.

Mere gods were no exception.

Venlyra trembled, but her eyes searched the void. "Sun Eater. What have you done to me?"

>*You have been shown the price of resistance.*<

The pain surged through her again, agonizing. Rather than falling, however, she moved to the bars. When she gripped the silver-red metal, her hand burned.

She didn't flinch away. She pulled with every bit of her might, because she understood that she was rapidly running out of time.

If the Sun Eater was speaking to her, then...

The metal strained against her strength. She could not call extra power to empower her form as Venora had, but her body was still divinely forged. No mundane material could match her.

>*A worthy effort, but pointless. You would not survive exposure to the outside.*<

"Very likely." She spoke aloud. "But if you wanted me dead, I'd already be that way."

The first bar snapped.

Brute force was rarely her preferred method of handling anything, but she had rapidly understood that sorcery would not avail her.

Not when she couldn't reach the stars.

Void was the bane of every sorcerer, mortal or deity. A sufficiently thick layer of void could prevent the use of any form of dominion sorcery. Spiritual arts and spells powered from internal essence could still be used, but those were not her areas of strength. Her opponent had known that, and he had placed her in a situation that would be nearly impossible to work around.

"You want me in your service. A mindless puppet, fulfilling your will. Death is preferable to such an existence."

>*You are wrong.*<

His voice was agony, spreading like fire inside her veins.

She would not scream, however. She would not fail.

She was working, and would not be interrupted.

She tore another bar from the cage.

>*You were born from the stars, a child of one of my compatriots. While Rendalir must end, you needn't end with it. You may join me in building a new world. A grander experiment. I will allow you to retain your sense of self.*<

Venlyra shook her head. "My role is to preserve. To guide. And even if it was not, I value the world that exists. I have seen how your experiments end, Sun Eater. When you bore of your next world, you will break it like you seek to break this one. Like a child who has lost interest in a toy."

>***Insolence.***<

The single word struck her harder than any statement before. Wounds opened on her skin, bubbling with black, tar-like fluid.

Still, she didn't scream. She tore away the next bar.

Almost enough.

>*Destroying yourself will serve no purpose.*<

Her eyes searched the void. There was no sign of her enemy there, so she looked inward.

"Won't it, though?" Her jaw tensed. "You know how my abilities function. Even if I chose to serve you, the moment the next season came, I would change — and Venora would never surrender. Venshara least of all. So, there's another reason you want me alive. You have something going that requires keeping me here for a long time. I don't intend to give it to you."

She tore another bar free. The pain and exertion were maddening, but now, she saw a way to flee.

That endless void.

She didn't know what would happen if she immersed herself in it. Perhaps her existence would end in an instant. Perhaps she would float, helpless within that void.

In a best case, perhaps she'd survive and find a way to navigate through it. Void was not one of her dominions, but it was not impossible to shape. Or perhaps she'd find a place where it was thin enough to call upon the stars, or the power within her.

>*You must not do this. If you persist in this foolishness, my true self—*<

Venlyra stepped into the void.

Never before had the winter felt cold.

Her body slowed, beginning to freeze, but beyond the bars she sensed something — a flicker of distant power. The void was not the only force suppressing her abilities; the prison itself had been.

She had mere moments to work before her mind and body ceased to function.

And so, she latched on to that distant force, the vaguest light of a faraway star — and hurled her spirit toward it with all of her might.

And in that moment, Vendria shattered into pieces.

***

Venlyra opened her eyes.

She was in a library. Not one of Ionel's, though. An unfamiliar one, with strange, white-stone architecture.

Where...

Something burned in her mind, a jolt of agony.

>***Return to your cage.***<

There was a flash of blackness. Pain. Her knees buckled, her eyes fluttered. As she began to fall, someone caught her arm and steadied her.

Venlyra blinked.

Her eyes turned upward. A spectacled woman with a stern expression was looking at her. Her scarlet hair was pulled upward into a neat bun, the kind she might not have found strange for a librarian to have...but no librarian she knew of wore glimmering silvery armor or an arming sword on their left hip.

"...Ionel?" She asked. Had enough time passed that he had changed his manifestation so?

"I'm Lydia Hastings. I'm in your mind. Or, perhaps, you're in mine. We're sharing for a bit. Forgive me for the intrusion."

She didn't smile, but there was something in the woman's matter-of-fact tone and demeanor that she could appreciate.

"A sorceress, then?" Venlyra frowned. "I'm sorry, I don't know what is happening."

>*Return to your—*<

Lydia pressed her fingers against Venlyra's forehead, and the voice — that terrible, all-encompassing voice — fell silent.

For the first time in...how long had it been?...the voice had ceased to scream in her thoughts.

And, along with it, her mind began to clear.

Lydia helped haul her to her feet.

"You must not stay here," Venlyra explained, as knowledge and memory began to flow into her. "It is not safe. I've been touched by the Sun Eater."

Lydia nodded in understanding. "I believe I can assist you with that problem."

"You have a cure, then? Has one been found?" Venlyra's eyes searched the library, intuitively scanning for relevant books nearby.

There were many books on the shelves, but she couldn't read the writing on the spines. Perhaps they were in a foreign language, but the more likely reason was that they were merely figments of the dreamscape. Representations of knowledge, not true books.

That was rather disappointing.

"Not a cure, no. But you are not infected in the traditional fashion. You have been separated from your other aspects, and I have one of them — Venora — with me. She is not afflicted as you are."

Venlyra processed that. "...Separated? The void. When I attempted to reach beyond it, I must have...ah." She nodded. "Fascinating. Ah, I believe I understand your intent. You believe you can reunite me with her?"

"That is the eventual plan, yes. Would you be willing to—"

The room around them darkened.

"...Are you seeing that?" Lydia asked.

"He's coming." Venlyra drew in a breath. "We haven't much time. You should separate your mind from my own as quickly as possible."

Lydia wrinkled her nose. "I think not. We are in a shared mindscape. I will fight this infestation along with you."

"You don't understand. He—"

>*You were warned.*<

Agony shot through every inch of her existence.

She stumbled, and this time, Lydia stumbled as well.

But when Lydia was afflicted, Venlyra saw a flicker of sparks in the air around her.

Some sort of...defensive spell, then? Was that even possible in a mindscape like this?

"Ah." Lydia's jaw tensed, her eyes searching the area. "I believe I understand now."

Lydia snapped her fingers. "Sorcerous shield. Mental barrier. Comprehensive barrier."

The air around Lydia glimmered with each phrase. Then she reached down and touched Venlyra's head again. "Sorcerous shield. Mental barrier."

Venlyra's head swam as the second effect took hold on her. The voice in her mind quieted once again, but she could already feel it scraping against the walls of the shield.

"Your sorcery is most impressive, Lydia Hastings, but it would still be wise for you to withdraw. If the infestation cannot assault us internally, I believe it will manifest in our shared mindscape more directly."

Lydia helped Venlyra steady herself again, then pulled her hand away and reached for the sword at her hip. "I understand. I'm counting on it."

"You will be at great risk. If he wins, your mind is likely to be subsumed, as mine has been for entirely too long."

Lydia smiled. "I accept the risks."

"Why? You do not know me."

The red-haired woman shook her head. "Irrelevant. You are being tortured and controlled by an external entity. It is my duty and honor to assist you."

When Venlyra heard those words, she heard something she had not felt in a very long time — resolve. It was one of her defining qualities, once. Now, she felt like just a withered husk of what she once was, incapable of such certainty.

But with Lydia beside her, their minds in this shared place...perhaps she could borrow a bit of that strength and make it her own.

She had little time to find that resolve. The world around them continued to darken, with lines of blackness appearing across the ground and collecting into a single terrifying figure.

The creature was a twisted mockery of the human form, standing half-again her height with spindly limbs and a jaw containing far too many vicious teeth. His hands were eight-fingered claws, his head dotted with horns, and he had bat-like wings and a spiked tail.

Though the creature seemed to be formed from shadows, his body became more solid with each passing moment. Darkness rippled like water, forming plate-like scales on the creature's body, which rapidly became more rigid.

Venlyra tried not to tremble as she looked upon him. Her memories of the creature were fragmented, but she knew this was the entity that had stolen her mind and power for centuries. Not the shapeshifter, but rather the being that had lived within the dagger that had pierced her other body.

"If you will not respond to my commands, perhaps I have allowed your consciousness to persist too long. A more direct approach may be warranted."

The creature opened his hands, and two spheres of black fire floated above them.

Lydia smiled, adjusting her glasses. "I'm glad you're here. I was hoping you'd show yourself directly. That simplifies this process considerably."

"Fool. I am the Sun Eater, creator and destroyer—"

Lydia shook her head. "I'm sorry, you can't actually believe I'm going to fall for that, are you? A true deity wouldn't need to be riding around inside Venlyra's mind like this. You're just another shade. A figment. Nothing more."

The creature growled. "I am more than a mere shade, human. While I may not represent the fullness of the Sun Eater's strength, I am a part of him. I am Em'rak, eighth and strongest of his fragments. And, when I take your body and leave this place, I will be one with him once again. And he will learn—"

A blast of light hit Em'rak from behind. He spun around, hissing, and hurled both blasts of flame toward the direction of his attacker.

The black fire found only a hovering book, which floated out of the way of the flames.

Em'rak spun back toward Venlyra and Lydia, readying another blast of fire but Lydia was already speaking.

"Theas' Introduction to Protection Sorcery."

A book floated off a bookshelf to hover behind her, then glowed brightly.

As Em'rak hurled another blast of darkness, the book glowed brighter, and a shimmering blue barrier appeared around Lydia. The barrier shattered, but the blast was diminished enough that it failed when it hit Lydia's *second* barrier, which she'd formed around herself earlier.

Lydia waved, and another book flew off a nearby shelf. "Hartigan's Essential Guide to Flame Calling."

The book opened and a white-hot blast of flame leapt out of the pages. Em'rak hissed, jumping to the side and avoiding the flames, only to be blasted again with a bolt of light from the book that still hovered behind him.

Em'rak howled, slamming his palms together. The floor of the room began to crack. "Your parlor tricks are infuriating, but they will not last for long. I will annihilate this place, and you along with it."

Lydia pointed to the ground. "Theas' Art of Structural Reinforcement."

Another book flew off a shelf, opened, and pressed itself against the library floor. It vanished, and the cracks in the library vanished along with it. The earthquake ceased.

The attacking books continued to barrage the shadow with fire and light, and Em'rak raised his arms to defend himself.

Venlyra was done simply watching the exchange. She'd been idle for far, far too long.

As Em'rak finally managed to blast the light-throwing book out of the air with a burst of shadow, Venlyra conjured a rain of frozen spikes above him. The lances of frost flew downward and pierced the shadow's body, pinning him to the ground.

Em'rak trembled, then shifted into a liquid state. The inky pool flowed along the floor, then re-formed into Em'rak right in front of them.

"Fools." Em'rak grabbed Lydia by her throat, reaching straight through the barrier around her and smashing her into a nearby bookcase. "I understand your tricks now. Your conceptualization of this place as a library has given you flexibility, but not power. And in this world, power dictates all."

Lydia coughed, struggling to tear free from the hand around her neck. After a moment of failing to speak, Lydia's eyes widened.

[Ah. I understand. Speech isn't necessary here. Choking me accomplishes nothing.]

A book floated off a nearby shelf.

[Tarren's *The Nature of Worlds*.]

Lydia vanished from Em'rak's grip.

Em'rak spun just in time for Venlyra to press a hand into his chest.

"Stop."

Ice covered the monster's body. The ice began to shake almost immediately as Em'rak began to break free.

Lydia appeared again at Venlyra's side. Or, rather, her sides — there were three copies of Lydia now, each holding out a hand toward the frozen shade.

"Eru volar shen taris."

Blasts of blue-white flame engulfed the ice and shadow alike. The creature within howled and writhed. As the ice melted, Em'rak began to burn, parts of him vanishing into nothingness.

Em'rak screamed, and the environment changed.

In an instant, the library was gone.

They stood on a handful of grey stone tiles that hovered within a seemingly infinite void. The darkness around them was oppressive, omnipresent.

It was the darkness Venlyra had seen in her mind for centuries, that she had screamed into without effect. And as she watched, the few stone tiles they stood on began to fade.

Two of the Lydia copies vanished, leaving only a single one, and an oppressive pressure manifested in the air.

Em'rak in front of them changed and twisted, growing larger and larger. "Human. You have fought well, but it is at an end."

The force around them intensified, pushing Venlyra and Lydia downward. Lydia's barrier spells manifested around them both, but it only dampened the effect. They were barely able to remain standing.

Em'rak smashed a huge fist into Lydia's chest, sending her flying back across the tiles. Venlyra moved a hand and raised a wall of ice, blocking Lydia from falling into the void.

Lydia began to push herself back to her feet, but the air continued to push downward on both her and Venlyra, making movement difficult.

And all the while, the darkness grew. "This is my true strength, mortal. You cannot stand against it alone."

Em'rak raised a hand, and Lydia floated off the ground. A burst of force slammed her against the wall of ice, leaving cracks in the frozen surface. Lydia coughed on the impact.

Venlyra fired a blast of icy knives at Em'rak, but they shattered harmlessly when they impacted against him.

Em'rak drew back an arm. The arm shifted into the shape of a spear, and it aimed for Lydia's heart and lunged.

Lydia didn't move. Instead, she closed her eyes.

A many-faceted green barrier appeared around her, deflecting the strike.

"Who...said anything...about being alone?" Lydia struggled, blood flowing from her mouth and nose. She resisted the force of Em'rak's pressure, pushing herself away from the ice wall, and raised her hand again. The glimmering barrier compressed, forming a shimmering field of green energy around her body.

Venlyra stared at the barrier in shock. She knew that technique; she'd seen it many times in fragmented memories of her mind.

It belonged to one of her other selves.

<Venora?>

[I am here, Venlyra.]

<How...why?>

Lydia pointed her finger at the titanic shadow again, and wisps of blue flame appeared around it. The flames grew brighter and brighter with each passing moment.

The shadow struck her again, cracking her green barrier and hitting Lydia hard in the chest. She coughed, stumbled back a step, and then steadied herself.

And still, Lydia's flames grew brighter.

[It would seem this one wishes to save us, Venlyra.]

<She must flee this place. She cannot succeed.>

The shadow lashed out with a lance-like arm, this time piercing through Lydia's barriers entirely. She twisted just in time to avoid a lethal blow, but a vast hole appeared in her left shoulder.

She staggered, gritting her teeth.

Still, her flames glowed brighter.

[She can. And she will — if we help her.]

He's too strong.

The shadow's lance came down again. This time, Lydia was too slow to dodge.

She didn't have to.

A wall of ice appeared in the way of the lance-like appendage, blocking the strike. As the shadow reared back for another attack, Venlyra conjured more spikes of frost and hurled them toward Em'rak's chest.

[We are stronger. Together.]

The spikes flashed green, glowing with inner light.

This time, they pierced deep into Em'rak's shadowy form, leaving wounds that bled inky fluid. Em'rak screamed, reaching for the largest of the shards and trying to pull it from his chest.

Lydia took that moment to strike.

She vanished, reappearing in mid-air in front of Em'rak, and placed a gleaming hand against the shadow's forehead. "Begone, monster."

There was a flash of white from Lydia's ring.

Then a sphere of purest white flame enveloped Lydia and Em'rak, exploding outward and consuming everything in its wake.

The darkness around them *cracked*.

When Venlyra's vision cleared, they stood not in the darkness, but atop a mountainside.

Lydia was lying on the ground, her right arm badly burned, and her chest still bleeding from the terrible wound she had suffered.

And standing above her, with a black dagger raised, was a hideous mockery of Tysus. His face was burned half-away, showing a blackened skull beneath. Black fluid dribbled from a massive hole in his chest, but even now, his body was beginning to repair itself.

"You...you have harmed me..." The false Tysus shuddered, the skull-half of his face hideously contorting along with his skin. "But I will end this. I will end *you*, in the same way that it all began."

He brought his dagger down to strike.

But as his hand descended, an arm grabbed him from behind.

Venora.

Venlyra had never seen her spring aspect in person before, only in images drawn by others. Her skin was the color of bark, and her hair a mixture of green and brown.

And more importantly, her fists were currently glowing with green light. "You will not harm her."

Venora's fist slammed into the Tysus, cracking his unnatural jaw. He stumbled backward from the strength of the blow, but quickly righted himself.

"You are a fool to show yourself here," he hissed. "I will take you as well."

"**No.**"

Spears of ice shot up from the ground, piercing the shadow's legs. Venlyra stepped forward. "You imprisoned me." She raised a hand, conjuring a wall of ice to surround the cage. "Suppressed me."

The cage began to fill with water. "Stole my body."

Inside, the trapped form of Tysus bashed against the wall of ice, making wide cracks.

"Stole my life." She propelled herself forward as the cage finished filling with water, then pressed a hand against the cracked icy wall. "Now, face your punishment. **Stop. Forever.**"

The water inside the cage froze.

And within it, the shadow stilled.

Venora stepped to the side of the frozen cage, placing a hand on it. A wall of stone formed around the ice, then a layer of wood formed and hardened around the stone.

Venlyra looked to Venora. "It is done, then."

Venora nodded. "It is. Save for one thing."

Then they walked to Lydia's wounded form and knelt beside her.

She lay unmoving in a still-growing puddle of blood.

"She has given too much for us. Her mind, spirit, and essence are in tatters."

They placed their hands on her together, then nodded to each other.

"We will repay our debt."

And with that, they began to work in unison.

CHAPTER XIX – JONAN V – WOUNDED BY A THORN

Jonan was a few hundred yards away from the Crescent Thorn when Velas appeared in front of him, just as expected.

He caught her as she stumbled, careful not to impale himself on the Heartlance in the process.

Velas trembled for a moment, then pulled free from his grasp. "Kestrian." She stumbled away from him, then caught herself with the spear. "We need to get back there. Now."

He put a hand on her shoulder. "No."

Velas spun around, batting away his hand with her only functional one. "Rialla. She's badly hurt. We need to go."

Jonan shook his head, reaching up to tap the earring he was wearing. "Heard the whole thing. We're leaving. You're in no shape to fight, and I'm not a fighter."

"No, no, no." Velas shook her head. "She took a knife to the chest, Kestrian. She's *dying*. We need to go now." Velas took a step away from him, turned, and started heading back toward the building. She leaned heavily on the Heartlance, careful not to put any pressure on her injured ankle.

"You're insane." Jonan walked in front of her. "Stop. You'll just get us both killed, too."

"She wasn't dead, Jonan!" Velas snarled. "If we go now, we might..."

"What are you going to do, bleed on the other Silk?" Jonan folded his arms.

"Do not press me right now, Kestrian. I am not in a pleasant mood." She tilted her head down and gave him her best glower, but it was somewhat less intimidating than usual, given that she could barely stay on her feet.

"If the Shrouded One wants her dead, she'll be dead long before we get there. If she wants her alive, we're just presenting extra targets right now. We stand no chance. Come with me, we'll get you healed, and we'll go rescue her together. *Later*."

"I..." Velas stared toward the Crescent Thorn, wavering. "I...I can't just leave her like this. She saved me, Jonan. She..."

Velas bit her lip, turning away. "I thought *she* was the other Silk. I didn't trust her. I didn't talk to her. If I'd believed in her, if I'd shared my plans...if we'd gone together from the start, maybe..."

She looked like she was on the verge of tears. Jonan was momentarily stymied by that, given that he'd never seen her with extreme emotions of that kind, and also because he was generally awful with people.

After a moment, he reached over, patted her on the cheek, and said. "Please don't get me killed with sentiment."

Velas stared at him incredulously for a moment, then snorted. "You...never change, do you?"

"Dying would constitute a change. An unwanted change. Can we go?"

She took one ragged breath, then nodded. "Right. We're going now."

He put an arm under her other shoulder, grimacing at the look of her broken wrist, and helped her limp toward the nearest alley.

From there, it was a very long, painful walk to the blacksmith shop where help was hopefully waiting.

***

"Oh, dear." Aladir took one look at Velas, grimaced, and then gestured at the floor. "You can lie her down. I'll need to get to work immediately."

"What, I don't even get a chair? What sort of doctor are you?" Velas grumbled.

"It's much harder to work on you while you're sitting. I do wish I'd prepared a better environment for this, but..." He gave her a sheepish look. "It is what it is."

Mairead Caelan sat nearby, in the one and only chair within the shop, sitting next to a line of weapons. An excellent position, in Jonan's judgement, for grabbing something to murder them all while they were in a vulnerable position on the floor.

Jonan went and leaned up against the wall near the weapons. "Where's your commanding officer?"

He knew better than to use Taer'vys' name when non-Thornguard were present. Aladir was nominally working with them at the moment, but that didn't mean they were going to share everything with him.

"Busy." Mariead offered him a strained smile. "Mind explaining all this?"

"Perhaps later." Jonan smiled. "For now, let's let the doctor work in peace."

"No, no, it's quite alright. Talk away." Aladir was inspecting Velas' wrist. "I won't be bothered."

Jonan was not an expert on healing, but he was reasonably certain that you weren't supposed to distract someone while they were working.

Is he trying to get us to say something while he's around? How uncharacteristically sneaky for a paladin. No wonder he's Lydia's partner.

After several minutes which were mostly filled with Aladir talking to himself, Jonan came to the conclusion that while Aladir was probably being sneaky, he was also just extremely talkative.

"Touch of Life." Aladir's hands glowed green as he touched Velas' wrist. He'd already physically adjusted the bones in her wrist, then used a different spell to force them to begin mending more quickly. Jonan hadn't watched — the sight was a little too disturbing. "...That should be it for the wrist for the moment. Don't use it, of course. I'll need to clean this off, then work on your ankle and burns."

Velas groaned. "Hurry. I need to get back out there."

"Absolutely not. You shouldn't be fighting again for at least three days."

Jonan suspected they'd be lucky to keep Velas from rushing out for three more minutes if they didn't do something to placate her. While she was clearly hurting more now that the adrenaline of battle had fled, there was no chance she would be willing to just sit around and wait while her friend was in danger.

"How many paladins do we have available, Aladir?" She asked.

Mairead raised an eyebrow, but said nothing.

"Not...many, in this city, I'm afraid. Lydia could call on more, but she's heading toward," he glanced at Mairead and Jonan, then back to Velas, "that other place, now."

"Get her back here. We have our target."

Mairead's look of concern intensified, but again, she remained silent.

"You can tell me all about it in the morning, after you've rested."

"No. Tonight. Now. Get Lydia back here, before it's too late."

Aladir frowned, finishing cleaning her wrist and moving down to work on her leg. "I have no way of doing that."

"I can send Lydia a message," Jonan offered.

Aladir gave him a look. "One that I provide?"

"Certainly. I believe we all have the same goal."

He was absolutely not certain that they had the same goal. In fact, he was rapidly having to evaluate if he even knew his *own* goal.

The conversation between Velas and the Shrouded One had been interesting. Interesting in the sense that it was awful, even more so than he'd anticipated.

There's zero chance that Aayara didn't already know the Shrouded One's identity. That means she deliberately pitted her two current apprentices against her old one.

She'd probably planned for some of us to die in that conflict. I'm not sure who she expected to lose, or if she even cared.

He continued to worry about that for the next hour, while Aladir finished his work.

After that, Aladir wrote a letter, which Jonan sent to Lydia via mirror, and they parted ways for the night.

"Mairead, I'll fill you in tomorrow. Velas, let's get you somewhere safe."

"Should you be moving anywhere tonight?" Mairead asked. "You can just sleep here. It's not comfortable, but it might be safer."

Jonan shook his head. "Can't. We have places to be. Resources to work on. Thank you, though."

Mairead nodded. "Be safe, then."

Velas gave Mairead an odd look, then nodded in return. "You as well. Thanks for the shelter."

With that, Jonan and Velas left the shop, and headed back out into the night.

***

"We're going for Rialla now."

"No, we're not."

This argument continued while they headed to a different safe house that Jonan had prepared, just in case they were being followed. He hid them while they walked with both invisibility and illusionary duplicates, but if the Shrouded One was following them directly, he knew it wouldn't be effective.

Eventually, they made it to the safe house, and Jonan opened it up and let them inside.

They checked through the building, insuring it was actually unoccupied, before Jonan finally dismissed his illusions, sighed, and sat down on yet another dusty and long-abandoned couch.

"You're awfully reticent to help someone who needs us."

Jonan folded his arms. "You're injured. I'm useless. We're waiting for help."

"What sort of help?" Velas sat down on the floor, wincing. Life sorcery was accelerating her healing process, but it hadn't fixed all of the damage.

"I requested some assistance from Velthryn a few days ago."

"Velthryn? That could take *weeks*!"

Jonan shook his head. "It's been expedited, and it should be ready soon. And it'll be useful. I have a plan to get us close to the Shrouded One without raising too many suspicions."

"She knows me now, it's a little late for that."

He shook his head. "No, this will probably work, unless she knows me on sight."

Velas frowned. "She very well might. She knew who I was. She said she'd killed a Velas Jaldin before, whatever that means."

"Any mysterious grandmothers missing in your family history?"

"Not that I'm aware of. I didn't think I was named after any predecessor. And," she hesitated for a moment, "I'm not really a Jaldin, anyway. I was adopted."

That's...awkward. Was Velas' name in those books...? I don't remember seeing her in there. Hm.

Jonan shrugged. "So was I, if you count Aayara's pulling me out of a burning home. Do you think what she said had some significance?"

"Don't know. Might have just been a simple intimidation trick." She frowned. "But one way or another, it shows she had an information source about me. She both knew my name and she knew to be waiting there for me. Who could have told her?"

"It wasn't me, before you ask." He frowned. "And I doubt it was Lydia or Aladir."

"Mairead, then?"

Jonan nodded. "A likely suspect. Or her commanding officer, Taer'vys. But I don't necessarily think someone told her. Not in the sense we're thinking."

"You're talking about those books you've been reading. The ones that mention the future."

"It may sound absurd, but if the leader of this cult is a vae'kes — and she had another vae'kes working for her — the plausibility of someone who can accurately foresee the future being involved is vastly higher than I would have thought before."

"You think there's something as minute as my position on a rooftop in those books?"

"Not in the books, but if someone — like the Shrouded One herself — can see the future, they might be able to catch glimpses of things like that. Your paladin friend can do things like that, can't she?"

"Asphodel's predictive abilities were unreliable when I was training with her. She also used to have trouble seeing me with her future sight at all, but maybe that's changed. I've heard she's gotten better. And I suppose if a vae'kes has that ability, and she's been training for hundreds of years..." Velas sighed. "How do you beat someone like that? How can we even try? She could be years ahead of us in planning."

"I don't think so." Jonan shook his head. "I mean, maybe she's planned for some things that far out, but the moment-to-moment actually sounds harder. You seemed to hurt her at some point somehow."

Velas frowned. "Yeah...I'm going to be honest, I'm not sure exactly what happened there."

"Start from the beginning. I heard a lot, but tell me in your own words. We should gather everything we can about the fight so we can strategize."

"Right." Velas nodded, winced again, and then steeled herself. "So, first, I landed on the rooftop..."

***

They met with Aladir again the next morning at a different house, judging that moving frequently was wise now that the older Silk was aware of Velas being present in the city.

"I've sent the message you requested, Aladir, but she hasn't replied."

Aladir gave a nod. "Her current task could take some time."

Velas tightened her jaw. "We're going without her, then. I'm not waiting any longer to get Rialla out of there."

Jonan glanced at Velas, considering before he replied. "Ordinarily, I'd urge us to wait...but Lydia wouldn't be able to help with my current plan, anyway. And I don't think it's worth waiting for any other approach."

More honestly, he couldn't take the risk of Taelien and Lydia retrieving the mask from Kyestri before he finished his own assignment. While discovering that the Shrouded One was the original Silk was something, it wasn't a complete answer.

Aayara would want a name, and he didn't have that.

That meant he was, unfortunately, going to have to take a risk. Failing Aayara was simply not an option.

Rescuing Rialla quickly would be an added bonus, if it was possible. But while Jonan had many illusions, believing it was likely Rialla had survived was not among them.

Fortunately, his preparations were finally complete. He hadn't heard from Lydia, but he had received a different message in the morning.

It's done. Both deaths have been confirmed.
-Scour

Jonan's contact in Velthryn had finished his assignment, and it was time to move on to the next phase of the plan.

Aladir looked to Jonan, then to Velas. "You should wait here. I'll accompany Master Kestrian for whatever this...plan, is."

Velas snorted. "Not likely. I'm itching for a rematch."

"You're not in any shape for one. Even after my healing, you've only had one night of rest."

"What, and you think you'd do any better? You're a *medic*." Velas scowled.

"I'm a *paladin*. A paladin who happens to have life sorcery, in addition to other skills." He raised his hand, and the thin wooden bracelet on his wrist glowed. A moment later, a gleaming sword appeared in his right hand, the hilt designed to look like the trunk of a tree. "We knew we might be running into a va'ekes up here. We came prepared for Sterling, but I suspect this will work equally well against a different one. And Rialla is my friend, too."

"A fancy dominion bonded sword isn't going to help you if you can't see her move. I'm handling this." Velas leaned forward.

"That's enough bickering." Jonan interjected.

Velas blinked in surprise.

"I have roles for you both to play."

Aladir frowned. "Go on. I'll listen to your idea, at least. But you're not my commanding officer."

Jonan nodded. "I'll explain the plan. I think you'll find the odds are better than a direct assault, but there are some risks..."

***

An hour later, Jonan and Aladir arrived at the back entrance of the Crescent Thorn, dragging a large cart. The cart carried two coffins, one of which was abnormally large.

A pair of guards stopped them at the door, of course. It was broad daylight, and they weren't concealing their movements. "Who goes?"

"Vincent Calloway and Lyras Luria. We've just completed an important assignment, and need to make a report."

One of the guards paled. "Lyras...Luria? As in, House Luria? My apologies, I didn't recognize you."

That was unfortunate, since Jonan thought his illusion that made Aladir look like Lyras Luria — or Eridus, as he'd been called back in Velthryn — was quite convincing.

Aladir smiled brightly. "No need to be concerned, friend. I've been out of the city until recently, doing some work for an important cause." He gave the guard a conspiratorial look.

"I...I, uh, understand. Please, wait here. I'll need to check some things."

"Of course, of course. We wouldn't want any mistakes to be made about something this important."

The guard hurried off.

A few minutes later, they were being escorted inside, wagon and all.

A few minutes after that, they found themselves in a small room standing across from a masked and hooded figure.

Flower Mask, Jonan remembered. *Although it could easily be a different person wearing the same mask I saw before.*

"I've been told you have a delivery?" The hooded figure asked.

"Yes. The same one I mentioned previously. It needs to go directly to the Shrouded One, however, for immediate authentication."

The hooded figure leaned forward. "What makes you think I'm not the Shrouded One?"

"You could be, but you don't match the description Sterling gave me," Aladir offered. "From your outfit, I'd wager you're one of the council members that's been sent to screen us. That's fine, you can look in the crates and verify our delivery first, but we're going to need to take it straight to the top after that."

Flower Mask gave a curt nod. "I'll inspect them first." They waved a hand, and a glimmering barrier appeared around them before they moved to the cart.

A sensible precaution.

"You said these were..."

Jonan waved to the coffin. "Nakane and Larkin Theas. Last two on the House Theas list. Page 374."

Flower Mask nodded. "I'm familiar, and I recall our previous discussion." She turned toward Aladir. "You were the one originally responsible for this, yes? These deliveries are significantly late."

"I, uh, ran into some difficulties." Aladir sounded sheepish.

"You were captured." Flower Mask shook his head. "You have much to answer for."

Aladir's eyes narrowed. "Don't get snippy with me. I work for Sterling, not for you. And the job is done."

"That remains to be seen." The figure stepped forward, opening the first coffin, and immediately stepped back with a hand over his face.

"Sorry, should have warned you about the smell. Neither of us is a stability sorcerer, so..."

The hooded figure slammed the first coffin shut, then moved to the next.

"That one isn't *as* bad," Jonan offered helpfully. "Nakane was a little more intact than her cousin."

Flower Mask opened the coffin, stared inside for a moment, and then shut it again. "She's older than I remembered."

"You've met her?" The surprise in Jonan's tone was sincere.

Flower Mask nodded. "Reconnaissance for the upcoming city-wide event. Continuity checks. You've done well to correct this mistake, it was one of the more serious problems with the scenario. This should reduce the probability that fate has been twisted beyond repair."

Jonan thought he understood most of that, but he didn't like the implications.

"Come this way."

Flower Mask led them to a spiral stairway. "The Shrouded One will see you on the top floor. Ah, I'm afraid getting that cart up the stairs might be somewhat difficult, however. Do you need some help?"

Jonan looked at the cart and the stairs, grimacing.

"We can handle it, thank you," Aladir answered.

Flower Mask watched them for just another moment, then nodded and walked away. "Good luck. You'd best hope she's in a good mood."

Jonan took a deep breath.

Honestly, I'm not even sure we'll survive making it up the stairs.

***

Dragging the cart up the stairwell was, predictably, tremendously awkward. It took several minutes just to get to the top floor, and that was *with* Aladir cheating and using some kind of levitation spell to help.

When they reached the top, they found a pair of bright red double doors waiting for them. There were no guards outside.

"Come in," a voice said from the opposite side. "It's unlocked."

Aladir and Jonan exchanged glances, then dragged the cart toward the doors. Aladir pushed the doors wide as they approached.

The room ahead was huge and ostentatious. The walls were white stone, but draped with numerous banners and paintings. Four high stone pillars led to the angled ceiling, and toward the back of the room, Jonan could see a small stairwell leading to a trap door that presumably led to the roof.

None of that was immediately important, however. Crimson carpet led across the room to end at a golden throne. Sitting on that throne was Silk — or, at least, someone who looked very much like her.

The Shrouded One. It should have been so obvious.

She was perhaps a bit shorter than Velas, however, and even lighter in build. Little more could be seen beneath the veils, however. Potent sight sorcery blocked any attempts to gaze at the person within. Jonan probably could have broken or bypassed that effect, but it would have been tricky to accomplish at a distance, and it would have been noticeable to everyone if he tried.

"You can bring that straight to me." The Shrouded One waved at them, holding a scepter shaped like a long-stemmed rose.

Jonan and Aladir dragged the wagon forward.

"The delivery, as promised." Jonan bowed his head. "If there's nothing else..."

"Stay." The Shrouded One commanded. "If you've actually completed this piece of the grand work, you should be rewarded, after all."

"Ah, many thanks." Jonan took a step away from the wagon.

The Shrouded One approached, then paused, turning her head toward Jonan. "You sound familiar...Virgil, was it?"

"Vincent," Jonan corrected, trying not to sound too nervous. "Ah, perhaps you saw me at Fort Kaldri?"

She was there visiting Captain Nolan, so maybe...

"Ah, yes, that must have been it." She snapped her fingers. "My, this coffin is *quite* large."

"Larkin was wearing full armor," Jonan explained. "We felt it was best to preserve the body with all the equipment."

"Prudent." She walked closer, reaching for the coffin. "I'll see—by the gods, what is that *smell?*"

Jonan winced. "Decomposition, I'm afraid. We didn't have someone with stability sorcery."

"Ugh." She pulled her hand away. "And the other one?"

"Not quite as bad, at least."

The Shrouded One groaned, then moved and opened the other coffin. "Hm. Nakane Theas, is it...? Interesting."

She took a few steps closer to Jonan. "You've done very well."

Jonan resisted the urge to flinch away. "Thank you, Shrouded One."

She's so close.

Her veils were floating inches away from him, almost within reach.

"I'm quite impressed that you did such a service to the cause." The Shrouded One stepped closer. "Tell me, what inspired you to go to such efforts?"

She leaned in. Her draping silks brushed against Jonan's shoulder.

A moment of concentration and a single thought was all it took for Jonan to brush past their sorcery and see within them.

And in that moment, he realized his mistake.

She was right in front of him. That dark hair, those burning eyes, that awful smile.

The same smile she'd worn when she'd burned his family to ashes.

Lavender.

"Ah...I..." he stammered, frozen in place.

Lavender's hand reached out, brushing his cheek. "No need to stutter. I already know the answer. I know what you want. I've known all along." Her hand moved down to his neck, then slowly tightened. "You want to kill me. But I should offer you a warning — I see the future, Jonan. I saw you coming here. I saw your little tricks, I saw your disguises, and I let you come here. And I've seen how this ends."

She leaned in and whispered in his ear. "There is no future in which you leave this place alive."

CHAPTER XX – TAELIEN VI – LORD OF STONE

Lydia collapsed the moment she spoke the words of her spell. Taelien couldn't catch her — not with a sword in one hand and a lantern in another.

Wrynn was not similarly encumbered, and she managed to move forward quickly enough to grab Lydia before she hit the ground. She was surprisingly mobile for someone with a hole in her chest, but she still winced at the extra weight.

Rather than collapsing like Lydia, Venlyra's body simply trembled for a moment then froze in the position it had been standing in.

That's...creepy. Like looking at a porcelain doll, but far too large.

Taelien kept his sword at the ready, preparing to strike Venlyra or the shades surrounding them if anything made a hostile movement. The shades seemed contented to simply circle around them now that Venlyra was inert.

"What's going on with them?" Taelien gestured toward the shades with the Sae'kes.

"You remember how I mentioned that they're controlled by some kind of dream sorcery? Lydia changed their commands with that dust she tossed around the area. Clever." Wrynn sniffed at the air. "More will be coming, and I don't know if her commands will spread to them or not. We should move."

Upon determining that the nearby shades were probably harmless, Taelien moved closer to Wrynn. "Are you capable of walking with an injury like that?"

Wrynn snorted. "I've had a lot worse, and I'm already getting better."

Taelien blinked as he examined the wound. It was covered by a black, shimmering substance now, which he belatedly realized was a piece of her tunic that seemed to have broken off and stuck to it. "Ah. One of your famous shadeweave tunics?"

Wrynn nodded. "Yep. They work quick, and I can regenerate even without it. I could heal myself faster if I could use my spirit arts properly, but I can't risk using more energy than I absolutely need to use. The chances of breaking my seal are too high right now."

Taelien nodded. "Okay. I should probably carry Lydia, though. Can I take her and pass you the lantern?"

"Sure, but let her keep her hand on the stone. I don't know what will happen if we break the connection."

"Okay. Does that mean we need to take Venlyra with us as well?"

Wrynn shook her head. "Nope. That thing is just a shell at best."

"Then how—"

A shimmering aura briefly surrounded Wrynn's hand. She brought it upward, cutting through Venlyra's arm at the wrist. Then Wrynn shifted, lifting up Lydia — with the crystal still gripped in her hand — and offered her to Taelien.

"That...works, I guess." Taelien sheathed his sword, set down the lantern, and took Lydia. Venlyra's severed hand remained clutched around the bottom half of the crystal, which looked a little creepy, but it began to melt almost immediately. Apparently, whatever force was keeping it frozen was disrupted by separating it from the main body.

He'd just have to deal with it for a little while.

He held Lydia carefully, prepared to shift her into an over-the-shoulder carry if he needed free use of one of his hands to fight.

Wrynn picked up the lantern. "Let's go."

They headed back toward the barrier.

The shades followed behind them. Taelien found that unsettling, but he knew they weren't hostile.

At least, *those* shades weren't. Other shades began to converge on them from all sides as they moved deeper into the woods. They didn't attack immediately, but that only made the unsettling feeling worse.

"What are the odds that Lydia's command has a time limit?" Taelien asked.

"Possible, but unlikely. It's more likely the other shades are simply waiting to have a critical mass to overwhelm us and the shades that are protecting us."

"Lovely." Taelien took a breath, then quickened his pace. Wrynn kept up easily in spite of her wound.

More shades gathered with every passing minute. Lydia showed no signs of waking.

When they reached the barrier, there was a small army of shades standing in the way. Dozens, maybe hundreds. They didn't look friendly. As Taelien watched, they began to spread out and raise their claws. In a few cases, he saw balls of darkness forming between their hands, most likely preparations for ranged attack spells.

That'd be fun to tangle with if I didn't have to worry about Lydia dropping the crystal if I get into a fight. As it is, I'm going to have to be careful.

He shifted Lydia to over his left shoulder, hoping she could maintain her grip from that position. Then he moved his hand to the hilt of the Sae'kes.

"Don't. Hold on." Wrynn stepped forward. "**Stop.**"

The shades ceased moving immediately.

Wrynn drew in a deep, ragged breath. "To the barrier, quick. I can't maintain this long."

Taelien blinked, then rushed to the barrier's edge. Wrynn stumbled along behind him. "Should I...?" He gestured toward the barrier.

"No, I've got it." Wrynn reached a hand toward Lydia, putting it on her forehead, and closed her eyes for an instant. "Reshape."

A hole opened in the side of the barrier, just as it had when Lydia had opened it before.

Taelien didn't wait — he rushed through the hole.

Wrynn followed behind him, but only barely. She was staggering now, clearly exhausted.

The barrier slammed shut behind them.

Beyond it, Taelien could see the shades beginning to move again — and throw themselves bodily against the shield. "Uh..."

The barrier flashed each time one of the shades made contact against it, and the shade fell back, writhing in agony.

After the first few shades crashed into it, cracks began to appear.

"That's...bad..." Wrynn managed before breaking into a cough. "Keep...moving..."

"If you can take Lydia, I can stay here and fight the shades. We don't want them to escape."

Wrynn shook her head. "Can't... Not enough..." She wobbled on her feet.

Taelien moved closer, using his free hand to steady her. "Okay, come on. I'll carry you both."

Wrynn considered that for a moment, then nodded. "Drop me...if anything attacks."

He wasn't planning to do that, but he nodded anyway, picking Wrynn up and putting her over his other shoulder.

"Now...*run*."

Taelien ran.

Maybe if I get out of sight, the shades will stop trying to break through the barrier.

He didn't know what the odds were of that happening, but either way, getting Lydia and Wrynn back to safety was the priority.

After all, the shades weren't the only thing watching them.

He made it a few hundred yards into the woods before things went from bad to worse.

A shimmering portal appeared in mid-air. Not a teleportation spell, but a two-way sorcerous gate, the kind that only the most powerful of travel sorcerers were capable of using.

A single figure stepped through the portal. His broad build was encased in glittering golden armor, but he still wore the same stone mask as the last time he saw him.

Perhaps more worryingly, he carried a massive two-handed hammer against his shoulder. Taelien recognized that just as quickly.

En-Vamir, the Hammer that Broke the Spine of the World.
Ooh.
I wonder if he's going to fight me with that thing.

A smile crossed his face at the thought, but he quickly reminded himself of just how precarious his position was, and that they were ostensibly supposed to be making a deal with Kyestri, not fighting him.

"Lord Kyestri," Taelien gave him a nod. "Please forgive me for not bowing, as you can see my hands are a bit too occupied."

"Of course, there is no need for such formalities." He lowered the tremendous hammer, laying the white stone head against the ground. The hammer's head was glimmering with light, the runes on it already active.

"May I ask why you're here?" Taelien scanned the forest, looking for signs of other people, but he couldn't see anyone from his current angle. That was both good and bad.

"I confess that I have been monitoring your progress, and when I saw how badly injured Prime Lady Wrynn was upon your exit from the barrier, I arrived as quickly as possible to offer aid. I have many potent healing compounds at home. If you'll follow me through the portal, we can ensure everyone's injuries are properly treated, and perhaps conclude our trade after you've had a chance to rest."

Wrynn didn't say anything. Either she'd actually lost consciousness or, Taelien suspected, she was simply faking it.

Even without her guidance, though, he could tell something was off. Not just the hammer — taking a weapon when leaving the house was a fairly reasonable precaution when you lived in a murderous death forest. He didn't know exactly what Kyestri was playing at, but if he'd wanted to offer healing items, he could have just brought them with him.

"Ah, I'm afraid that won't be possible right now. You see, Miss Jaden has to be returned straight home. Her injuries are not a concern. She's having problems with her...condition."

Well, that was probably the most vague and awkward bluff anyone has ever made, but hopefully he'll buy it.

"Ah, I do understand. My manor is a bit out of the way...but I could have a carriage prepared for you if you'll come with me briefly? I'm certain you must be tired, and carrying two people for that distance would be quite a challenge, even for a paladin of your stature."

Taelien shook his head. "No, I'll be fine. I do, however, need to hurry. I'll look forward to meeting with you again to secure our deal after we've had a chance to rest."

He continued walking down the path, watching Kyestri closely.

"You know, I really don't think that's the wisest course of action you can make right now, young paladin." Kyestri lifted the hammer again, propping it against his shoulder. Whether or not it was Koranir's actual hammer, it looked tremendously heavy, and Kyestri was holding it in one hand with seemingly no effort.

With the hammer in hand, Kyestri stepped right into the middle of the road.

Taelien sighed. "Look, even on my best day, I'm no good at political talk. I'm tired, injured, and carrying two friends. Either take a swing at me or get out of my way."

Wrynn whispered something in Taelien's ear. He stiffened, gave a slight nod of affirmation, but didn't otherwise react.

"Very well." Kyestri shook his head. "I was truly hoping we could find an amicable arrangement, but alas." Kyestri snapped his fingers.

Taelien was ready for Kyestri to attack. He wasn't quite ready for the barbed spear that flew out of the still-open portal, straight for the center of his chest.

Both his hands were occupied, and jumping to the side risked crushing one of the people he was carrying.

Instead, he concentrated.

Magnetic repulse.

A burst of metal sorcery deflected the hurled projectile, sending it to crash into a nearby tree.

Kyestri's mask-covered-face turned toward the tree. "Hm. Your metal sorcery skills are perhaps a bit better than advertised."

"I'd like to think I'm getting better all the time." Taelien smirked. "You'll be an interesting challenge. Metal against stone."

"Is that what you're expecting?" Kyestri shook his head. "Foolish. I am no ordinary sorcerer. You'll soon see that your powers are feeble compared to my own."

"Spooky. I'll look forward to letting my sword prove how wrong you are in a moment. Before we get this dance started, though, I have to ask, though — what's your goal here? The Sae'kes?"

"The Sae'kes?" Kyestri snorted. "You think overmuch of yourself, child. Not everything is about you. No, you've simply stumbled upon something I've been looking for, and I could not allow you to hold onto it."

"I was hoping for a more descriptive monologue, but I guess that's a good enough starting point. Okay. I guess if you're going to be vague, I suppose I can be the one who tells you something."

"Oh?" Kyestri sounded amused. "And what would that be?"

"Spears are great throwing weapons. But you know what's better?"

Kyestri was silent for a moment, then replied in a confused tone, "If you're going to say swords, you're definitely—"

Taelien threw Wrynn Jaden at Kyestri.

She spun around in mid-air, her right leg already glowing with inner light. Her boot slammed into Kyestri's mask, snapping his head back and leaving deep cracks in the surface of the stone. He staggered back a step, but he was already swinging his hammer before Wrynn even landed.

The hammer didn't connect, but it didn't have to.

There was a crack of thunder the moment Kyestri brought the weapon down. The ground beneath him shattered, leaving a massive crater, and a spherical burst of force surged outward and blasted Wrynn from the air. She flew backward, slamming into a nearby tree, which cracked at the force of the impact.

Even Taelien, standing several feet away, was knocked backward by the sheer force of the swing. And, as he quickly realized, that was a mere casual flick of the hammer, not a direct attack.

Ooh. I like that thing. Definitely don't want to get hit by it, though.

He spared a single glance toward Wrynn, who was already groaning and picking herself up from the ground, before rushing for cover. He ducked just in time to avoid what happened next — Kyestri swung the hammer again, this time horizontally, and a compressed wave of pressure rippled through the air toward him. As it went above him without making contact, he still felt the crushing force pressing down on him, threatening to push him against the ground. When the pressure wave hit a nearby tree, the portion of it that the wave struck collapsed inward, like it was being crushed by a gigantic fist.

Hm. Tree cover isn't going to do much, I guess.

He ran behind a tree regardless. Protection wasn't his goal, he simply needed a moment of cover.

Wrynn was up again, rushing at Kyestri and flicking her wrists. A pair of glittering knives flew from her sleeves, smacking against Kyestri's mask and leaving gouges in the side.

He grunted, then started to swing his hammer again. Wrynn jumped, surged forward in a blur, and landed atop the hammer. Then she kicked him in the face, hopped off, and kicked him again from behind.

Kyestri swung around, letting out a growl of annoyance, but showing little real harm. "You're more spry than I would have expected, Prime Lady Jaden, given your injuries."

"I'd like to think I keep in good shape for my age." She grinned.

Taelien finished finding a satisfactory spot and laid Lydia down against the ground. Then, he pulled Sculptor from his hip and concentrated on the earth.

Reshape.

The stone shaping knife assisted his focus, allowing him to quickly raise a section of the ground into a curved wall that sheltered Lydia's unconscious body. With an additional moment of focus, he concentrated on hardening the earth he'd raised as much as possible. Then, he returned Sculptor to the sheath on his belt.

Hopefully that'll protect her from collateral damage, at least. I doubt it would take a direct hit from that hammer, but if it gets a direct hit, that means something has gone very wrong.

With Lydia being at least somewhat secure, he stood just in time to see a barrage of stone projectiles flying in his direction.

His hand shot downward and drew the Sae'kes, bringing the blade upward and into the first of the projectiles. The sword's destructive aura ripped through the stone before it touched the metal, and he quickly repeated the process, swinging the blade in a flurry of cuts.

Kyestri wasn't even looking at him — he'd commanded the stone with a simple gesture in Taelien's direction. His focus was on Wrynn, who was hounding him with a series of rapid punches, her fists now enshrouded in an inky black aura.

"You're quite talented, Prime Lady Jaden. I would feel much more threatened if you were actually capable of using your true strength. With that seal of yours, you can't hope to harm me." Kyestri gestured to the ground. The dirt beneath Wrynn liquefied, then flowed upward and solidified around her legs.

Wrynn put her hands together and shoved them outward. "Oh, you might be surprised." A dozen ribbons of darkness emitted from her palms, slicing through the air. When they hit Kyestri's armor, they left deep furrows in the metal and blood streaming from the wounds inflicted on the person beneath.

Taelien rushed forward, closer to the fight, his sword raised. For the moment, the Sae'kes aura was largely under control, with five runes lit. He could have controlled it better by passing it between his hands, but he didn't have the time.

Kyestri swung his hammer at Wrynn, and with her legs bound by stone, she was in no position to dodge.

Instead, she simply raised her arms in an x-shape in front of her body, a thick veil of shadow flowing over them.

The hammer connected. There was a tremendous *crack* on the impact as an explosion of conflicting forms of power ripped the air around Kyestri and Wrynn asunder. The resulting blast of cutting shadows and pressure spread rapidly across the forest glen, leaving meter-wide cracks in the ground and shearing through entire trees and rocks.

Wrynn took the worst of it. The shadows around her arms might have diminished the impact, but they couldn't possibly stop a direct hit from a weapon of that level of power. The impact bent her backward and smashed her forearms hard, leaving them bleeding and very likely broken. She collapsed to the ground after that, unmoving, a pile of rubble around her from where the stone surrounding her legs had shattered apart. From her position, dodging or blocking another attack looked nearly impossible, and Taelien couldn't tell if she was still conscious.

Kyestri was clearly staggered by the explosion as well, reeling backward, with a small crack visible in the shaft of his hammer. He was recovering quickly, though, and preparing to take another swing.

Taelien instinctively side-stepped a cutting wave of darkness that emitted from the impact and rushed forward to close the distance. By the time Kyestri was swinging around, Taelien was in the way.

He didn't raise the Sae'kes to block. Blocking was never really Taelien's style.

In Taelien's mind, the best way to stop a devastating attack was to hit it with even greater force.

Body of Iron.

He brought the Sae'kes down in a two-handed swing, focusing the destructive aura into the point of impact where he slammed it into the shaft of Kyestri's hammer.

There was no concussive shockwave as one legendary artifact met another. No mutually-destructive wave of power as one or another powerful item shattered on impact.

Taelien had aimed for the crack in the hammer's shaft. And when he struck, he cleaved straight through without resistance.

Legendary artifacts, it seemed, were not all built to identical specifications.

As their momentum continued, the still-glimmering head of Kyestri's hammer flew off harmlessly into the distance, crashing into a boulder that crumpled inward like a ball of paper on impact.

Taelien's swing, conversely, continued through the shaft of the weapon and cut a gouge straight through the armor on Kyestri's right arm and into his bicep. He deliberately pulled the swing to avoid cutting all the way through Kyestri's arm, then swung the point upward to rest it at Kyestri's neck. "You've lost. Surrender."

Kyestri's other hand shot out, grabbing Taelien around the neck. "I think not. **Petrify.**"

Taelien's eyes widened as his throat suddenly felt constricted. He understood what was happening in an instant, bringing his sword down and severing Kyestri's left arm at the wrist.

Then he fell backward, pulling Kyestri's severed hand off his neck.

...But it was too late. The spell had already taken effect, and his body was beginning to turn to stone.

Taelien released his left hand from the grip of the Sae'kes, gripping at his throat as he began to choke.

Stop, he commanded the spread of stone. It was stone sorcery, after all — he could feel the stone essence spreading throughout his body, and he could resist it.

But he wasn't strong enough. He was no Prime Lord of Stone, and the potency of the spell was beyond his current strength. He was able to slow the progression, but failed to stop it.

As he watched in horror, Kyestri sighed, discarded the useless shaft of his hammer, and began to change.

His body seemed to liquefy, turning into something resembling flowing mud. The armor he was wearing fell into a pile, his broken mask falling alongside it and finally shattering apart.

The mud-form moved to the side of the pile, then re-solidified into a taller and more bestial shape.

He stood nine feet tall, still vaguely humanoid, but with vicious fangs and four glowing red eyes. His skin had turned to dark blue, with bits of armor-like carapace forming over it. His right arm now ended in a six-fingered claw, spikes protruded from his back and forehead, and a spined tail sprouted from his back.

His left wrist still ended at a stump, and as he glanced down at it, he let out a hiss. "*Destroyed.* Your weapon is potent." Kyestri — or whatever had been pretending to be Kyestri — turned toward him. "I will enjoy using it."

Taelien fell to his knees, his vision briefly going black. In desperation, his free hand fumbled across his belt until he found a hilt.

He grabbed Sculptor, drawing it and pressing the blade against his neck. The knife bit into the bare portion that remained flesh, drawing blood. And with that, he could feel the power of the knife flowing into his body.

Stop. Reverse.

With Sculptor's aid, he began to push the petrification spell back.

That did, however, take all of his effort. He had no way of raising his sword to block or counter when Kyestri surged forward far faster than he'd moved before, then took a claw and raked it across Taelien's face.

Blood flowed across Taelien's face. Blood flowed from open wounds where claws gouged him, but none of them went particularly deep.

The impact jarred Taelien's hand, moving Sculptor out of position and leaving a red trail across Taelien's neck. Fortunately, his Body of Iron was still in effect and prevented it from cutting deeply.

Instinctively, he jabbed upward with the knife in response to the attack, but Kyestri merely gripped his wrist. "**Petrify.**"

And with that, Taelien's left arm began to turn to stone.

Taelien swept the Sae'kes upward, swinging for Kyestri's other arm. Kyestri was faster, releasing Taelien's grip and avoiding the swing, then jumping backward as a boulder smashed the ground where he'd been standing a moment before.

Wrynn?

But Wrynn was still on the ground nearby, unmoving.

Then who—

Taelien coughed, his vision blurring. The petrification spells were both spreading again now, and he needed to concentrate to try to stop them.

Through his distorted vision and the haze of pain, he barely understood what happened next.

A glowing figure flew in front of him, shimmering with green and white energy. She was wreathed in a halo of leaves, and when she raised her hand, a tiny sphere of light appeared above her palm. "Ancient servant of the Sun Eater, you have no place in this world. **Begone**."

The speaker was Lydia, but the voice was not her own.

Still, Taelien recognized it. He had heard the faintest whispers of it in his mind when he'd first carried a green gemstone out of the Paths of Ascension in Orlyn.

Lydia closed her hand into a fist, then reopened it. A spiraling nimbus of green-white energy shot forward. Kyestri's eyes widened and he stomped the ground, raising a stone wall between them. The blast tore straight through the wall and struck him in the chest, leaving a gaping hole.

Taelien continued concentrating on the stone essence in his body. With Sculptor still in his grip, he was barely holding the two spells at bay, and his breathing was labored by the portion of his neck that remained in a stone form.

Release Body of Iron.

Body of Stone.

It was a risky move. By flooding more stone essence into his body, he risked worsening the spell if he lost control.

But this stone essence was *his*, invoked by his own sorcery. He sent the conjured essence toward the petrification spell, then forced the energies into contact and willed the petrification spell to *change*.

His body and spirit trembled with effort.

Kyestri stumbled back from his broken wall, clutching his chest. He spat blood, growled, and then bent double with pain. He shivered for a moment, then rose again.

The hole in his chest had closed, as if it had never been there.

"Shapeshifting to heal your injuries? An advanced technique." The voice was Lydia's this time, at least at the start. "I will not allow it to continue," she continued in the *other* voice.

Kyestri spoke her name, confirming Taelien's suspicions. "Vendria. Or, Venora, I should say. It seems you have found a host body." He snarled, turning his head to the side. "No matter. With only two pieces, you are still out of balance. Your power and control will be weak."

Lydia floated to the ground. "You've missed a key detail." She pointed at herself. "This mortal body is not a mere 'host'. She has shared her strength with me, and I with her. And together—" She pointed her finger at Kyestri, "We have made a new whole."

Another blast of light flashed from her finger. This time, Kyestri dove aside, swinging his own hand. His shattered stone wall separated into spikes, flying at Lydia.

They crashed into her and splintered on contact without any effect.

Lydia snapped her fingers.

The ground beneath Kyestri transformed into crystalline chains, which shot upward and entangled his body. He struggled against them, but more chains fell into place with each moment.

"I will learn why you are here." Lydia floated forward, still glowing with bright light. "And you will be punished for harming my friends."

Then she whispered to herself, "Your turn."

The aura around her changed in a moment. Instead of a vital aura of glimmering green, it was blue and white. The temperature in the forest dropped precipitously, with the ground beneath her freezing solid. The tips of her hair turned frosted white.

As Kyestri struggled to swing at her, she effortlessly grabbed his hand.

"**Freeze.**"

Kyestri froze solid in an instant, his body a statue of ice.

Lydia turned away from him, shivering for an instant, then the glowing aura around her faded as she settled down against the ground. She blinked, scanning the area and seeming to see it with new eyes. "Taelien!" Her eyes settled on him and she began to walk forward. Her leg very nearly buckled as she stepped forward. "Ah. Easy to forget about that. Hold on, I'll help you." A stone staff formed in her right hand, and she began to use to it walk forward toward where Taelien was still focusing on the ground.

Change.

He continued to will the petrification spells to shift at his command, and they continued to resist him. Perhaps if Lydia could reinforce his efforts with her newly-gained stone sorcery, together they could...

"Look...out..." Taelien barely managed to choke out the warning, his vision flashing red from the effort of speech.

Lydia spun just in time to see what he'd seen — a second figure emerging from the still-open portal that Kyestri had opened.

"Well, well. It seems you've started the party without me, haven't you?"

Jonathan Sterling smirked as he stepped out of the portal, a gleaming white-bladed sword rested against his shoulder. "Can't have that. I've been waiting for this for entirely too long."

CHAPTER XXI – VELAS V – THE SECOND SILK

Jonan had the hand of a vae'kes around his neck, which was never a good start to a fight.

Still, Velas would work with what she had.

Slowly...

She had to remain undetected, and that was harder than usual. Using any sound sorcery to mask her movements would unveil her presence.

Aladir moved first. "Unhand him." The bracelet around his wrist flickered, and it vanished, a gleaming sword manifesting in his right hand.

"If you insist." The Shrouded One spun, hurling Jonan straight into Aladir. They crashed together on the floor in an unruly pile.

The Shrouded One stalked closer as they tried to disentangle themselves and rise. She wasn't even armed, but she didn't need to be.

She raised a hand and conjured a ball of flame. It grew larger — and hotter — with every passing moment. "I'm grateful, Kestrian. I'd always wanted to finish what I'd started, all those years ago. Now, you've given me a chance to tie up a loose end."

Jonan and Aladir rolled apart. Jonan was just pushing himself upward when the Shrouded One moved to hurl the globe of flame in his direction.

Jonan snapped his fingers. The fireball exploded before it left the Shrouded One's hand.

She fell backward, screaming, as Jonan pushed himself to his feet. "I hate fire. You *made* me hate fire, Lavender. But that anger, that resentment — that drove me to *learn*."

The flames ignited the Shrouded One's glove and veils. She snarled, hurling the glove and veil free. Beneath the veils were a black-haired woman. Velas didn't recognize her, but she did note the presence of old burn scars all across the right side of the woman's face.

Lavender. So that's her name. A flower name, meaning she works for Jacinth.

Velas felt along the wood beneath her, searching, until she heard the 'click' of a switch and a compartment opened. Her hand grasped her weapon, and slowly, she began to rise.

Jonan was on his feet now. He ran straight at Lavender, his hand wreathed in fire.

Lavender shoved her hand straight through his chest...then snarled as Jonan vanished, and a blast of flame smashed into her from the side.

"Illusions." She waved a hand. Velas couldn't see the real Jonan's location, but she heard him fly backward as a blast of force from the Shrouded One smashed him backward into a nearby wall.

Another wave of Lavender's hand sent a blast of flame in the same direction as the sound of the crash. For a moment, she could see Jonan's profile outlined in fire, then the flames faded.

He managed to disperse her attack, but he got burned in the process, Velas realized. *He's not strong enough to repel her attacks directly. I need to help.*

Within those few moments, the burn wounds from the explosion and Jonan's blast of fire had already healed.

Oh, and she's regenerating, too. Just perfect.

Aladir was on her a moment later, swinging that gleaming sword of his. He was much faster than Velas would have expected from a healer, but Lavender still dodged his swing easily, then slammed a palm into his chest. He flew backward, then drove his sword into the ground to slow his movement. In a moment, he was up and swinging again, a crescent-shaped wave of light following his swing.

Lavender side-stepped that attack as well, but it put her right where Velas needed.

Enhance.

Lavender began turning as soon as Velas activated the spell — she must have sensed it. But Velas was already moving, jabbing the Heartlance upward from her position in the coffin.

The strike wasn't perfect. She was aiming from the ground, with too little room to move a spear properly, and Lavender was fast enough to try to move out of the way.

Those factors meant that rather than impaling Lavender outright, Velas had to settle for simply jabbing the Heartlance through Lavender's right shoulder.

Lavender screamed, stumbling back, her shoulder bleeding. She ripped herself free from the weapon as she fell backward, pressing a hand to the wound and staring at it in disbelief. "You...you weren't supposed to be here."

Velas hopped out of the coffin, then tapped the end of the Heartlance against the floor. Gold flowed across the shaft of the spear and into her body, further increasing her speed.

"Turns out it's very hard for oracles to see my future. Don't know why, but Jonan and I knew we could use it. See, we knew you'd predict him coming up here. And we knew, being the arrogant monologuing villain type, you'd probably let him." Velas smirked. "Thanks. Fate might not be very predictable, but *you* certainly are."

"Eru volar proter taris." Phantasmal armor solidified around her. "Tell us what you've done with Rialla, and maybe I'll be merciful, just this once."

The Shrouded One laughed. "Rialla Dianis? You're here for her? You're *far* too late."

Velas snarled. "Thought so. Guess it's just time for some old fashioned revenge, then." She leveled her spear, then jabbed again, this time aiming for Lavender's leg.

Lavender blasted herself backward with a burst of kinetic energy, no different from the type Velas used herself.

Aladir launched another crescent of light at Lavender as she moved, but she raised a hand and formed a sphere of blackness, which spread out into a shield that nullified the attack.

A blast of flame hit Lavender from behind a moment later. She snarled and spun again, swinging a fist at the empty air. There was a grunt from an invisible Jonan as a crushing burst of force slammed into him, then he went silent.

Velas lunged at Lavender from behind.

Lavender blurred and vanished.

A moment later, Velas felt something smash into her jaw. She stumbled backward, nearly losing her grip on her spear. Then something hit her again, too fast for her to get her guard up. A sharp pain spread through her chest, and she knew that without her armor spell, a strike with that level of force might have pierced straight through her body.

Listen.

Instinctively, she enhanced her hearing to try to trace her invisible attacker, but it didn't matter. She realized too late that as another sound sorcerer, Lavender must have already silenced her own movements. Lavender struck her again, this time in the throat.

She fell, gasping, and her grip on the Heartlance slipped.

The moment the spear hit the floor, it vanished.

Velas reached for the spot that it had been, but she felt only solid ground. A moment later, she blasted herself backward, growling. "You stole some of Jonan's sight sorcery."

"I admit, it always irritated me that he'd been able to hide from me as a child." The voice came from her right.

...But that was an obvious trick. She could sense the sound sorcery that had thrown the voice, and she could sense the path it came from.

Push.

She shoved herself in the direction the sorcery had emanated from as hard as she could, swinging her fist.

Her swing caught resistance. Lavender flickered for an instant, but didn't appear completely.

Velas missed that momentary window, but Aladir didn't.

Roots burst from the stone below Lavender, wrapping around her leg and pulling downward.

Lavender vanished entirely again a moment later, but Velas could still see the roots moving — Lavender was still there.

Velas jumped backward, avoiding a swipe from the Heartlance that she'd seen coming in the moment when Lavender had been visible, then pulled her fist back and called as much force as she could muster.

"You can't hurt me with that," came Lavender's voice from behind her.

Velas ignored it. The roots were still moving, snapping apart as Lavender struggled.

Aladir slashed the air again, creating another shockwave. A shadow shield appeared to block it again, but that meant Lavender was distracted.

Velas launched her blast of force. Not at Lavender herself, but at the floor beneath her, already damaged by Aladir's roots.

The floor beneath Lavender collapsed.

The fall wouldn't do much harm, but Velas had accurately assessed Lavender's instincts. Lavender released her grip on the Heartlance and grabbed onto the side of the hole as it appeared to stop herself from falling.

In that moment, the Heartlance reappeared, and Velas threw a smaller blast of force from her other hand to send it across the room. It flew until it cracked into the side of the second coffin, still unopened.

There was the sound of someone — presumably Jonan — snapping their fingers. Lavender reappeared, fully visible. Her invisibility had been dispelled.

Lavender hurled herself upward from the side of the hole, flying into the air.

With a whisper carried by sound sorcery, Velas sent a message.

Now.

The second coffin exploded.

And before Lavender had even landed, the figure within that coffin had grabbed the Heartlance and hurled it at her with tremendous force.

Lavender blasted herself backward. The Heartlance crashed into the ceiling, embedding itself deeply into the stone.

When she landed, she was forced to dodge immediately. Dozens of floating swords were whipping at her from all directions, each burning with blue-green flames.

"*Harvester*," Lavender hissed.

The Wandering War stood among the ruins of the coffin, brushing himself off with one hand while controlling his floating swords with the other. "God-child. I will be your opponent."

As one of the blazing swords flew at her, Lavender stepped beyond it, then grabbed the hilt. The sword vanished, then she had conjured one of her own in her hands a moment later, using it to deflect the rapid strikes of the others.

Velas launched herself upward, ignoring the growing pain in her chest.

Surge.

She flew toward the ceiling, but a blast of flame from Lavender forced her to adjust her trajectory before she could reach the Heartlance.

"Touch of Life." Aladir's hand glowed as he briefly touched someone Velas couldn't see.

Jonan must be badly hurt from those blasts that hit him earlier, she realized. *And he must have excluded Aladir from his invisibility. Wish I could see him, it'd be easier to coordinate.*

Lavender burst through a growing tide of conjured blades, aiming her own conjured weapon straight at the Wandering War's chest.

He drew a gleaming greatsword from his side, red runes shimmering on the black surface of the blade.

"You made a mistake coming here, Harvester." She brought her sword down, but he parried the strike easily.

Lavender's conjured weapon shattered, and War countered with a slice aimed at her chest.

She blocked with one arm. His attack drew a bloody line, but stopped before cutting deeper.

And with her other arm, Lavender reached forward and grabbed War's wrist. "You're the worst possible match against someone like me."

War trembled. His shoulders sagged as essence rapidly flowed from him into Lavender's hand.

He pulled back, opening his mouth—

A conjured dagger appeared in Lavender's other hand, just like the kind War used. She slashed it across his throat, and blood flowed freely from the wound.

War let out a gasp, clutching his neck feebly, and collapsed to the ground.

"Fool." Lavender kicked the fallen Harvester's body, then picked up his greatsword.

"No!" Aladir screamed, sending a shockwave in Lavender's direction before she could raise her sword to bring it down on the Harvester's fallen form.

Lavender swept the Harvester's sword through Aladir's projectile, cutting it in half.

Velas landed a moment later, swinging a punch at Lavender. She barely managed to pull herself back as Lavender swung upward, nearly cutting off Velas' hand at the wrist.

As Lavender swung the greatsword at Velas' chest, Velas flung herself backward, aiming for the ceiling again.

A hail of swords glowing with blue-green fire appeared around her.

"Oh, resh—"

With a motion of her hand, Lavender brought the swords down.

Velas was cut a dozen times in a moment. Her phantasmal armor offered some protection, turning deadly blows into shallow cuts, but the force of the barrage still drove her back to the ground.

She pulled a knife and hurled it as Lavender stepped closer, but Lavender deflected it effortlessly.

"Spirit, give me strength!" A soft glow surrounded Aladir's body as he charged into sword range again, swinging his glittering blade. In the rapid exchange of strikes and parries that followed, Aladir came inches from landing a blow to Lavender's wrist, only to have it deflected with a floating sword that appeared in the way.

A second floating sword hit him in the back of the arm a moment later, then a third pierced through his shoulder. The blades pressed downward, pinning Aladir to the ground.

Velas had to jump backward to dodge several more floating swords. They were pursuing her now, seemingly of their own accord.

I...can't keep this up much longer. I have to end it here.

Velas surged in.

She didn't aim for a punch this time.

Instead, she simply slammed straight into Lavender and wrapped her arms around her in an attempted grapple. Velas was bleeding badly, and didn't have the strength to hold her for very long. In a moment, Lavender had slipped an arm free, and she was maneuvering it to grab Velas' throat.

Fortunately, that moment was all she needed.

Her injuries were ebbing at her strength, but Velas hadn't forgotten her last encounter with Lavender.

Expulse.

Every bleeding wound was a place where the strange power living inside Velas could escape.

In the moment of Velas' command, she was bathed in a flood of light as power escaped from every wound in her body.

Lavender screamed, struggling with great strength. Velas pulled her tighter.

Expulse.

Another flash of light. Another scream. Then an elbow buried itself in Velas' chest, and she fell backward with a gasp.

Lavender's body was covered with burns. And, unlike the burns caused by ordinary flame sorcery earlier in the fight, these weren't healing closed.

Velas didn't have a chance to celebrate. A moment later, Lavender slashed War's greatsword straight across her chest.

There was a moment of shock as the wound spread. Then Velas felt herself falling, her legs no longer capable of holding her.

She hit the ground hard, a pool of blood rapidly spreading around her.

No...it can't...

Her vision blurred. She strained to lift her hand.

The greatsword came down, aiming for her neck.

A blast of force carried Lavender out of the way. The greatsword cut into the floor next to her, briefly getting stuck.

Then Jonan was there, fully visible. His shirt was torn and bloodied, and his skin was badly burned. A glowing rune was visible on his arm, the one he'd used to conjure that force.

And as his eyes narrowed, a new rune appeared on his arm, flashing with a crimson glow.

Flames ignited around both of his hands. Red, orange, then brilliant white.

She'd never seen fire glow that brightly.

A dominion mark for flame sorcery? When did he get that? And how is he using it without speaking?

Jonan stepped toward Lavender, the runes on his skin and the flames around his hands growing ever brighter. "Lavender. You—"

Lavender ran him through.

"—always fall for the same tricks."

The false Jonan vanished.

White flames crashed into Lavender from behind, then engulfed her entirely. The stone beneath her melted, and Velas' skin cracked and broke just from proximity to the heat.

Seconds passed. Then she heard a grunt, and her fading vision turned to where Jonan materialized nearby.

A floating sword had pierced through his back.

The white fire faded.

Jonan collapsed to the ground, the sword still embedded in his back.

Aladir was still pinned to the stone, other conjured weapons piercing through his arm and shoulder.

Lavender was standing right where she had been, encased in armor of half-melted ice. She was badly burned beneath that ice, presumably from the first few moments of the attack, but those burns were rapidly healing.

No...that's...

The remains of the ice armor fell away. Lavender smiled, striding forward, resting War's sword against her shoulder. "I suppose I should be grateful your friend came to rescue you, Velas. Without her ice sorcery, I might not have survived that."

"You..." Velas clenched her fist, but she couldn't find the strength to even raise it.

"I confess, you gave me more of a fight than I expected. As a sign of respect to another Silk, I'll make it quick." Lavender raised War's greatsword.

Velas tried to call on the power within her again.

Please. One last time. Even if I die, let me do something. Let me avenge the others.

Please...

But her body, and the power within it, didn't care about sentiment.

Nothing happened.

Lavender's sword came down.

Roots burst from the ground beneath Lavender, catching her wrist. She glared at Aladir on the ground, waving her other hand.

"Lissari, take my breath to heal those who need it," Aladir whispered. With Velas' still-enhanced hearing, she could just barely make out the words.

She felt the slightest rustle in the air, then her wounds began to close. It didn't heal her much — it was too difficult to properly channel energy without physical contact, even for a veteran like Aladir. Still, some of the pain from her injuries diminished.

A moment later, two more swords shot downward and pierced through Aladir's body. He shuddered for a moment, then his eyes closed.

No...

Lavender pulled free of the roots. She didn't bother saying anything else, she simply raised her sword again.

The sound of a voice made her pause.

"Open...the...other...door..." Jonan mumbled, barely audible. He was still on the ground, a phantasmal sword pinning him to the floor, and his words were pained. "I...get it now." He let out the slightest chuckle, then broke into a cough. His hand extended upward from the ground, pointing. There was a burst of motion sorcery from his hand, then a crack as wood splintered.

The door to the roof shattered to pieces, and a look of shock crossed Lavender's face.

Asphodel descended from above. She had wings of glimmering amethyst protruding from her back. Her entire body was shimmering with power.

And her once bright crystalline hair was almost entirely grey.

"You. The other oracle." Lavender snarled, her grip around her sword tightening. "You're too late."

"No." Asphodel smiled softly. "I believe I am precisely on time."

With a wave, Lavender sent a dozen black swords in Asphodel's direction.

With a single beat of her tremendous wings, Asphodel had flown out of the way, her hand reaching up and grabbing something from the ceiling.

As she descended in a lunge, golden light flashed along the surface.

The Heartlance.

Asphodel's lunge was deflected by a swing of War's sword, but a second jab followed, and a third.

Lavender stumbled back. Her burns and cuts hadn't entirely healed, and the wounds that Velas had inflicted with her strange light hadn't healed at all.

After a momentary exchange, Asphodel was pushing Lavender back.

A flick of a wrist changed that. Asphodel flew backward, and a wall of icy spikes appeared behind her.

She swerved, her wings buffeting her out of the way of the icy wall, only to have Lavender appear right behind her.

She...teleported.

More of Rialla's sorcery.

Asphodel ducked a swing aiming for her neck, but took a blast of fire straight to the chest.

Need...to help...Asphodel...

Velas grunted, attempting to push herself back up, but a surge of pain through her chest made it clear that was impossible. Even with Aladir's last healing breath, it took every effort just to remain conscious.

Asphodel winced, then parried a swing from War's sword with the Heartlance.

Lavender vanished again. When she reappeared, she found Asphodel already lunging for her. Lavender barely managed to raise the greatsword in time to parry, and even then, it skidded along the edge and jabbed into her left arm. She staggered back with another bleeding wound.

Lavender blasted herself backward, snarling. "Enough of this. I only have to touch you once, delaren. You're just as vulnerable as War was."

Asphodel nodded. "I know. You won't."

Lavender screamed in fury, vanishing.

She reappeared only inches from Asphodel, her hand reaching out.

Asphodel used her free hand and smashed a vial in Lavender's face.

Lavender stumbled back, screaming, black fluid trailing over her face. "This is...what have you..."

"The same thing Susan Crimson did to me. Void essence. And while Sterling might be a void sorcerer with some resistance to it, you, Shrouded One, are not."

Lavender lashed out blindly. Even without her sight and with her sorcery weakened, she was tremendously fast. Asphodel managed a parry, but only barely.

And then, before Asphodel could recover, Lavender stepped forward and grabbed the Heartlance by the shaft with her off-hand.

Asphodel struggled, but even empowered by her transformation, she couldn't match Lavender's strength. The Heartlance slipped from her grasp.

There was a critical moment as Lavender wrenched the spear backward with her single-handed grip. An instant in which she'd thrown herself off-balance.

And in that moment, two people struck.

Asphodel surged forward, smashing Lavender in the chin with a fist. The blow caused little harm, but it served as an ample distraction.

Velas wasn't able to stand, but she could see the battle clearly enough to sense an opportunity.

Her hand clenched and she focused.

Motion sorcery could do more than just push. She remembered when The Wandering War had used it during the paladin trials to tear her out of the sky mid-jump.

And, as much as she loathed to mimic one of Taelien's tricks, she had to admit that pulling could be just as useful as pushing at times.

Pull.

With a surge of every bit of essence she could muster, she wrenched the Heartlance from Lavender's hand. The spear few from Lavender's grip straight to her own.

Lavender struck again a moment later, the blackness of void already beginning to fade from her face. Asphodel tried to dodge, but her movement seemed sloppier than usual.

She can't predict Lavender's movements. Their oracular abilities don't work on each other.

War's sword scored a gash across one of Asphodel's forearms. Asphodel's jaw tightened, but she said nothing. She simply circled to the right, looking for a window to strike.

Lavender didn't spare Velas a glance. She put every effort into cutting her last opponent down, swinging furiously. Asphodel could find no window to counter, more cuts managing to make their way through her guard every few moments.

Velas focused on the spear in her hand.

This had better work.

"Blood of the fallen, ignite my spirit."

It was the command that Jonan had written for her — one to unlock some hidden latent power within the Heartlance. As a technique made for an esharen wielder, she knew it had the chance to harm her as much as help, but she could see no alternatives. If it failed, she saw no chance at victory.

The spear glowed brightly for an instant with inner light.

...And then nothing else happened. She felt no well of inner strength, no further healing of her wounds, no change in the power of her spirit.

Then the glow faded, and she was once again helpless on the ground.

Lavender tossed a glance in her direction, raising an eyebrow. Asphodel surged in again, trying to take advantage of the distraction, but earned only a slash that cut a chunk off of one of her crystalline wings.

Then Asphodel was falling back again, avoiding another swing.

No. We can't win this way. I need...

A deep voice caught her by surprise. "An...interesting...technique..."

The voice came from a figure on the ground nearby.

The Wandering War was looking up at her, his eyes glimmering faintly. One of his hands was still clutching at his throat, but the damage seemed less than she'd seen before.

With his other arm, he was slowly pulling himself along the ground toward her.

He's...alive?

There was a pool of blood where he'd fallen, his face was contorted with agony and exhaustion. But he lived, albeit barely.

And he was crawling toward her with every bit of strength he could muster.

Aladir's healing spell must have caught him, too, Velas realized. *But it wasn't enough to get either of us back in the fight.*

"War...what are you...?"

He was near her now, almost within reach.

Asphodel took a cut to her other wing. She hurled another black potion, but Lavender dodged it, and it exploded harmlessly on the ground.

"The spear..." He reached for it. "Please."

Velas narrowed her eyes. She didn't like the idea of passing the Heartlance off to anyone. She didn't like giving away her last weapon, the last symbol of her strength.

But when their eyes met, and she saw his pleading and resolve, she made a decision.

I can't win this on my own.

This time...I'm going to give him my trust.

With the last of her strength, she pushed herself forward and passed him the spear.

A thin smile crossed his lips, though they still trembled with agony.

"Thank...you...Velas. The technique...requires sacrifice." He coughed, producing blood. Then, shaking, he moved the spear.

"With this...perhaps I'll be able to fight him again...someday..."

And then, with a single movement, he drove the Heartlance into the center of his chest.

The entire room darkened. A red aura crackled in the air around War.

And in the space of another instant, his body crumbled to dust.

The Heartlance clattered to the ground in front of Velas. The metal glistened blood-red.

Pull.

The Heartlance flew to her hand, easily this time.

And when her grip tightened around it, she felt a surge of strength like she'd never known.

The golden lines across her skin faded, replaced with trails of black and red. The air around her ripped apart, and the ground beneath her crumbled. A swirling aura of flame ripped around her.

When Velas stood, Lavender was staring at her, jaw agape.

Surge.

Velas flew forward, slamming the shaft of the staff into Lavender's face. The vae'kes fell backward, staggering. Lavender clumsily raised War's sword to parry the next swing.

But Velas was already behind her, jamming the Heartlance into Lavender's leg.

Lavender screamed, falling to the floor.

She swung her sword upward, but Velas was gone, already moving to Lavender's other side.

The shaft of the Heartlance came upward, slamming underneath Lavender's jaw and snapping her head back.

Lavender hit the ground hard, then snapped her fingers and vanished.

She reappeared near the chamber's entrance door.

I won't let you run.

Surge.

The command shifted Velas faster than she'd ever believed possible. She was in front of Lavender in the moment, raising her spear again.

When she jabbed again, Lavender was ready this time. She abandoned War's sword and grabbed the shaft of the spear with both hands, grunting with effort.

"I'll...take that." Blackness welled around Velas' hands and she understood what Lavender was trying to do.

But it didn't matter. The power burning within Velas didn't dim. It burned brighter with every passing moment.

With a single movement, she wrenched the spear out of Lavender's hands. "This is for Rialla."

She jammed the spear into Lavender's right shoulder.

As Lavender fell backward in shock, Velas struck again.

"This is for War."

She smashed the spear's haft across Lavender's throat. Lavender choked, raising her hands to her neck.

"And this..." Velas spun the spear, her hands clenched tight. "Is for Garrick Torrent."

With all the strength she could muster, she slammed the Heartlance into the side of Lavender's head.

Lavender crumpled, insensate, to the ground.

Velas raised the spear again, her jaw tight...then jammed it down into Lavender's arm, pinning it into the floor. "That should keep you from leaving."

When she released her grip from the spear, she realized her mistake.

In a heartbeat, her new strength had fled her.

Asphodel caught her before she could fall.

"You did well." Asphodel said.

Pain was rapidly returning. "I..." Velas coughed. Her vision reddened.

"You'll be fine." Asphodel helped Velas into a sitting position, then turned to Lavender. She retrieved another handful of black vials from her pouch, then smashed them all into Lavender's unconscious form at once. "That will hold her for a while."

Velas nodded blearily, her vision swimming. "I..."

The glowing swords that had been pinning Aladir and Jonan to the ground vanished, the source of their essence exhausted.

"Wait there." Asphodel instructed.

Asphodel raced toward Aladir, reaching into her bag and retrieving a red potion. She poured it across his back.

We...did we...win?

That was the last thought that crossed Velas' mind before her eyes closed.

CHAPTER XXII – LYDIA VII – A PATH TO VICTORY

Lydia's jaw tightened. "Sterling. I'd suspected your involvement with Kyestri, but I couldn't be certain."

"Well, well. You've managed to make a real mess of things here, haven't you?" Sterling clapped his hands, stepping away from the portal. "As usual, it seems I'll need to clean up after your messes."

Lydia glowered at him. "Clean up? You *killed* a friend of mine."

"Oh, Torrent? That was unfortunate. I should have gone straight to the source of the problems." Sterling raised his glimmering golden sword. "Really, such a waste. You would have made an excellent servant."

Lydia snapped her fingers. A dome of stone appeared around Sterling, encasing him in an instant.

Still, she knew it wouldn't hold him for long, and her body surged with pain from the effort.

Her strength was already rapidly fading.

She turned her head from side to side, searching. She could sense other figures in the distance, but they weren't the immediate concern.

Wrynn Jaden was groaning and sitting up. Her forearms were both bleeding badly, but the bones that Lydia had seen protruding from them seemed to have vanished back into her arms.

A powerful regeneration effect, Lydia realized. *But even with that, I doubt she's up for fighting. She taxed herself tremendously in the battle with Venlyra and maintaining the barriers in the forest.*

Taelien was still down, too. He'd released the Sae'kes and had one hand pressed against a wound on his throat. That would have been alarming enough in itself, but a voice informed her that was not the greatest problem.

[A petrification spell. He's resisting it, but with difficulty. It's too soon to say if he will succeed on his own.]

Thanks, Vendria. Can you help?

[If we can get close, yes. Just touch him, I'll do the rest.]

Lydia nodded, turning toward Taelien and hoping that the stone dome would hold Sterling a few more moments.

Predictably, she hadn't moved a step before Sterling appeared right next to her, shaking his head. "Speaking of Torrent, he *did* leave a lasting impression on me."

Lydia swung her stone staff. The conjured weapon was crude, but she'd left her sword cane behind when she'd floated, half-aware, toward the fight with Kyestri earlier.

Sterling deflected the staff with a flip of his sword, then riposted. Sparks flew as his sword scraped against her barrier. It left cracks, but she was uninjured.

He hopped back before she could swing again, but that wasn't her plan.

She dropped the staff, pointing her ring finger at him. "Eru volar—"

There was a flash, then her barrier cracked and her finger was missing.

Lydia screamed, stumbling back.

A second, green barrier fell into place as she stumbled, just in time to block Sterling's follow-up lunge.

[Can't...do...much more. Tired.]

Her bleeding wound froze a moment later.

<I am no healer, but I can stop the bleeding,> Venlyra's voice explained in her mind. <This may be the last of my strength as well, however. I'm sorry. I used too much in the previous battles. I must rest.>

Lydia gritted her teeth. The numbness that settled into the stump where her finger had been diminished the pain, but didn't stop it entirely.

"*Lift.*" She commanded the air, feeling her throat tighten. The wind carried her off the ground, and as Sterling swung again, she flew out of the way of his swing. He pursued relentlessly, but with a wave of her hand, she blasted him backward.

He vanished, reappearing right behind her.

Lydia flew to the side, earning a glancing cut off her barrier as she moved. She fumbled for the pouch of dust at her side, but with a missing finger, even the simple motion to get it open was agonizingly difficult.

Sterling readied himself for another lunge, smiling. Then something crashed into him from behind, sending him stumbling forward.

When he spun, Wrynn was there, surrounded by an aura of floating knives.

"Hi."

She pointed. Dozens of knives slammed into Sterling, flashing with elemental energies as they made contact. A blazing knife set his shirt aflame, and another cut a length off his hair.

Sterling snarled, tossing off the burning shirt. The knives spun around in mid-air, crashing into him again, but not a single one broke through his skin.

Lydia finished opening her bag. There wasn't as much dust left as she'd hoped, but it was still far from empty. With a gesture, she carried the dust on the wind.

As Sterling lunged for Wrynn, dust settled on his skin.

For a moment, his eyes fluttered, his charge abruptly stopped.

"...What...What was I...?"

Wrynn vanished, moving too fast for Lydia to follow. When Lydia saw Wrynn again, she was launching a kick straight at Sterling's chest, her leg surrounded by a black aura.

Sterling blearily raised a hand to block the incoming kick, but he was too slow. The sheer force of the impact blasted him backward, straight back through the portal.

Lydia glanced toward Wrynn.

"Get Taelien on his feet and get out of here," Wrynn said. "That won't keep him for—"

A black-bladed sword flew out of the portal, straight at Wrynn. She dodged to the side, but it cut a long gash along her left arm.

She winced, slapping her other hand over the injury. "Void," she hissed. "I'm..."

She bent over double, gritting her teeth.

Sterling walked back out of the portal a moment later, his sword once again sheathed at his hip.

Lydia flew toward Taelien as fast as she could. He was still writhing on the ground, struggling to breathe. His face was bright red.

Sterling continued to ignore Lydia, facing Wrynn. "Ordinarily, I'd be quite concerned to tangle with you directly. But you're injured, exhausted, and don't have access to the overwhelming majority of your powers. I've been watching. You're struggling with that seal of yours." Sterling smiled at her. "If you keep fighting, you'll just wear yourself out."

Wrynn grimaced. "Suppose you're right. Do you really want to back me into a corner and see what happens?"

"You're assuming I'm afraid of the consequences of breaking your seal." Sterling pressed his hands together, forming a sphere of utter blackness between his hands. "You're mistaken."

He hurled the orb, and Wrynn's eyes widened as she recognized it, just as Lydia did.

More void sorcery. If he keeps hitting her with that...

Wrynn leapt out of the way of the orb, but as she jumped, Sterling lifted his left hand, vanished, and appeared right below her. He redrew his golden sword in a classic execution of the Instant Striking Style, slicing upward. An aura of burning light covered the blade as he swung.

Wrynn reacted in an instant, a barrier forming around her arms as she blocked his swing. There was a flash of light from his sword on impact, cracking the barrier, but failing to break it. The force of the impact still carried her backward, and she landed in an uncharacteristic stumble. It was only after she landed that Lydia saw the real damage — that flash of light had blasted several holes in the shadeweave tunic she was wearing. He hadn't worsened her injuries much, but now she had more clear vulnerable points for Sterling to target with future attacks.

As Sterling lunged for another swing, something caught him from behind — a solid shadow, grabbing underneath his shoulders.

Wrynn flicked her wrist. A dagger with a silvery blade flew out of her sleeve.

Sterling raised his left hand and vanished again. "Irritating." Sterling appeared right in front of Lydia, smashing a fist into her chest. She flew backward, crashing into a nearby tree. Venora's barrier had absorbed much of the force of the punch, but the impact still sent a jolt of pain through her body. She groaned, her vision swimming.

Then Sterling vanished again, appearing in front of Wrynn and swinging his sword at her chest.

Wrynn hopped backward to avoid the blade, bringing her hand forward as she moved. A burst of tenebrous force erupted from her palm, slamming into Sterling a moment later.

Sterling ignored her attack entirely, walking right through it. "Miss Jaden. Wrynn. Can I call you Wrynn?" He smiled. "You're not in any condition to fight me right now. Withdraw, and I'll allow your involvement here to be forgotten."

Wrynn responded by snarling and blurring forward, shoving an open hand into the center of Sterling's chest. There a web of shadows spread over his body, then anchored themselves into the ground.

Sterling was immobilized, but only a moment. When she swung her other hand, blazing with fire, he shifted his arm, vanished, and appeared behind her.

Lydia grunted, barely finding the strength to push herself off the ground.

Need...to...get...help...

She waved her hand, lifting the remaining dream dust with the wind. Then, with a gesture, she sent it deeper into the woods.

Wrynn spun around, smoothly continuing her attack, but Sterling simply vanished again and appeared a few feet further away. "Tsk. You can't hit me like that, Wrynn. And even if you did, nothing you have here can harm me."

Sterling flicked a finger in Wrynn's direction. A blast of light shot out from it, piercing through her right shoulder, where her tunic had already been burned away. Wrynn gasped and reached upward, a glow forming on her hand that Lydia suspected was a healing spell.

She didn't have time to finish it before Sterling swung again, leaving a long cut across her forearm.

Wrynn jumped back, a blast of energy at her feet carrying her a dozen feet away. Sterling jumped right after her.

Lydia's eyes found the Sae'kes, still inches from Taelien's hand.

Taelien was still dozens of feet from her. She couldn't touch him to reverse the petrification...but the sword was lightweight.

Gods, forgive me for this transgression.

She whipped her hand in a cutting motion toward Sterling. And, carried on the wind, the sword followed.

Sterling's eyes widened as he saw it flying toward him. He vanished, appearing a few feet away.

Wrynn blurred forward with breathtaking speed and hurled herself on top of Sterling. "*Void.*"

Her hand shifted to the same color as the sword that had cut her, and for a moment, that darkness spread into Sterling.

Lydia twisted her hand. The floating sword turned, aiming straight for Sterling.

Sterling reversed Wrynn's grapple, spinning her around to put her in front of him and restrain her. Wrynn struggled against Sterling, but failed to free herself. "Stop," he hissed. "You'd have to go through her."

The sword floated in front of them both.

Wrynn snarled, then turned to Lydia...and nodded.

Lydia lifted her hand, bringing it backward and preparing to sweep it forward in one final, definitive strike.

Then stone burst from the ground, moving upward and wrapping around the hilt of the Sae'kes, locking it in place.

Lydia's heart sank, and she understood — her time had run out.

Kyestri was free.

He stood in his monstrous form, shaking off the last pieces of ice that had entombed him. With a crack of his neck, he turned toward Sterling. "You should have come immediately."

"I like to wait and make my entrance at the most dramatic moment possible. Excellent work on your part, by the way. You're just in time for the finale." Sterling pulled Wrynn closer, speaking directly into her ear. "Now, I've always wondered...just how powerful is a rethri prime lord? I suppose I'll find out."

Lydia commanded the wind to push the Sae'kes, but it accomplished nothing. Her spell wasn't strong enough to break it free from the stone.

"No, stop. The *seal.*" Wrynn managed to wriggle a single arm free, waving it frantically, but to no noticeable effect.

"I think I've already made it quite clear I don't care about that little issue. Now, let's begin."

Wrynn screamed.

Lydia shuddered. She couldn't see what was happening, but she remembered how it *felt*.

I need to stop this.

The sword is trapped. Taelien is still down. I need...

Her eyes searched, and she found it.

Her hand whipped upward, and once again, the winds answered her command.

A moment later, the massive head of En-Vamir, the Hammer that Broke the Spine of the World, slammed straight into Sterling's back.

There was a loud *crack* as the runes on the hammerhead flashed, and then a blast wave shook the forest.

Sterling stumbled forward, and Wrynn slipped free from his grasp, crumpling on the ground.

"That..." Sterling coughed, spinning toward Lydia and gritting his teeth, "...actually hurt."

"Good." Lydia twitched her hand. The hammerhead flew at him a second time, straight for his head.

Sterling caught it in a single hand, shaking his head. There was a crack on impact, but as the pressure built, it seemed to soak backward — straight into Sterling's hand. "No." He narrowed his eyes. "I don't think you understand who you're dealing with."

There was another flash from the hammerhead.

Then a different sort of crack as the runes on the hammerhead began to flicker, and Sterling's hand began to grow brighter.

No.

Lydia shifted the winds, but they couldn't tear the hammerhead from his grip. With every passing moment, the artifact's power weakened, and Sterling's grew.

I'm not strong enough to tear it from him, and I can barely move. I need to move it faster, but how? I don't have motion sorcery like Velas, and—

And then she remembered. A spell used on her before, that she understood, but had never used.

Casting a spell based purely on what she'd interpreted from Comprehensive Barrier was difficult, but not impossible.

Casting a spell from a dominion she wasn't familiar with was always a risk.

And casting a powerful spell without trying a weaker one first was, as a general rule, a terrible idea.

But while Lydia was usually averse to risks, she was even more averse to Sterling stealing the last remaining threads of power from a legendary Tae'os artifact.

So, she concentrated and whispered, using the winds as a medium.

"Superior Teleportation."

It was Erik Tarren's spell, the one he'd tried to use to move her from his home. An extreme manifestation of travel sorcery, one far too advanced to use properly without practice.

But she understood it intuitively. She'd been reading Tarren's books on theory since childhood, watched Garrick practice his spells, and experienced teleportation directly. She understood the function, and the exchange.

En-Vamir's flickering hammerhead vanished from Sterling's grasp.

Lydia felt a surge of pain in her muscles and bones as the spell extracted its cost. She sagged, even as the hammerhead reappeared, falling to crash into the ground in front of her. It formed a small crater as it landed.

She was exhausted. Her body burned. But she couldn't rest, not yet.

Venlyra, I need a little help. Anything.

[I will do what I can.]

She felt a pulse of strength filling her as she reached for the hammerhead. The winds carried it toward her, and she drew from the strength Venlyra had given her to form another stone object. Not a staff, this time.

Instead, she formed the haft of a hammer. It connected with the hammerhead securely, locking it in place. Then she pulled the hammer back to swing.

Sterling's head turned toward her, and he raised his right hand. She knew what was coming next — he telegraphed the same way each time.

When Sterling reappeared right behind her, she was already swinging.

En-Vamir cracked straight into the center of his chest.

There was a burst of pressure on impact. Sterling flew backward, but landed on the ground in a slide, growling.

The hammer had hit him hard, but not hard enough. He'd already stolen too much of its strength for it to do him much harm.

Still, there was nothing saying she couldn't hit him more than once.

When Sterling teleported again, she knew simply spinning wouldn't catch him a second time. So, when she spun, she whispered as well.

"Superior Teleport."

She reappeared behind him, still swinging. The hammer cracked into his back, knocking him down to his knees.

"Agh!"

She lifted the hammer again, but Sterling turned and grabbed the shaft. He snarled. "You...you *hurt* me. Me!"

In a moment, the stone handle was crushed to powder. Then with a gesture, he sent her flying backward. She crashed into the ground only a couple feet from Wrynn, who was still writhing on the ground in agony, presumably due to the damage to her seal.

She impacted hard, but her shield and Venora's strength spell kept her from losing consciousness.

Sadly, she only held a half-piece of the stone shaft of the hammer in her hand. The hammerhead had fallen on the ground where she'd stood before.

I don't have enough strength left for another teleport, she realized. *It might kill me. I'll need to go another route.*

Lydia flicked her hand upward again.

Her ring began to fly toward her, only for another burst of stone to erupt from the ground and encase it.

"None of that." Kyestri said, striding toward her. "You're done."

Sterling appeared right in front of her, smiling and raising a fist. Compressed power flowed around it, growing by the moment. "I'd stop to steal your sorcery, but we've already danced that dance, haven't we? I think it's enough to just kill you here. Goodbye, Lydia Hastings."

When he pulled back his leg to swing, he frowned and looked down.

Wrynn had grabbed him around the leg. "*Void. Stop.*"

Black energy shot through his leg, then ice spread across his body.

He swung his fist downward, but stopped mid-way as the ice encased him.

Wrynn collapsed again, her eyes closed.

Kyestri glanced at them, made a dismissive "tsk", and then turned toward Lydia. "That won't last long, but I suppose this leaves me with a brief window to pursue some revenge of my own."

There was a flash of steel as a knife flew through the air.

Not one of Wrynn's.

Sculptor flew from Taelien's outstretched hand, cutting straight through the stone that had trapped Lydia's ring.

She shot him a glance. He was still on the ground, breathing heavily, but the stone around his neck and arm were gone. He'd broken the spells himself.

His hand moved, then the trajectory of the knife changed, whipping through the air to cut through the stone below the Sae'kes.

Both ring and sword fell toward the ground.

"Lydia!" He yelled.

She understood. With a gesture, the winds answered her call again, though she knew they would not much longer. Her breathing was rapidly weakening.

Her ring, still partially encased in stone, flew to her hand.

Taelien's sword flew toward his — only to stop part-way, as more stone erupted around it.

Kyestri strode forward, shaking his head. "I don't believe I'll allow that."

Taelien stood up, glaring at Kyestri, then a smirk crossed his face. "Then I suppose we're doing this the old fashioned way."

"This time, I will break you to pieces, fool." Kyestri surged forward, grabbing Taelien around the neck. "*Petrify.*"

Stone spread across Taelien's neck briefly...then stopped. Then reversed.

Taelien stared at his opponent silently.

Kyestri squeezed down on Taelien's neck to no apparent effect.

Taelien reached upward, casually grabbing Kyestri's wrist and bending it downward.

"Ah...ah..." Kyestri grunted. "...How...?"

Taelien pulled Kyestri downward, bringing them face to face. "As it turns out, your spell is actually pretty similar to something I use. Took me a while to figure out the best way to handle it, but to summarize, you just made me stronger." His smirk broadened. "Oops?"

Then he slammed his fist into Kyestri's gut. The huge monster bent over double, coughing.

Crack.

Another of Taelien's punches carried Kyestri off his feet, sending him to sprawl, insensate, out on the ground.

"Now, to deal with—"

Sterling appeared next to Lydia, his sword flashing toward her neck.

Lydia wasn't anywhere near fast enough to stop it. Her barriers were gone, and there was nowhere to dodge.

His sword paused mid-swing. Sterling made a confused expression, seeming to struggle against some invisible force. Then he snarled and turned toward Taelien. "When did you...?"

Taelien stepped closer, the Sae'kes in one hand, the other empty and outstretched. "That's one of Kyestri's weapons, the Descent of Twilight. I suspected he was going to betray us. I lightly magnetized all the weapons he let me pick up in his gallery."

"And since you altered the metal, it doesn't feel like a spell." Sterling growled. "Fine. Take a few more moments to die."

Sterling swung a fist in Taelien's direction. A blast of compressed force surged outward, knocking Taelien backward.

Then he spun toward Lydia, only to find a hand wearing a silvery ring in his face.

"Eru volar shen taris."

A blast of blue-white flame flashed forward, right into Sterling's face.

He stumbled backward, raising a hand to his face and screaming.

When the flames cleared, his hair was burned away...but there was no obvious sign of harm.

Sterling snarled, blinking reddened eyes. "You...nearly blinded me..."

Lydia took the moment she had to act. "Sorcerous shield. Comprehensive barrier."

Barriers flickered into place around her. She didn't have to hurt Sterling — she just had to survive what came next.

Sterling charged at her, sword raised. She ducked. His first swing was sloppy, likely on account of his still-recovering vision. He missed her entirely.

"You...probably hoped to kill me with that." Sterling laughed. "I'm surprised. I didn't think you had it in you, paladin. Perhaps a year ago, you could have. But I saw you use the ring before. I prepared."

"You talk too much." Taelien put a hand on Sterling's shoulder, spun him around, and slammed a fist straight into his face.

And, when Sterling reached upward, there was blood flowing freely from his nose.

Sterling staggered backward, raising a hand. "You..."

"Yep, me." Taelien threw another punch, but this time Sterling swung his glimmering sword between the two of them. Taelien tried to side-step it, but Sterling was faster. He left a shallow wound across Taelien's left side.

Taelien grimaced, then took a cautious step backward, raising his left hand.

The Sae'kes, still encased in stone, shook but failed to break free.

Venora, Venlyra, can you help with that?

There was no reply. The stones had run out of power, at least for now.

Sterling raised his left hand, seemingly trying to teleport again, but Taelien stepped forward. He took a cut in the process, but managed to get his hands around both of Sterling's wrists.

Then Taelien bashed his forehead into Sterling's already-bleeding nose.

Sterling snarled, slipped his empty hand free, and raised it. He didn't teleport, though. He collected another wave of concussive force and slammed it straight into Taelien's shoulder.

Taelien flew backward, hitting the ground hard. When he cracked against the ground, it looked like his left shoulder might have been dislocated from the punch.

Sterling groaned, raised a hand to wipe the blood off his face, and then turned toward Lydia. He flicked his sword upward and a cutting wave of light shot forward.

Lydia raised her arms in front of her face, concentrating on her barriers. The attack diminished as it went through them, but cut through all the same, leaving bloody gashes across both her forearms.

When Sterling strode forward, she discarded her usual strategies for a different one.

With a blast of wind, she slammed straight into him, carrying the two in a tumble to the ground.

"Sleep." She pressed her bleeding hands against him, focusing her power. "Sleep. Sleep. *Sleep!*"

Sterling groaned, his eyelids fluttering...but again, the spell failed to take hold.

In a moment, she was hurled away, crashing painfully to the ground.

When she rolled over, face-up, she could barely open her eyes. Her wounds just hurt too much.

Sterling was looming over her a moment later, then there was a flash of silver and Sterling let out a hiss, stumbling backward.

Taelien was right above her, too. And he finally had his sword.

Lydia could barely process the rapid exchange of bladework above her. But when their swords caught for a moment and pressed, it was Sterling that fell backward.

Taking inspiration from Wrynn, she grabbed Sterling's ankle from the ground. "Sleep."

"Ugh!" Sterling faltered and stumbled.

That moment was all Taelien needed. With an extra press of force, Sterling's sword fell into two pieces.

Then the Sae'kes was at Sterling's neck. "I'm giving you one chance to surrender."

Sterling raised his left hand and vanished.

Taelien spun around, searching. Lydia groaned and sat up.

Sterling had appeared right by Kyestri's fallen body.

"Stop. You won't escape," Taelien stepped forward, raising the Sae'kes in a striking position. Kyestri and Sterling were far from reach, but Lydia had seen Taelien project blades of force from a distance.

"Escape?" Sterling scoffed, reaching down. "No, no. Just getting a quick pick-me-up."

Taelien swung, but too late. His shockwave of force cut through empty air.

Sterling reappeared next to the portal, then surged forward and pulled Kyestri through it.

For a few moments, there was silence. Lydia painfully forced herself back to her feet, only to stumble and nearly fall back down.

Taelien moved into a defensive position next to her, watching and waiting.

Lydia heard something moving in the woods nearby. Not Sterling. "Taelien. As soon as he emerges, plan C."

There was a look of surprise on Taelien's face, then a smile crossed it again. "Got it."

She pressed a hand against his back. "Sorcerous shield." She trembled, then fell to her knees. "I'm sorry. I'm..."

"You've done your part." Taelien raised the Sae'kes, watching the portal. The blade of the sword seemed to be glowing brighter and brighter with every passing moment. "We'll handle things from here."

Sterling stepped back out of the portal. The blood on his face was gone, and he had a massive greatsword leaning against his shoulder.

"World Cutter," Taelien mumbled. "Couldn't magnetize that one. He wouldn't let me touch it."

Sterling strode forward, looking confident. It was easy to see why.

His exposed skin was *gleaming* with new power.

"Did you...kill Kyestri?" Lydia broke into a cough as she asked.

He shook his head. "No, no. The creature is still useful. I merely took *most* of his power." He raised the tremendous sword with a single hand, pointing it at Taelien. "More than enough to finish this, I'd say."

Taelien took a few steps forward, watching Sterling carefully. "You'd think that, but I have a habit of breaking things. Other swords. Valuable artifacts. People who gloat too much."

"Come on, then." Sterling smiled. "Break me, if you can."

"Sure. But you should know," he glanced toward the Sae'kes, then back toward Sterling. "I wasn't just standing around while you were away."

Lydia saw it clearly, then. The aura around the Sae'kes was flickering violently.

And not a single one of the runes was lit.

"I might have broken this just a little bit, too."

Taelien swung his sword.

The world around him disintegrated. Everything in a five-foot sphere — everything up to just in front of where Lydia was lying — simply vanished.

That was only the backlash.

Everything in a line in front of where he swung was severed. There was a shimmering crack in the air, a tear where space itself had been rent apart, that went on for dozens of feet.

The attack was soundless and near-instant. There was no visible shockwave to dodge, no telltale blast of flame to absorb.

He had simply cut, and the world was changed.

Sterling reached down, searching for injuries, and finding none. "You...missed?"

Taelien's forehead was matted with sweat. His hands trembled on the grip of his weapon. In spite of that, he smiled. "Nah."

The portal behind Kyestri and Sterling had been cut in half.

A moment later, there was a crack as the damaged portal collapsed in on itself. The air around it distorted, then seemed to shatter apart.

Sterling was the only one still standing near it. As the air rippled and pulled inward, he lost the grip on his greatsword, and it flew dozens of feet away to land harmlessly on the ground.

In spite of the sheer force of the implosion, Sterling was unharmed. He balled his hands into fists, concentrating power within them. The air around his hands warbled and cracked.

Taelien raised his sword again. "I just cut off your escape route. And that," he waved his sword in a small circle, "was the signal for our reinforcements to attack."

A dozen glowing golden blades appeared in the air around Sterling. He smashed the first two with the explosive force emanating from his hands, but more appeared in their place.

Metal spikes appeared from the ground beneath him, pinning Sterling's legs in place.

Three figures stepped out of the forest, opposite Taelien and Lydia.

Keldyn Andys was in the front, holding his hand up as he concentrated, his dozen swords already moving closer to pin Sterling in place. "You're going to pay for what you did to my team, monster."

Behind him were three others. Kestrel Makar and Gladio Gath stood in defensive stances in front of Bobax, the illusionist that Taelien realized had been keeping them near-invisible all the time they'd been following Lydia. Gladio was holding a black-bladed sword marked with silvery runes, and Kestrel was wielding a two-handed blade of light, like a much larger version of the ones Keldyn was commanding.

Lydia didn't see the rest of their squad. Presumably, Finn and Durias were still invisible, waiting in reserve.

Sterling glanced at the newcomers. He vanished...

...then reappeared right where he'd been standing.

Gladio Gath raised the black sword he was carrying, pointing it at Sterling. "Teleportation anchor. We remember who you stole from. We remember who you killed. We came prepared."

Sterling ducked, ripped one of the metal spikes from the ground, and hurled it at Bobax with lightning speed.

Kestrel stepped in the way, cutting the projectile in half. "That won't work." She gave a slight shake of her head. "Can you, uh, please just surrender now?"

Bobax snapped his fingers and a glowing series of letters appeared in front of Taelien. They vanished a moment later.

At the same time, a blur shot through the opposite side of the forest. Taelien barely had time to turn before Dyson was next to him, kneeling at his sister's side. Then his arms slipped under her, and he lifted her from the ground. "I've got her."

"Dyson..." Lydia managed.

"Ssh. It's okay. We're here now." He flashed a grin at her. "You should have called us sooner. Or let us follow closer."

"Couldn't risk Kyestri or Sterling noticing. Even with Bobax's sorcery, there was a high chance scrying would catch you."

Taelien gave Dyson a nod. "Get her clear."

Taelien advanced to where Sterling was still surrounded by a dozen floating blades. Sterling tried to grab one of out of the air, but it simply bobbed back out of his reach. As Taelien grew closer, Sterling charged more force around his hands. "Stop. If you want to continue this, you'll have to kill me. And I'll take *many* of you with me."

Taelien offered a simple shrug, raising the Sae'kes. "I was given orders to use lethal force. That includes you, if you don't surrender immediately."

"I..." Sterling glanced around. Wrynn stirred on the ground, reaching for one of her knives. Kestrel and Gladio were slowly approaching from his rear, and Taelien from the front. "You wouldn't cut me with that sword. You wouldn't dare. It would be an act of war."

Lydia gave Taelien a nod.

There was a flash of silver, then Taelien lowered his sword.

A gash opened across Sterling's cheek, bleeding freely. Sterling raised his hand to his cheek, then glanced at his blood-stained fingertips. "You…"

Taelien leveled his sword, putting it at Sterling's throat. "Surrender. Now."

For a long moment, Sterling's eyes met Taelien's. Sterling's jaw tightened…then, after a moment, he seemed to relax. A smirk crossed his lips.

The glowing sword fell from his grip.

And then he raised both empty hands and said—

"You win. I surrender."

***

For the first time in hours, Lydia could take a moment to breathe.

The battle was over.

Wrynn was back on her feet within a couple minutes, using her strange "spirit arts" to provide some minimal healing. That was enough to prevent any of her injuries from being life-threatening, as well as to close the nasty gash on Taelien's neck. It wasn't enough to reattach Lydia's finger, though. She found that on the ground, bagged it, and hoped that Aladir would be able to reattach it if they got to him quickly enough.

Her abilities are very strange. I'll have to see if I can use Intuitive Comprehension to figure out how it works after I've rested. For now, I don't think I can cast one more spell without collapsing.

Wrynn practically collapsed again after that. Her tunic was working to close her injuries, but it couldn't repair the damage to her seal. She looked awful, but Lydia didn't have any way to help her immediately.

While Taelien hovered within sword reach, Dyson's squad set up a teleportation ritual around Sterling. The materials involved cost a fortune, but they'd transport a small group directly back to the Citadel of Blades.

Once there, they'd shove Sterling directly into a specially-prepared cell.

She watched, exhausted but relieved, as they worked. Two more figures emerged from the woods before they finished — Durias Moss, the communication paladin who had served as the announcer during the arena battles, and Finn Pine. The pair reported that they'd successfully finished re-sealing the barrier to keep the shades from breaking through.

Minutes passed. Dyson insisted on carrying Lydia around, which admittedly was rather nice.

Sterling was atypically quiet as the majority of the paladins stepped into the ritual area and spoke the words to complete it.

Moments later, they were gone.

"It's done, then. He's gone." Lydia breathed a sigh of relief.

How long they could keep him confined was, unfortunately, an entirely different question.

I'll need to head back to Velthryn as soon as I've checked in with Aladir and Velas.

That way, if — or more likely when — he escapes, I can be there to begin tracking him immediately.

She had his blood now, stored in a vial. They hadn't managed to get much of it, but even a bit was enough to use as a component for a potent tracking ritual. Even Sterling's natural defenses and void sorcery would be unlikely to stop it.

When he broke out of their prison, she'd be ready to follow him. Then she'd find who had been pulling his strings in the first place.

Dyson grinned. "What, were you doubting us?"

"Yes, Dyson. I was doubting everything. I still am." She sighed. "But for the moment, at least, things are better. Thank you and your companions for the help."

"So formal, Sis. Geez." He smiled. "But you're welcome. I'm sure the others were glad to be here."

While Dyson held Lydia, she cradled the hammerhead of En-Vamir in return. Even with part of the essence drained out of it by Sterling, she knew how valuable it was, both in terms of power and religious significance.

"Still, I appreciate all their efforts. I'm aware this was not a typical assignment."

"Pfft. Those are the best kind. We should get going, though. That finger isn't going to reattach itself." Dyson turned toward Taelien. "You sure you don't want to tag along with us, at least as far as town?"

Taelien shook his head. "No. Wrynn and I need to get to Kyestri's manor. At the moment, he's still probably incapacitated."

"I could get there faster," Dyson offered.

"*You* need to take Lydia to get medical help," Wrynn replied. She turned to Lydia. "The art I used on her should keep her stable, but she really needs to see a dedicated healer. I'm sorry I can't do more, but I can't risk weakening my seal further. Even as it is, I need to go do something about that as soon as Kyestri is dealt with."

"Seal?" Dyson raised an eyebrow.

"I'll explain later," Lydia told him, then turned back to Wrynn. "I wish I understood the seal well enough to assist with it. When Venlyra recovers, perhaps we could manage a stasis effect."

"We can discuss that later. For now, Sal and I should get moving."

Dyson frowned. "You sure? You're not in much better shape than Lydia is. If you give us a week or two to prepare, we could just storm the place with a big group."

"He'll be gone by then." Wrynn shook her head. "Probably to another world entirely. He's almost certainly an agent of the Sun Eater. That's why he was after those stones."

[Agreed. I don't know why he wanted us in specific, but that was definitely a karna.]

The same one that stabbed you with the black dagger?

[No, his true form was different, I think.]

Lydia nodded. "Venora concurs."

Taelien drew in a breath. "And Sterling was working with him. Do you think Aayara was aware?"

"Absolutely," Lydia replied without hesitation. "Jonan knew."

Taelien frowned. "And he told you?"

"Not precisely. We'll get into that talk another time. For the moment, secure the mask. Then, go to the place we discussed back in Wrynn's place."

"The place we...ah, on the card?"

Lydia nodded. "Don't say anything else. Too likely we're still being watched."

Taelien groaned. "Understood."

Lydia turned toward her brother. "We're lucky you arrived when you did, Dyson. I don't know if we could have handled Sterling without you."

"Luck had nothing to do with it, sis." Dyson grinned. "All skill."

Taelien rolled his eyes. "Give Bobax my compliments on his tricks. Even knowing you were out in the woods, I never could find you."

Dyson snorted. "No problem. I'm sure he'll be thrilled. And hey, those tricks fool the best of us. Not me, obviously, but the best non-me people."

Lydia chuckled. "Of course." Her vision swam. "Ugh. Not to alarm anyone, but I think I might need that medical help sooner, rather than later."

Taelien gave her a concerned look. "Be safe, Lydia."

Lydia nodded. "You be careful, too. I'm sure I'll see you again soon."

Taelien gave her a bright smile. "I certainly hope it won't be too long. I missed you."

CHAPTER XXIII – TAELIEN VI – CLEAN UP

Dyson left with Lydia almost immediately, heading toward Selyr, where Aladir was supposed to be staying. Even while carrying Lydia, he was able to run at prodigious speed.

Be careful, you two.

"Phew. Just us now, eh?" Wrynn glanced around the battlefield. "That's good. We get some time alone for the most important part."

Taelien blinked. "...Which is...?"

"Looting, obviously!" Wrynn beamed. "Look at all this *stuff!*"

After a moment of appraisal, Taelien nodded. "...I get the swords."

***

Taelien did not, in fact, get the swords.

Given their injuries, Wrynn ended up stowing all of the littered objects on the battlefield — the broken remains of Kyestri's armor and stone mask, her own knives, Void Branch, and World Cutter — inside the Jaden Box.

Lydia had left with the single most valuable item already; she was still carrying the remains of En-Vamir. He hoped she wouldn't have to use it again any time soon.

By the time they'd reached Kyestri's manor, Taelien was exhausted, but still feeling ready for a fight. He approached the front door with his sword already drawn, scanning from side-to-side for threats on the way in.

Wrynn checked the door for traps before they burst inside, but didn't find any. Then, with great alacrity, they searched the building.

Kyestri was already gone. The servants were all gone, too. Wrynn even risked using another spirit art to search the place, but found only the lingering traces of another portal spell.

Taelien tightened his fist. "I should have hit him harder."

"You might have killed him if you had." She patted his arm. "And that's never been what you're about."

"You're...right." He took a breath. "Maybe I should have made an exception for him, though. Kyestri is going to be trouble in the future."

"Maybe, but nothing immediate, I suspect."

Taelien raised a hand to his chin. "It just doesn't feel like we've done enough to prevent him from just coming back and causing more damage. Hm...maybe..."

"Whatcha thinking?"

He grinned at Wrynn. "Still got more room in that box?"

Wrynn's eyes glittered. "You know I do."

***

It took a number of hours to loot the entire building. The vast majority of valuable items went into Wrynn's box, though she promised to hand a portion of it over to the Paladins of Tae'os later.

Taelien would have carried more of it himself, but his shoulder was still terribly sore from being dislocated, and his destructive aura was being particularly difficult to control after the fight. He'd taken a real risk by suppressing the runes on his sword completely for that attack on the portal, and now, it was taking a great deal of effort just to keep his aura from burning through the floor beneath him and the clothes he was wearing.

He did take one thing, though — the Mask of Kishor. He was confident that the artifact could handle a bit of exposure to his aura, and it was what he'd come for in the first place.

With the whole building stripped of valuable enchanted items, there were two more things left to handle. "What should we do with the menagerie of monsters?" Taelien asked.

"I can get them transported somewhere they can be handled safely. It won't take long, I know a guy."

"What about the servants? Do you think he kidnapped them?"

Wrynn shook her head. "I think they were other shapeshifters like him. I'll investigate, though."

"...What about the actual Kyestri?"

"Long dead, I think. I'll do some digging on that, too. If we need to do a rescue mission, I'll let you know."

Taelien nodded. "Thanks. One last thing...those creepy, human looking statues..."

"I don't think they're people. I know he tried to petrify you, but it would be a little too brazen to put real people out front, even for him."

"Let's at least do a cursory check."

Using Sculptor and his own stone sorcery, Taelien inspected the statues, but couldn't find any indication they were anything other than solid stone. If they were petrified victims of Kyestri, they were beyond his help. "Can I get you to look into this further after I leave?"

"Sure. I can get a memory sorcerer to check on them, if it's important to you."

Taelien nodded, then flipped Sculptor around and handed it to Wrynn. "Take this, then. Might help with breaking them out."

"What, you don't want to keep it?"

"I do, but my aura is going wild right now. Don't trust it not to break. You can give it back to me later if you feel like it." After a moment, he removed two more items from his bag — Arturo's Amulet of Sanctuary and the map that came along with it. "Hold on to these for me, too. Maybe pass them to Lydia if you see her before I do."

Wrynn nodded. "Okay. We can make a list of how we're splitting all this stuff up while we walk...but if we're not fighting Kyestri, I really need to get back."

"Let's head home, then."

***

They headed back to Wrynn's tavern. From there, Taelien escorted her back to the vault. "You going to be okay once you get in the pool?"

Wrynn nodded. "This is...bad, but I'll recover, given time. I'll plan to meet up with you sometime soon so we can split up all this loot properly. If there's anything you particularly want, you can write me a note."

"The swords, Wrynn. It's going to be all of the swords."

Wrynn snorted. "You've got a one-track mind."

"Nah. I like hugs, too."

"You're adorable. C'mere." Wrynn stepped forward, wrapping her arms around him and hugging him tight. "I'll see you soon, okay?"

He smiled, pulling her close. "You'd better. You still owe me stories about Artinia and my parents."

"You bet. I'll look forward to it."

With that, he watched Wrynn step into the side of the stasis pool, and headed off for his next part of the journey.

EPILOGUE – VELAS – LEGACY

The pain returned to her first. Other senses came more gradually.

She heard voices, whispering far too loudly, but she couldn't make them out.

Where...what...

Her eyes fluttered open.

She was in a bedchamber. A nice one, with heavy covers pulled over her, and several pillows beneath her head.

A familiar figure sat next to her, holding her hand.

"Hey, there." Landen smiled, leaning down. "Thought I told you to be careful out there. For future reference, being very nearly cut in half does not count as careful."

Velas groaned. "You're...cheerful."

"Of course I'm cheerful. You're alive. I...well, it wasn't looking good there, for a while." Landen took a deep breath. "Don't try to move yet. Or, uh, probably for a while. Sorry."

"Where..."

"Still in Selyr. I just arrived a few hours ago. Nakane paid to have us teleported here after we heard we could stop hiding. It was pricey, but we both wanted to check in on things."

Velas shut her eyes, suddenly feeling exhausted. But she couldn't sleep again. Not yet. "The others..."

"Asphodel got Aladir back on his feet first. He healed the rest of you as best he could, but...it was bad, Velas. Aladir healed remarkably fast — benefits of having a lot of life essence, I guess — but the others...your

Thornguard friend may be blind in one eye. And War..." Landen shook his head.

"He...died to help me." Velas felt strangely conflicted by that. She wasn't close to War. She didn't even know if she liked him. But there had been a bit of a kindred spirit between them in their shared love for battle, and she would regret not being able to fight him again. "What happens to harvesters when they die?"

Her gaze shifted to a corner of the room, where the Heartlance laid against a wall. The metal had lightened back to silver, but retained a hint of a crimson tint.

"I don't know." Landen shook his head. "Sorcerous theory never was my thing. Lydia might know better."

Velas nodded weakly. "I...didn't know him very well."

"I don't think any of us really did. Aside from Sal, maybe." Landen sighed. "He's not going to be happy when he hears about it."

"Sal...what happened with him?"

"Well, while you tangled with The Shrouded One, his group got Sterling."

"Is he...?"

"Sal is fine. His group got pretty beaten up, too, but no one died. And they got Sterling. Captured him, I mean."

Velas took a deep breath. "Good. Have you figured out what exactly Lavender was trying to accomplish with all this fate and prophecy stuff?"

Landen shook his head. "No. She didn't talk."

She felt her jaw tighten. "I'll *make* her talk."

Velas heard Landen sigh. "Won't be able to. She's gone."

"...What do you mean, *gone*?"

"We made a trade. If you were conscious, I think you would have agreed with it."

She sat up in her bed, wincing at the pain that shot through her body as she did so. "A trade? After all we went through, someone *traded* Lavender away? What could possibly be worth that?"

Landen sighed. "Come with me."

***

"...Oh."

Rialla Dianis was in a bed in the next room. She was pale, and a wet towel was draped across her forehead.

Aladir sat next to her. He raised a finger in a gesture of 'quiet' when Velas walked in the room.

Velas rushed to her side. "She's alive..."

Aladir raised his finger again.

Contain sound.

Velas rolled her eyes. "There. I've put up a field to keep sound from escaping. We can chat without waking her."

"You really shouldn't be using sorcery again so soon." Aladir gave her a weary look. "You shouldn't even be out of bed."

Velas ignored him. "How is she?"

Aladir winced. "...Not good."

"But she'll live?"

"...For a while."

Velas narrowed her eyes. "What does that mean?"

"Lavender took every drop of sorcerous power Rialla had. In doing so, she broke Rialla's bond with her dominion. For a rethri, that means..."

"*Uvar.*" Rialla winced. "She's *uvar* now, like her brother. No sorcery, and a limited lifespan."

"Critically limited. It's amazing that Elias survived as long as he did. Rialla's condition is worse. She was in an unstable condition for hours before we made the prisoner exchange."

Velas tightened her jaw. "Who did you make the exchange with?"

"Aayara."

Of course Aayara got her hands on Rialla somehow. Probably right when we were in the middle of fighting Lavender...assuming Lavender didn't just hand her over to Aayara earlier than that.

Her fists clenched. "How long does Rialla have?"

"I don't know. A few days, maybe. She needs stability sorcery more than healing, and that's not something I have access to. Lydia has an item that might be able to help, but it's recharging, and won't be ready for weeks. Months, maybe. It's...a seasonal thing, I guess."

Velas nodded. "Keep an eye on her for me. Where'd you meet with Aayara?"

"I didn't, Lydia did. But my understanding is that she's at some sort of tavern. The...perfect something?"

"Perfect Stranger. I know the place."

"She might be gone by now. And you're not in any condition to—"

"Don't try to stop me." Velas turned, stood, and reached over to put a hand on Rialla's cheek. "I'll be back for you."

***

Wrynn Jaden wasn't tending the bar at The Perfect Stranger when Velas arrived, but she knew a few of the other workers. She waved someone down as soon as she walked in. "Is Symphony still here?"

She got a nod. "She's been expecting you. Back room."

Of course she's been expecting me. She's been playing us all from the start.

She gave a friendly wave and headed to the back room.

Aayara was reclining in a huge chair, sipping wine from an expensive bottle she probably hadn't paid for. A set of crimson veils — a portion of Aayara's Symphony outfit — were folded neatly on the table. "Darling! You're looking unwell. Sit."

Velas wrinkled her nose, leaning up against the nearby wall instead. "I'm not here for idle banter, Aayara."

"Oh?" Aayara's eyes scanned her. "Not in a fun mood? I suppose I wouldn't be if I was in your boots, either. You're probably still weak from all that blood loss."

"Rialla is dying."

Aayara gave a nod, tipping her bottle toward Velas. "That she is."

"Fix it."

After a moment of pause, Aayara tilted her head to the side quizzically. "Pardon?"

"She's dying. She's one of your agents — an 'ess'. You brought her into this, you get her out."

"On the contrary, I do believe you brought her into this. Well, a combination of you and Scribe. He recruited her, and you got her killed with your lack of caution."

Velas snarled. "She's not dead *yet*. And she worked for you. She was doing her job, and you have an obligation to help her."

"Do I? What if I told you that she was ordered not to help you, and did so anyway?"

"...What?"

"I instructed her to observe you, but not to interfere. That's why she's dying. She violated her orders, and now she faces the consequences. Now, I do have a reward for you for—"

"Stop. Unless that reward is help for Rialla, I don't want to hear it."

"You're sure? It's something *quite* significant."

Velas folded her arms. "No games, Aayara. Help Rialla, then we'll talk."

"Hm. What makes you think I *can* help her?"

"That was the entire premise of her working for you, wasn't it? Finding a way to fix *uvar*. She's *uvar* now, and I'll wager you have a method for treating that. Maybe you did from the start. Now, I need you to deliver on that."

Aayara set her wine bottle down. "I don't like your tone, young lady."

"Aayara—"

She tilted her head downward, making a dangerous expression. "You're not calling me 'Auntie Ess'."

Velas drew in a deep breath. "Auntie Ess. *Please*. Help her. I...it's my fault."

Aayara stood, approaching and putting a hand on Velas' cheek. "You're right, dear. It most certainly is your fault. You were weak, too weak to handle Silk on your own. And planned inadequately. There need to be consequences for things like that."

"Fine. I'll pay the consequences. Don't make her suffer for my mistake."

Aayara gave her a sad look, pulling her hand away. "I suppose you may have been unsuited for what I was planning."

"What's that supposed to mean?"

"Your reward, dear." Aayara gestured at the folded garments on the table.

"You want to give me some colorful clothes? I don't need new veils, I need you to *help my friend*."

Aayara sighed. "No, dear. Who wears *those* veils?"

"You do. But—oh." Velas felt her heart sink. "No. That's...is that what this was? Why you had me fight Silk? This wasn't just a petty game, it was..."

"A succession test." Aayara's hand drifted to the top of the pile of clothing, patting it.

"You want me to take your place as Symphony."

Aayara shrugged. "I did. But it would appear that your priorities are your personal attachments. A shame. With the previous Silk finally taken care of, I was hoping for a chance to distribute some of my responsibilities."

"Can we talk about this another time? Rialla is *literally* dying right now, and I don't know how else—"

"I won't help her. You don't have the resources to do it yourself. What will you do?"

Velas narrowed her eyes, then stomped forward.

With a swift movement, she snatched the crimson veil off the table. "This discussion isn't over." She glowered at Aayara, then lifted the silk to her face.

Aayara smirked. "Congratulations on your promotion, dear. Now, off you go. I believe you have some work to do."

EPILOGUE – JONAN – TRAVEL PLANS

Blinking was much more uncomfortable with only one usable eye.

I'll fix it somehow, he told himself for the hundredth time.

He knew it wasn't likely. Eyes were notoriously difficult to heal, and he'd been overusing powerful sight sorcery for years. Every power had a cost.

Still, thinking of his eyes was a good distraction. The futility of fixing his vision was nothing compared to the other challenges he knew he'd be facing soon.

Jonan was waiting outside when Velas stepped out of the room carrying Symphony's veils.

He'd heard everything. Aayara hadn't bothered to shield the room from sound. She'd wanted him to hear.

She had, however, sealed the room to prevent him from actually going inside and interfering.

Velas turned her head when she saw him sitting at the nearest table. "Jonan. You—"

"I heard. We can talk while we walk. We need to move her right away."

"Move her? Where?"

"Here." Jonan tapped on a table.

Velas gave him a confused look.

"Come on. I'll explain while we walk."

***

"You've been keeping secrets." Velas folded her arms as they headed back toward Selyr.

Jonan blinked. Darkness again. It was irritating. "Of course I have. What in particular were you thinking of?"

"You've got more dominion marks. I saw you use one against Lavender."

"Two, actually." He rubbed at his arm absently, which only made it hurt more. "No, three, now that I think about it."

"And?"

"And what?"

Velas jabbed him with a finger. "And knowing about them might have been relevant to our strategy?"

Jonan winced. "Yes, I suppose you're right. But neither of us is exactly good at trusting, are we? And beyond that, we haven't had any chances to discuss it while we weren't potentially being observed. I couldn't risk Lavender finding out about them if she'd been scrying on us while we chatted."

Velas lifted a hand to her forehead, looking frustrated. "Fine, fine. But I know about them now, and so does she. So, tell me. What have you figured out? Do you know enough to save Rialla?"

Oh. Is that why she's so upset?

Jonan shook his head. "No, sorry. I know Edon was researching using dominion marks to cure the *uvar*, at least in theory. But my own angle of research has been somewhat different. I will study Edon's notes and try to finish the process, but I'm not at that point now."

"So what did you figure out, then?" She made a gesture at his arm. "What's with the new marks?"

"Put a field of silence around us first, please." It wasn't a perfect precaution, but some was better than none.

"Fine." Velas waved a hand unnecessarily. "It's done."

Jonan could feel something in the air around them, but he still wasn't effective enough at sound sorcery to be able to discern much about it. That was a little annoying, but he trusted that the spell was what she'd claimed. "You recall that I spent some time studying in the restricted section of a Thornguard library?"

Velas nodded.

"Well, there were some items being stored there for research. Dominion marked items. Mostly things the vae'kes wanted more information about, like a replica of Hartigan's Star that Jacinth made for Aayara. And I wasn't allowed to take them out, but..."

Velas stared at him. "You *didn't*."

A smirk crossed his face. "I did. I was under observation, and in a room surrounded by void, but I was still able to cast spells inside." He lifted up his sleeve, displaying the ugly marks on his right arm. Dominion marks had to be in a specific shape to function — he still wasn't sure why — but they didn't have to be traditional tattoos.

"I branded myself while five feet away from a man who could have killed me in a heartbeat if he'd wanted to. I don't think he even noticed. I had sight sorcery to make it look like I was simply reading a few feet away, and sound sorcery to conceal the sounds of me being in, well, frankly terrible pain."

"That's a pretty dangerous move, Kestrian." She nudged him. "I'm impressed. But I didn't think you could pull off sound sorcery?"

"I can't on my own." He lifted up his other sleeve, displaying another rune. "I cheated. This rune links me to the helmet from your old suit of armor — the one that uses sound sorcery to change voices. I was able to figure out how to get it to silence my voice instead."

"And the other runes?"

"One of them ties me to that Hartigan's Star Replica. That's how I was able to enhance my flame sorcery enough to hurt Lavender. The other is tied to an amulet that protects the wearer's spirit and essence."

Velas examined him for a moment, seeming to consider that. "Is that how you retained your sorcery after Lavender grabbed you?"

"I think that's a part of it. Also, she threw me almost immediately. Even without the mark, I don't think she would have had time to drain my sorcery entirely...but I'm still glad I had it."

"Were you *planning* to be grabbed by a vae'kes? Is that why you got so close to her?"

"Oh, Vaelien, no. That was me having terrible combat instincts. You should understand that I'm not a fighter like you, Velas. I never should have gotten anywhere near her." Jonan sighed. "I'll need to be more cautious in the future."

"You're a strange one, Kestrian. Half the time I think you're brilliant, the other half..."

"I get the idea." Jonan smirked. "I'll try to be more careful. Maybe in a few years I'll be brilliant fifty-five percent of the time."

Velas snorted. "I don't think it works like that, but sure, you go ahead and try." She paused, seeming to process everything they'd just talked about. "So, the dominion marks are neat, but they're not your current plan to help Rialla. What is?"

"We need to get her back to that tavern."

"Why? Do you think Jaden can do something?"

Jonan shook his head. "Not precisely. There's a Xixian vault under her inn, and it has a stasis chamber in it."

"...What?"

Jonan nodded. "Yes. It won't fix Rialla's condition, but I think stability sorcery on that scale will keep her, well, stable. We can use that time to find a more permanent solution."

"How'd you know all this? Did you get your mirrors to convey sound as well as sight?"

Jonan snorted. "No. I'm still working on that, and maybe you can help me with it later. Lydia just told me about the stasis pool. I chatted with her briefly after Aladir healed me."

"Oh." Velas blinked. "That's significantly more mundane."

"Sorry to disappoint you." Jonan sighed. "I suppose that's my lot in life."

"Oh, cut the self-deprecation, Kestrian. This plan is more on the brilliant side of things. And if Rialla actually lives through this, the new Symphony will owe you one."

"That sounds more intimidating than reassuring."

Velas smiled. "It was supposed to."

***

With Symphony's veils and Jonan's illusions to nudge things further, Velas was Symphony, the Lady of Thieves. No one in Selyr would dare to deny her.

Aayara had to know we'd work together to make this happen. She's been driving us together from the start.

They arrived together at a certain blacksmith shop, invisible. When Jonan used a basic sight spell to glance through the walls, he felt a sharp spike of pain in his remaining functional eye.

Still, when the haze of pain cleared, he could see who he wanted inside.

He made a gesture to Velas, who slipped behind him, still invisible. Then he appeared and knocked on the door in the proper sequence.

Taer'vys opened it a moment later. "Kestrian. You survived. And I heard there was quite a shake up with the Disciples of the First?"

"I'll inform you about the details later. For now, there's someone you need to meet."

"Oh?" Taer'vys raised an eyebrow.

"Hello, Taer'vys."

Velas had slipped behind Taer'vys during the conversation, concealed by both invisibility and her own silence spell.

Now, as she spoke, her voice was a perfect copy of Aayara's.

When Taer'vys spun around, his hand went to his hip in a flash — and then he froze as he processed the crimson veils in front of him.

"I heard you were interested in meeting me. Please, come inside." She gestured toward the interior of the building, as if she was the one who owned it.

Taer'vys didn't spare Jonan another glance as he stepped back inside, following "Symphony".

"It's a pleasure to finally meet you in person, Lady Aayara."

"Please, darling. It's Symphony right now. Now, have a seat. I have a few tasks for you."

A grin stretched across Taer'vys' face. "Anything you wish, Symphony."

***

It took all of ten minutes for Taer'vys to arrange for a travel sorcerer that would transport them and Rialla Dianis back to The Perfect Stranger tavern outside town, no questions asked.

It took an extra dozen to extract a *substantial* amount of gold from the local bank, which she knew she'd need shortly thereafter.

The hardest part was convincing Aladir to let them take her.

"We gave up the Shrouded One to get Rialla out alive. You could just be taking her back to Aayara. We know you work for her."

He...has a point, Jonan had to admit.

After a few more minutes of banter, they simply agreed to allow Aladir to go with them to the tavern and the vault.

"You should be aware that Wrynn has the whole place trapped," Aladir explained.

"Of course she does." Jonan groaned. "Do you know how to get through them?"

Aladir shook his head. "Sorry. Taelien is the only one who accompanied Wrynn all the way into the vault. We'll have to break our way inside, then apologize to her later."

That is, perhaps, the worst plan I've heard all week. And I have heard some truly terrible plans. I've made them. I've experienced them. This is the worst.

Fortunately, by the time they arrived, Wrynn was back to tending the bar. She looked like she had a terrible hangover, but she was on her feet.

As they carried Rialla inside, Wrynn gave them a quizzical look.

"Can I...help you?"

Velas walked over, dropped a sack full of gold coins in Wrynn's hands, and said, "We need to use your swimming pool for a little while."

Wrynn raised an eyebrow, lifted the bag of money, tilted her head to the side appraisingly, and then said, "Follow me."

***

"It won't fix her condition, you know." Wrynn was sitting with Aladir, Velas, and Jonan on the first floor of the vault. Rialla had been placed inside the water upstairs, and it appeared to work just as Lydia had described — she appeared to be in a state of suspended animation.

I wonder how Wrynn manages to get out of that pool on her own? Maybe she has a way to set the enchantments on the pool to turn off after a set time? Or some kind of inherent ability that lets her remain partially conscious inside? Or maybe she sets a golem or a shadow to pull her out after a while...

He shook his head. It didn't matter at the moment. Rialla was stable, but they still had problems to solve.

"I have Rialla's notes from what she'd discovered about her brother's condition, as well as what I could find from Edon's old journal. We have a starting point." Jonan looked at Wrynn, then gestured at her arms. "And you have some interesting marks there. Would those happen to be related to dominion marks?"

"Ah, not these. I have some of those, but..." Wrynn frowned. "I can't help. The majority of my powers are sealed, as no doubt you've already heard. If I had a solution to the *uvar*, I would have used it years ago, believe me. Maybe between the lot of us, we can put something together, though, if you're willing to put in some work."

"We'd appreciate your help, Witch of a Thousand Shadows." Aladir gave her a smile.

"Please, it's just Wrynn. I mean, unless you're flirting with me. In which case use as many titles as possible."

Aladir blushed. "I, uh..."

Wrynn laughed. "You're adorable. Okay. Are you willing to share your notes with me?"

Velas and Jonan exchanged glances. "If you think you can solve this. What's this idea you were talking about that involves 'work'?"

"Well, I know *something* that might be able to help your friend. But it's going to take some traveling, and there are risks."

"Why's that?" Velas asked.

"Because these types of powers," she gestured to the marks on her arms, "aren't from around here. You'd need to go to Kaldwyn or Artinia to get anything like them."

Jonan took a deep breath. "Well," he glanced at Velas, "Then I suppose one of us is probably going to have to go to another continent at some point, aren't we?"

Velas nodded. "We can flip a coin for it."

EPILOGUE – LYDIA – HOME

Lydia spent much of the day after the battle with Sterling discussing what had happened with Aladir while he treated her wounds. Given how badly injured he had been during the fight with Lavender and how many other people he had to heal, he had little essence to spare for her, but a few minor regeneration spells helped supplement what Wrynn had already done to help her.

That hadn't fixed her finger, though. Apparently, the dominion marked sword that Sterling had severed it with had damaged it too badly to be properly reattached. She'd most likely be missing that finger permanently.

She had little time to mourn the loss.

Just after getting healed, she'd been approached for a deal. She'd negotiated trading Lavender for Rialla with significant reservations, but she felt it was the right choice. Saving a life was always a priority for the Paladins of Tae'os, and more importantly, she was not at all convinced that they could keep Lavender captive.

They'd prepared a special prison in Velthryn for one vae'kes, not two. An oversight, in retrospect, but she hadn't known that the Shrouded One would be another vae'kes with any certainty. It was one option that had been considered, but even if they'd known, the resources to prepare multiple cells — and multiple transportation rituals to move the prisoners — were beyond what they could have amassed without alerting the entire paladin order to the situation.

Even after the trade, they'd made several important gains. They had Sterling, another piece of Vendria's fragmented form, and Wrynn had sent a message indicating she would be visiting to discuss the distribution of spoils she'd picked up with Taelien after she'd rested.

She had En-Vamir, too. The hammer wasn't a perfect weapon for her — she could barely lift it without Venora increasing her strength — but it was a tremendously powerful relic, even in its damaged state.

And, perhaps most importantly, they'd discovered much of Lavender's agenda. She still didn't understand it entirely, but from what Jonan had told her, Lavender seemed to be pushing toward a very specific set of events that she believed needed to happen. They could use that information to try to predict any future movements the Disciples of the First attempted to make.

She couldn't take any direct actions against the other members of the Disciples of the First — she didn't have any local authority. Fortunately, Jonan and Velas seemed to have that in hand. They didn't tell her any details, but apparently Velas had somehow gained some influence with the local Thornguard, and arrests were being made.

I'll need to ask her about that later, but for now, it seems like we're on the same side.

All in all, it had been a productive journey, even if she mourned the loss of another ally. The Wandering War had been a strange one, but she'd seen value in his life all the same.

With her business in Selyr concluded, it was finally time to go back home. She had a great deal of preparation to do.

***

"Hello, Sterling."

Lydia was carrying En-Vamir over her shoulder as she walked to the edge of his cell. She was positively brimming with protective spells, as well as boosted strength from Venora. She wouldn't take any chances if he somehow had managed to break free from his bonds.

For the moment, however, Sterling didn't make any hostile movements. He simply sat on the bed of his cell, his hands and legs shackled to the wall, allowing enough freedom of movement for him to lie down or pick up the nearby books or food if he needed it.

"Lydia. I was wondering when you'd come and visit." Sterling smiled. "I'd tip my hat, but I'm afraid they've taken all of my personal belongings. Now, I'm forced to sit in this terribly unstylish prison garb."

"I'm afraid we couldn't take the chances that any of your clothing had enchantments we couldn't detect."

Sterling smiled. "You're wise to be thorough, even if it's irritating. So, how can I help you?"

"Lavender was working from history books that appeared to be from the future. She appeared to be ordering people — including you — to ensure that specific events occurred. Why?"

"Ah." Sterling nodded. "Finally, someone is asking the right questions. We're trying to save the world."

Lydia raised any eyebrow. "Trying to save it from who? Or what?"

"Fate." Sterling folded his hands together in front of him, staring at Lydia. "I resisted the idea at first. Most people do. But if you've seen what I've seen, century after century...well, time has a way of changing us all."

Lydia frowned. "So, your plan was to follow this book like an instruction manual to avoid some sort of terrible fate?"

"That's a good way of thinking about it. I'm sure you've talked to your oracle friend about the consequences of resisting fate."

Lydia nodded. "I'm aware of her background. She tried to save a little girl, and after she did, she learned that nearly all of the girl's family members had been killed the next day as a result."

"Right." Sterling snapped his fingers. Lydia braced herself for a spell, but apparently it was just a gesture this time. "You push up against fate, and eventually it pushes back, harder. I like it as little as you do, but I've lost enough to know when it's time to concede. Have you?"

Lydia shook her head. "I don't believe in people being pushed around by concepts. There must be an architect to what you speak of."

"Maybe." Sterling shrugged. "But it's beyond you. Beyond me."

"I'll evaluate that as I learn more. The books that speak of the future. Where do they come from?"

"I'm afraid that's one of the questions that I won't be able to answer."

Lydia nodded, unsurprised. "And do you know anything else related to what is going to happen, aside from what is written in these books?"

"Sure. I know all sorts of things." Sterling smiled.

"Such as?"

Sterling leaned back against the wall of his cell, pulling his hands behind his head to use them like a pillow. "Velthryn. This mighty city of yours...it's going to burn. It's going to burn to the ground."

Lydia felt a shiver as he spoke. There was something about his tone that felt...final.

And, perhaps more worryingly, it felt *familiar*.

"How?"

Sterling shook his head. "You can't stop it, Lydia. Trying to is only going to make it worse."

"I can make a choice when I have more information."

"I think you're going to be a little biased. But you know what? I'm feeling generous. And, I'll admit, maybe even a little curious. So, ask me your questions, and maybe I'll answer. You may want to pull up a chair, though. You have a lot to learn."

Lydia nodded. She gestured to one of the nearby guards, who brought a chair for her to sit in.

She sat, draping the hammer across her lap, and looked at Sterling.

"So," Sterling stared back at her. "Where should we begin?"

Lydia reached up and adjusted her glasses, taking a breath.

"Tell me everything you know about the Fall of Velthryn."

EPILOGUE – TAELIEN – ENDINGS AND BEGINNINGS

Taelien walked through the streets of Selyr, still keeping his hand floating near the sword at his side. He'd grown up near here, but he couldn't trust the area to be safe. Not after everything that had happened.

He wore the cloak the Wandering War had given him to conceal the sword at his hip. He didn't need any extra attention.

The cloak didn't seem as hot as it once had. The sorcery within it had faded, leaving only a memory of the warmth it had once contained.

Maybe I'll ask him if he can heat it up again next time I see him.

The streets were busy with ordinary people, but that didn't mean he could count on getting help if something happened. This was a Thornguard city. The vae'kes were like gods to them, and it was possible someone had already put a warrant out for his arrest if they'd learned he'd hurt one.

He was almost to his goal when he heard a set of footsteps fall into sync with his own. He was being followed.

Nope, not being subtle about this.

He spun around, coming face-to-face with what looked like a young woman with shining blonde hair. She wore a rapier on her hip and the leather garb of a stereotypical rogue.

"Aayara." It took great effort to keep himself from pulling the Sae'kes out of its scabbard immediately.

She raised a finger to her lips. "Not so loud, dear. I wouldn't want to draw too much attention. Come, this way."

Aayara waved a hand, leading him to what was among the world's most conspicuous dark alleys. "Perfect." She leaned against a wall nearby. "A clandestine meeting between paladin and rogue. This is nostalgic."

He folded his arms. "What do you want, Aayara?"

"I believe you have something for me?"

Taelien tightened his jaw. "You set me up to fight Kyestri and Sterling."

"Yes, obviously. But do you have the mask?"

Taelien sighed. "Yes. But I'll need to talk to my superior officers before handing it over, given that you were clearly being duplicitous with your deal."

Aayara gave him an appraising look, then shrugged. "Very well. I didn't need the mask, anyway. You can keep it. I suppose that concludes our business."

"Wait." Taelien stepped forward. "Sterling...he was one of yours, wasn't he? An 'ess' name, not a flower or a gem like the ones that work for Jacinth. Was he working with you from the start? Was he working for you when he killed Garrick Torrent?"

"Oh, I don't believe I owe you any answers on that, dear." She winked. "Our contract is broken, after all. You'd be wise to get on your way before I decide to extract a fee for the breach."

"I don't appreciate being threatened and manipulated, Aayara."

She shrugged. "Then get strong enough to do something about it. Right now, however, you're not worth another moment of my time."

Aayara snapped her fingers and vanished.

After a heartbeat, he heard her voice whispering in his ear. "...Not one more moment of my time, but my siblings may disagree. I'd give you less than half an hour before they arrive. You may want to run. Good luck."

Taelien scanned from side-to-side, cursed, and resumed the walk toward his destination.

He wouldn't run.

If Vaelien's children wanted a fight, he'd gladly give them one.

A few minutes later, Taelien knocked on the door of the house listed on the card Lydia had given him.

Erik Tarren opened the door a few moments later. "Come in. I've been expecting you."

Tarren led him into a sitting room, then gestured to a pair of chairs that sat on opposite sides of a Crowns board.

"Is Lydia already here?" Taelien asked.

"No, not yet. I'm afraid you probably won't have a chance to see her again for a time."

Taelien quirked a brow. "And why is that?"

"I have a task for you. One that will require you to travel to another continent. It may take some time to complete, I'm afraid."

Taelien folded his arms. "I'll consider it."

"I would certainly hope so. It would be...most unfortunate, if you refused."

Taelien felt his hand drifting to his side. "Is that a threat?"

Tarren raised his hands in a defensive gesture. "No, no. Forgive me, poor phrasing. I didn't mean to imply I would do you or anyone else harm. Rather, it's that your help is very much necessary for something important."

"And that would be?"

Tarren smiled. "Would it be overly clichéd to say it involves saving the world?"

"Yes. Definitely. Give me something a little more plausible."

The old sage nodded his head. "I suppose I should be more direct. Very well. Are you familiar with the continent of Kaldwyn?"

"Only in passing. My history lessons on other continents were pretty sparse."

Tarren gave him a sad look. "Unfortunate. I'll be succinct, then. There's an ancient goddess that lives there, one who has cut herself off from all others. And we are in dire need of her help."

"For what purpose?"

Tarren's shoulders sagged. "You may not believe the world is at stake. But could you, perhaps, believe that you may have just been involved in sparking a war that your people cannot win?"

Taelien nodded. "The vae'kes. They're going to attack because we hurt Sterling." It was more a statement than a question. Sterling had made it clear enough that they should expect consequences for hurting him, and Aayara had implied much the same.

"Ah, I suppose you haven't heard yet. Sterling is a part of it, yes, but some of your friends also hurt the one called Lavender. You would have heard her referred to as the 'Shrouded One'."

Taelien froze. "Wait. They already found her? And fought her?"

I suppose it's good that I didn't hand the mask over, then.

"Indeed."

"Who was there?"

"My sources indicate that your friend Velas was involved, but that the principal architect of the Shrouded One's defeat was the oracle Asphodel."

Of course. That's why she's been gone.

She wasn't planning for fighting Sterling when she was sparring with me. She knew she was going to be fighting a different vae'kes...or guessed it correctly, at least.

"Velas and Asphodel...are they okay?"

"Injured, but alive. They will both recover from their wounds."

Taelien let out a sigh of relief. "Okay. And they hurt this 'Shrouded One' badly enough that you think a war is brewing?"

"I know that one is. And I can tell you, with the utmost certainty, that it is a war that the Paladins of Tae'os have no chance of winning without significant help."

"What about the Tae'os Pantheon? You must know something about them. You're the one Aendaryn apparently handed me off to, after all."

Tarren winced. "I...don't believe they'll be able to help as much as you'd like. Lydia will explain more to you when you see her next; I've already filled her in on what I can."

"I'd like to know more right now."

"I will tell you some things, but I will need to prioritize. We need to get you off this continent soon. And by soon, I mean within the next few minutes."

Taelien tightened his jaw. "I suppose she was being literal, then. It's fine. I'll fight them." Taelien stood up. "The vae'kes aren't invincible. We've already beaten two of them."

"Ah, yes, and you're to be commended for your role in that. But when I say 'they will be coming', I don't mean one at a time. I mean they'll come with a dozen. Overwhelming force. Even if I tried to assist you directly, we would be overwhelmed."

"Why now?" Taelien frowned. "They could have gone for the sword when I was a child. I was near Selyr, and they had to know."

"Politics. You've caused one of them direct harm today. They have the justification to strike back. Moreover, fear. They've seen that you're a potential long-term threat now. And with the mask, you can potentially disappear. Do you know how it works?"

"It's an anti-divination device. It prevents people from recognizing the wearer and blocks forms of scrying in a large area around it."

"Good. Once you're on the other continent, you'll largely be safe. They're unlikely to pursue you there quickly, since the local goddess, Selys, is extremely hostile toward vae'kes. They'll take some time to plan before pursuing. But if you sense any hint of them nearby, put on the mask and flee. You may be strong enough to fight one or more vae'kes by yourself someday, but you are not yet."

Which...it seems like Aayara wants me to do. She could have taken the mask. She's much stronger than Sterling, I wouldn't have stood a chance.

That means she wants me to get away. Why? What's her angle? Using me against Jacinth, maybe, or even Vaelien himself?

He shook his head. He'd need to gather more information to figure out her motives, but now wasn't the time. "So...I'm going out there alone, trying to, what, recruit some goddess? I'm not a politician, Tarren. That's not my skill set. I *fight*."

"You won't be alone. I'll be sending Miss Jaden there shortly. Kaldwyn may have some locations that can help with her condition. And I plan to send some of your other friends there as well, given time. For the moment, all you would need to do is gather resources and information, while staying safe from the vae'kes. Your sword *must* not fall into their hands."

Taelien's hand tightened. "How much of all of this was your doing? You just told me the name of the Shrouded One — did you know in advance?"

"I had suspicions, but I wasn't certain. One of my agents reported her identity after her defeat."

"Fine. But you had an idea of where this was all leading, didn't you? Before you spoke to Lydia — you knew we'd probably be fighting one of the vae'kes, and where that would lead."

"Yes." Tarren acknowledged. "But I suspect you knew that as well. Once Sterling harmed one of you, there was little chance for this to end any other way. Now, we must all play the roles we've been given." Tarren gestured toward the Crowns board in front of them for emphasis.

Taelien took a breath, then moved his hand.

A moment later, the Crowns board fell apart, sliced neatly into two halves. Broken pieces fell off both sides of the table.

He hadn't drawn his sword.

"I refuse."

Taelien stood up.

"If you want me to cooperate with you, it will not be a game. It will not be based on half-truths and vaguely-worded prophecies. And if you continue to try to play me like a game piece," he leaned forward, "I will break the hand that tries to move me."

Tarren pulled back, raising his hands in front of him in a warding gesture. "I...didn't mean..."

"You did, though. You've been toying with me from the beginning. Not just me — perhaps I could have forgiven that much. But you've been manipulating others, too. Including Lydia. And I don't take kindly to people who try to manipulate my friends."

Tarren winced. "You're making a mistake. I'm not your enemy."

"Then prove that to me. No more games. Tell me about my parents, and tell me about my sword. Then maybe, just maybe, I'll consider doing you a favor on my own terms."

Tarren took a breath. "Very well. We have limited time, but I will give you what answers I can."

"Good. Now, who are you, really?"

Tarren considered, then answered. "The name I've given you is true. It was my name as a youth, and as a mortal. But you would know me also by another name."

"Eratar?"

Tarren nodded. "Is it truly so easy to guess?"

"You might have wanted to change at least a few more letters. Why are you concealing your identity?"

"Because we have lost, Taelien." Tarren sighed, deflating. "We lost long ago."

"Lost...to who, Vaelien?"

"It is so. When Aendaryn came to me, injured, that was not the beginning of our failures. It was the last of them. Others had already abandoned the cause long before. The others, those that live, are scattered. Lydia knows more, but our time is limited. Ask the questions you truly wish to ask."

"What can you tell me about the Sae'kes? Is it true that it was built by the Tae'os Pantheon?"

Tarren shook his head. "No. It is far older than we. Have you heard of the Dominion Breaker?"

Taelien frowned. "I've heard the name, but that's an old legend. One about a sword made before our world was first formed. Are you saying it is the same?"

"It is. The Sae'kes was a weapon forged by four worldmakers — Kelryssia, Velryn, Caerdanel, and Delsen — for the protection of the new world they were creating. They hoped the sword would never be used. It was intended to be a symbol of our strength. An unused threat."

"A threat? Against who?"

"The Sun Eater." Tarren sighed. "I presume I don't need to explain that further."

"He'd destroyed one world. They didn't want him to destroy another. Sensible." Taelien nodded. "Is it truly strong enough to be used against someone like that?"

"It is. Unfortunately, no one alive can properly wield it, as you yourself have found. Even the God of Swords himself was never able to fully unlock its powers. This is both a matter of strength and an issue of design. The greatest abilities of the weapon were sealed away, with one fragment of the key given to each of the worldmakers. And when they died..."

"Those keys were lost." Taelien nodded. "I've heard about some of that before. I simply didn't realize they were the same weapon, but it makes some sense."

"I can tell you more about the sword, but we only have a few more minutes. I would advise you to use that time wisely."

Taelien nodded. He knew what he had to ask.

"Who am I, really? *What* am I?"

Tarren took a deep breath, then answered. "I have suspicions, but I cannot be certain."

"Just say it."

Tarren nodded, more to himself than to Taelien. "I believe you inadvertently just gave me an important clue. Have you ever noticed any strange interactions with objects in your possession?"

Taelien frowned, surprised by the style of question. "My aura has been gradually damaging things I've been wearing. It's getting worse since my last fight."

"And what aura is that?"

"One similar to the one the Sae'kes generates. I'm making it on my own now, even without the sword."

"Like how you cut my poor Crowns board with your bare hand just a moment ago." Tarren gestured. "Tell me, why do you think that is?"

"Essence has been leaking from the sword back into me. Because it's damaged."

Tarren nodded. "I believed your sword was damaged when we last spoke about it, and that may still be the case. But I do not believe that is the reason you can use the aura in that way. If it was leaking essence into you of that type, an ordinary human — or even an ordinary *demigod* — would have simply died. Your connection goes deeper."

"I've used the sword since I was a child. I've bonded with it."

"That was my belief as well, at first. But upon further consideration, I find fault with that being the entire explanation. The aura of the Sae'kes is known to cut through anything — body, essence, and spirit. The only thing it does not cut is the sword itself. And, it would seem, you."

"Because I'm generating the same type of essence...but the aura never harmed me. Not even as a child." Taelien glanced down at the sword, then back to Tarren. "Wait. You're not saying..."

"The Sae'kes is not harming you because it *is* you. Or a part of you, at least."

"That...doesn't make any sense. I..." His hand moved to the hilt of the weapon. He felt the essence flowing between him and the sword, even when it was sheathed.

He felt the aura around his body, and the sameness of the sword within.

"I have seen similar things, though not on the same scale." Tarren shook his head. "Luck's Touch is a sword that speaks to the wielder, for example."

"And one of Vendria's forms was capable of making and controlling bodies." He lifted his hands, staring at them. "What does that mean, then? Is this body just...a puppet for the sword?"

"No, I don't believe so. You bleed, yes? If I am not mistaken, you would be something like a sword elemental. A person manifested from the will and the spirit of the sword."

That...is that why the Wandering War calls me cousin?

Am I a harvester, like he is? A harvester of...swords, perhaps? Or another elemental type entirely, like a gatherer or a star?

Taelien trembled. "If I'm some sort of elemental...how was I born? Aren't they usually from other planes?"

"I do not know how you were made. Perhaps elemental is the wrong term...sword spirit might be more appropriate? The Sae'kes already possessed a spirit when it was first made, but it was not self-aware. Perhaps Aendaryn and Karasalia granted the sword awareness through some sort of ritual, and it formed a body on its own. You."

"But that...why? For what purpose?"

"To continue their fight." Tarren seemed more certain now. "To succeed where they could not."

Taelien shook his head looking down. "...So, I was nothing but a weapon to them as well?"

"I am sorry, Taelien. Truly. But you should know that they were good people, and they—"

"I don't care." Taelien shook his head. "No one should be created solely to fight someone else's battle." His hands tightened. "I...think I've heard enough."

Tarren nodded slowly. "Please believe that I would have told you sooner if I had known. And, even now, I cannot be certain of this. It simply fits the pieces we've learned."

Taelien shook his head. "It's fine. You're not the one I blame." He drew in a breath, then stood up. "I'll find what happened to my parents. They're the ones that will have to answer for creating me."

"You may not like what you find."

"I expect I won't." Taelien cracked his knuckles. "But I won't hide from the truth. In the meantime, however, I believe I have more pressing business."

"You'll do it, then? You'll go to Kaldwyn and help convince their goddess to assist us?"

"If there's a threat to my friends from the vae'kes, I can't ignore that. I'll fight for my own reasons."

Tarren nodded. "Very well. I would advise you to travel in disguise. It will take some time for the vae'kes to follow you there, but it will happen. You should choose a new name and find some ways to change your features, aside from just the mask."

Taelien glanced down at the sword at his hip, then with a moment of concentration, he altered it. Metal from the hilt stretched over the pommel, concealing the large blue crystal. The blade shifted as well, with metal stretching over the seven runes in the blade. And finally, the shape of the hilt shifted, retaining a winged shape but with a thinner and more elegant look. "A new name...hm. Maybe something similar to Aendaryn?"

"Perhaps a bit too obvious, I suspect, as you pointed out in regards to my own pseudonym."

"Fair. Hm...I suppose you said his traveling name was 'Vel'...but that's too much like Velas." Taelien shook his head. "Maybe something based on my mother's name?"

"Karasalia was never as broadly known, since she didn't join the Tae'os Pantheon. That would be safer." Tarren nodded.

Taelien nodded absently. "What's the male form of Karasalia...? Keras, right?"

"Yes. A common enough name that it would not be suspicious. I approve."

Taelien felt a smile crossing his face. "Keras...and for a surname, I suppose something equally generic. Keras...sword-something? No, too obvious. Keras of Selyr?"

"Given that Selyr is on this continent, that may be too direct as well. Selyrian would be appropriate for the same concept, but without being so obvious."

"Keras Selyrian." Taelien turned the name over in his mind as he spoke it aloud. "I like the sound of that."

THE END

APPENDIX I – MAGICAL ITEMS
Notes by Wrynn Jaden

Sal has a habit of running into magical items and legendary artifacts. I'd be a little jealous if I didn't have a pretty impressive hoard of them myself.
Let's talk about some of the fanciest ones, shall we?

The Sae'kes is Sal's sword, and it's obviously the most famous item on the list. It's got this weird warbly killy aura around it, which lets it cut through, well, literally anything as far as I can tell. Magical barriers, solid objects, even other magical artifacts — provided he can focus the essence around the sword enough. Big problem is that it seems like it's leaking a bit, and uh, that could be kind of bad for him in the long run.

Of course, it used to belong to the Seven-Branched Sword Deity, better known as Aendaryn on this continent. When Aendaryn used it, it had all sorts of other abilities...but Sal hasn't quite figured those out yet, and I'm not sure it would be best for me to explain. I'm a little worried that if he tries to use them when the sword is like this, he might, well, explode or something.

Then there's the Heartlance. Once the symbol of the gods of Orlyn, it somehow ended up in the hands of a paladin named Velas. It's popularly known for preventing injuries it causes from healing, but while it might have some properties that slow healing, it definitely doesn't actually do that. The main function seems to be some kind of haste effect when the wielder taps the bottom of it on the ground, but I suspect it has other abilities. Maybe something involving blood sorcery, given the name.

DEFYING DESTINY

Vendria is a talking gemstone, and one of at least three, maybe more. So far as I can tell, they all used to be a single entity from the distant world of Rendalir. Still sorting out all the details there.

En-Vamir, known for the overly-fancy title "The Hammer that Broke the Spine of the World", once belonged to Koranir, the God of Strength. Its powers involve being able to crush things it comes in contact with. Most people believe this is simply some kind of direct application of force — meaning the dominion of motion — but my experience tells me it's more akin to gravity. I think the dominion of tides might be involved. Sadly, I haven't had a chance to get my hands on it yet, but maybe if I make a few trades...

Anyway, I've saved the most important item for last. My box! The Jaden Box, because, well, it's named after me. It lets you store items in an extra dimensional space and retrieve them at will. And, perhaps more importantly, it has a long-distance summoning function. Sadly, that function takes a long time to recharge, but it's really useful! All I need is some blood or hair or something from someone and I can pull them over from anywhere I want. (Don't look at me like that, it's not creepy for me to collect blood and hair from my friends. It's practical, okay?)

There are lots of other interesting items lying around on Mythralis – World Cutter, Sculptor, Void Branch...but I'm bored now, so I'm gonna just end this note here. Bye!

APPENDIX II – NOTABLE PERSONAGES

Paladins of Tae'os
- **Lydia Hastings (aka Lydia Scryer)** is a Paladin of Sytira, the goddess of knowledge. She was badly injured by Jonathan Sterling, but has been spending the last several months training to recover and enhance her skills. She is a practitioner of several forms of sorcery, most notably Protection, Knowledge, and Dreams.
- **Taelien Salaris** has only been a member of the paladins for about a year, during which time he's been hunting for dominion bonded items and artifacts for his branch, the Paladins of Aendaryn. He carries the Sae'kes Taelien, which is believed to be the sword that Aendaryn himself once wielded. He is a talented user of metal and flame sorcery, and also possesses some stone sorcery. His most unique power comes from his destructive aura, which appears to be similar to the aura emitted by the Sae'kes itself.
- **Velas Jaldin** is a former member of the Queensguard of Orlyn, as well as an agent of Aayara, the Lady of Thieves. Her name when working for Aayara is Silk. She wields the Heartlance, a legendary spear, and utilizes motion and sound sorcery in combat.
- **Garrick Torrent** was in charge of Taelien and Velas' training when they were taking the tests to join the Paladins of Tae'os. He was killed by the vae'kes Jonathan Sterling.

- **Aladir Ta'thyriel** is Lydia's paladin partner and a tremendously powerful healer and spirit sorcerer. He is the son of Ulandir Ta'thyriel, one of the most notable spirit sorcerers on the continent.
- **Landen of the Twin Edges (sometimes Landen of the Twin Blades)** is a Velthryn-native swordsman who adopted the name Landen after leaving his old life behind. He is Velas' closest friend and companion, as well as a cousin of Nakane Theas, the current heir to House Theas.
- **Asphodel** is a delaren, a species with crystalline hair that generates sorcerous essence. She possesses a powerful talent for destiny sorcery, allowing her to continuously see a few seconds into the future, as well as concentrate to see visions on specific subjects. Because of this, she is referred to as an oracle. Others that sleep near her are sometimes visited by dreams of the future as a manifestation of one of her oracular talents.
- **Keldyn Andys** is a swordsman with the ability to use the Dominion of Blades, which is believed to be a gift from Aendaryn, the God of Swords. This allows Keldyn to conjure and manipulate multiple phantasmal swords. It is believed that this is one of the few types of sorcery that could potentially harm a vae'kes, who are otherwise nearly invincible to conventional harm.
- **Kestrel Makar** is the only other active paladin with the ability to utilize the Dominion of Blades. Her manifestation is somewhat different, allowing her to create a single phantasmal greatsword that she wields directly, rather than conjuring multiple floating swords like Keldyn. She was adopted by paladin commander Rowan Makar, but her original surname was Haven — the same as the legendary Aayara Haven, the Lady of Thieves. Because of this, Kestrel has come under some scrutiny as a potential agent of Aayara.
- **Dyson Hastings** is Lydia's younger brother and a Paladin of Eratar. His tremendous speed is believed to be a gift from Eratar, the God of Freedom.

- **Herod Morwen** is a former Paladins of Tae'os officer that still oversees training for some new potential recruits in an unofficial capacity. He was one of the commanding officers during the fall of the capitol city of Xixis.
- **Alaria Morwen** is Herod's daughter, and a Lieutenant in the Paladins of Tae'os. They're known to have a had a falling out years ago.
- **Cassidy Ventra** is a squire for the Paladins of Tae'os.
- **Durias Moss** is a paladin specialized in communication sorcery.
- **Gladio Gath** is a paladin with a talent for metal calling, minor protection sorcery abilities, and a dominion bonded sword that serves as an "anchor" to prevent teleportation spells when active.
- **Bobax** is an eccentric paladin who specializes in illusions using light, shadow, and sight sorcery.
- **Finn Pine** is a paladin with talents for fist fighting and ice magic.

Thornguard and Servants of Vae'lien

- **Jonan Kestrian** is ostensibly a member of the Order of Vaelien, the non-military branch of servants of Vaelien, the deity worshipped in the Serelien ("Forest of Blades") region. He works directly for Aayara, the Lady of Thieves, under the name of Scribe. He is a potent sight sorcerer, but also possesses a talent for flame sorcery, which he loathes to use.
- **Aayara,** also known as Symphony or the Lady of Thieves, is the patron deity of thieves on the continent of Mythralis. She one of the eldest of the vae'kes, who are believed to be the children of Vaelien. Like all vae'kes, she possesses the ability to permanently steal sorcerous power with a touch. As a tremendously ancient being, she is one of the deadliest known entities on the continent. Even gods fear her. Aayara's followers use "ess" names (meaning they start with the letter "s") as code names, such as Silk (Velas) and Scribe (Jonan).

Characters that use "ess" names are collectively called "esses".

- **Jacinth,** also known as the Blackstone Assassin, is the other of the eldest vae'kes. The two are known for their legendary rivalry, often going to great lengths to disrupt the plans of the other. Jacinth's followers use code names related to gemstones or flowers, such as 'Diamond' or 'Lavender'.
- **Jonathan Sterling** is a vae'kes, one of the children of Vaelien. He infiltrated the Trials of Unyielding Steel — a contest to join the Paladins of Tae'os — and used that opportunity to attempt to assassinate Landen of the Twin Edges, one of the few remaining members of House Theas. While Landen survived, Sterling killed Garrick Torrent, earning the enmity of the surviving paladins.
- **Captain Nolan** is a Thornguard commander that works in Aayara's service.
- **Taer'vys Ironthorn** is an ambitious member of Thornguard military intelligence. He has an interest in forbidden knowledge, such as time and void sorcery.
- **Mairead Caelan** is Taer'vys' adjutant. Her abilities are largely unknown.

Deities

- **Vaelien**, the King of Thorns, is the patron deity of the Serelien region of the continent. His children are the vae'kes. He is believed to be the god of fate, time, shadows, and nature.
- **Aendaryn** is the God of Swords and leader of the Tae'os Pantheon.
- **Sytira** is the Goddess of Knowledge and Sorcery. She is a member of the Tae'os Pantheon.
- **Eratar** is the God of Freedom and Air. He is a member of the Tae'os Pantheon.
- **Koranir** is the God of Strength and Stone. He is a member of the Tae'os Pantheon.

- **Xerasilis** is the God of Justice and Fire. He is a member of the Tae'os Pantheon.
- **Lysandri** is the Goddess of Water and Clarity. She is a member of the Tae'os Pantheon.
- **Lissari** is the Goddess of Life and a member of the Tae'os Pantheon.
- **The Sun Eater** was one of the creators of another world, Rendalir. He slew the other worldmakers of his planet and brought destruction to his entire world. According to legend, he was then sealed away by the efforts of the worldmakers of other worlds.
- **Kelryssia** was the Worldmaker of Destiny and the Stars. She is an ancient deity, now mostly forgotten. Even less is remembered of her contemporaries Delsen, Caerdanel, and Velryn.

Others

- **Edon** was once the ruler of Orlyn, until he was deposed in a coup only about two years ago. He was the leader of the pantheon of self-made "deities", who used a form of sorcery drawn from dominion marked items to empower themselves.
- **Byron** is the current king of the nation of Orlyn, after the machinations of the Thornguard and vae'kes deposed the previous ruler, Edon.
- **Tylan** is Byron's mother, and ruled as the queen regent for many years. She was also one of Edon's "deities" when he was in control of the city.
- **Blake Hartigan** is one of the three legendary immortal sorcerers of Velthryn. He has accepted Lydia as an apprentice, and is teaching her powerful new sorcery.
- **Erik Tarren** is one of the three legendary immortal sorcerers of Velthryn. He handed Taelien to a rethri family when Taelien was a newborn, after supposedly being given Taelien by Aendaryn, the God of Swords. A famous scholar, he writes books on sorcerous theory and other worlds.

- **Edrick Theas** is one of the three legendary immortal sorcerers of Velthryn. His daughter, Nakane, is his last remaining heir.
- **Nakane Theas** is a young sorceress and last heir to House Theas. She possesses an exceptional talent at spirit sorcery, much like her father and late brother.
- **Wrynn Jaden**, also known as the Witch of a Thousand Shadows, is one of the prime lords of the rethri. She has tremendous sorcerous powers and a habit of collecting enchanted curios.
- **Korus Kyestri**, also known as the Titan of the Northern Reaches, is the Prime Lord of Stone. He's an eccentric, known for his sculptures and his menagerie of monsters.
- **Karheart** is the Crown Prince of Keldris, a city to the south of Selyr. He is also the Prime Lord of Deception and fond of pranks.
- **Vendria** is a sapient gemstone, reportedly once from the world of Rendalir, which was destroyed long ago. Originally, she was a seasonal entity, with each aspect having different personality characteristics and abilities.
- **Venora** is Vendria's spring aspect, possessing healing and defensive sorcery.
- **Venshara** is Vendria's summer aspect. Her capabilities are unknown.
- **Venlyria** is Vendria's winter aspect, possessing ice and stability sorcery.
- **Tysus** was a legendary hero of Rendalir, thousands of years in the past. He was a lover of Venora, Vendria's spring aspect.
- **Em'rak** is a being that claims to be a fragment of the Sun Eater.
- **Rialla Dianis** is a powerful young rethri sorceress from House Dianis. She left home at a young age to protect her younger brother, who was born without a bond to a dominion. She seeks a way to help with his condition, which is slowly killing him.

- **Elias Dianis** is Rialla's younger brother, and an uvar, meaning a rethri born without a bond to a dominion.
- **Liarra Dianis** is Rialla's twin sister and a powerful healer.
- **Torian Dianis** was Rialla and Liarra's father. He was one of those responsible for the assassination of members of House Theas. He was killed by Rialla.

A NOTE FROM THE AUTHOR

First off, I'd like to give my sincere thanks to everyone who has read through this trilogy. It's been a life-long dream of mine to publish a series like this, and I appreciate everyone who has supported me along the way.

This concludes the *War of Broken Mirrors* proper, but there is more content coming in the same universe.

The *Weapons and Wielders* series picks up with Taelien right after this book ends. The first book of that, *Six Sacred Swords*, is already out.

At present, I'm planning to write other books to follow the other characters (although some of them may show up in *Weapons and Wielders* as well). I don't want to say too much more on that right now, but rest assured that more content is in the works.

The *Arcane Ascension* series also takes place in this universe, although in a different location and time period. If you enjoyed these books and haven't read those yet, you may want to check them out. You'll see some familiar names and faces, but not directly as you will with *Weapons and Wielders*.

There may be a "Book 4" of the *War of Broken Mirrors* eventually, but don't expect that any time soon. These other series will be my focus for the foreseeable future.

Thank you all again for reading to this point. I hope you enjoyed the book, and if you're interested in reading more, I hope you'll take a look at my other books.

If you want to see what Taelien is up to after this book, *Six Sacred Swords* is already out — or you take a look at the preview chapter for it just ahead.

PREVIEW CHAPTER – SIX SACRED SWORDS

I've always had a complicated relationship with magic swords.

There's a magic sword at the very start of my personal story, but I'm not going to start there. You wanted to know about how I'd encountered Dawnbringer, one of your six weapons of legend.

That's a much better story.

Let me tell you about when I first came to your lovely continent of Kaldwyn.

***

I awoke in the Whispering Woods. I didn't know the name at the time, of course, but I trust that you've heard of them.

Most of it looked pretty standard as far as forests go, at least at first. Tall trees, occasional patches of high grass, a few mysterious blue flowers growing to the side of where I woke.

Mist. Lots of mist. I could see a good twenty feet though, so it didn't add any particular sense of danger. The forest I grew up in got misty at times, too.

I pushed myself off the ground and wondered how in the name of the gods I'd gotten there.

My head swam as I rose, teetering on my feet.

My stomach grumbled.

How long had I been out?

I wiped the dirt from my hands off on my tunic, then spent a moment just rubbing my temples. It didn't help much, but my mind was clearing even if the pain wasn't fading.

I scanned the area. I didn't recognize my surroundings. The tree bark was a light shade of green, almost as bright as the grass below.

I need to break the habit of letting old sages teleport me to strange places.

I didn't notice any immediate dangers, fortunately. Based on the disruption in the foliage, I suspected I was on a path. The brush had been cleared in a broad enough swath that I suspect it was a human trail rather than animal trail, but I didn't see any boot marks or other clear indications to confirm that.

No other people around. That was irritating, because a distinct lack of people would make my job harder. I needed to gather information about the continent and local customs. That generally required people to talk to.

I remembered the last thing the sage told me.

"I'm sending you to another continent. Your objective will be to gather information and resources before I send the rest of your team. After your friends arrive, you must meet with their goddess and bring her to join our cause. Without her help, we stand no chance against the threat that is to come."

Lesson One: Old sages will *never* tell you the full story.

This didn't look like a good place to find information and resources. True, he hadn't said he'd be sending me to a major city, but he hadn't warned me that I'd be in the middle of nowhere, either. So, either the sage had omitted some key information or something had gone horribly wrong.

I didn't know which was worse.

Either way, no one was nearby. I'd have to search the area and see what I could find.

At least I was intact. No horrifying teleportation damage to my person, as far as I could tell without a mirror.

I checked my side. The sword was there, as it always was, and locked firmly in its scabbard.

Good.

Couldn't let that thing escape. There was no telling what it would get up to if I wasn't around to keep it reined in.

I still had my backpack on, too. I *had* been preparing for a journey to another land, even if I'd expected to show up somewhere a little bit more civilized.

I checked my pack.

I had most of the basics. A little bit of food, little bit of water, gold coins, bandages, healing ointment, slightly magical rock, rope, mask of a long dead god, that sort of thing.

I heard something *crack* behind me.

I dropped my pack, spun, and drew my blade in a flash of unparalleled grace.

The squirrel was unimpressed.

I sighed, sheathing my weapon slowly to prevent any damage to the nearby terrain, and then picked my backpack back up.

Fortunately, I didn't have anything particularly breakable inside.

Unfortunately, I didn't have a tent with me, so I was going to need to find shelter pretty fast.

I glanced left and right. I couldn't see any clear signs of human traffic in either direction, nor could I hear the sounds of water, so I picked a direction at random.

Left it is.

Before I wandered off, I set up a small pile of rocks to mark the spot in case I ended up wandering back there. It was easy to get lost in the middle of a forest, especially the particularly misty kind.

After that, I headed left.

The path was dirt and grass, almost completely straight, surrounded on both sides by forests. It was just broad enough for two people to walk abreast comfortably. It felt cultivated. Deliberate.

That wasn't worrying in itself, though — manmade paths often were deliberately cultivated. Maybe this had been a common path to a town at one point, and someone had cleared out the trees and foliage on this path a year or two ago.

No, the worrying part was that it felt too *similar*. After walking for just a few minutes, I felt a bit dizzy, and I had the unnerving sensation that I'd seen each and every tree in the path before.

"Trespasser, turn back. Before it is too late."

The voice sounded like it was coming from all around me, but I couldn't see a source. I pointed at myself. "Me? I mean, I assume you mean me, but if there are invisible people around, maybe you could clarify?"

I glanced around again. No source, no reply. I'd dealt with invisible adversaries before, and usually I could catch a hint of movement from the sound of footfalls. Maybe even a blur of motion, if the caster was less experienced. I didn't catch any of that, though.

I kept walking.

My earlier assessment was accurate. A few minutes after that, I walked right back into the glade where I'd started, coming into it from the opposite side. I wasn't imagining it. I found the cluster of stones I'd set as a marker.

That seemed...odd, though. The path was almost perfectly straight. I'd placed the bed of rocks because it was easy to get lost in most forests where there weren't coherent trails or where there were lots of branches in the pathways that did exist.

I hadn't taken any branches from the path. I'd seen a few of them, but I'd gone completely straight.

I ducked down, inspected the group of rocks to make certain they were the same ones, and headed off again.

"Turn back."

The same voice. It didn't alarm me quite as much this time, but it still grated on my nerves. Now it seemed like I was being followed, or maybe observed from a distance. I'd seen some spells that could be used to watch people from afar and send sound to a remote area. Maybe that was what was happening?

"Do you mean 'turn back' as in 'leave this place, pitiful mortal'? Or is it more of a 'turn back, you're going the wrong direction, and make a left at the fork'? If you're just being helpful, some clarity would be appreciated." Again, I looked and listened for movement, but I found nothing.

I resumed walking.

It took me about the same amount of time to end up right back where I started. If there's anything worse than a mysterious misty forest, it's a *magical* mysterious misty forest.

I tried walking the opposite direction. Same result. Pushing through the forest in one of the other two directions was tougher, so it took me a little longer to appear back in my starting location.

The same voice spoke to me about mid-way. The message was different this time, at least. "This is a sacred place. You are not welcome here."

It had been obvious the voice wasn't just trying to give me directions, of course, but the fact that this was a *sacred* location? That was new and interesting.

I tried replying each time, of course. Not just to be polite. I was trying to get a reaction, just in case anyone was physically present. I was leaning toward the explanation that whoever was watching me was in a remote location, and since they didn't appear to be responding directly to what I said, I wasn't sure if they could even hear me.

I tried going part way down each path, then taking one of the branches. That got me a little bit of new scenery, but I still ended up in the same grove somehow. After four attempts at trying branches of the path, I knew the brute force approach of just trying every trail was going to take too long.

I kept getting one message with each trip.

"Turn back."

"This place is deadly to outsiders."

"There is no treasure here, only death."

"The Whispering Woods are not for your kind."

I finally knew the name for the area after that one. And I had to admit, it was pretty apt. I might have gone for "Nameless Voice that Growls Angrily at Intruders Woods" since it wasn't really whispering, but I had to admit that the original name was a lot easier to remember.

I tried tying a shirt over my eyes and walking down the path blind. That was slow going. When I finally took off the makeshift blindfold, I was in an unfamiliar location...but after I walked a bit further, I still ended up back in the grove.

I tried it a second time, keeping the blindfold on longer, but it didn't help. By this point, I was starting to recognize all the surrounding areas as well. The area I was looping through was maybe half a kilometer in each direction, and I was routinely running into landmarks, including my own tracks.

With a frustrated groan, I took off my backpack and sat down to think.

What's causing this? A confusion spell? A teleportation spell that spins me around?

Memory alteration? Maybe I'm making progress and then forgetting about it. Ugh, that'd be awful.

Guess there could be several places that just look identical...but no, that probably wouldn't work with the rock cluster. Hm.

Whatever is happening, it probably has to do with the mist.

Okay, I can work with this. The area isn't that big. Just need to try a few more things.

The voice kept "whispering" at me each time I walked through the area, but with no indication that it was hearing my replies. That was a shame, because some of my remarks were pretty amusing, and it was unfortunate that my foreboding observer wasn't getting to enjoy them.

"Is it your job to just watch people and...be creepy at them? Or is this more of a hobby? Because if it's a job, I could probably find you a better option. Not to be rude, but you clearly have a talent for growling at strangers, and I can think of some people who could use that."

I consoled myself with the fact that this whole experience was probably even more repetitive for them than it was for me.

I opened up my pack, found parchment and a quill, and started working on a map. I counted paces in each direction. It took me an almost identical number of paces to get back to the glade regardless of whether or not I went left or right, and it felt like the same amount of time.

That made it likely that the glade was physically at the center of whatever effect I was in, and that the effect had something to do with my location, not the amount of time that was passing.

Once I'd done that, I started dragging a stick behind me to make a line in the dirt. If I'd planned better, I could have just paid attention to my boot trails, but I'd walked over the area so many times now that it wouldn't work for this particular test.

I glanced behind me periodically, watching the line I was making.

I'd walked just about halfway through the total distance of the loop when I realized that the line behind me was gone, with the exception of the last few feet I'd just drawn.

I turned around, walking back the way I came...and there was the longer line again, leading a long way down the trail in front of me.

I felt a renewed wave of nausea hit me and paused to take a drink.

That was when I noticed a small cluster of rocks that I hadn't placed.

Foregoing the drink, I walked over to the rocks and knelt down to inspect them.

I found runes carved into the one in the center.

There you are.

I didn't know exactly what the runes did. Wasn't my area of expertise, and honestly, I don't even remember what they looked like. Sorry, Corin, I know you like adding to your rune collection.

I do remember the cathartic feeling when I smashed the rock, though. Mm. Breaking things.

There was a flash of light when I shattered the stone, then I was elsewhere.

My stomach briefly protested in response to the teleportation effect, but fortunately, there was nothing immediately dangerous to assault me during my recovery.

I took in my surroundings. Same forest, or one designed to look similar. Now I was on the border of a hillside, though, or maybe a mountainside. I couldn't determine the scale due to the mist.

Either way, the stone outcropping near me had a conspicuous-looking cave with an obviously humanoid sized entrance.

I almost avoided it out of irritation. I didn't like playing so directly into someone else's hands, but I had a job to do. I'd been told that the goddess I was looking for had a thing for presenting challenges, but I wasn't expecting anything quite this obvious...or something quite so soon after my arrival.

I'd hoped to end up in a nice town, with some time to plan and gather information.

Hope can be a source of strength, but when it fails to deliver what I want, I've found a good degree of stubbornness to be an appropriate substitute.

So, I walked into the cave.

The mist was even thicker inside. I could only see a few feet in front of me, and even that was hazy.

I could feel the moisture in the air, and that moisture made it easier to pick up the scents around me. Moss, feathers, a hint of death.

Good. Maybe there's something I can fight in here.

My hand settled on the sword on my left hip out of instinct, but I didn't draw it. There was no need to make things worse.

I was tempted to conjure a bit of flame to disperse the mist around me and provide some much-needed light, but the cost of maintaining it for a trek of indeterminate length was more of a risk than I was willing to take.

Instead, I walked back out of the cave for a minute or so, found a branch of about an arm's length, broke off the little twigs protruding from the sides, and tried to light it with the flint and steel from my pack.

After about a minute of trying to get a spark to catch on the wood, I gave up and just ignited the top of the branch with sorcery. A chill ran down my spine as I felt the spell's cost, but it wasn't much of a burden. A mere flicker of fire wouldn't drain my strength as much as maintaining a ball of flame would have.

The branch blazed brightly as I strode deep into the depths of daunting darkness.

Oh, come on. I'm not being *that* dramatic. A little bit of narrative flavor never hurt anyone. You could use a little more of it when you tell us the next part of your story, Corin.

Anyway, cave. Right.

With the makeshift torch, I could see a little bit further — just far enough to notice the trail of bones. I could also see that the cave went deep into the mountainside, expanding beyond the human-sized entrance into a vast cavern with an open area ahead and what looked like a couple different possible paths.

I ducked under a stalactite, reminded myself not to stand straight up, and knelt next to the first skull I could find.

Deer, I think. Looks about adult-sized.

I inspected some of the other large bones nearby, frowning as I took in the size of the gouges on the ribs. They'd been pushed inward, and I could see marks on several of them where something sharp had cut into the bone.

Crushed by claws, and big ones. Large enough to wrap around the entire torso of the deer, I think.

Either that, or five people with clubs and axes.

Going to go with claws.

I stood up, hit my head, and died.

Kidding, kidding. I didn't die until much later.

Didn't even hit my head. I'd been climbing through enough caves that I knew to exercise due caution. I remained in a crouch until the cave widened and the ceiling was high enough to stand back up without bashing my head.

It was fortunate that I was close to the ground for a while, because that made it easier to notice the spine crawlers.

What are spine crawlers, you ask? Why, they're like centipedes, only three feet long, about eight inches thick and, as I learned, swift to anger.

Their gray skin blended near perfectly with the stone floor — it was the glint from the light reflecting on their carapaces that gave them away.

By that point, it was almost too late. I was only inches from a nest, and one was slithering toward my feet.

I backpedaled because, well...no one wants to get eaten by giant poisonous worms. That took me into the *other* monster nest.

Vines wrapped around my legs as the winged beasts descended from the ceiling. They looked like bats, but with wings that were more birdlike, if bird feathers were metallic and razor-edged.

Also, given how rapidly the vines were moving from the cave floor to encircle me, one or both of the monster types could use nature sorcery.

Well, I'm surrounded by monsters. That was quick.

I smirked.

Time to get started.

I tugged on the vines. Animated or not, they were vines, and not particularly strong. I snapped one just in time to see one of the razor bats — no idea if that's what they're typically called, just going to go with that name — flapping its wings in my direction.

Which, predictably, sent a wave of razor-sharp feathers in my direction.

The feathers weren't actually metal, so I couldn't turn them aside with metal sorcery. I resisted the instinct to draw my blade and hurled myself out of the way, narrowly avoiding the quills.

The few lingering vines wrapped around me weren't sufficient to hold me in place, but the ones I snapped were quickly replaced by more. And now I was on the ground with razor bats above me, and a spine crawler, well, crawling closer.

I flared my aura, surrounding my body in a silvery blur. Vines disintegrated. Inches of stone beneath me vanished, not even dust left in my aura's wake.

I rolled in the opposite direction of where the vines had been, my right hand burning from the power I'd just used. I didn't even have time to regret it before I was pushing myself to the side, failing to avoid another barrage of feathers entirely. A quill glanced along my back, drawing a trail of blood.

I rolled, grabbing the quill with two fingers and hurling it right back at the bat.

It missed. I'm a good shot, but it was a feather, not a throwing knife.

I threw the knife from my belt next. I hit the bat that time, and it fell.

The spine crawlers were on top of it in seconds, biting with venom-laced fangs. I scurried backward, retrieving my fallen torch, and watched as another spine crawler dislodged its jaw and sprayed acid on the still-wriggling razor bat.

A good portion of the bat melted away before it ceased struggling entirely.

A smaller portion of my knife melted along with it.

And I *liked* that knife.

Rather than extract revenge for the vicious daggercide that had just been committed, I took the more cautious course of pushing myself to my feet and inching away from the scene. The spine crawlers didn't seem to notice me at all now that they had easier prey, but I didn't want to risk aggravating them further with any sudden movements.

Burning through those vines with my aura had been...unwise. Overusing it was dangerous in a different way from conjuring too much fire. It wouldn't harm me.

Not physically, at least.

Practicing any type of sorcery generates essence — what you'd call mana where you're from — of that type in the body. That essence changes you; subtly with some types of mana, more overtly with others.

I could use three fairly common types of sorcery: flame, stone, and metal. I wasn't really sure what the first one did to my body, but stone and metal essence both worked to reinforce skin, muscles, and bone. I'd practiced metal sorcery daily since childhood, and that had made my body both stronger and more resilient than any ordinary human.

I'd disintegrated the vines using another, lesser known type of sorcery. I'd practiced it unknowingly for years by using the sword sheathed at my side, and during that process, it had bled into my essence.

Now I was generating some of that type of essence myself all the time, even without the sword.

That wasn't a good thing.

The aura that was around me at all times?

It breaks things.

Anything I'm in contact with for long enough wears down. Food, clothes, armor, weapons — it all breaks. I'm not talking about just accelerating the normal passage of time, either. That'd be ruin sorcery, which is related, but *less* dangerous.

My aura is gradually cutting through everything around me — erasing pieces of everything it touches. This is not convenient.

For example, if I wear items that generate protective sorcery, like a shield sigil?

My aura breaks the barrier down in minutes, rendering the item worthless. Even the magical object itself will gradually break down, unless the item is shielded well enough to prevent the aura from cutting through it. Very few defensive spells are that resilient.

I had precisely three things on me that were powerful enough to survive long-term exposure to my aura without harm. My sword, the scabbard designed to hold it, and a weird mask I really shouldn't have held onto.

My aura was already too strong for me to suppress it entirely at any given time. It was cutting away at my backpack, my boots, everything around me, just very slowly. I probably had about two or three weeks to get to a town before my equipment fell apart.

Any time I used that type of sorcery, I'd make the problem worse. Permanently, unless I also improved my degree of control over the aura, and that was easier said than done. Drawing the sword involved the same type of risk; a portion of that destructive magic would leak into me any time it wasn't sheathed.

If I didn't find a solution, I'd eventually get to the point where I couldn't touch non-magical objects at all.

Or people.

I didn't exactly care for the idea of never being able to embrace my friends or family again.

The old man who had sent me to this place?

He was a famous scholar of sorcerous theory, and one of the few people who might've been able to help me.

But there was always a price.

And with that in mind, I continued into the cave. My back still ached from the brush with the razor bat's quill. I waited until I was several minutes in before pausing, putting down the torch, and digging bandages and ointment out of my bag. The wound was relatively shallow, but not shallow enough that I could ignore it entirely. I applied the ointment and bound the wound, then continued on.

Hopefully there'd be something a little bigger to fight deeper inside, if I was lucky.

"**Turn back.**" The voice boomed, and it sounded like it was coming from directly in front of me.

I saw the pair of glowing motes of light — presumably eyes — in the distant mist a moment later.

I waved my off-hand. "Oh, you must be the creepy fog voice! I was hoping I'd eventually get to meet you."

The twin lights blinked.

I walked closer, passing the torch to my off-hand. I wanted my sword arm ready, but I didn't move it close to the hilt. I didn't want to appear threatening.

"**Leave.** This is your final warning."

I ducked under another low portion of the ceiling as I approached. The cavern walls encroached around me until I could barely fit down the tunnel, then widened again into a massive, almost circular chamber. The mist was the thickest I'd seen so far. I could feel the moisture on my skin, taste it with every breath.

I could vaguely make out the outline of a humanoid figure ahead of me. That was a bit of a comfort, since I wasn't sure I should expect anything close to human. Plenty of monsters could produce a human-sounding voice.

"I'm sorry to intrude. I don't mean to be rude." I grinned, pausing now that I was close enough to get a good look at who I was talking to. I could see the outline of hair, almost floor-length. Slender arms and legs...did those hands end in claws?

Yeah, those were definitely claws.

Nice.

The figure must have been wearing white. They blended in with the mist so thoroughly that I couldn't make out any other details. I guessed they were probably about ten feet away now, which was about the farthest I could see in the haze.

"Then you should have left when you had a chance." They raised a clawed hand. "Prepare yourself."

As much as I *wanted* to fight, I couldn't jump right into it. I'd finally found someone I could talk to, and I needed information.

I raised a hand. "Wait a moment, please. I was teleported to this forest, and I'm lost. I'm supposed to be gathering information about the area. I've been told there's a goddess called Selys, I believe? Are you her?"

The figure tilted its head to the side. "...Are you mocking me? Is that a serious question?"

"Completely serious."

The person...creature...thing exhaled heavily enough that I felt it. The air pushed me back a step. I steadied myself, bracing for an attack, but realized they had just *sighed*.

Humanoid or not, this thing really knew how to breathe. "I am not the goddess, but I do serve her. I am the guardian of the Shrine of the Dawnbringer, one of the Six Sacred Swords."

I nodded. I was finally making some progress here. "Okay, great. If you're in her employ, could you direct me to where I can find her?"

"If thou dost seek the goddess, thou must climb the Soaring Spires. For the goddess resides in the skies above, and only atop the spires might one glimpse upon her greatness. But, be forewarned, ere false hope be thine — centuries live and die between the successes of heroes who seek to reach the spire's summit."

Yeah, they actually used 'thou'. Apparently they had penchants for both growling *and* theatrics. Maybe if I was lucky I'd get a prophecy at some point, too.

"That's great, thank you for that. So, there are a few of these spires?"

"Six are the spires, as six are the sacred swords."

"Huh. Sounds like that's not a coincidence, then?"

The figure lowered their head, as if in prayer. "Atop each spire lays one of the god beasts, ferocious guardians that await those who would dare to seek an audience with the goddess. None would stand a chance against these beasts, save for the sacred swords — one blade forged to survive the power of each beast."

Ooh, god beasts sound like they'd be fun to fight. And I do love collecting magic swords.

I was starting to get more excited. Maybe the sage hadn't sent me to such a bad location after all. "Got it. That makes sense. And you're the guardian of one of the swords?"

"So I am. Since time immemorial, my people have served here."

I frowned at that. "And you're okay with that? Servitude?"

"My task is a *sacred* calling, given by the goddess herself. Thy banter and jesting are what bore me. Either flee from my sight or challenge me properly. Those are your choices."

I frowned. This was not going where I wanted it to. "Sorry, didn't mean to sound insulting. Okay, challenging." I cracked my neck. "What are the terms? Could we have a match to the first successful hit of any kind, for instance?"

"We would fight until one of us could fight no longer. I would not be gentle. Face me and you should expect to lose your life."

I winced. I loved fighting, but I was strictly against killing people without a good reason. "Could I convince you to alter the terms to a middle ground? First blood, perhaps?"

"The terms are set down by tradition. They cannot be altered."

I nodded sadly. "I expected as much. And the sword is right past you?"

"It is not far. I am not the last of the challenges, but I am the greatest. It lays in the grove of three virtues, untouched in the two decades since it was last claimed."

So, someone had the sword twenty years ago, but it's been hundreds of years since someone successfully reached the top of a tower. That means even having the sword is far from a guarantee that we're going to be successful at finding this goddess. Wonderful.

"Okay. And just to be clear, your responsibility is to guard this specific tunnel?"

"Such is the path to the sword."

I focused, trying to peer through the mist as best I could. I thought I could just *barely* make out an exit tunnel on the opposite side of the chamber, maybe twenty feet away.

I picked my torch back up, waved, and shifted my stance as if I was about to turn around. "Okay, thanks for all the information."

I hated to leave a potential fight behind, but I couldn't accept the offered terms.

"You're...leaving?"

I think they actually sounded a little disappointed. In truth, I was disappointed, too. "Yep. I'm not going to invade someone's home and kill them just so I can walk through a particular cavern. I figure now that I broke your teleportation rune, I can probably just walk out of the forest and find a town. But you're a great storyteller — that part about the spire was riveting. You're welcome to come with me if you'd like."

"You...mock me."

I shook my head. "Nope. I just don't think anyone should have to live their life in a cave because a goddess told them to, and I'm certainly not going to kill you just because a goddess put you here."

The creature in front of me growled and lowered their stance. "You insult me and the goddess alike."

"I don't mean to be insulting." I raised my off-hand in a defensive gesture. "Just sympathizing. My own life has been largely dictated by the whims of the gods, and I'm tired of it. If you'd like to get out of this situation, I'd be glad to help you."

No growl that time, which was progress. Just a tilt of the head to the side, maybe a bit of introspection. "I will not leave while my task remains undone."

"I understand." I nodded affably. "Well, I'm leaving then."

"See that you do not return unless you are prepared to face my challenge."

"Right. That won't be a problem."

I shifted to the left as if I was turning around...and rushed forward at top speed.

I'd gone left because the torch was currently in my right hand, and as I sprinted past the creature, I waved it right in front of their eyes. Not close enough to hit them — I was just going for momentary blindness.

They roared, far louder than their body should have been able to, and the entire room shook. Dust and debris rained from the ceiling. Fortunately, I was used to sprinting across uneven terrain, and I maintained my footing. I turned toward the exit tunnel as I moved, finding it easily as I approached.

I was only a couple feet away when a wall of stone shot upward from the ground, blocking the path.

I spun just in time to dodge a spiked tail that was arcing toward my face.

"Coward! Craven!" The creature roared, lunging at me with clawed hands. As they drew closer, I got a better look. They had a human-looking face and body, but they were covered from head to toe in white scales, and they had a serpentine tail covered in wicked six-inch spikes.

I side-stepped the lunge and the creature missed, stumbling. I realized they were probably still half-blind from the torch, and they had probably responded to my movements through hearing or another sense.

That didn't stop them from whipping their tail around the moment they failed to connect with me, though. It was a low sweep, so I hopped over it, backing up and keeping the torch in front of me. "A little redundant there. Coward and craven are pretty much the same thing. I appreciate alliteration, though."

They just roared at me in reply. They were done talking for the moment, it seemed.

I considered sprinting back toward the entrance, but they were in reach of me now, and faster than I'd expected. I wasn't confident I could outpace them, especially after they recovered their sight.

Instead, I stepped to the side and began to circle them, moving gradually back to the area that had been sealed by the wall. I wasn't a master of stone sorcery, but I *could* use it. If I could find a few moments, maybe I could make a gap big enough to climb through.

"I'd really like to avoid—"

They swiped a claw and knocked the torch right out of my hand.

I stared blankly for a moment as the light source clattered across the floor, then punched the scaled creature in the face.

Hard.

The creature staggered back, raising a hand to their cheek. Their expression changed.

To a smile. "**Better.**" Their blue eyes seemed to shimmer in the dark. That was not a good sign.

I'd learned to control my swings a long time ago, because I liked being able to spar with humans without crushing their bones to powder.

But I'd taken that swing out of instinct. It wasn't quite my full strength, but I would have put my fist through the stone wall without any difficulty.

They weren't even visibly bruised.

Their return punch came a moment later, and I raised an arm to block. The blow carried me off the ground and threw me back a good ten feet. I landed in a slide, my arm aching from the force of the impact.

Motion sorcery, I realized. No amount of pure physical strength would have knocked me upward like that. Instead, the strike had carried with it a blast of magic that enhanced and spread out the impact.

I knew what was coming next.

They blurred, flashing forward in a burst of kinetic energy, closing the gap between us in an instant.

But I'd fought motion sorcerers more times than I could count. Even before they landed, I was rotating my hips for a *real* punch, the kind I used to practice tearing through breastplates.

I hit them dead-on in the solar plexus. That actually slowed them down. They doubled over, clutching their chest and coughing.

For a moment, I was concerned that I'd misjudged and hit too hard.

Their tail whipped over their head, spiked tip arcing toward my throat. I grabbed it just in time, cutting one of my fingers on a spike in the process. They jerked the tail back, but I maintained my grip and stumbled forward.

With my free hand, I tried to throw another punch, but they grabbed my arm with both of theirs. We were practically on top of each other at that point, so I threw a knee upward. They countered by raising their own leg to block, which I hadn't expected.

They snarled, biting at me with a set of teeth that were just *slightly* sharper than human ones. I stepped back to avoid the bite, and they finally managed to pull their tail free from my grip. Before they could swing it again, though, I slammed my boot down on their foot.

That got my hands free while they recoiled, and I used that freedom to back off a few feet. My left hand was still bleeding from where it had brushed against a spine, but not badly.

They backed off as well, apparently assessing me. That *seemed* good, until they kept backing off to the point where they disappeared into the mist.

I glanced around for any signs of my opponent, then headed for where I'd dropped the torch.

It went out before I reached it.

Resh.

I was plunged into darkness. I couldn't see anything, but I could hear something moving to the side of me.

Something *big.*

I heard a growl, followed by what sounded like bones *snapping* to my side.

I continued to inch toward where I'd last seen the torch. Since blinding the creature had seemingly worked, it was possible the creature would have a tough time finding me in the dark, even if their night vision was better than mine.

I was pretty close to where I'd thought the torch was when I ran into something much larger than I was.

I took a step back. I hadn't remembered a wall there. I raised a hand and ran it across...scales. Large scales, each the size of my fist.

Uh oh.

I stepped back just before something slammed into me the size of my entire midsection, hard enough to throw me almost ceiling-high. I landed hard and fell on my side, rolling a few feet across the floor.

That *hurt.*

I barely managed to push myself to the side before something landed on the stone where I'd been moments before, smashing the stone of the cavern floor.

Even without the light, I was close enough to get a glimpse of the clawed appendage that landed near my face. It was even bigger than what I'd felt connect with me, probably about the size of the upper half of my body.

I'd been thrown and battered by nothing more than a glancing blow.

I pushed myself to my feet with a cough, raising my left hand.

The darkness wasn't slowing this thing down as much as I'd hoped, but it was making it impossible for me to evaluate my opponent effectively.

Burn. A sphere of flame the size of a watermelon appeared in my hand, and a chill ran down my spine as the spell extracted its cost. I rarely conjured fire on this scale due to the tax on my body, but I needed this flame for two reasons — both to see, and as a potential deterrent to further attacks.

"**Foolish human,**" they spoke, the room trembling with each word. "**Had you chosen to fight me honorably from the outset, I would not have used this form.**"

As they spoke, I took in what I was looking at.

A huge, serpentine head with a pair of vicious horns, each of which was large enough to impale me with ease.

A leonine body covered in hardened scales, with four massive clawed hands. Though standing on four legs, they were still twice as tall as I was.

And their wings were vast, at least twenty feet in total span, nearly brushing the ceiling and walls.

They were a creature of legend.

Unfortunately, I had no idea what I was looking at.

They don't have dragons where I come from.

ACKNOWLEDGEMENTS

A lot of the characters in this trilogy were based on player and non-player characters in role-playing games I ran over the years. Some of the locations and historical elements were also drawn from these campaigns.

I'd like to thank everyone who I drew inspiration from, including but not limited to: Mowi Reaves, Carly Thomas, Andrew Warren, Joshua Noel, Rachel Noel, Kieran Brewer, Danielle Collins, Justin Green, Emily and Trevor Gittelhough, Robert Saunders, Robert Telmar, Morgan Buck, Mackenzie Jamieson, Alex Arjad, Edward Fox, Rob McDiarmid, Eric Maloof, Joslyn Field, Michael Kelly, Rebecca Nieto, Michael Corr, Chris Ruffell, Devin McCarthy, Amanda Mielke, John Lin, CW Fox, Ali Buntemeyer, Anthony Scopatz, Shannon Kirkwood, Brittany "Emma" Brooks, and Jess Richards.

My beta readers were also tremendously helpful. I'd like to thank Brittany Chhutani, Jess Richards, Bruce Rowe, Christine Rowe, Samuel Williams, Rachel Noel, and Will Wight, as well as all my other beta readers.

I'd like to thank everyone at Podium Publishing for their help with the audio versions of these books and Nick Podehl for his amazing narration.

Daniel Kamarudin has been my cover artist since the very first book in this series, and his amazing artwork has helped bring my characters to life in ways I never imagined. Thanks, Daniel. I look forward to working with you for many more series in the future.

I'd like to thank my partner, Jess, for reading all these books and giving me amazing notes and feedback over the years. You've helped me build my writing skills up from, well, a pretty low level, and I appreciate all your tireless support.

Finally, I'd like to thank my brother, Aaron, for playing D&D with me as a kid, and my parents, for always supporting my reading and gaming habits. Without them, this never would have been possible.

Thank you all, as well as all my other players and tireless staff members, for helping to contribute so much to my world.

ABOUT THE AUTHOR

Andrew Rowe was once a professional game designer for awesome companies like Blizzard Entertainment, Cryptic Studios, and Obsidian Entertainment. Nowadays, he's writing full time.

When he's not crunching numbers for game balance, he runs live-action role-playing games set in the same universe as his books. In addition, he writes for pen and paper role-playing games.

Aside from game design and writing, Andrew watches a lot of anime, reads a metric ton of fantasy books, and plays every role-playing game he can get his hands on.

Interested in following Andrew's books releases, or discussing them with other people? You can find more info, update, and discussions in a few places online:

Andrew's Blog: https://andrewkrowe.wordpress.com/
Mailing List: https://andrewkrowe.wordpress.com/mailing-list/
Facebook: https://www.facebook.com/Arcane-Ascension-378362729189084/
Reddit: https://www.reddit.com/r/ClimbersCourt/

The next book after this one chronologically is Six Sacred Swords, which is already out! Click here if you want to check it out.

OTHER BOOKS BY ANDREW ROWE

The War of Broken Mirrors Series
Forging Divinity
Stealing Sorcery
Defying Destiny

Weapons and Wielders Series
Six Sacred Swords
Diamantine (Coming Soon)

Arcane Ascension Series
Sufficiently Advanced Magic
On the Shoulders of Titans
Arcane Ascension Book 3 (Coming Soon)

Printed in Great Britain
by Amazon